D0065440

THE PRICE OF PLEASURE

THE PRICE OF PLEASURE

JOAN ELIZABETH LLOYD

KENSINGTON BOOKS
http://www.kensingtonbooks.com

KENSINGTON BOOKS are published by

Kensington Publishing Corp.
850 Third Avenue
New York, NY 10022

ISBN 0-7394-2678-8

Printed in the United States of America

THE PRICE OF PLEASURE

Chapter

1

Erika Holland flipped off her blow-dryer and ran a final comb through her carefully styled shoulder-length mink brown hair. She had considered wearing it up for the evening, but she knew that Clay Williamson liked it loose, falling softly around her face. He had often said that he loved to imagine running his long fingers through it. And, after all, he was paying for the evening.

She closed her eyes, the color of aged brandy, and smiled as she remembered her most recent evening with Clay, two months earlier. He had come to New York from his company's office in Silicon Valley for a high-level strategy meeting and afterward had needed to blow off steam.

"Erika, love," he had said on the phone having awakened her from a sound sleep, "I need you. I know it's late, but I have to talk to someone sane. I'm at the Plaza. Can you come over?"

Erika, who had gone to bed an hour earlier after a rare evening to herself, rubbed her face and made an effort not to sound sleepy. "Of course." Erika had Clay's credit card number on file so she made a mental note to take care of business the following morning. Clay might be a friend, but both of them knew he was also a customer.

She always awakened easily so it took only a moment until she was fully conscious. It was almost midnight so, rather than risking being unable to get a taxi, she called her limo service and asked for a town car to be sent to her building in fifteen minutes. Never careless about her appearance when meeting a client, especially one she liked as much as Clay, Erika dressed in a long, flowing, floral silk skirt and a soft cotton blouse the color of ripe peaches, which flattered her creamy skin and pale brown eyes. After she carefully applied her makeup, she threw a long, black silk raincoat over everything. By the time the uniformed doorman opened the heavy glass door of Erika's trendy apartment building on Riverside Drive, a sleek black automobile was waiting.

Half an hour later she knocked on the door to Clay's hotel room and he answered with a wide smile. Almost dragging her inside the large two-room suite, he grabbed her in a bear hug and buried his face in her neck. "Oh love, you have no idea how delicious you look and feel and smell." He kissed her deeply, threading his fingers through her hair. "And you taste wonderful." With a hand in the small of her back, he pressed her body against his. "Better. You make me feel better just by being here."

With a deep sigh of contentment, Clay took Erika's coat and tossed it over a chair. "The hotel had a great red wine on their list, a 1994 Shiraz. I got some black caviar and those crackers you like, too." Arm in arm they crossed the room to the linen-covered rolling table room service had brought. Erika watched as Clay deftly half-filled a stemmed glass for each of them. Clay was six inches taller than her own five foot six inches, with deeply waved chocolate brown hair with drifts of silver at each temple. He wasn't handsome in the classical sense. He had a long nose and a heavy, five o'clock shadow, but his soft gray eyes and full mouth were extremely sensual. She watched his long fingers as he covered a cracker with the black fish eggs, then added a bit of chopped hard-boiled egg and several small capers. As she held her hand up, he said, "I know, no onion."

He extended the cracker toward her and she gently held his wrist as she bit off half of it, pursing her lips around his fingers. Then he popped the remaining cracker into his own mouth. As Erika licked her lips and watched his tongue slowly circle his moist mouth, she felt herself dampen. God, he was a sexy man. She would probably entertain him for free, but, after all, a woman had to make a living. "You always know how to please me," she said, "and I want to please you, too, but I know you need to talk first."

"I do need to vent, and I need for you to listen and tell me whether I'm totally out in left field."

For the next half hour, as they shared several glasses of rich ruby wine and nibbled crackers piled with caviar, Clay railed about his frustration with the company's plans while Erika asked probing, often insightful questions.

"You're right, you know," he said finally. "Putting my nasty thoughts in writing isn't the answer and I can't rat them all out to the stockholders." He rested his elbows on the arms of his Louis Quatorze–style chair. "It's the wrong way to go. Maybe your idea of a face-to-face with the CEO is a good one. He just might listen."

She sat propped against the head of the king-size bed, her long legs stretched out on the satin quilt. "If you handle it right you have little to lose, and if things go well he might just thank you in the end."

"Thanks for coming over, Erika," Clay said with a sigh. "As always, you've helped me a great deal. Not only do you keep me sane, but you challenge me and force me to think everything through. I know you don't know much about silicon chips, but you do understand people."

Her smile slowly changed from understanding to erotic. "I understand you well enough," she said, toeing off her black pumps and wiggling her stockingless toes. Slowly, she stroked one instep with the ball of the other foot and watched as his eyes were drawn to the rhythmic motions.

"You're an oversexed bitch, you know," Clay said, his tone changing from business to pleasure. "You certainly do know how to change the subject, just with that delicious body of yours."

"I know," she said, still stroking one foot with the other. "And I'm doing it deliberately. It's time to put an end to work and begin other things." The tone of her voice left no doubt as to what those "things" were.

"I don't know whether I prefer your mind or your body." With a wolfish leer, he continued, "Let's find out. Come here, woman."

Erika slid off the bed, allowing her skirt to slide up her legs, giving Clay a good view of her naked calves. She pressed the button on the top of the bedside radio and tuned it to a station that played easy-listening music. With a soft smile, Clay stood and she melted into his arms. He held her, moving his feet only slightly in time with the music. She slid her hands to the back of his neck and raised her face, pressing her breasts against his chest, nuzzling his mouth and flicking her tongue over his lips.

"You always know just the right things to do," he said, cupping her face and deepening the kiss.

After a few minutes, she said, "Let's do this a better way." She unbuttoned her blouse, let it drop to the floor, then unfastened his shirt and pulled it off. She quickly removed her lacy bra and again wrapped her arms around him, pressing skin against skin. Sinuously Erika rubbed her body against Clay's, feeling her breasts swell and her nipples contract as they scratched against his chest hair.

His voice hoarse, Clay said, "You make me crazy, lady."

"I hope so. I just try to make you as crazy as you make me." She swayed, rubbing against him like a cat, feeling her blood ignite. Sometimes sex was just a job, but with Clay it was pure pleasure.

"I love making you crazy." He cupped her buttocks and lifted slightly, rubbing his hardness against her. "That's how nuts you make me. God, I always swear that I will take my time, but my body can't seem to cooperate." He buried his face in the curve of her neck and bit the tight tendon. "I just want to devour you."

Laughing with the sensual joy of it, she said, "Go for it. I love it when you devour me." She scratched her long deep-red nails down his back, hard enough to make his skin tingle yet not hard enough to draw blood. She wasn't averse to rougher play, but she knew exactly how Clay liked it.

He cupped her breast with one hand and lowered his head until he could reach her nipple with his mouth. He used his other hand to massage the small of her back, rubbing his cloth-covered cock against her mound. As he filled his mouth with her flesh, she felt her heart pound and it became difficult to draw a deep breath. He nipped and bit her breast-flesh, then licked across her collar bone. "So good," she purred, arching her back and allowing her head to drop back so he could kiss and lick her throat, while his fingers pinched her nipples. "God, you're fabulous."

Finally, when they were both trembling with need, Clay moved them to the bed and lowered her onto the quilted spread. With rapid movements he pulled off her skirt and she watched him gaze hungrily at the triangle formed by her tiny lace panties before dragging them down her legs. While her eyes roamed his flushed skin, he removed his slacks and then hooked his thumbs in his shorts and tugged them down, allowing his erection to spring free. Finally, as he stood before her, Erika gazed hungrily at his rampant cock, thrusting from its nest of curly hair. Knowing exactly what he liked, she spread her hand on her belly, then slid her red-tipped fingers downward into her carefully trimmed bush.

"Show me, baby," Clay groaned, stretching out beside her.

"Yes, show me where you want me." He placed his hand on the back of hers.

"Here, darling," she purred, enjoying the feel of her fingers playing with her soaked, swollen flesh. She parted her inner lips and slid two fingers deep inside her soaked pussy. "I want your hard cock. Right here." She wrapped the fingers of her other hand around his shaft and squeezed while rubbing her thumb over the already oozing tip. "And I know you want it too."

"Not yet." He went to his suitcase and pulled out a small parcel wrapped in golden paper. "I brought you a present."

"I don't need presents from you," Erika said.

"I know, but I saw it in a magazine and thought of you. I had it made just before I left."

Erika unwrapped the parcel and withdrew a handful of slender gold chains that Clay took from her. "Let me show you how to wear them." He untangled them and said, "Stand up."

She stood and Clay wrapped one chain around her waist and clipped it closed with a tiny clasp. Another chain hung behind her and Clay drew it between her legs and pulled it tightly against her wet lips, clipping it in front of her to the center of the waist-chain. "How does that feel?" he asked.

"Ummm," Erika said. "It catches me in just the right place." She wiggled her hips. "Oh yes, it feels really hot."

"It looks fantastic against your skin. I wonder how it will feel when I make love to you."

"Let's find out." She stretched out on the bed, spreading her legs so he could see the golden chain winking from between her nether lips. She slipped her fingers through the hair on her mound, sliding them along the chain. She crooked one finger beneath it and pulled, enjoying the tug against her heated flesh.

"God, I can't wait to have you," Clay said.

"Ah, but you must," Erika replied, grinning as she reached for her purse. She opened the foil package she found and placed the still-rolled condom against the end of his staff. "Patience, love.

You have to learn patience." She leaned close to him and slowly, agonizingly slowly, unrolled the condom over him.

He grabbed her wrist, urging her to hurry. "Baby, you're driving me crazy," he moaned.

Erika giggled. "And the problem with that is?"

Clay's sudden laugh was rich and warm. "No problem. Just a news flash."

The condom was halfway down his shaft. "Good. Then I won't rush."

"The hell you won't." He pulled her hand away, pushed the condom all the way on, then shoved her onto her back. In one motion he drove himself into her until he was deeply imbedded. "I can feel the chain against my cock." Erika thought the chain was smooth enough not to puncture the condom, so she moved her hips to rub it against the length of him. Instead of thrusting into her, Clay became totally still.

Erika reveled in the feel of him fully lodged within her and clenched her inner muscles over his erection, driving herself higher. When he didn't move, she wiggled her hips to feel him more fully. "Come on, Clay," she whined as he stoically remained still. "You're torturing me." She pulled on the waistchain but still he didn't move.

"Patience, love," he said, mimicking her earlier words. "You have to learn patience." He pulled back slightly, then slowly slid his cock more deeply into her tight channel.

"Not a chance when I know just how good you feel." She wrapped her legs around his waist and thrust her hips against him, knowing how ready he was.

"Shit, baby." Unable to hold still any longer, Clay pulled back, then drove into her over and over until, with a roar, he came. Without withdrawing, he slipped his fingers between them, found her swollen clit and rubbed it with the chain. "Oh yes," she screamed as he caressed her, "do that. Just like that. Just . . . like . . . THAT." With a crash, the waves consumed her, slashing through her like liquid lightning, her spasms milking his cock. She never had to fake it with Clay. Unlike many of her customers, he always made sure she was satisfied.

"Oh God, I love being inside you when you come," he moaned. "If I hold very still, I can feel every movement of your body."

Returning to the present Erika smiled and put the blow-dryer into the drawer of her vanity. Tonight would undoubtedly be just as climactic. She laughed inwardly at her deliberate pun. How many women get to have hot, steamy sex with rich, powerful men like Clay and get paid great money for it? She glanced at her watch. Almost five-thirty. She didn't need to be at the Waldorf until seven so she still had a few minutes.

As she considered what to wear that evening, her personal phone rang. She tightened the sash on her old blue terrycloth robe, one she had had since the old days, and crossed the large bedroom, her bare toes sinking into the thick pearl gray pile carpeting. "Hello," she said, her voice schooled to be soft and melodious.

"Hi, it's me." Erika's body relaxed as she recognized the voice of her best friend, Brook Torrance.

"Hi yourself." She propped the cordless phone between her ear and her shoulder and walked to the small refrigerator in the corner of the bedroom. "What's up?" she asked as she pulled out a half-full bottle of white wine and deftly pulled the cork from the neck with her teeth.

"Nothing much. I'm just getting ready for Howard this evening."

Erika chuckled as she poured herself half a glass of Fume Blanc, all she allowed herself before a date. "Is he really as much of a bore as you paint him to be?"

"I'm afraid so." Erika could hear Brook's sigh. "His idea of a great evening is to sit over a dinner of giant slabs of red meat and a bottle of red table wine, telling me all about the big deals he's cooking up. You know, if I were into insider trading, I could make a fortune from what he says. And Erika, if that cell phone of his rings one more time while we're having dinner, I think I'll ram it down his throat. I must spend hours staring at my food while he wheels and deals and the people around us glower and go 'Shhh.' "

"During dinner?"

"Constantly, even at the best table at one of the finest restaurants in town. He's always in the middle of some big something-or-other. At my prices he'd be richer if he just stopped hiring me and talked on the phone alone all night. He wouldn't miss the sex either, I'm afraid. It's barely mediocre. Stuff it in, wiggle it around until he's satisfied, and that's that. An inflatable doll would do just as well, but for some reason he wants me."

Erika giggled and stretched out on her bed, tucking a strand of hair behind her ear. No matter what, Brook could always be counted on to be Brook. "Of course he wants you. I just wonder why you continue to go out with him," Erika said, knowing the answer. Fifteen hundred dollars was more than enough compensation for spending a boring evening with a guy.

"The usual. The money's really difficult to pass up and, all in all, he's undemanding and harmless. Anything new with you?"

"Just the usual craziness. Hank Talbott called. He's got another guy for next Thursday night. Some CFO is bringing a vice president, so he needs one more woman for the party. Fortunately, Carolynn is free and is more than willing to accept another client. Greg Haslett canceled for next month as I was sure he would. Luckily I didn't firm up many plans."

She heard Brook's sigh. "I don't know how you put up with all that detail stuff."

Erika took a quick swallow of her wine. "I like to complain, but you know as well as I do that I enjoy most of it, and the money's terrific." She looked around her spacious bedroom in her luxury apartment. The building was completely secure, with a twenty-four-hour doorman and a daytime concierge who did everything from delivering the daily papers to walking the tenants' dogs. When she arrived home in the wee hours, as she often did, the night doorman informed the concierge the following morning, so when Erika opened her apartment door two flaky croissants and a large container of steaming cappuccino awaited on the pie crust table beside the elevator.

Her apartment contained only the best. Her furniture had been carefully selected by a prominent decorator to enhance the few pieces she'd brought from her old apartment. Erika especially loved her bedroom, with its queen-size brass bed. Its multicolored quilt contrasted with the gray of the chaise longue and the soft gray tailored drapes that were usually left open so she could gaze at the Hudson River and the Palisades beyond. Somehow the fussy eighteenth-century vanity with wide mirror and tiny bench the decorator had found worked with everything else to create a comfortable, if eclectic, room.

Her gaze shifted to the mirrored doors on the wall of closets in the dressing room. She loved designer clothes and had the money to indulge herself; her closets were filled with outfits for all times of the day. They were created by the best designers and were bought at the best shops in New York. Yes, she admitted, she enjoyed the good life and the sexual entertaining that paid for it.

The company she owned and ran, Courtesans, Inc., now employed more than thirty escorts, all satisfying the cravings of men and women who could afford to indulge their pleasures at the cost of one to three thousand dollars a night. Again Erika sipped her wine. "Anyway," she said into the telephone, "think of all the men and women who'd be out of jobs if I quit."

"I know. I know. Speaking of your employees, how did your interview go this afternoon?"

Erika grimaced. "Ms. Kallinski won't be joining us."

"Why not?" Brook asked. "Paula was so high on her, and I

know you could use another woman or two. She sounded so perfect."

Erika pictured the upscale blonde she had spent nearly an hour with earlier that afternoon. "She sounded perfect in the interview, too," Erika answered. "Cornell alumnae with a degree in economics, four years with a major international bank. She told me she needed some extra money to help her father through some tough times with a tax man. A familiar story, but somehow she sounded just a little too perfect. She asked a few too many questions about what Courtesans, Inc. actually does." She took one last swallow, then put her empty wineglass on the table beside the bed. Sue Kallinsky had left a bad taste in her mouth. "She kept mentioning prostitution and I kept insisting that we are an escort service and nothing more. I don't think she believed me and I didn't much care. She just felt wrong to me."

"You think she might have been a cop?"

"Or a friend of Sean Fredericks." Sean Fredericks was a tall red-headed reporter for the *National Informer*, new at the scandal sheet and trying to make his mark by getting hold of her client list with the lurid details of their escapades with her high-priced courtesans. She knew he'd do almost anything to find out about the sexual exploits and unusual practices of her high-profile customers.

"You think the *Informer* would try to get you to hire someone like that?"

"I wouldn't put it past them. The woman might be on the up-and-up, but over the past ten years I've learned to trust my gut and my gut said no."

"Then no it is." Since neither woman liked to consider how precarious their business made their lives, Erika knew that Brook would deliberately change the subject. Predictably her friend said, "The weather's supposed to be really dreadful later tonight and I'm trying to figure out what to wear. I don't want to soak my shoes and freeze my feet, but I hate wearing boots."

"Phone a cab or a limo service and just add it to the bill. From what you've told me, Howard should have no problem picking up the tab for it, and if he's too cheap to spring for service, then maybe it's time to ditch him. It's not as if you don't have other opportunities." Brook was one of her most popular escorts. Seldom did a man spend an evening with her and not request her the next time he called. "What are you wearing tonight?"

"I guess I'm in denial. I haven't thought about that yet."

"How about that new apricot wool you showed me a few weeks ago? Howard will really love it." The dress was classically simple, bias cut with elegant lines that accentuated Brook's shapely body.

"If Howard notices." She paused. "It might work, but I never know what color shoes I should wear with it."

"Didn't we get you a pair of antique gold pumps last month? They might really dress it up. And maybe add your wide gold belt instead of the apricot one and your gold Cleopatra collar."

She could hear her friend tap her fingernail on the receiver as she considered. "Yeah. That might really work out well. Big gold earrings too, our lucky ones maybe. Nice."

Erika remembered the times either she or Brook had worn what they called their lucky earrings—large, chunky, gold free-form shapes—costume jewelry but classy and effective. She had worn them on her first evening in the business. "With you inside it, the dress will be smashing. Maybe you'll get lucky and he'll decide to move to the West Coast or something."

"If he did, he'd come back every month just to haunt me." Girlish giggles filled the phone line as they continued to discuss their respective evenings.

Steeling herself for the inevitable discussion with her best friend, Erika said, "I had a quick lunch with Stuart today." Stuart Dunlop, medium height, warm smile, carefully cut deep-brown hair shot with gray, and wonderful warm blue eyes behind rimless glasses. At forty-nine, he was five years older than Erika and they had been friends for more than ten years. "He showed me the latest pictures of his granddaughter. Oh, and Kevin's wife is expecting again."

"Tell him congratulations for me. You know, the three of us should get together more often."

"I know, but working out the logistics with our busy schedules has been really difficult. Let me try for dinner some time next week."

"You two have been friends forever, and I know you're sleeping together. Have you ever considered making your relationship more formal? Maybe living together, or even more."

"You mean marriage? I'm not sure I'd want that, even if he were interested."

"Why not? Although I don't know him particularly well, he's a great guy and you're good together. He makes you happy."

"He certainly does, but I just don't know. He hasn't mentioned it, but I must admit that I've thought about it. I couldn't give up Courtesans and I don't think he could deal with it if I kept working."

"Come on. He's the one who got you started with Courtesans. Do you really think he'd object?"

"I don't know. Maybe *I* would. After all, marriage should be one woman, one man. Not one woman and dozens of men. It wouldn't be fair to Stuart."

Brook's voice lowered. "You're sounding deliberately negative. Is some of this because of Rick? Not all men are shits, you know."

"I know. I just want to think about it."

"You love him." It wasn't a question.

"Yes, I do. There's so much more, though. Rick, Rena. I made such a mess out of my marriage," she paused, "that I don't trust myself any more. Not about serious stuff."

"You know what's best for you, but life is really long, and can be very lonely."

"You're not lonely, Brook," Erika said quickly.

"Not yet," Brook said, "but I've accepted the fact that not too many men want to marry women who've led lives like ours. I just wonder where I'll be in twenty years. Where will you be, Erika?"

"Loneliness isn't a reason to consider marrying Stuart. It has to be right."

"I understand and I wouldn't presume to think for you." Changing the subject, Brook continued, "Call me in the morning. I found a new little lingerie shop in the East Fifties. You'll love it."

"Great," Erika said. "Enjoy your evening . . . as best you can."

"You too. Take good care of yourself."

"Take good care of yourself too." They had been ending their conversations with that phrase since the business began, and although neither really heard it any more, it was a serious warning. Dismissing any dismal thoughts, and vowing to think about Stuart later, Erika tossed her head and settled at her vanity to put on her makeup for the evening.

While she applied soft brown eyeliner, she pressed the *play* button on her business answering machine. "Erika, darling. It's Andy Kremins." As Erika stroked mascara along her pale brown lashes, she pictured the sports agent, a long-time customer. "I've got a guy coming into town in about three weeks. Have you, by any chance, got a girl who really knows basketball? The guy's a big-time promoter from Atlanta who does me lots of favors. I want to keep him happy, if you know what I mean. Let me know." He repeated his phone number and hung up.

Diane Murray was an avid fan of almost every sport and very knowledgeable. One client had called her a walking sports encyclopedia. As Erika made a quick note, the machine continued. "Erika, Marty McDermott here. You know that party you're helping me out with in Atlantic City next month? The one for all the high-rollers? Well, I need two or three good-looking talented guys. I want the husbands to be free to play, so I want to enter-

tain the wives—and I don't care how, or how much. Actually, neither do the husbands, I'd guess. Call me."

As Erika completed her makeup and dabbed a tiny touch of
Rive Gauche behind each ear and deep in her cleavage, she listened to the remainder of her messages and made an occasional
additional note. She'd be busy tomorrow adjusting schedules,
but that was what made Courtesans, Inc. thrive. Before she finished dressing, she lifted the chains Clay had given her from her
jewelry box and fastened them around her waist and between
her legs. Sometime during the speeches, she'd remind Clay she
was wearing them. That ought to keep him hot and hard.

Many hours later, after a predictably dull corporate evening
followed by a delicious hour in his hotel room, Clay Williamson
stood in front of the Waldorf clutching his suit jacket tightly
around him, trying to cover his only partially rebuttoned shirt.
"This weather really sucks," he said, his breath forming smoky
puffs in the frigid air. "I don't understand why you don't move to
California. You could run your business just as well out there."

Clay waved the doorman aside and held the taxicab door open
himself so Erika could slide into the warm interior. "I really like
New York, sleet, snow, and everything," she said as she brushed
a few shiny ice crystals from her shoulders, then ruffled several
snowflakes from Clay's hair.

"Okay. It was worth a try," Clay said. They had had this discussion many times before. "I'll be back in town next month and
I'm going to plan to have an entire day free. I'll let you know exactly when and we'll make plans." He leered and waggled his
eyebrows. "We may even leave the hotel room." He leaned into
the dark interior of the cab and kissed Erika soundly. "God, I
love these evenings. You are one hot lady."

"Don't sell yourself short, darling," she said, using her long
fingers to push a lock of deep-brown hair off his forehead. "It
takes two to tango, or whatever it was we were doing." She gazed
into his smokey gray eyes, then winked. "Give me as much

warning as you can when you're coming back into town. That way I'll make sure to be available. All day."

"I will. Get home safely."

As the door of the car slammed, Erika switched her attention to the driver. "Good evening," she said cheerfully. "Or maybe not so good. I'm glad you came along."

"Evening," the driver said in a thick Indian accent. "Where to, lady?"

"Riverside and eighty-eighth, please," she said, "and there's no need to hurry." Erika put her beaded evening purse on the seat beside her and lowered the hood of her plum wool cape. She reached for a seat belt but found none. Oh well.

"You got it, lady," the driver said with a bright smile.

As the cab lurched into the street, she unfastened the frogs on the front of the cape, exposing the full-skirted black wool dress beneath. Erika considered telling the cabbie to slow down but, not wanting to backseat drive, she kept still and carefully gathered her skirt around her long shapely legs. "It's a terrible night. I just came out of the hotel and saw the sleet. How long has it been doing that?"

"About one hour," the driver answered. She glanced at the identification card on the front dashboard. Ashok Bansal. Swarthy complexion, thick black hair, and serious five o'clock shadow.

Erika watched as the taxi wove around other cars crawling along Park Avenue, her entire body tense, her hands balled into fists in her lap. She stared out the front window, watching glistening bits of ice pelt the pedestrians as they hustled toward their destinations all around her. "Are the roads very slippery?" *Please*, she thought, *slow down*.

"Yes, lady, but don't be nervous. I'm a very good driver." He gazed at her in the rearview mirror and nodded almost imperceptibly. "And I can be a slower one."

She felt him ease his foot off the accelerator and, with a sigh of relaxation, let her body lean back against the seat. "Thank you so much." She played with the strand of pearls that set off the neck-line of the dress. The evening had gone well. She and Clay had sat through the long meeting applauding at the right points, laughing behind their hands at Clay's witty comments about the speakers. Afterward they had adjourned to his hotel room for over an hour of superior lovemaking. Her body was deliciously tired, her thigh muscles just a bit sore. She turned her lower body slightly sideways and stretched her legs, making idle small talk with the driver as he made his way uptown, then turned west on Seventy-Sixth toward the Seventy-Ninth Street transverse through Central Park.

Erika closed her eyes and focused all her thoughts on the double-size mug of Earl Grey tea and the handful of Milano cookies she would grab from her kitchen when she arrived at her apartment. Then she would crawl into bed, enjoy another chapter of the novel she was reading, and allow herself to completely unwind. Fortunately, she could sleep as late as she wanted in the morning.

Suddenly she felt the taxi swerve, heard the blast of a horn and the shout of the cabdriver for her to hang on. Frantically she looked around and saw, to her right, a large, black Chevy Suburban hurtling toward the taxi, its wheels obviously getting no traction on the icy roadway. Erika quickly realized that the skidding vehicle was going to hit the cab in the door beside her. Unable to move, she watched the taxi driver's body as it bounced, his foot obviously pounding the brake, his hands frantically spinning the steering wheel, his actions having no effect on the cab's trajectory. "Lady, hang on!" the taxi driver screamed.

Erika stared at the headlights of the oncoming SUV. She wondered how many times had she used the phrase *deer in the head-lights* not really understanding what it meant. Now she knew. She was unable to react, paralyzed yet knowing something disastrous was about to happen. Then she felt the impact, the entire cab thrown sideways, the door beside her pressing into the passenger space. Her body was thrown across the seat, then forward onto the floor. As she fell, she saw Stuart's loving face smiling at her. Then her head smashed into the support for the front seat and she felt nothing more.

Almost an hour later, Brook stood in front of her bathroom mirror wiping off several layers of eye makeup. The evening had been the usual with Howard. Smith and Wollensky for noise and steak. Although she vastly preferred lighter fare, she would never criticize a client's restaurant selection. The wine had been unusually good however, and Howard's conversation, though predictable, was mildly entertaining. His cell phone had been blessedly silent all evening. He really was a harmless man, with large amounts of money to spend. She smiled at the slender gold bracelet that he had given her to celebrate their three-month anniversary. And, of course, there was the check for fifteen hundred dollars.

After a thorough cleansing, she opened the medicine cabinet, pulled out a jar of Estée Lauder renewal cream and spread it liberally over her skin. As she rubbed it into her face and neck with practiced upward strokes, she gazed at herself in the mirror. Not too shabby, she told herself. She wasn't gorgeous. Actually, if she were being honest, she wasn't even pretty. However, with her country-girl blue eyes and baby-fine straight blond hair, carefully styled to curve against her neck and bring out her high cheekbones, she was certainly good-looking enough for any man. Smiling, she thought about the rest of her week. She had plans for both Saturday and Sunday evenings and with quick mental calculations she realized that she'd make almost four thousand dollars more by the end of the weekend. Not bad for a thirty-nine-year-old woman from a California commune.

The jangle of the phone startled her, but she did occasionally get calls from clients late at night. She had become quite accomplished at phone sex, and although she sometimes charged for the hour, she just as often enjoyed getting both herself and a man excited until they masturbated together without charge. As she crossed the bedroom, she pulled her robe tightly around her and glanced at the clock. Almost one. It could also be Erika with gossip about her evening.

"Hello?"

"Is this Brook Torrance?"

Brook dropped onto the edge of the bed, listening to the unfamiliar woman's voice. "Yes."

"You're a friend of a woman named Erika Holland?"

Brook's grip on the phone tightened and she swallowed hard. Had Erika been arrested? Was she in trouble? "Yes. Is something wrong?"

"I really regret the need to call you like this," the woman said. "I'm calling from the emergency room." She mentioned a prestigious midtown hospital. "I'm sorry to have to tell you that there's been an accident. We found your name on the emergency card in Ms. Holland's wallet so we thought you'd want to know that she's in critical condition and being transferred to the OR for surgery."

Brook's brain refused to function. "Operating room?"

"She's got a serious head injury, and the doctors need to relieve the pressure on her brain. She's holding her own right now, but we won't know much more than that for several hours."

Brook tried to picture Erika, vital and vivacious, now unconscious and being wheeled down a bright white corridor by some nurse who didn't know her. She'd need her friends. Brook felt her brain clearing, cataloging the things she needed to do. "I'll be right over. What happened?"

"The taxi she was riding in was broadsided by another car."

"I can stop at her apartment on the way over. What should I bring for her?"

"She won't be needing anything just yet," the calming voice said. "And please take your time getting here. It's very icy out and your friend will be in surgery for quite a while."

"I have several phone calls to make," she told the nurse, "and then I'll be there. Where should I go?"

The nurse gave her the hospital's address and details on where to find the waiting room. "Try not to worry, she's in good hands. The best neurosurgeons on staff are with her. Please believe that we're taking very good care of her."

"Thank you. I'm sure you are." Slowly Brook lowered the receiver to the cradle, then sat, trembling, on the edge of the bed. *Shit. Erika. Why now, when things are going so well? Damn.* After several minutes of blankness, Brook took a deep breath and found her address book. There were so many people who would want to know, want to be at the hospital to do whatever was necessary to help.

She flipped pages and began to dial.

Shara Marques was sprawled across the hotel bed, her café au lait skin bathed in perspiration, her short, tight ebony curls damp. Two French automobile executives lay panting, one on each side of her. Even after an evening of wine, dancing, laughter, and two hours of great sex, she still couldn't remember which was Georges and which was André.

After several minutes' rest, one of the men—she thought it was Andre—stood up, padded to the dresser, and handed her a stack of traveler's checks from his wallet.

"Thank you for an amazingly wonderful evening," he said, his accent thick. "Can I, or we, look you up when we're back in town?"

"Of course. I'd love to spend another evening with either or both of you, but right now I'm exhausted. You two wore me out." She stood, unself-consciously naked, and smiled. "When you're back in town, you know how to get in touch with me, through Courtesans, Inc." Allowing them another moment to admire her shapely body, she walked slowly into the bathroom and spent several minutes getting cleaned up. When she returned to the bedroom, she posed for a moment in her panties and thigh-high stockings, then slowly redressed in a long, white, beaded evening dress and found her matching purse. She opened it and, as she put the checks inside, noticed that there was a voice mail message on her pager. Snapping the purse shut and slipping on her shoes, she kissed each man good night and dropped an embossed business card on the table beside the bed. *Courtesans, Inc. Exclusive Escort Service.* "Be sure to call. I'm looking forward to seeing you again."

When the hotel room door closed behind her, Shara quickly pulled out the pager and pressed the *review* button. "Bad accident. Erika in OR. Call for directions to the waiting room." A phone number followed. "Don't call my cell phone, it'll probably be busy. Brook."

Shara's knees buckled and she slumped against the wall of the hotel corridor. *Erika. Accident.* The words kept swirling in her head. *Erika.* She couldn't be badly hurt. She just couldn't.

Shara found a soft upholstered chair beside the hotel elevators, scrubbed her hands over her face, and pulled out her cell phone. Desperately wanting to believe that things weren't as bad as they seemed, she called the hospital number and was told that Erika was still in surgery. As she pulled a small pad from her purse and wrote down the directions she was given to the waiting area, she pictured Erika's face, smiling as if sharing a joke with the world. Erika. Shit, bad things couldn't happen to such a good person. They just couldn't.

She slowly stood up, slipped her arms into her coat, and pulled it tightly around her as if to protect her from whatever lay ahead. Standing as tall as her five-foot, three-inch frame would allow, she pressed the elevator button.

Alex Kosta sat across the small table from a jewelry-laden woman about twenty years older than his thirty-one years. It was amazing how his Mediterranean good looks allowed him to appear to be as old or as young as he wanted. Tonight, in a dark suit, crisp white shirt, and striped tie, he could easily pass for forty-five. "I know what you mean, Dorothy," he said, fixing her with his intense gaze. "It's so difficult finding a reliable broker. I finally had to resort to doing my own research."

"When my Phillip died, he left me with absolutely no one to fall back on. I've just kept my accounts with the man who's always handled them. But—well, how is one to know?"

Alex placed his hand over Dorothy's and gazed deeply into her eyes. He knew how to play the game and he loved every nuance. He had spent countless evenings with wealthy women who wanted men to pay attention, listen, sympathize, and make love to them until they screamed in a most unladylike fashion. He could do all of those things and lots more, and he was well paid for his time. If he knew his women, and he did, he and Dorothy wouldn't end up in bed this evening. She'd be cautious, not wanting to seem as hungry as he knew she was. She'd tell herself that she wanted companionship and nothing more, although her body screamed for sex. She'd wait a few days, then get in touch with him and set up another evening similar to this one. Dinner and a play with drinks, talk, and this time sex afterward for two thousand dollars a night.

Alex didn't begrudge his women a single minute. He loved talking to them, being with them, making love to them. He loved the way they looked and smelled and tasted. He loved the way their skin glowed, their nail polish shined, their hair was always just so. He had loved women all his life, now he just made a business of it, thanks to Erika Holland.

As he held Dorothy's hand, he felt his pager vibrate.

Mei Lee was in a hotel room discussing the late evening's activities with a tall, angular financier with a hawklike nose and granite chin, a regular customer from Seattle, when her pager beeped. "I'm so sorry, Frank. I must have forgotten to turn the thing off."

"It's awfully late. Nothing bad I hope." They had been together every evening for the past four. "I know you have wonderful plans for me for the rest of the evening." He stroked the front of his carefully tailored slacks.

"Let me turn this thing off," Mei said, glancing at the screen of her pager as she pressed the power button. "Erika, critical." She blanched, scanned the rest of the message, then quickly pulled herself together. She was a professional, after all. "It's nothing that can't wait, darling. Just something I'll have to attend to later." She schooled her features, smiled, and returned to the conversation as if nothing untoward had happened. As soon as she was finished here, she'd find out the details and head directly over to the hospital.

"We have to talk about your behavior." She focused her attention on Frank and gestured. Quickly he knelt before her, his deep blue eyes gazing devotedly up at her. She had dressed especially for him in a tight black leather vest with one button holding it closed over her naked breasts and matching short skirt with nothing beneath. Her knee-high black boots gleamed as she slowly spread her legs and picked up a black wooden paddle from the table beside her. "We have to deal with the fact that you've been a very naughty boy." She smiled, smacked the paddle against her palm, and watched as he lowered his head and shuddered in delicious anticipation, particularly thrilled to be dominated by a four-foot-eleven Asian woman who looked sweet and innocent.

Later she'd see about Erika; dear Erika who had been there for her in her worst times. "What would be an appropriate punishment for your misbehavior?"

Stuart Dunlop was already asleep when his phone rang. Groggily, he reached for the receiver. "Hello?"

"Stuart, it's Brook. I'm sorry to have to wake you, but I thought you'd like to know. Erika's been in an accident. She's in surgery. We're gathering in the waiting area and I thought you'd want to be there."

"Of course." Stuart listened to what details Brook had, then hung up and sat on the edge of his bed, his head in his hands. Oh my God, Erika. He felt the telltale prickling at the back of his throat, the quiver of his lower lip. Grown men didn't cry, especially him. He felt a tear slowly trickle down his cheek and dashed it away with the back of his hand. She wouldn't want me to be like this, he thought, standing and purposefully straightening his spine.

Erika. There are so many things left for us to do. So much of life yet to be lived. He turned on the light and headed for his closet to dress.

In Chicago it was almost twelve-thirty when the phone rang. Rena Hughes rubbed the back of her neck and looked up from her computer screen, staring at the jangling instrument. "One minute," she called at it as she dumped several papers on the floor of the small second bedroom she had converted into an office. Although she'd had a modem line installed, she hadn't gotten an extension of her regular phone line and the cordless was in its charger. "I'm coming." Who could be calling her after midnight? As she stumbled through the living room of her small apartment, her mind clicked through the friends and relatives who might be in trouble.

The answering machine clicked on. "Hello, you've reached 312-555-1648. I can't come to the phone . . ." She grabbed the receiver. "Hello? Don't hang up. Just let me turn this thing off." She found the *off* button and heard the machine click into silence. "Hello?"

"Is this Maureen Hughes?"

"Yes. This is Rena."

"Are you the daughter of Erika Holland?"

At the mention of that name, Rena froze. She hadn't spoken to her mother in several months, and if she had her way, she'd keep it like that. "She and I aren't in contact." *And if there's trouble, I don't care.*

"I've called three M. Hugheses in Chicago and I'm glad I finally found you. Rena, my name is Brook Torrance. You don't know me, but I know quite a bit about you from your mom. I don't know how to make this easier. There's been an accident. The taxi your mother was in was broadsided by a car and she's in critical condition."

Rena couldn't think of anything to say. She opened her mouth but no words came out. *Mother.* That word wasn't part of her vocabulary. She hadn't seen Erika in almost two and a half years. Just before her college graduation, Rena had made it clear that her mother's visits were no longer welcome. Since then Erika had phoned several times, but the three minutes of torture hadn't done anything to heal the breach between the two women.

"I don't know whether you're interested in coming to New York to be with her," the woman's voice said, "but in case you are I just thought I'd give you a number where you can reach me." Brook gave Rena her cell phone number and the number of the hospital and reflexively Rena wrote them on a slip of paper. "You can get updated information about her condition from me or from them. I'll leave your name as next of kin so they'll keep you updated."

Rena cleared her clogged throat. Why did she care? Did she care? "Thank you for letting me know." *Next of kin,* she thought as she hung up the phone. Yes, she guessed that was true since there was no one else. Certainly not Rick, Erika's ex-husband, Rena's father. Had there been anyone else, Rena wasn't sure she would have been listed in her mother's address book at all. The phrase *She talks about you frequently* echoed in her head. She talks about me? I wonder what she says. What does she know about me anyway?

"Damn." Rena slammed a fist into the arm of the chair, then strode back into her office. She dropped into her desk chair but was unable to return to what she had been doing. She didn't need this. She was busy, happy, successful. She didn't need complications and that was all her mother had ever been to her, a complication. They were complications for each other, awkward remnants of a past that neither of them wanted to think about.

Staring at the computer screen, Rena remembered her mother as she had last seen her at her, poised, confident, dressed to kill. Damn. She didn't want any part of any of this, but she knew that the following morning she'd be on an eastbound plane if only to tell the woman how she felt one last time.

When neurosurgeon Ira Freed walked into the waiting room just after 4:00 A.M., he saw a cluster of about a dozen men and women, many dressed in trendy evening clothes, sitting, drinking coffee, and talking in whispers. One woman, a handsome blonde who stood out both for her good looks and her Donald Duck shirt and jeans, spotted him and stood up, quickly followed by the others. "Doctor," she said, "do you have news about Ms. Holland?"

"Are you all here for Ms. Holland?"

The woman looked at the concerned faces on the people who now clustered around. "Yes. I'm Brook Torrance and we're all Erika's friends. You might even call us family. Please, Doctor, what's happening?"

In addition to the good-looking blonde and the other women, the group contained a handsome man in a dark suit who could have been a Greek god and a rumpled, professorial looking man in his late forties. Amazed by the incredibly mixed assemblage, the neurosurgeon rubbed the back of his tension-tight neck and said, "I'm Dr. Freed and I operated on your friend. She's out of surgery and in recovery." He looked at all the concerned faces. No false hope, yet somehow he wanted to paint a slightly upbeat picture for these people. "She had an epidural hematoma as a result of the accident; that's a blood clot that forms on the surface of the brain. We had to operate to relieve some of the pressure. It was a long procedure, but it went as well as we could have hoped. Now all we can do is wait and let her body try to heal."

"Heal? Does that mean she's going to make it?" the professorial type asked.

"Don't jump to conclusions. She's unconscious and we don't have any idea whether she'll come out of it and, if she does, what condition she'll be in."

A spectacularly good-looking black woman with soft, toast-colored skin and liquid brown eyes said, "You mean she may never wake up?"

"I have to be honest with you. There's no guarantee of anything, and we won't know much for several hours at least. It will be days before we've got any real idea of her future. You all might as well go home and we'll get in touch when we know more."

"Thank you, Doctor," the blonde said. "We'll work everything out. Someone will be in the waiting room at all times, so if there's any change, just come here. May we see her?"

"She'll be in recovery for several hours. When we get her settled in ICU, one of you can go in for five minutes. She won't be able to respond, but she might be able to hear you. You can have a positive effect on her recovery if you're strong, upbeat, and supportive."

"Thank you, Doctor. Please keep us informed, even if it's just to say that nothing's changed."

"I'm afraid I didn't catch your name the first time around," he said to the blonde.

"It's Brook, Brook Torrance."

"Ms. Torrance," Ira said. Since she had seemed to be the spokesperson for the group, he assumed she was the closest to the woman in recovery. "Could I speak to you in private for a moment?"

"Of course," Brook said, following him into the hall. "And it's Brook. Is there something you didn't want to tell everyone else?"

"In a way," he said, stopping by a linen closet. He hoped he could handle this with delicacy. "I'm taking a bit of a risk here, Brook, but I think you're the one whom Ms. Holland would want to have this." He pulled a handful of gold chain from his pocket. "The nurses in the ER gave me this." He felt his face flush. "I gather it was, well, intimately arranged around her waist and other places."

He watched Brook's face ease and a hint of a smile curve her lips. That smile warmed him and, despite three hours of surgery and Ms. Holland's critical condition, made his body react in a sensual way he thought he'd forgotten. How could he have sensual feelings at a time like this? he wondered.

"Thanks," she said. "That's Erika's." She extended her hand and Ira dropped the chain into her palm.

"She must be quite a woman." He wondered whether Brook was wearing a chain like that, but shoved the thought from his mind. Bad timing.

"Yes, she is definitely quite a woman," Brook said, dropping the chains into the pocket of her jeans. "Thanks." Ira guided her back toward the waiting room with a hand in the small of her back, enjoying the play of the muscles beneath her shirt as she walked. *Stop it*, he told himself. *Just cut it out.*

Ira looked around at the group of visitors, all looking drawn and drained, some clasping hands, others holding shredded tissues. "Thank you for everything," Brook said.

"You're quite welcome. I'm glad that Ms. Holland has so many friends."

In the recovery room, Erika was beyond knowing how many friends she had. Her head swathed in bandages, she lay on the crisp white sheets, deeply unconscious, no sound in the room except the incessant beep and whine of monitors and machines. She knew nothing of the outside world, nothing about all the people sending prayers and love in great waves toward her. She felt only the pull of the light at the end of the long road she drifted along. Toward . . . From . . .

It had been such a long, bumpy road. Who would have considered ten years earlier that she would be where she was, who she was today. Such a long road.

Chapter

2

Ten years earlier

"Erika," Jarred McKay of Harcourt, Fried, Murray, and McKay said, "I wish I had better news."

Erika sat in the deeply padded leather chair before the lawyer's wide antique partners desk and crossed her long shapely legs. "I was afraid of that," she said with a long sigh, fighting tears of desperation, "but I had hoped . . ."

She had only about three months before her money ran out. The attorney's sizable retainer had almost depleted the proceeds from the sale of the Long Island house and its furnishings. She had sold all her good jewelry to pay for her move to a tiny one-bedroom apartment on the upper west side of Manhattan. Now the only cash she had left in the bank was what remained from the sale of her six-year-old Mercedes. If Jarred couldn't get her any alimony or even part of what she had helped Rick earn during their marriage, then she would have to resort to the *New York Times Classified*. And what skills did she have to get a job with? *What the hell am I going to do?*

As she felt her breathing quicken and her palms begin to

sweat, she straightened in her seat. *Panic is useless,* she told herself. She would figure something out, she had to. She purposely released some of the tension in her body and stroked her palms over her skirt. She had lost more than ten pounds since Rick's departure. Despite her extensive wardrobe, she had been very limited in her choices of what to wear this afternoon. She had settled on a dusty rose silk suit that used to be slightly tight and selected a black silk shell to wear beneath the boxy jacket. She had put her hair up in a tight French twist and had polished her nails in the exact shade of the suit. She thought about her clothes, classics from the best designers. Eventually she could send them to a consignment shop but she wasn't ready to take that final step just yet. And anyway, although she had spent a great deal on her wardrobe, the small amount she might receive would only delay the inevitable. She had to think about a more permanent solution, but not right now.

"I'm afraid your husband's tied everything up really tightly," Jarred said, jerking Erika back to reality. "You know the story as well as I do. Although he's drawing a seven-figure salary in Switzerland, it's from a Swiss subsidiary rather than the New York corporation and there's no way we can touch any of it. We'll get a judgment of divorce, of course, and on paper you'll receive half of everything you've helped him accumulate over the years of your marriage and alimony that would support you in the style, et cetera, et cetera. But that's only on paper and it's unenforceable unless your husband returns to the U.S. I know you've sold all the assets you could get your hands on, so in reality I'm afraid you're on your own."

Erika sagged against the back of the chair. Of course she had known all of what Jarred had just told her but hearing it aloud was so final, so definite. She had taken her wedding ring off several weeks earlier, but she found that, when she was upset she still played with the indentation where it had been. "What about my thirteen-year-old daughter?"

Erika needed her daughter and Rena needed her, whether the girl knew it or not. A teenaged girl should be with her mother, so Erika could help her through the awkwardness, the misery of being neither a child nor an adult. The school she was in was the best money could buy of course, but school in France was out of the question now. However, maybe she could stay for the rest of the semester and then come home once Erika was really settled and had her finances better organized. She'd have a job by then.

It would be such a change for Rena, from the fancy school in the small village in France to a New York City public school. From a cottage with three girls her own age to Erika's one-bedroom apartment on West Eighty-Seventh Street. Rick would probably at least send child support, which would allow Erika to work only part-time and be there when Rena got home from school. Although he obviously hated Erika, he loved his daughter . . . didn't he?

Jarred absently smoothed the sides of his carefully blow-dried hair with the palms of his hands. "Your husband has made it quite clear through his lawyer that he'll continue to pay whatever bills are necessary to support his daughter in school in France, but if she comes home to you, he'll pay you nothing."

"She can't come home?" Erika was dumfounded.

"Not if you want her to continue at that private school," Jarred said. "Your husband says that school is what you two decided was best for Maureen, and he sees no reason to change things." He cleared his throat. "He's doing this all on spite, of course, but again there's little we can do."

"She isn't coming home?"

"Unless you want to try to support both of you. If you let her stay in France, he says he'll take care of her during vacations and see that she wants for nothing."

Erika clenched her teeth. She had finally adjusted to the fact that the man she had lived with for almost fourteen years was no longer the man she had fallen in love with, but she had thought he'd agree that Rena should be with her mother. With another long sigh, she accepted the fact that Rick was trying to keep mother and daughter apart, using Rena to punish her. But why? Why was he so angry that he was trying to hurt her in every way possible? It must be more than just a thirty-seven-year-old man with a midlife crisis. He had been the one with girlfriends and the secret apartment in the city. He had been the one who came home less and less frequently, citing work and late-night meetings so he could be with some woman or another. He had been the one who finally decamped one afternoon with a would-be trophy wife, leaving Erika terrified until she received a formal letter from his attorney. He had been the one . . . but there was no use crying about what was in the past. "So I'm left with nothing. No money, no home, no alimony, no nothing." Her eyes filled. "And no daughter."

Jarred's voice sounded carefully calming. "You can and will stay in touch with your daughter, Erika. There will be phone calls and letters and, when you get back on your feet, trips to visit her. It will all work out eventually." He leaned forward in his wine-colored leather chair and propped his elbows on the desk. "You're an attractive woman and now you'll have your freedom. From what I've heard about your soon-to-be ex-husband, that's long overdue."

Was it long overdue? Erika wondered. How long had their marriage been empty? How long since there had been any genuine affection? She had spent quite a bit of the past four months looking back and she had finally accepted that there had been no real marriage for many years. Just cohabitation.

In the beginning it had been wonderful. Okay, they hadn't married under the best of circumstances; she had been pregnant with Rena. But they would have married anyway when Rick graduated from Harvard Business School and she from U.C. San Diego. His career certainly hadn't suffered from their slightly premature marriage; if anything she had helped him, molding herself into the ideal corporate wife and mother. She had supported him in every way she could think of, learning to play good bridge, adequate tennis, passable golf. She had listened and absorbed enough about his business to speak with some knowledge with Rick's associates, and had taught herself to entertain in the lavish style that was expected from the wife of a man who was "partnership material." She had seen that Rena went to gymnastics class with one partner's daughter and took tennis lessons with another. She had lunches at the country club and was a member of several charitable committees. Erika had been happy in those early years, when she really seemed to matter to Rick, before she'd become someone he either ignored or tried to work around.

Erika looked up and was startled to find Jarred seated in the chair beside her. "Erika," he said, leaning close and taking her hand, "it's really not that bad. You're charming and intelligent. You have so much to look forward to. Try to think of this as the beginning of something rather than the end." His blue eyes gazed deeply into her light brown ones.

"I know, Jarred," she said, enjoying the warmth of a man's touch. In the past four months, except for her new best friend Brook, she'd had very little contact with people. When word of Rick's transfer to Switzerland and the fact that he had left his wife for his executive assistant had gotten around, Erika had become *persona non grata* in the social circles in which she had traveled, as if a husband's defection might be catching. She had called Rena at school every weekend, but even her daughter had seemed distant and awkward, busy with her friends and unwilling to talk about more than the most superficial aspects of her life.

Erika focused on Jarred. "It's just that it's really been difficult adjusting and now to hear that I won't even have Rena. . . ." When she felt her eyes filling again, she pulled away, turning her face toward the windows, not seeing the spectacular view of midtown Manhattan. "I'm sure you go through this every day."

Jarred cupped her chin lightly and turned her face so she looked at him again. "Not with someone so attractive and so deliberately wronged. Your husband is part of your past, and that's behind you. You have a future, a long and eventful one. Erika, it's time you remembered that you're a woman, a beautiful, sexy woman." The touch of his fingers was warm as he gently stroked her jaw. "Let me prove it to you. Have dinner with me."

Have dinner with me. Erika closed her mind to the past and future and concentrated on the present. If she were being honest, she had half-expected his dinner offer. Jarred had been not-so-subtly coming on to her since her first visit to his office and, although he was a bit smarmy, he was an attractive man. He was offering dinner, but it was obvious that he intended for her to be dessert.

Why not take him up on his offer? She was only thirty-five and she needed to prove something to herself. She was going to do what she wanted for a change. That was why she had dressed so carefully today, she realized. She and Rick had had a rich and varied sex life, which, at the end, had been the only good part of their marriage. She could almost feel his fingers, his mouth, his body. God, she realized, she had missed it during the four months since his departure. Although she had never been with anyone but Rick, for this moment she needed to feel like a grown-up woman who wasn't the loser that her soon-to-be-ex thought her to be.

Erika gazed at the attorney's perfectly styled pale brown hair, his lightly tanned skin, his penetrating blue eyes, and knew exactly what she would be getting herself into. Not love, not commitment. Just sex, pure and simple. As she felt her body respond, she uncrossed and recrossed her legs, rubbing her stocking-covered thighs together. He might be using her, but she was going to use him as well. A small smile curved the corners of her mouth and she didn't break the eye contact. "Jarred . . ."

He took her hand. "Please. Let me help you celebrate the beginning of Erika Hughes, phase two."

"Holland. Erika Holland." She looked down and saw that, while Jarred held her right hand, she was playing with the empty ring finger of her left. No. That married woman was gone now. "Erika Hughes is history. I want my maiden name back."

Jarred reached over and scribbled a note on his pad, the only thing besides her divorce folder that lay on his highly polished desk. "No problem. It can be handled at the same time as the divorce." He turned back to her, propped his elbows on his knees, and took both of her hands in his. "Tell me you'll have dinner with me."

Erika's smile widened. Rick was gone. She had gone through the denial and the grieving. Now she was beginning to accepted the fact that she really didn't want him back. As the cliché went, This was the first day of the rest of her life. It was time to become Erika Holland. "I'd love to have dinner with you, Jarred."

The following afternoon Erika stood at the sink in her tiny apartment, filling a teakettle with water. "You know, Brook," she said to her friend who leaned against the kitchen counter, "I feel better today than I thought I would. Actually knowing that there's no money is a relief in some ways. I know where I stand and I can move on."

Erika's best friend was the only good thing to come out of her divorce. Brook, a free-spirited child of the sixties, had knocked on Erika's door two months earlier on her first Saturday in her new apartment. "I saw the moving men bringing in some of your boxes," Brook had said. "I live upstairs, so I thought I'd say hello and welcome you to the neighborhood." That wonderfully cheerful voice had been the first crack in Erika's depression and had started her climb back to the real world. A naturally charming, open, honest woman in her late twenties, Brook had a no-nonsense way of looking at the world and the people in it. They had become friends and confidants almost immediately.

"The sex last night was obviously great," Brook said now.

"What sex?" Erika said, trying to look innocent.

"Don't kid me, babe," Brook said, sorting through a basket of herb teas. "Fess up. You and the hunky lawyer got it on last night. It's written all over your face."

As she put the kettle on the burner and turned the knob on the two-element stove, Erika thought about denying everything. But in the few months the two women had known each other, they had gotten so close that lying was out of the question. Instead she blushed. "Okay. Yes, we did, and the sex was wonderful." Brook handed her a bag of Cranberry Dream and Erika dropped it into her cup. "God, I hadn't realized how much I missed it."

Jarred had taken her to a small but very fashionable local restaurant that specialized in northern Italian food. They had eaten slowly and shared a bottle of wonderful Cabernet. Mellow and relaxed for the first time in months, Erika enjoyed Jarred's attention and his obvious desire for her. Seated side by side on an elegantly embroidered banquette, she had felt him press his muscular thigh against hers. As the evening progressed, his warm hand had wandered slowly along her leg, making her skin tingle with expectation. She had felt a sexual excitement she hadn't felt in a very long time, an anticipation of something intense. She had also flirted outrageously, and her hand had found his leg and the hardness beneath his suit pants. She had hungered and felt herself getting wet, and she had enjoyed it.

Later they had arrived at Jarred's apartment and ripped each other's clothes off in their mutual frenzy. Together they had fallen on the thick carpet, Jarred's fingers unerringly finding her opening and plunging inside, pistoning in and out while her hips bucked and her chest heaved. She had come almost immediately; then he moved so he could lap at her juices while she licked his hard cock. A small part of her registered that he didn't feel or smell like Rick and his lovemaking was very different, but it hadn't mattered.

God, he felt so good, the skin on his penis smooth and velvety with the steely hardness beneath. She parted her lips and flicked her tongue over the tip of his cock while he sucked and licked deep between her legs. She pursed her lips and kissed his cock-head then created suction so he was drawn into her wet mouth. Over and over she pulled back, then sucked him in.

"God, Erika, you're marvelous," he said, lifting his head and panting. "Let me get something." He rummaged in his wallet and found a condom, quickly covering his cock and positioning it at the entrance to her sopping pussy. "Now, lady, I'm going to fuck your brains out."

"Do it," she yelled, her voice harsh and needy. "Do it." He filled her and she thrust against him, meeting his every plunge. Their lovemaking was fierce and almost savage. She wrapped her legs around his waist and pulled him more deeply into her, her blood boiling. She guided his hands to her breasts. As they found their rhythm, he pulled at her tender flesh. "Yes," she screamed as she writhed and strained beneath him. "God, yes." As he climaxed, she came again.

"Earth to Erika," Brook said as the kettle bubbled. "Come in, Erika."

Erika blinked and returned to the present. "Sorry. I drifted off."

"You certainly weren't here, and you were grinning."

"I was not," Erika said, tightening the muscles around her mouth.

"Yeah, you were, and that's great. It's about time you accepted that sex is a necessary part of every woman's life. So tell me everything, babe," Brook said, tearing open the wrapper on a bag of English breakfast tea and dropping it into her cup. "What's the sexy attorney like in bed?"

Erika momentarily regretted telling Brook about Jarred, but it was also delicious to share something so exciting. She'd never really had a girlfriend to share with. She relaxed and her smile almost split her face. "We never made it to the bed, but he was pretty darn good, actually." She rubbed the base of her spine.

"Rug burns?" Brook asked.

"How did you know?"

"Been there, done that," Brook said with a grin. "Was he better than Rick?"

Erika thought about it. "Jarred was hard and hungry while Rick was creative." Not wanting to discuss *creative*, she snorted. "I wonder whether Sandy is any good between the sheets." Sandy Braverman was Rick's twenty-four-year-old ex–executive assistant, now Swiss roommate.

"Ah yes. Sandy of the perky breasts and flat belly with no stretch marks." Brook had listened to Erika complain about the younger women so often that she mirrored all of Erika's feelings. "Sandy the slut," she muttered, making Erika snicker.

"You've got to stop calling her that."

"Why? It makes her easier to hate that way."

"I know, but if I were being honest, some of the divorce was my fault too."

"Probably, but who has to be honest? And stop changing the subject. Tell me about last night. I want details."

"No details. Suffice it to say that he was hot and hard and very satisfying. And God, it's been so long."

"I know it has. You said he's attractive. Does he look good naked? So many men look great in clothes but dressed only in skin? Some men I've been with should have kept their clothes on while fucking."

"Brook! You're outrageous."

"I'm just being honest and really curious. How did he look? This is important stuff here."

In spite of herself, Erika relented. "Yes. He looks as good naked as he does in a suit and tie." She paused then continued, "Part of me is really embarrassed about all this."

"Don't be, just keep talking."

"He kept telling me how beautiful and hot I was. Sometimes it sounded so corny. I'm sure he does this with every willing, newly divorced woman who enters his office, but I wanted it and I took it." He even had a convenient pied-à-terre like Rick did, she thought.

"Who gives a shit who he does it with? Last night was good for you and you look really alive for the first time since I've known you. Let's have more details."

Erika giggled. "You really are nuts. Do I look like the type of woman who would kiss and tell?"

"Of course. What good are friends it they can't compare men and techniques?"

"Enough, Brook," Erika said as the kettle's whistle startled them both.

"You're no fun at all." She looked at Erika as her friend filled the cups with boiling water. "You're not having second thoughts about last night, are you?"

"I should be, but I'm not. Yesterday I got the final word, the bad news about Rick and about my finances and I should be down about that, too, but I'm not. I feel free somehow."

"So forget the 'shoulds' and just let yourself be whatever you are."

Following Brook, Erika wandered into the living room, set her cup on the coffee table and settled on the worn chintz sofa. She looked around at the comfortable couch and matching over-stuffed chair covered with faded cabbage roses, the scratched end tables and the coffee table covered with white cup-rings, all left by the woman from whom she had taken over the apartment.

The furniture was all one step up from the Salvation Army, but it was hers now. She was free, independent, and—she had to admit—happier than she had been the previous day. She'd move on. She had to. No more "shoulds." Thoughts of Rena flashed through her mind, but she squelched them. She'd keep up their relationship as best she could, but Rena would stay in school in Europe while she made a life for herself in New York.

Erika tucked her feet beneath her. "Now I have to get a job and figure out what I'm going to do with the rest of my life. And I've got to talk to Rena, try to get her to understand that I realize that I was a fool to send her away to school but that right now I can't have her here. I know now that I made a lot of mistakes and I just want a chance to make it up to her." She started to get teary, her emotional roller-coaster plunging again.

"Are you going to tell her that her father will only pay as long as she stays in France?"

"What's the point in that?" Erika said. "She'd resent him for it and since it's really for the best I'll let it go. She needs the stability that the school can offer, and Rick will be there for her. As much as I love her, the more I think about it, the more I realize that I can't handle her right now."

"She needs to know that and that you want her."

Erika's eyes filled. "I know, and I do want her, but I also need to find out who I am and doing that, broke, with a teenager just seems so daunting." She swiped at her tears. "Am I wrong? Should I bring her here?"

Brook squeezed Erika's hand. "You've made that decision, so stop revisiting it."

"I guess." Erika grabbed a tissue from the box on the end table. She'd used a lot of them in the past few months.

"We'll have none of that," Brook snapped. "There's no use crying over things you can't change. We'll do some serious thinking about how we can fund a trip to Europe for you. I wish I could help you more, but my savings aren't in much better shape than yours. You know, of course, that anything I have is yours."

Erika reached out and hugged her friend. "Oh Brook, I couldn't take your money. I'll find some other way."

"For the moment, just keep calling every week and let Rena know you care. Do you have any idea why Rick is being like that? I know men are often really hard-nosed about alimony but not letting her live with you . . ."

Erika swallowed hard, then took a sip of her tea. "I don't really understand it. Midlife craziness maybe. Maybe he never loved me and just married me because of the baby. Maybe he got a taste of what life could be without a wife and child. Who knows, and in the end it doesn't really matter. Jarred will get all the paperwork in order so that if Rick sets one Gucci loafer in the U.S. he's toast, but as long as he's willing to stay in Switzerland we can't touch him and that's that."

"How bad are your finances really?"

"Bad. Most of the money I ended up with after everything was sold is gone. I can last a couple of months, but I have to find a job."

Brook settled back and looked at her thoughtfully. "Okay, so what can we find for you to do to make a living?"

"You don't have to be part of this, Brook. It's enough that you're such a great friend."

Brook puffed out her ample chest. "That's what terrific friends like me are for. Let me try to get you something at Juskowitz," she continued, referring to the advertising agency she worked for.

"It's not going to be easy," Erika said. "I don't have any skills, unless you include knowing which wines go with which foods or entertaining twenty at dinner."

Brook looked suddenly hopeful. "How about being a catering consultant, something like that?"

"I didn't really enjoy it when I did it for Rick and me, and I know I'd hate doing it for strangers. I would if I could, of course, but to do that sort of thing you need contacts and I'm pretty much out of touch with my old crowd." She sipped her tea slowly.

"Okay," Brook said, "you're right about contacts, so that's out. You're a bright woman with most of a college degree. We'll think of something."

"Yeah, most of a college degree in art history. I don't have"— she made quote marks in the air—"skills like typing or taking shorthand. I don't even know how to use a computer."

"There must be things you can do. We'll come up with something." Her eyes lit up. "While we search, I've got some teach-yourself tapes that I got with my computer. I'll bet you could learn basic word processing and stuff. If I can do it, you certainly can."

The roller-coaster climbed again. "Thanks. That would really help. Maybe I'll eventually have something to offer besides being a corporate wife."

"Tomorrow we tackle the classifieds."

The following morning, Brook rang Erika's doorbell at 10:00 A.M., several pounds of *New York Times* under her arm. Erika welcomed her friend dressed in black-and-tan plaid slacks, a soft tan sheer-wool shirt, and black flat-heeled shoes.

"You put me to shame," Brook said, looking Erika up and down. "I just love your wardrobe." She put the paper on the coffee table.

Erika eyed the faces of Donald and Daisy Duck and the words *So Many Ducks and So Little Time* on the front of Brook's sweat-shirt and said, "I love the way you can wear the most outrageous things and come out looking great." She led Brook into the bedroom and opened the closet doors. "As for my wardrobe, I certainly won't need to spend any money on work clothes for the next century."

"Holy shit," Brook exclaimed, her eyes widening at the amazing assortment of clothing. "I never dreamed anyone could have so much stuff."

"In my old life I spent a large part of my time shopping." Erika looked embarrassed. "I've got a lot more stuff in the storage room in the basement. I keep thinking that if I get really desperate I can send some outfits to a consignment shop, but I don't think they would be worth much used." She smiled ruefully. "I have to admit that I really like nice clothes. Once I gain back some of the weight I've lost I'll be able to wear them again." She fingered a blue satin evening dress and then looked at Brook. "You know, we're about the same size. You can borrow anything you need any time."

"You wouldn't kid a friend." She stroked a soft green wool suit. "I might just take you up on that." Brook closed the closet doors and the two women walked back into the living room. Brook rifled through the newspaper and, pulling out the classified ads, said, "So where's my tea?"

Later, as she did every Sunday afternoon, Erika called Rena's school. "How are you, honey?" she asked, the phone connection making communication difficult.

"I'm fine, Mom," Rena said, her voice sounding tight and controlled.

"How's school going?"

"Fine."

How did one communicate with a thirteen-year-old? With only short conversations each weekend, they had little to talk about. "I've begun to look for a job. It won't be easy to find one, but I'm going to learn to use a computer. I'm a bit intimidated."

"Oh, Mother, really. Anyone can do it. Even you."

Even you. "Any tests lately?"

"Sure. Every week. They're okay."

"How about your teachers? Anyone giving you problems?"

"Nah. They're okay too."

"Have you thought about the summer? Maybe you could come home and be with me for a few weeks."

"I'm going to Japan with Dad for six weeks. And Sandy's going, too."

Erika didn't like the nasty note of triumph in her daughter's tone. Had they grown so far apart? "You mean there isn't any time for me in all that vacation?"

"Oh Mom, be real. I've only got a few weeks and the Japan trip will take most of it. Actually I'm going to miss the first week of school as it is."

"Is missing school really a good idea? The first week is when everything gets set up for the year."

Her voice firm, Rena said, "Dad says I can, so I'm going to."

There was no hesitancy in her voice. The decision had been made by the only ones who were important to her, her father and herself. "Well, maybe I'll be able to come to France to see you soon."

"Whatever. I've got to go now. Julie is waiting."

"Who's Julie?" Erika said, then realized that the line was dead.

During the next several weeks, Erika split her time between interviewing for jobs and practicing with Brook's computer. She bought a learn-to-type program and dutifully did hours of exercises until her fingers could find the correct keys most of the time. Then she moved on to *Teach Yourself Word Processing in 12 Hours*, mastering the techniques of creating and editing documents. Finally, after six weeks of exhausting job hunting and interviewing, she landed a position as the executive assistant to the vice president of the Proxmeyer Insurance Agency. She quickly realized that she was, in reality, a gofer who got Dave Proxmeyer's suits from the cleaner and bought birthday gifts for his children, but the weekly paycheck was just enough to support her apartment. She was making it. Herself.

Over many dinners in Erika's or Brook's apartment and drinks in small local watering holes, the two women really got to know each other. Brook had grown up the child of free-spirited parents who exerted very little control of their daughter's personal life. As a child and young adult, Brook had been able to do what she pleased, except when it came to education. Her mother, Blossom christened Bertha, had been a schoolteacher before her marriage and saw to it that her three children as well as all the other children of the commune received a thorough education until Brook went to public high school.

As a teenager, Brook had had only two interests: reading and sex. Her insatiable appetite for books and almost photographic memory resulted in an amazingly eclectic collection of information on topics as diverse as seventeenth-century French history and the greenhouse gases on Venus.

Her other interest—members of the opposite sex—had begun when she turned thirteen and graduated from high school boys to the yuppy Wall Street types she now dated for periods lasting from one date to several weeks, seldom longer. "I guess I've made love to hundreds of men through the years," Brook said one hot summer evening over a beer at Gerald's Place, "and I never tire of it. Frankly, I think it's high time for you to get back into the game. I'm sorry that you never repeated your evening with the sexy lawyer."

"Jarred was just a one-night stand, a notch on his bedpost and mine, and we both knew it. Sure, it was wonderful and it was perfect for me at that moment, but he was just a horny divorce attorney taking advantage of a recently separated, hungry woman."

"But the sex was explosive," Brook said, shaking her head in amazement. "How can you be content to just give it up? Don't you need regular doses of hay-rolling?" She sipped her beer.

"It certainly doesn't seem so. I look at the guys you pick up and they do nothing for me."

"You know, I find that when I have to do without for a while I seem to lose interest. What you need is a hot date that ends with some great sweaty sex to get you back in the swing of things."

Erika raised an eyebrow. "What I need is to take my time. When it happens, it will happen."

"Not! You can't be happy without good sex. That's Aunt Brook's first law."

"Listen, Aunt Brook," she said warmly, "I'm fine. Truly."

"What about Stuart? He's really sweet and all, so how about him?"

Stuart Dunlop. He and his wife had three boys ranging in age from several years older than Rena to a little younger. Stuart had been a business partner of Rick's. Over the past few months, he had been wonderful about helping her deal with the details of starting over. He had helped her find the apartment she was now renting, recommended Jarred, guided her with her limited finances, and most important, he had been supportive, kind and a good friend.

Erika had hardly known Stuart before Rick decamped but only a week after his departure, Stuart had shown up at her door asking to help. He had made it quite clear that he was ashamed of Rick's behavior and was trying in some way to make it up to her. "I mentored him when he first joined the firm," Stuart had told her, "and I told him then that if he just kept them discreet, his little dalliances would be overlooked. I really hate myself for that now, but it was, and still is, the company line. Several of the partners have relationships on the side." He had sighed. "That advice sounded fine at the time but I never considered who might get hurt. Helping you is partly for your sake and partly penance for me."

Since then Erika and Stuart had had dinner together every week or so. At first she had needed his advice on various money matters, but now that she was feeling capable of managing her own affairs they were just friends getting together for good conversation. Although she had to admit that she found him attractive, he was very happily married and thus strictly off-limits.

"He's not going to be in my bed. Period. He's not interested, I'm not interested and he's married to a terrific lady. Butt out."

Brook looked momentarily chagrined. "Okay. I will butt out for the moment, but you're on my to-do list from now on. You need things that I can help you with and I'm not going to let you spend the rest of your life working and not rewarding yourself."

Erika took Brook's hands across the tiny table. "Thanks. You really are a good friend and eventually I know I'll be ready for hot sweaty sex. You'll be the first to know, I promise."

One Tuesday evening after Erika had been living in New York City for almost five months, she met Stuart after work at the Pagoda Palace, a neighborhood Chinese restaurant around the corner from her apartment. Decorated like every other Chinese restaurant, with watercolor paintings of Chinese life, storks, and dragons, the place was small and comfortable, and the food was sensational. It was an unseasonably warm late-September evening and while Erika was dressed casually, Stuart wore his standard suit, dress shirt, and tie.

They met outside, embraced as old friends do, bussed each other's cheeks and immediately began to catch up on news about their lives and gossip at the firm. "How's Rick doing in Zurich?" Erika finally asked as their appetizers arrived. She was amazed that she could now talk about him without much pain.

"Actually," Stuart said over steamed dumplings, "he's doing well."

Why she wanted to know she couldn't fathom, but she asked, "What about Sandy? Are they still an item?"

"I'm afraid so. I have no idea what he thinks she's got that you don't. You're quite a woman and it's too bad he forgot that over the years. Sometimes you remind me to notice how wonderful Lorraine is."

She tucked one leg beneath her. "Thanks for that, Stuart. You've really been a lifesaver. I don't know what I would have done without you."

"I've thought about that," Stuart said, "and I've decided that you'd have been just fine. Maybe you'd have moved a bit more slowly, but you'd have pulled yourself together and done okay, even without me. You're a survivor, Erika, and whatever you set your mind to will happen."

Stuart always seemed to say just the right thing. "Thanks for that, too."

They chatted about many things over a dinner of kung pao chicken and orange beef. When the fortune cookies arrived Erika cracked hers open and read aloud, "There are new and wonderful things in store for you."

"That could be true, Erika," Stuart said. "Actually I've got something to discuss with you and I need you to have an open mind and not judge too quickly."

Totally puzzled, Erika chewed her cookie. "Sure. Shoot."

"Cadmire," he said, referring to the investment banking firm he and Rick worked for, "is having a very important dinner party for two European bankers. Greg Wolfe will be there with his wife as will Mark and Stephanie Harris. I'm bringing Lorraine. I want you to come and even the boy-girl ratio a bit."

"I don't know, Stuart. It's been a long time for me, and I'm not sure I want to make nice with Greg and whoever else. I've still got a lot of issues with Cadmire and the way they seemed to condone Rick's leaving me penniless."

"There's money in it for you."

"Excuse me?"

"We'll pay you for the evening. Cadmire often hires very high class women to even the odds at dinners like this. They are highly paid escorts, intelligent, classy, able to take an equal part in conversations, like that."

Erika gasped and tossed her napkin on the table. "Paid escorts?" she hissed. "You mean hookers. Are you suggesting that I become a prostitute?" She started to stand up, trying hard to control her fury.

"Sit down and listen," Stuart snapped as everyone turned to stare. He lowered his voice. "You know me better than that."

Slowly, Erika settled back into her chair. Glaring at Stuart, she said, "Okay. Explain."

"I'm talking about a paid escort not a bed partner. Only you can decide how far you want to go with any man, but that's not included in the price. We pay these women five hundred dollars for an evening. Notice I said evening, not night."

"Five hundred dollars?" Erika gasped.

"Precisely."

"Okay, if they aren't spending time in bed, what are they hired to do? That's a lot of money for just an evening of pleasant conversation."

"To be entertaining, charming and intelligent like the old Italian courtesans or Japanese geishas. You've been at dinners like the ones I'm talking about, and frequently there were paid escorts invited. I don't think you knew the difference, did you?"

She remembered attending and enjoying many dinners of stimulating conversation with intelligent people. Rick had always praised her ability to find an interest she shared with a dinner companion. As she mentally cataloged the attendees at the most recent evenings she could think of, she couldn't remember noticing any women who looked like paid escorts. "You're kidding. Paid women? At those business dinners that Rick enjoyed so much?"

"Absolutely."

Erika mentally shook herself. At first she had thought Stuart had lost his mind and she couldn't decide whether she was incensed or hurt. Now, as she allowed the idea to bounce around in her mind, she understood that he was asking for something quite different. She focused on the last such dinner she and Rick had attended and thought about the women at the table. Three of the six had been wives or girlfriends of the partners, but the other three had been introduced as friends of someone. She hadn't thought a thing of it and the women had fit right in. Paid courtesans? She still couldn't quite digest it. "Why does the firm pay?"

"It's really bad policy and quite awkward to have several more men than women at things like this. It puts the clients off, makes them feel awkward and out of place when we want them to be happy. Very happy. Years ago, we scrambled, asking the partners' wives to find friends to invite. That worked, up to a point but then, I don't know who made the connection, someone found out that for a modest fee . . ."

"Five hundred dollars is a modest fee?" Erika gasped.

"It is for us. Remember these men represent millions of dollars in bottom line profits, and as you of all people should know, the bottom line is everything. This isn't charity we're talking about here."

"Okay. I'm listening. Go on."

"We began to hire women for our gatherings. We sprinkle the Christmas and summer parties with them and use them at dinners like the one next Wednesday. When I found out about this particular evening, I thought of you for several reasons."

"I'm unattached and probably horny," Erika snarled.

"That's not worthy of you, Erika, and not very complimentary of me either."

Erika lowered her gaze. "I'm sorry, Stuart."

He took her hand. "I know you are and I'm sure this is a bit of a shock to your sensibilities. I thought of you because you're a high-class woman quite comfortable at the kind of dinner we're having. As Rick's ex-wife, you've got the credentials and I can bring you as a friend who is just returning from a sort of self-imposed exile." He paused. "There's another reason, too. To me it feels like a wonderful way to get even with the senior partners. Paying you with even a tiny part of Rick's profits amuses me. If I made a mistake, I'm truly sorry."

Erika was silent for several minutes. She was tempted for all the reasons Stuart had mentioned. What a kick being paid with

Rick's money. "You make it sound positively reasonable." Her expression softened. "And I do love the idea of spitting in the firm's eye. I don't know whether I'm ready for that kind of thing, though. I'm really out of practice."

"Please," Stuart said waving his hand, "you don't forget how to behave. It's part of you. If you want to do it you'll be perfect, and if not, that's all right too."

"Do the men in question know that the woman are paid?"

"Sometimes yes, sometimes no."

"If they know we're paid escorts, don't they expect sex?"

"If they know at all, it's completely understood that if they hit it off with a particular woman, they can suggest whatever they want. But it's *not*, I repeat, *not* part of what the ladies are paid for. Confidentially, I think most of the women make extra money after our evening ends, but that's between the parties involved."

"So what if someone thinks I'm dessert?"

"You do whatever you want, but it's not expected or compulsory. A gentle no will suffice."

"What you're suggesting sounds illegal and immoral."

"I guess that if, after dinner, he and she exchange money for sex it's technically illegal but that's between them. As far as morality goes, what's the difference between accepting dinner and a movie in exchange for some time in bed or taking the cash."

Erika gasped. "Stuart. You sound as though you're advocating prostitution. I never would have expected that from you."

"I'm honest with myself. Lorraine and I have a wonderful marriage, and I wouldn't dream of going outside of it. However, there are lots of lonely people in the world who just want someone to be with or make love to. What's the harm? Who's hurt? Certainly not either party in the transaction."

Presented like that, it sounded so reasonable. Erika's mind was scrambled. Stuart was challenging some of the things she had always believed. Prostitution was bad. Period. Wasn't it?

Things were just true because they were true. "Society's hurt. It demeans women. I don't know. The men's wives are hurt because they lose part of their husbands."

"That last one is probably true and I certainly don't advocate men cheating on their wives. When you think about it more carefully, however," he continued, "legalized prostitution makes sense. If a guy's going to do it anyway, maybe it's better that he does it with a professional who knows the score than picking some innocent up in a bar who's going to be hurt. If two people want to have sex for money, how does that demean women? These women are doing it by choice and many of the high-class call girls make a fabulous living doing it. Anyway, what I'm talking about isn't prostitution."

She shook her head slowly. "Stuart Dunlop, boy radical. Somehow I don't see you that way."

His expression eased. "I take it you're not too angry with me."

Erika felt her body relax. "Of course not. It's an interesting offer and I have to think about it. Can I let you know in a day or two?"

"I need to know by Friday, so I can plan something else if your answer is no. Do give it some serious thought. It's just one evening after all. Think about it and call me."

"I'll do just that," Erika said, her mind already whirling.

Just one evening. Erika thought of little else after Stuart walked her to her building. It was just an evening of pleasant conversation, not unlike dozens she and Rick had spent over the years. And Stuart had assured her that there need not be any hanky-panky. Five hundred dollars. Erika had been trying to figure a way to travel to France and visit Rena but hadn't yet managed to save enough to cover even part of the plane fare. An evening like this would go a long way toward covering her expenses. *Stop it!* she told herself. *You're justifying doing it and that's stupid. Either do it because you want to or don't, but don't bring Rena into it.*

Admit it, she said to herself. *You're intrigued*. She decided to use Brook as a sounding board.

"I need someone to talk to," she said when Brook answered the phone. "Can I come up?"

"Sure, babe. I'll put on the kettle."

Erika trotted up the two flights of stairs to Brook's apartment and when she arrived the door was ajar. "I'm finishing the tea," a voice said from the tiny kitchen. "Make yourself comfortable."

Brook's apartment was identical in layout to Erika's but that was where any similarity ended. Where Erika's was neat and organized, Brook's living room was a jumble of books, newspapers, and magazines. Her computer sat on a desk in the corner covered with boxes of disks and instructions on various programs. Two walls were covered with bookshelves containing everything from romance novels to tomes on European history. The clothes Brook had worn that day were scattered on the sofa and her dinner dishes were still on the card table beside the sofa. An old window air conditioner hummed in the corner, barely combating the muggy night air.

As she had many times, Erika picked up several items of clothing and compulsively folded them before piling them on the arm of a worn butter yellow leather chair. She thought about all the contrasts between herself and Brook. Erika carefully logged every cent that passed through her wallet and bank account in a notebook. Brook's checkbook was such a disaster that she had finally asked for Erika's help. Erika's makeup was done with a light touch, but it was always perfect and she touched up her lipstick several times a day. Although she was from California, Brook had Midwest farm girl good looks that needed almost no makeup. Erika knew that her friend started the day with a coating of pale gloss, but after a few hours it was gone, not to be replenished. How they had become such good friends was a puzzle, and a miracle. Erika kicked off her shoes, settled on the textured oatmeal sofa, and tucked her feet beneath her.

"I assumed hot tea despite the temperature," Brook said as she walked in from the tiny kitchen, holding two steaming mugs. She handed her friend a cup of Cranberry Dream. "So what's up? Stuart make a pass?" She was wearing a pair of loose orange shorts and a faded green T-shirt with a picture of Winnie the Pooh on the front. Her reading glasses were perched on top of her head, and her long hair was pulled back in a pony tail with a purple scarf.

"Not a chance. He's happily married and totally monogamous."

"How dull. So what's the problem?"

Briefly Erika outlined the situation as Stuart had explained it to her. "Not prostitution exactly, but it feels like it."

Brook had remained silent until Erika finished. "There's no sex unless you and he want it, right?"

"Yeah, but it still feels dirty somehow."

"If it feels dirty, then just say no and that's that. What do you need me for?"

Erika stared at her hands. In a small voice she continued, "Part of me is intrigued by the idea."

"Bravo!" Brook said. "There is life in the woman yet. I wouldn't have pushed you to do it if you hadn't had the spark, but if you think you might be interested . . ."

Erika pulled on the little cardboard tag, dunking the tea bag over and over. "You sound as if you approve."

"I do. Go. Have a great evening and get paid by the company that has happily screwed you. Then pocket the cash and buy yourself something outrageous with it. Or go visit your kid."

"What if the guy wants more? What if he offers me money to go to bed with him?"

"You can decide that when it happens. Do whatever you want. If he's a drag, tell him no. If he's attractive, go dancing and see what develops. If he knocks your socks off, fuck his brains out but don't forget to take the money. Oh, and bring protection in case he doesn't have any."

Erika snorted. "Just do it. Just like that."

"You know I cruise for company," Brook said, her voice tinged with wistful longing. "I love men. What's so different between what I do and what you're contemplating? I do it for the fun of it, but I'd give my left arm to get paid for it, too."

"So *you* go."

"I'd love to," Brook said, "but I wasn't invited and you were."

"I was, wasn't I," Erika said, looking very pleased with herself.

"So when is the big night?"

"Next Wednesday."

"Have you decided what to wear?"

Without hesitation, Erika responded, "I have a simple deep-blue dress. . . ."

"Gotcha. You've already decided to go, haven't you?"

Erika sighed and took a swallow of her tea. "I guess I have. It's really scary, but I have to admit that it sounds exciting, too."

"So go and have a blast and let what happens after dinner take care of itself."

"Yeah," Erika said. "Yeah."

Chapter

3

Erika changed her mind a dozen times before Friday, and each time she had a long conversation with Brook. Over and over her friend assured her that whatever she did was fine and that she really had to make her own decision.

Friday afternoon Stuart called. "I need to know about next Wednesday evening one way or the other, Erika," he said, "so I can make other arrangements if you don't want to do it."

"Won't everyone there know I'm being paid? I couldn't let Greg or anyone else find out."

"I've thought about that. I can take care of it and get the money to you privately. The only issue here is whether you want to do it. Do you?"

Erika let out a long sigh. If she were being honest, she really wanted to, but somehow she didn't want Stuart, or herself for that matter, to know that.

"It won't make me think less of you," Stuart said after a long silence. "I love you and I'll abide by whatever you want, but I think it would be good for you to get out, even without the money." She could hear the warmth in his voice. "And the money's quite an incentive, too."

"It is and I really want to do it."

"I'll take that as a yes and hang up now before you can talk yourself out of it again. Good-bye, Erika."

Feeling good inside, she said, "I love you, too, Stuart. I'll see you Wednesday," and hung up.

For the remainder of the time before the "big day" as she had taken to calling it, she worried about how to behave, what to talk about, and exactly what to wear. Finally, on Wednesday, she left work early, took a long bubble bath, polished her fingernails and toenails and styled her hair in the same type of slick twist she had worn to Jarred's office. Was this for the same purpose: to make a man want to take it down and play with it? To expose her neck so that some man would want to nibble on it? After a light coating of hairspray, she vowed not to play shrink games with herself. She could probably psychobabble herself into a breakdown without too much effort.

At six, Brook charged through Erika's bedroom door wearing a Mickey Mouse T-shirt and tight black leggings. She found her friend putting on eyeliner in front of the bathroom mirror. "You *are* here," Brook said, sounding surprised. "I knocked, and when you didn't answer I was sure you had chickened out and were hidden in the corner of some local bar nursing a martini. I used my key and was going to give you hell when you got back from wherever you had run to."

"I'm sorry, but I'm a bit preoccupied and I guess I didn't hear the bell. I've thought about calling it all off at least a million times, but I promised Stuart and I'd be leaving him in the lurch," she sighed. "So here I am, quivering, with sweaty palms, but here, nonetheless." She was wearing only a deep-blue lace bra, matching panties, and a blue satin-and-lace slip. Brook picked up the panty hose container from Erika's bed and stood in the bathroom doorway shaking the plastic egg. "You're not going to wear these things, are you?"

"What things?" she asked, looking at her friend in the mirror.

Brook tapped the capsule and snapped, "If there was ever a man-hating deterrent to fooling around, these are it. A twentieth-century version of the chastity belt, without a key. You need a pair of thigh-high stockings with elastic tops to hold them up."

"Brook, I'm not doing anything after the dinner so stop trying to dress me like a prize bull."

"Heifer, love, heifer, or is that the lady cow who's been fixed?" Momentarily she looked puzzled. "Anyway why the hell not be prepared? You've got nothing to lose. If you come home as pure as Snow White, no one will know or care what you've got on under your clothes. And if you choose not to remain virginal, so much the better." Before Erika could respond to the "virginal" crack, Brook dashed out of Erika's room and returned several minutes later with three unopened packages. "What color?"

Erika put the finishing touches on her makeup and inspected herself in the mirror. Not bad. She looked like the old Erika, a corporate wife ready to take on the world of big business. She walked out of the bathroom, opened her bedroom closet door and pulled out a deep-blue crepe dress with short sleeves, a scooped neckline, and softly flared skirt with handkerchief points. "Okay. I get your point. What color would you wear with this?"

"Nice dress. What color shoes?"

"I have a pair of gold sandals if you don't think it would be too much."

"You've been to more of these things than I have. What would you have worn if you were going with Rick, the shit?"

Through her laughter, she said, "Stop calling him that! And I guess I would have worn the sandals."

"Then wear them." Brook picked up one of the packages and thrust it toward her friend. "These." Erika pulled on a silky toupe stocking that stayed up due to a soft elastic-lace top. As she drew the second stocking on, she admired her legs. Not too shabby. As if reading her mind, Brook said, "You really do look terrific, all over."

"Thanks. I can't tell you what a help you've been these past few days. I know I've driven you crazy but this is really difficult for me."

Brook dropped onto the edge of the bed. "I know, babe, and I sympathize, but it's all going to be great. You'll see."

"I'm sure it will be."

While Brook sat on the bed, Erika finished dressing, then twirled so Brook could get the full effect. "The dress is great," Brook said, "and it fits like a dream. Now add these." She pulled a pair of chunky gold earrings and a heavy gold necklace from her pocket and held them out. "We wouldn't want anyone there to look down their nose at you. Costume, of course, but pretty good stuff. Cost half a week's salary and I think you'll look smashing. They've always brought me luck."

Erika smiled at Brook. "You're really the best." She put on the jewelry and stood for inspection. "What's the final vote?"

"I think you look wonderful. I hope you feel as confident as you look."

"I feel like Jell-O but I'm ready to go anyway."

Half an hour later, Erika climbed out of a taxi and entered Prima Donna, a new and very "in" restaurant in the East Fifties. She looked around at the open, airy interior and stared at the wall of windows that allowed the diners to see into the kitchen. Why, she wondered, watching several sweaty chefs rushing around arranging vegetables on plates, would anyone want to do that? She remembered something she'd heard once; anyone who loves sausage or the law should never see either being made. She decided that went for restaurant kitchens, too.

With a shrug, she handed her coat to the checker and asked the maitre d' for the Cadmire party. As she was led to a large table in the rear of the restaurant, she tried valiantly to quiet the herd of kangaroos once again bouncing in her belly. Stuart rose as she approached. Dear Stuart, his open smile quieted her nerves a bit.

"Erika, it's so great that you decided to join us." He turned to the rest of the diners. "Greg, Mark, you remember Erika Holland."

"Of course," Greg Wolfe said as he rose. "Stuart told me you'd be joining us. I'm delighted to see you."

Greg was Cadmire's CEO, the one who, despite Rick's despicable behavior, had appointed him to head the Swiss office. *It's always the bottom line in this business,* she thought. Rick was very good at closing the big deals especially since he has the morality of an alley cat. Was Greg's smile covering a bit of embarrassment? She hoped so. Enough of that! He took her hand.

"It's Holland now? You've dropped the Hughes?"

"I'm a new woman," she said, plastering a confident smile on her face, "with a new name. It's good to see you again."

Mark Harris, an executive vice president, stood beside him, both men wearing the uniform: dark suits, pastel shirts, striped ties. They could have been brothers, blow-dried, nicely tanned from tennis every Saturday morning, corporate posture. As she thought of Rick, she realized that he had had the same cookie-cutter looks. Beneath the old-boy cheerfulness, however, she thought that they both looked a bit uncomfortable. Somehow, their discomfort strengthened her resolve to take the money and everything that went with it. Suddenly she found she was enjoying herself and her smile widened.

"We haven't seen you in several months," Greg said. He motioned toward his wife who wore an off-white sheath dress with an olive green sequined jacket. Erika couldn't help the flash of cattiness as she noticed that the green washed out her ash blond hair and slightly sallow complexion. "You remember my wife, Beth, don't you?"

Beth Wolfe had been one of Erika's closer friends *before*. Since Rick's departure, Beth hadn't called or even dropped Erika a note. Erika turned her charm up several notches. "Of course. How have you been, Beth?" Her voice sounded sincere and friendly despite her real feelings.

"Just fine, and you?" Beth rose slightly and offered her hand.

"Just great." Erika took her hand and clasped it as if in genuine friendship. The woman reminded her of a chameleon, her face changing to adapt to any situation. *Did I used to look like that, too?* Erika wondered. Probably.

"You're looking well," Mark's wife, Stephanie, said.

You mean in spite of everything, Erika wanted to say, but she kept smiling. "Thanks, Stephanie. How are your wonderful children?"

While Stephanie took a moment to extol the virtues of her two teenagers, Erika glanced over at Stuart's wife, Lorraine, who rolled her eyes and winked. Not to be outdone, Beth added her voice to the discussion, bringing out photos of her three boys. "And how is your wonderful daughter?" she asked as she returned the pictures to her evening purse.

Keeping her voice soft and her tone even, she said, "She's spending the summer with Rick in Japan and then returning to school in France. I would have loved to have her here with me, but I just couldn't deprive her of the wonderful opportunity to continue school in Europe."

"Of course not," Beth said, returning to her conversation with Stephanie.

Greg began to introduce Erika to the others who sat at the table set for a dozen. She met a senior vice president from a large financial center bank and her husband, whom Greg introduced with great deference. *I wonder how Greg feels having a woman sit next to him who wields as much power as he does?* Erika mused.

Greg continued on to an executive from a large client's Paris office who spoke with a thick accent, there with a woman introduced as Belinda Peters. Erika wondered whether she was another paid courtesan.

"You know Stuart and Lorraine, of course." Greg continued. Lorraine stood and warmly embraced her. "It's great to see you, Erika." *Sotto voce*, Lorraine said into her ear, "Stuart keeps me up-to-date on your progress. You've really blossomed."

"Thanks, Lorraine," Erika said softly. "Stuart's been a great help."

"By the way," Lorraine whispered, "Greg was really upset that Stuart had invited you. He was afraid you'd make a scene in front of the others. I love seeing him uncomfortable."

"He's being ridiculous, of course," Erika whispered. "I couldn't be anything but charming and he knows it. I do, however, love to see him squirm."

"And this is Paul Johansen," Greg continued. "He's from Richards, AG, here on sabbatical from their Oslo office for a few weeks. I kept the seat beside him for you. I thought you two would have a lot in common. If I remember correctly, you studied fine art in college. In his spare time," Greg raised his eyebrows at the idea that anyone in the upper echelon of corporate politics could have any spare time, "Paul paints and has studied many of the masters."

Erika made her way around the table to stand next to Paul. Richards, AG, was one of Cadmire's biggest accounts. She must be here to keep Paul amused for the evening. "It's wonderful to meet you, Paul." She quickly gave the man the once-over. Just a bit taller than she was, he had blond curly hair, wide-set sky blue eyes, and a cleft in his chin. Although he wasn't classically handsome, his direct gaze made her toes curl. "Is this your first trip to New York?"

"I must admit that I plan a trip to New York every year," he said with only a trace of an accent. "I love the fall especially. I try to get enough time to rent a car and drive upstate to see the foliage." He pulled out the chair beside his. "It seems you already know most of the people here, so I'm going to spend some time getting to know you myself."

"I'd like that," Erika said, settling into the chair between Paul and the bank executive's husband.

Directly across the large round table, Stephanie leaned toward her and said, quite loudly, "How is Rick doing, dear?"

Despite her revulsion, Erika arranged a placid expression on her face, raised one eyebrow, and said softly, "Frankly, Steph, I don't give a damn."

Stephanie had the good grace to look embarrassed, while Lorraine mouthed, "Good for you."

"Marital problems I would guess," Paul said softly. "You have some history here, I gather."

She tried not to let her distaste show. "Once, not any more. My ex-husband is Rick Hughes, the partner in charge of the Zurich office."

"Ahhh," Paul said, suddenly putting the pieces together. "Well, his loss is certainly my gain." He paused, then looked chagrined. "Sorry. That was a terrible line as were a few before that. I sound like someone who's trying to pick up a good-looking woman in a bar. I sincerely apologize."

"It's all right. I considered it a compliment."

"It was meant as a compliment, but it's not all right. Let's start again." He extended his hand. "Hello. My name is Paul."

Suddenly the mood was light again. Paul was a pleasant man, and she was going to be able to enjoy his company for the evening. "Mine's Erika," she said, taking his hand. His grip was strong yet not overpowering. She liked the way his touch made her fingers tingle. Interesting. "It's really nice to meet you."

For the next several hours, Erika earned her money. She made light conversation where appropriate and talked with knowledge about international trade finance when Paul brought the subject up. Over coarse paté and Sauvignon Blanc, they discovered a common interest in eighteenth-century French painting and an even more intense love of the decorative arts of the same period. They had a spirited discussion about whether their furniture was more decorative than functional that the others at the table were unable to follow.

Through rack of lamb française, petits pois, pommes au gratin, and a fine 1988 Merlot, she was charming and just a bit flirtatious. He was an attractive man, after all, and it was fun to play the game that unattached men and women play. Whether it was the wine or Paul's company, Erika realized that she hadn't had such a delightful evening in a long time. Both made her feel sensual and a bit daring, which was wonderful for her ego.

"I'm enjoying myself so much, Erika," Paul said as the dinner wound down. "I discovered a small club a few nights ago just around the corner. Do you like jazz? They play until one."

"I love jazz," Erika said. Actually she barely tolerated it, but she didn't want the evening to end yet either.

The club was small and dark and the music was surprisingly good, a quartet of piano, soft drums, a bass, and a xylophone-like instrument. She and Paul talked very little, just relaxing with drinks and the dreamy music. As the minutes passed, Paul slid his chair close to hers and placed his hand on her back, idly stroking the skin above the neckline of her dress. The club was overly warm so it must have been Paul's fingertips that made her shiver and her nipples pucker beneath her dress. She shifted in her chair, but the hand remained on her spine.

She glanced at him, but he appeared to be concentrating on the musicians so she closed her eyes for a moment and enjoyed the sensations. Was he playing a game? Did he want her? He seemed to be saying he did. Did he think she was bought and paid for? He took her hand. When he scratched his fingernail across her palm, she shivered. Did she want him? If he asked and she agreed to make love with him, would he think she was a hooker? Did she care what he thought of her? Did she care what she thought of herself? So many questions with no answers. *Relax!* she finally told herself. *Let things go wherever they will and answer the questions as they come up.*

It was nearly one when the musicians said good night and began to pack up their instruments. As Paul motioned for the check, he leaned over and whispered, "I'm reluctant to let you go. I'm staying in a suite at the Carlisle. You understand there's a living room we could talk in and a bedroom with a door that we could keep closed. Would you come back there with me? I'd just like to talk for a while, maybe have one last drink."

Oh shit. There it is. The bought-and-paid-for part, the expectations. He sounds sincere, she told herself. *No sex, just a drink and conversation.* Being honest with herself, she found she didn't want the evening to end either. "I'd like that," Erika said, silencing all the conflicting voices echoing in her head. In for a penny . . .

As the hotel suite door closed behind them, Paul moved behind Erika and started to help her off with her black silk raincoat. As it slipped down her arms, she felt his breath on the side of her neck. "I lied," he whispered. "I don't want to talk for a while. I want to make love to you."

Thinking that she should be outraged, Erika froze.

"I'm sorry," Paul said, suddenly contrite and still behind her. "I thought you felt it, too. But I'll put your coat back on and you can leave if I'm out of line here." When the silence lengthened, Paul added, "Haven't there been delightful vibes bouncing between us all evening or is my radar totally out of whack?"

Up against an honest question, Erika found she couldn't lie. "No, you haven't been misreading things. It's merely been awhile." She thought of Jarred.

"I find you a very attractive woman and, to be frank, you turn me on." Remaining behind her, he dropped her wrap on a chair and slipped his arm around her waist, gently pulling her against him. "Oh Erika, you turn me on a lot."

Erika felt his breath on her ear as he lowered his mouth to her skin.

"Please. Let me turn you on," he said, his lips caressing the side of her neck.

She let her head fall back against his shoulder as he pulled the pins from her hair, allowing it to fall softly to her shoulders. He threaded his fingers through it and purred, "Better. Much better." He paused and nipped her earlobe. "Yes?"

At that moment, Erika decided that it was all okay. He was unattached and so was she. If they had been out on a date, there would be no layers of doubt and, she admitted, no shame. It was all silly and she was turned on, she did want him. So why not just enjoy each other? "Yes," she said softly, covering the hand at her waist with her own. As he nuzzled her shoulder, she felt her zipper slide down its track. Quickly her dress was pooled at her feet and as he turned her to face him, he lifted her slip over her head.

She watched his face as he looked her over, standing in her bra and panties and Brook's stockings. "I love it that you're not wearing those panty hose things," Paul said, stroking the white skin at the inside of her thigh above the stocking. "I think this is the sexiest part of a beautiful woman. Come here." He pulled off his jacket and drew her into his arms. Tangling his fingers in her hair and softly stroking her scalp, he held her head still as his mouth moved to cover hers.

The kiss was all Erika had expected it to be, deep, hot, hungry, yet not demanding. He asked and what she gave he took readily. She parted her lips but rather than plunging his tongue inside her mouth, he nipped at her lower lip. He took his time, kissing her in every way possible, with his mouth, his teeth, his tongue, his hands never still. And she returned what he gave with equal pleasure, her hands cupping his face, her head moving to taste every part of his mouth. Soon she was light-headed, her breathing almost as rapid as her heart rate. Just from kissing.

Without parting their lips, Paul released his tie, unbuttoned his shirt and pulled it off. Skin. His skin was smooth, his body firm, and she wanted to touch all of it. She rubbed her palms over his upper arms and his back. She pulled him closer and rubbed her lace-covered breasts over his hairless chest, feeling his bare abdomen against hers. She thrust her hips forward, pressing her mound against the ridge of hard flesh beneath his trousers.

"Woman," he said, his voice shaky, "you're incredible. You make me so hot."

"Only half as hot as you make me," Erika said, hardly recognizing the gravelly sound of her voice.

He guided her into the bedroom and settled her on the edge of the bed. As he dragged at his belt, Erika gazed at him, smiling. She slowly reached around behind her and, as he watched, unhooked her bra. He froze, staring, his belt dangling from one hand, his zipper half undone, as she slowly slipped the straps down her arms, freeing her breasts. She cupped them, watching his eyes. "You're magnificent," he murmured, slowly dropping the belt.

"I want you to think so," Erika said, feeling a power she hadn't known she had. Money or no money, this was something she enjoyed, and she had a right to it. She loved the wetness between her legs, the tingle in her nipples, the pressure building deep in her belly. Her evening with Jarred had been a beginning and nothing more. This was good, steamy sex, the way she liked it.

She stood and, as Paul finished undressing, she lowered her panties. Then she ran her fingers down the fronts of her stockings. "You say you like stockings. Shall I leave these on?" she asked.

"Please," he murmured. "I love the feel of silky legs around me when I make love."

"You're beautiful," she said, her eyes now free to roam his naked body. He was all man, with wide shoulders, narrow hips, and very little fat. Her eyes finally settled on his erection.

He blushed. Actually blushed. "I'm not used to being looked at like I'm a strawberry shortcake," he said.

"I'm sure you're much tastier than that," she said. Corny, she thought, but she watched his cock twitch. She slipped to her knees and licked the tip of his erection, but he pulled her to her feet. "If you do that, I won't last a moment, and I want this to last."

They stretched out on the bed and his mouth found her naked breast, feasting as his fingers kneaded her hot flesh. His suckling drove shafts of pleasure through her, causing her back to arch and her fingers to tighten in his hair. "Oh God," she yelled, on the edge of climax from his mouth alone. He pinched her other nipple and she could control it no longer. She screamed as the spasms ripped through her. "Yes," she cried. "Oh God, yes."

"My God, Erika, I've never known a woman who came from just what we're doing. It must have been a long time."

"Don't demean yourself," she said, panting, her body still cresting, "you're amazing."

As her spasms continued, his hand found her pussy, driving into her channel with first one, then two and three fingers, thrusting in and out, prolonging her climax. It was almost too much, as if she were unable to come down, his mouth on her breast, his fingers deep inside her.

"You are so sexy," he growled as he put on a condom. With a swift movement, he flipped over on his back, lifting her so she sat astride him, then drove his cock up into her heated channel. "I like it like this," he growled, his large hands squeezing and kneading her buttocks. "I like to give a woman the power to take as much as she wants."

Erika used her thighs as leverage and raised and lowered her sopping pussy onto his rigid shaft as she continued to come. Faster and faster she rode him, conscious of the increasing rate of his moans. "I can't get enough," they said together, then laughed. Laughter and climax proved to be a fabulous combination. His body tensed and his hips thrust upward. Moments later she felt his shudder and she collapsed on top of him, her palms splayed on his chest. "Mind blowing," she murmured.

Sometime later he pulled the bedspread over them and they dozed for a while. Later she padded to the bathroom, cleaned herself up and dressed. As she emerged from the bathroom, Paul opened sleepy eyes. "You're leaving?"

"I have something I have to do first thing tomorrow morning." Like a job.

"Can't you stay?" He sounded genuinely disappointed, which pleased Erika tremendously. "We could have breakfast together."

"I'm afraid not."

"I'm leaving tomorrow evening for the West Coast. I'd like to call you when I'm back in New York."

For a price, she wanted to say. I get paid for this, or at least I'd like to. Instead she merely wrote her phone number on the pad beside the bed. "Call me when you get back into town. Good night." She walked through the suite and out into the hall.

"I couldn't ask him for money!" she shouted into the phone. As she had promised, although it was almost three, she called Brook the moment she got home. "It was so awkward. I just couldn't say, 'Excuse me, that will be five hundred dollars.' I just couldn't and he didn't volunteer."

"First of all, it's a thousand dollars. I know you're worth that much."

"Okay. A thousand. Whatever. But I don't know how to ask. And since I know him indirectly through the firm, I couldn't have word get back to anyone that I'm doing this for money."

"Yeah. I wondered how that was going to work. Well, you made your five hundred and that's something. Good sex. Right?"

Erika paused. "I had great, sweaty, heart-pounding, earth-moving sex. Right!"

"So nothing was lost after all. You two could have been on a regular date and gone to bed afterward and you'd have had nothing to show for it. This way you have part of the airfare to France to see your daughter."

"True."

"So give me all the details."

Erika gave Brook most of the details of the evening, without going into the actual lovemaking. That part was too personal. At the end of the recital, Brook asked, "Do you think this will happen again? The dinner thing, I mean."

"Probably not and I'm not sure I can go through something like that again anyway."

"The sex? Or the being paid aspect?"

"Actually neither one. It's worrying that someone at Cadmire will find out. If they do, it will get back to Rick, and he'll have a field day trying to keep me from visiting Rena. I can't risk that."

"I hadn't thought of that. Of course you can't."

"Well, it was fun while it lasted, and the money's tucked away for my first trip to see my daughter."

Stuart called the following evening. "You were a tremendous success," he said. "Everyone said how well you fit into the group."

"Does this kind of thing happen often?" Erika asked.

"More often than you'd imagine." She heard him hesitate, then plunge onward. "Are you interested in doing something like that again? I've got a few connections in that area."

"I think I am. I had a delightful evening. Paul is a doll."

"He is, isn't he? But you know that not all the men you'd meet will be dolls."

"I know. You understand that it can't be with any of the Cadmire folks ever again. I can't risk that. If Rick finds out . . ."

"Of course. I understand. Let me give it some thought. Can we have dinner one evening next week?"

They made plans for the following Tuesday. "Give Lorraine my love. It was so great to see her last evening. She looked fabulous and she's such a lady."

"I'll tell her you said so. You looked pretty good yourself."

She and Stuart had dinner the following week, but the subject of her "entertaining" didn't come up, which was a mixed blessing for Erika. She'd like to earn money as an escort, but there were too many dangers if she traveled in Rick's circles.

Weeks passed and Erika settled back into her routine, with her five hundred dollars in a special savings account. She added what she could to it, but the account grew very slowly. Paul had phoned her about a week after their evening together to say that he had been called back to the home office and was disappointed that he wouldn't be stopping off in New York. She admitted that she was also saddened and asked him to let her know when next he was in the area.

Almost a month after the dinner with Paul, Stuart called just as Erika arrived home from work. After a few minutes of small talk, he said, "You said you might be interested in doing the escorting again and if you're really interested, I've got a friend who might be able to help you out. Her name is Valerie DeShields. She helps Cadmire find ladies for their parties from time to time. She's an unusual and delightful woman and she called me today because she's in a bind and wondered whether I knew anyone who could attend a large party this weekend. Nothing at all to do with Cadmire. I didn't directly mention you, but I said I might have an idea. So here I am. The evening pays seven hundred and fifty dollars, but I have to tell you that it will be a little different from the Cadmire dinner party. The guys know that many of the ladies who attend unescorted are paid courtesans and they will feel free to invite you to bed, for an additional price. That's sort of understood up front. You can say no, of course, but not too often."

"Why did Valerie call you?"

"Okay, let me be honest. I've talked to her about you, but I didn't want to make any promises and she hasn't had any need for another woman until now. It was through her, by the way, that you got paid for the Cadmire dinner. Anyway, she must have liked the little she heard about you from me, so she called and wondered whether you'd be interested in another evening with the understanding that sex was anticipated."

"You mean I'd be a high-class call girl."

"A high-class entertainer, and I'm not insulting you by asking," he said, his voice a bit stern. "You know my views on this. I don't think there's anything wrong with it. Like last time, this is a one-time shot and you can say yes or no. I need to know soon, however, before she finds someone else."

"Can I meet this Valerie beforehand?"

"It's pretty short notice, but let me see what I can do." His voice softened. "She's quite a woman. You'll like her. Let me call her and get back to you."

Half an hour later, Stuart called back. "I talked to Valerie and she'd very much like to meet you, too. She's still looking for someone for Saturday, so she suggested that you two might meet later this evening. That way you can kill two birds with one stone. Okay with you?"

Erika glanced at her watch. It was only six-thirty. "Sure. She's free this evening?"

Stuart snorted. "She's never 'free' if you know what I mean, but she'd love to meet you and she doesn't have another date tonight. I'm a big fan of you both, and I know you two will hit it off. Shall I have her call you?"

"Sure. Why not?" Why not indeed.

As she hung up, Erika couldn't help the picture that formed in her mind. Something out of an Old West brothel, a woman with slightly frowsy hair, just a bit too much makeup and a voluptuous figure. She'd call everyone "Honey" and talk a little too loudly.

Several minutes later her phone rang. "Hello?"

"Is this Erika? Hi, I'm Valerie DeShields."

"It's nice to meet you," Erika said. What do you say to a hooker, high class or not? This was too weird.

"I talked to Stuart and he suggested that we meet. Are you free for dinner?" Her voice was melodious, her tone softly modulated and cultured. There was none of the breathy Marilyn Monroe sound about her. Of course, if she entertained the rich and famous, she'd have to be more than an old-fashioned madam.

She's never free, Stuart had said, and Erika chuckled. What the hell. "Sure. Where?"

"I live in the East Fifties and I'm not going to be able to get out of here for a while. Can we meet near me? There's a great little Italian place on Fifty-second between Second and Third. Would eight o'clock be too late for you?" Valerie asked.

"Not at all," Erika said. "I'll see you then."

As soon as Valerie hung up, Erika dialed Brook's number and told her the entire story.

"Interesting," Brook said. "I wish I could be a fly on the wall. How did she sound?"

"Normal. She sounded like a real person."

"What did you expect, the Happy Hooker?"

Erika's mood lightened. "Maybe. I know I'm being silly, but I'm really nervous about this. I don't know what to expect, and I don't know whether I'm interested in this party on Saturday. It's so sleazy. Would you come with me?" Erika stretched her legs and propped her feet on the coffee table.

"Of course not, I wasn't invited. This is a meeting for you and her. Anyway, I'm not even in your league, and I wouldn't want to spoil it for you."

"Nonsense. You're in any league you want to be in. I just can't imagine myself making pleasant conversation with a madam, one on one."

"You could make pleasant conversation with the devil himself, so don't sweat the small things. I think it's a great opportunity for you, but you have to feel your way through this and see how it works out, one thing at a time, without me looking over your shoulder. Everything about this will be your decision."

"Oh God, Brook." She closed her eyes. "What have I gotten myself into?"

"Nothing but a congenial dinner. And if it's not congenial, you can leave anytime."

"I know. But what if she's . . . Well you know. Over the top."

"Stuart knows you very well, doesn't he? He's your friend. Would he suggest something he knew would upset you?"

Erika let out a long breath. "No. He's a pussycat."

"Well then?"

"Okay. You're right. Let me see what happens. I don't have to make any decisions just yet."

Erika considered what she should wear and finally decided to leave on the clothes she had worn to work: slender black slacks with a knit cotton sweater the color of crushed strawberries and a heavy gold neck chain with an irregularly shaped golden pendant suspended from it. Just before eight o'clock, Erika arrived at Villa Maria and asked for Ms. DeShields's table. "I have her reservation, but I'm afraid she's not here yet," the maître d' said, showing her to a quiet table in the back of the restaurant. "May I get you a glass of red or white wine while you wait?"

"That would be nice." She needed it. "White."

As the maître d' disappeared, she looked around. The restaurant was small, with ersatz red brick and murals on the walls to simulate the central plaza of a small Italian town. Waiters in large white aprons, red-and-white-check tablecloths, candles in wine bottles, all very predictable, yet somehow Erika suspected there was more to this restaurant than met the eye. If the smells were any indication, the food was good and the place was packed with yuppy couples consuming large amounts of regally presented cuisine.

Her wine arrived and she sipped, trying not to prejudge the woman she had arranged to meet. "You must be Erika." Erika's head snapped up as a woman slipped into the seat across from her. The stereotype evaporated. This woman was reed-thin, small-busted with curly black hair, pale ivory skin, and deep hazel eyes. About thirty-five, she was dressed in a maroon fleece jacket and matching short-sleeve top over slender black-denim pants with ankle-high black boots. She extended her hand, her fingers long and slender, her nails soft mauve. "I'm Valerie." She had an unconscious grace and, although she wasn't conventionally pretty, she had style, using large hoop earrings to accentuate her prominent cheekbones.

Erika took her hand, enjoying the woman's soft voice. "Nice to met you." Without thinking, she blurted out, "You're not at all what I expected."

Smiling, Valerie said, "I can tell that from your face. What did you think I'd look like?"

Erika was too embarrassed to speak. How could she tell this pleasant woman what she had been thinking? She was saved from answering by the waiter, who brought Valerie a Kir Royale. "Thanks, Jimmy."

"Are you ready to order, ladies?"

Valerie looked at Erika. "I'm ravenous. Shall we split an antipasto to start? It's really good here."

When Erika nodded, Valerie ordered. "Extra olives. Oh, and bring an order of garlic bread Parmesan."

As the waiter left, Valerie leaned forward and said, "I can't eat garlic when I have a date, so I make it a point to indulge when I have a night off."

"Right," Erika said, still trying to get her balance. This lovely woman was nothing like what she had expected.

"I won't embarrass you further by asking again what you expected. I can certainly understand." Every time Valerie smiled Erika felt herself calm another notch. "I gather you're an old friend of Stuart's. He's such a great guy and Lorraine's a sweetheart. She's a really classy lady with none of the corporate wife syndrome."

"Corporate wife syndrome?"

"You know. Stuffy. Only interested in clothes and jewelry and who's getting it on with whom at the office." Suddenly Valerie blanched. "I'm sorry. I didn't mean that the way it sounded."

Erika gasped, then couldn't keep the laughter inside. "Oh God, you're so right, and my ex was one of the premier getting-it-on guys." She studied Valerie, then asked, "Have you been to any of the Cadmire parties? You look vaguely familiar."

"I thought you looked familiar too. Oops! Were you one of those women I just insulted? I will now attempt to pull my foot out of my mouth."

"No need," Erika said, still chuckling. "Yes, I guess I was. My name used to be Hughes."

"Rick's ex? I get it. Stuart didn't tell me much about your history and with your different name, I didn't make the connection. I've heard a lot of rumors, though. The breakup was his idea?"

"Oh, indeed. He just left one day, never to reappear. Took off to Switzerland with all our assets and his busty blonde executive assistant. Left me feeling like a lost soul, but I pulled myself out of that morass and here I am. Job, friends, and a life of my own without a man." Why had she said all that to a perfect stranger? There was something about this woman that made her feel accepted for whoever she was. She would have made a good shrink. Maybe that was part of what a good hooker was.

Valerie reached across the table and patted Erika's hand. "Good for you. It's nice to stand on your own feet without anyone else to prop you up. Then if you fall, you know you can get up again all on your own."

Erika lifted her wineglass and extended it. "Here's to getting up all on your own."

Valerie took her Kir and touched the rim to Erika's glass. "Amen."

Their bread and antipasto arrived. The huge plate of appetizers was covered with two kinds of cheese, prosciutto, three kinds of olives, paper-thin slices of salami, and two other meats Erika didn't recognize and garnished with assorted vegetables, anchovies, and roasted red peppers. "My God," Erika said. "Does anyone ever eat a main course after that?"

"Frankly, I usually don't but maybe if we split this, we can split some pasta. And, of course, the bread."

The two women parceled out the antipasto and bread and chatted about everything from politics to the unusually mild weather. Eventually they ordered a bowl of linguini with white clam sauce to split and cleaned off their plates with final chunks of bread. Valerie ordered a cappuccino and Erika ordered herb tea. They agreed to skip the dessert cart and, stuffed to her ears, Erika leaned back in her chair. "I don't know how you can eat all that food," she said, "and stay so slim."

"A fortunate metabolism. I seem to be able eat anything I want and not gain weight. I don't know what I'd do if I had to watch my weight. You don't have to, do you?"

"Not yet." Erika decided it was time to get to the business at hand. "Tell me about this party Saturday night and how you're involved."

Chapter

4

"What you really want to know is how a nice girl like me got to be a madam."

Erika gulped and, although she tried to look appalled, she realized that that was exactly what she wanted to know. Recovering quickly, she said, "Of course that's not what I want to know."

"I hardly know you, except through Stuart, but I have a feeling that we can end up good friends, so let's be honest with each other from the start." As Erika started to protest, Valerie held up her hand. "Don't. I'm happy to tell you all about myself and my business but"—she glanced at her watch and grinned—"I don't have that much time right now. It's a really long story, so let's save it for another time. For now, let's just get to Saturday evening and what it's all about. We'll save the life histories for an evening when we can drink fine wine and laugh about what got each of us to where we are right now. I'll show you mine if you show me yours."

Erika couldn't help but like this charming woman. "Good idea," she said, laughing.

"The party Saturday evening is for a group of venture capitalists from all over the country. It's an early holiday gathering being thrown by Regency Software, a firm that wants to expand and is hoping that the guys with the checkbooks will sign on the dotted line and the bottom of big checks."

Erika's face dropped. "I know nothing about computers and software. I've just barely learned to use a word processor."

"No knowledge is required, just an intelligent mind and the ability to be charming. Although I don't know you, I can tell right off that you've got both of those in quantity."

Surprised, Erika said, "Thanks."

"You're welcome, but it's not a compliment; it's a statement of fact. I don't know whether true charm comes with mother's milk or can be learned, but you've got it. You look me in the eye when we talk and you're honest with me. You lean forward and seem to be interested in everything I say. You don't fidget or look around and you ask intelligent questions. Believe me, I meet lots of women who don't have any of that." Again she held up her hand. "Don't thank me again for something you've got little control over. You can thank me for telling you about things you do have control over. You're not gorgeous, but you use cosmetics to make the most of yourself. You've got a good figure, from what I've seen, and you dress with class. You've got a Jackie Kennedy timelessness, a classic simplicity."

Erika looked down at her clothing. It wasn't anything special, but she realized that, without thinking about it, her clothing was as Valerie had described it.

"There is one thing I need to know," Valerie continued, "and I need an honest answer if we're to continue. Although I run what is called an escort service, I'm sure you've gathered that there is usually sex afterward. It's not mandatory for every date, but for most it is expected. Let's be honest. A man who's paying—or whose company is paying—upward of a thousand dollars a night isn't only interested in good conversation and a charming dinner partner. How do you feel about that?"

Erika took a deep breath. Valerie was being amazingly honest, opening herself up to a charge of pandering, but somehow, in their short acquaintance, they had developed a rapport. "You certainly are blunt. How do I feel?"

Valerie chuckled as the coffee arrived. "You're stalling..."

"Okay. I am." She put sweetener into her cup and said, "Let me answer this way. I love great sex, and during my marriage I had a lot of it. Recently I've had a couple of one-night stands but that's about it. I miss it."

"What about those one-nighters? Were they good?"

Erica couldn't keep the grin from spreading across her face. "They were very good. They reminded me that I'm a woman, and a sensual, attractive one at that."

"That's one of the great things about sex. It does wonderful things for the ego. So you wouldn't be averse to that aspect of this?"

"No, but what about kinky sex? I don't think I could get into whips and chains. Don't most of the guys want really strange stuff?"

"Strange stuff? Okay, I won't kid you, some of the guys who use my escort service want the unusual, and I cater to those wishes when I can. Many of my ladies enjoy the"—she searched for the right word—"off-center. However, this party isn't like that. It's just to impress the visiting royalty. If you fit in the way I think you will, and you're interested in—well, let's just say expanding your horizons—we can work that in easily. If not, that's fine too. For now, unless we've agreed on something specific, feel free to say no if sex ventures into an area that makes you uncomfortable."

Erika thought about it. She was being offered a job as a highclass prostitute. She stalled. "Is it dangerous?"

"Everything in life has its dangers, but if you mean will some cop bust you for solicitation? No. My clients are established organizations, companies I've done business with for a long time, or people recommended by people I trust. To the outside world, we are an escort service, providing classy, intelligent, charming women like yourself for parties or for men who want a woman on their arm for an evening, weekend, or whatever."

"Weekend?"

"Sometimes longer. Several men have asked that one of my ladies accompany them on a cruise or a trip out of the country. If the woman is willing, I get part of the fee. It's just that simple."

"Simple. It doesn't sound simple to me."

Valerie sipped her cappuccino. "Okay. It isn't simple. It's hard work, frequent last-minute scrambling and a lot of worry, but it's worth it, for me and for the women who work for me." She winked. "And it's great money, but enough beating around the bush. I asked you a question and I need an honest answer. Are you averse to the sexual side of this arrangement?"

"I don't think I am, if I have the right to refuse if a man just plain turns me off."

"You do. Absolutely. I would hope you would do it gently and not make the man feel bad about himself. It's quite unusual for any of my ladies to refuse, but it does happen. Remember we've signed on to provide escorts. We're not an outcall service. Just keep in mind that these men are clients or friends of clients and I have a business to run, then suit yourself. I know you'll be as flexible as you can be."

"Of course. Tell me about the financial arrangements."

"I am paid from six hundred to a thousand dollars for a woman for an evening, not including sex. I keep twenty percent which leaves between five and eight hundred for you. If you arrange something more afterward, the usual fee is a thousand and I trust you to pay me my share."

"That part is all done on faith? You are a trusting lady."

"I guess so, but if I couldn't trust the women I deal with, I would be out of business in a hurry. If you're willing, this Saturday evening would be a first try for you and if you enjoy it, we can work out what evenings you're available and see what develops."

"How many women work for you, Valerie?" Erika asked.

"About twenty, but it varies. The average life span of a woman in this line of work is only two to three years. Some are married or have boyfriends who eventually want them out of the business. Others build up their bank account to a certain level and retire. Many just get tired of being charming all the time."

"Married? Aren't all of the women single?"

"Not at all." Valerie gazed into space for a moment. "Of the twenty-three right now, eight are married and four more have permanent relationships."

"Their husbands don't mind what their wives do?"

"I assume not. Occasionally one of my ladies has a problem at home. She cries on my shoulder and I try to give sound advice, but eventually the situation solves itself. Either she leaves or he gets used to the idea. Sometimes a relationship breaks up over this, but that's really not my problem. My ladies are capable of making their own decisions."

When Erika was silent, Valerie continued, "I know it sounds hard. I'm not as callous as I seem. I hurt for many of my friends when they have problems at home, but I can't be them. I counsel, I hug, but in the end I can't solve their problems. I can only give them the advantage of my wisdom and my experience, however valuable that is. Other than that, they're on their own."

"Has anyone ever been arrested?"

"Nope, and I don't expect it to happen. We're as safe as we can be in a dangerous world. I've got a few connections who can help out in a pinch, but it's never been necessary."

Erika decided to be blunt. "Isn't it dangerous to be talking to me like this? Aren't you admitting to prostitution and pandering?"

"I'm not really admitting anything, and it would be your word against mine. Somehow, though, I feel I can trust you."

"How can you? We just met."

"I know, but I trust Stuart and I've learned over the years to trust my stomach. My insides say you're okay."

"Any rules I should know about?"

"I have only a few rules and some very serious advice. The rules are simple. No drugs! If I ever get wind of any of my ladies doing drugs of any kind, they are out. And no gossip about any of the clients or their preferences, with anyone at any time. Their privacy is part of the reason they use my services."

Valerie continued, "I prefer that my ladies not smoke. Nothing turns a lover off faster than the smell of stale tobacco smoke that always surrounds a smoker, no matter how often he or she showers."

"I don't smoke, and I never have."

"Great. Get used to using a diaphragm at *those* times of the month. It makes it difficult for me if plans have to be changed at the last minute because you've gotten your period." When Erika nodded, Valerie continued, "My most important advice is this. Don't ever have unprotected sex, except with your husband or whatever. Always carry your own. You can't count on a man to have any with him, and you want to be sure to always use the best and freshest. The world of casual sex is a dangerous one."

"I know that and I would never dream of not having the man use a condom. What about oral sex and disease. Isn't that dangerous, too?"

Valerie sighed. "Frankly, I don't know. I do know that no man wants a woman sucking his cock with a layer of latex between them and they are paying big bucks for it. To the best of my knowledge, none of my ladies cares about unprotected oral sex, but I guess that has to be up to you."

"I don't think that would be a problem for me either."

"That's fine," Valerie said, obviously relieved.

Erika thought about her problem with Paul. "That evening after the Cadmire dinner I went to bed with the guy I was supposed to be with. I don't think he knew I was being paid and since I hadn't a clue how to ask for money, I didn't. What do you say when a guy suggests sex and you want to be paid?"

"That's the thousand-dollar question. Most of these men will know you're a professional hired for the evening. You can softly say that you're a paid escort and sex isn't included. He'll smarten up real quick and you can make your own arrangements. If a thousand dollars doesn't seem right, ask for more or less, whatever you think makes sense. I ask only for twenty percent of whatever you negotiate. The important thing is never ask for money first. Let him talk about the price. That way you have the best bargaining position and, on the off chance he's a cop, his mentioning it first makes it entrapment. If *you* talk money first, that's prostitution."

"What if the guy doesn't know I'm being paid?"

"That does happen occasionally, but it's rare. In those cases, you can roll in his hay for nothing or just tell him that you're not that kind of girl."

Erika's eyebrows lifted. "Not that kind of girl?"

"You're certainly not the kind of girl who has sex with a guy for free. Unless you want to, of course."

"Can we get back to kinky stuff for a moment?"

"Kinky is in the eye of the beholder, in my opinion," Valerie said. "If a guy asks for something—well, let's just say *unusual*—if you want to do it, go for it. If not, politely decline. If you're willing but it seems above and beyond, ask for more money. That usually separates the men from the boys, so to speak."

Erika couldn't believe she was having this conversation. She was actually getting rules for being a hooker. She could hear Stuart saying, "Why shouldn't a lonely man be able to offer a woman money for sex? No one's being hurt." And Brook's voice echoed, "I let guys pick me up and we end up in bed. Is that so different, except that I'm not financially better off afterward?"

Erika focused on Valerie and said, "I'm still having a bit of trouble taking this all in."

"I know. It's different from what well-brought-up women have been told all their lives. But it's real, and it's out there if you want to take advantage of it."

For what she'd earn in a few nights, Erika could plan a trip to France to see Rena. That was a good reason to say yes. More important, she wanted to do it. If she allowed herself to be honest, it sounded like fun. "Done," she said. "What time and where Saturday?"

"Cocktails at seven and dinner at eight-thirty. It's usually good to arrive a bit late. Make an entrance." Valerie gave her the details. "The evening won't be difficult. Just look classy and be charming; two things I know you're good at."

"I still can't believe I'm going to do this," Erika said to Brook the next evening as they sat in Brook's apartment sipping tea. She had spent the previous half hour giving her friend all the details as Valerie had told them to her.

"I can't either. It sounds almost too good to be true."

"It does, but it scares me to death, too. What have I gotten myself into?"

"Fun and games, with the accent on the games part. What have you got to lose? One evening, one nice guy, and one choice. You can play it by ear from there on."

"It's really not a choice. From the way Valerie talks, there is one. But it seems to me that a company that's spending that kind of money will want the guy to get his pound of flesh at the end and will be pissed as hell if he complains."

"Pound of flesh is a pretty negative way to describe it. If you feel that way, why are you doing it?" Brook asked.

Erika heaved a big sigh. "You know, I vacillate from moment to moment. One minute I think it's all fun and games and what the hell, then the next I think I'm becoming a whore and it doesn't feel good at all."

"It seems to me," Brook said, sipping her tea, "that you have to make that basic decision before you go any further. Will you be a whore? That's a pretty strong word for what you'll be doing. It's all semantics. If this thing makes you feel like a whore, cheap and—what's a good word, *tawdry*—then forget the whole thing. Nothing, including seeing your daughter, is worth cheapening your feelings about yourself. If, on the other hand, you feel that it's your body to do with as you like, and if you get paid for it, so much the better, then decide that's what you're going to do and stop overthinking. You'll drive yourself crazy."

Erika stretched her legs out on a stack of magazines on Brook's coffee table. "You're right, of course. I just have to learn to turn off my brain. I really want to do this for lots of reasons, some good and some maybe not so good, but what the heck. In for a penny, in for a pound."

"Is that a firm decision?"

"I hope so."

"Then the most important thing now is to stop remaking the decision over and over."

"Okay. I'm going to do it, and I'm going to enjoy it. Period."

"Period."

The days until Saturday passed quickly. Although she had second and third thoughts, Erika took Brook's advice and turned off her brain as much as she could. She had made up her mind and vowed she wouldn't deviate.

Saturday, freshly bathed and made-up, Erika put on the same cocktail dress she had worn to the Cadmire dinner. After all, it had brought her luck. Brook had lent her the same jewelry. As she gazed at herself in the mirror and combed her fingers through her shoulder-length hair, Erika decided that she looked pretty good.

The dinner was being held in a small room at Tavern on the

Green. When she arrived, she handed her invitation to the tuxe-doed man at the door and was directed to the bar. "Valerie's taste is wonderful as ever," a voice said in her ear as she waited in the short line.

She turned and her gaze met that of a man in his early fifties. His face was deeply tanned, with tiny laugh lines at the corners of his soft brown eyes, a slightly hooked nose, and a neatly trimmed beard. His tuxedo fit his medium frame as if it were custom-made. "Valerie?" she asked.

"Unless there's been a great mixup, your invitation indicated that you're one of the ladies hired to make charming conversation with my guests." He extended his hand. "I'm Craig Mc-Donald and this is my shindig."

Erika appreciated his strong handshake, his work-roughened hands indicating that he hadn't sat behind a desk all his life. "Very nice to meet you," she said. "I'm Erika Holland." She had thought for a long time about whether to use her real name and finally reasoned that it would be too confusing to keep changing names. She had had an unlisted phone number since her divorce so she thought that she had little to worry about.

"I thank you so much for coming. I'm sure that, if you just stand here, you won't lack for company."

"Thanks so much for having me. By the way, how did you know I was a friend of Valerie's?"

"We color-code the invitations. The ones in dark-blue ink are for the guests, the ones in dark-green ink are for Valerie's ladies. The guy at the door gives me the high sign so I can be sure to welcome you and point out the people of particular interest." They had reached the front of the line and Craig asked for a glass of red wine. "And for you?" he said to Erika.

"I'll just have a Perrier with lime."

Craig relayed the order to the bartender, then indicated the men she was to pay particular attention to. "Enjoy," he said, finally, as he took his wine and melted back into the crowd.

Of course, Erika thought, *color-coded invitations. That's how it's done. Very clever.* Erika knew that Valerie had sent four other ladies to this party. She was curious which of the fifteen or so women had the other green-inked invitations. She wondered exactly how to approach the men in question, but she thought she'd give herself a minute to blend in. Playing it by ear, she hung the chain strap of her beaded evening purse over her shoulder and, holding her drink, wandered through the crowd of smartly dressed people.

A short, balding, slightly overweight man with a red-and-black plaid tie and matching cummerbund beneath his well-tailored tuxedo caught her eye. With a remark that made all the men and women he had been standing with laugh, he separated himself from the group and made his way toward her through the crowd. "Good evening," he said. "We haven't met yet, something I'm about to rectify. I'm Jonas Stewart." He seemed to be in his early sixties, with lots of unruly gray hair and deep green eyes. Good, she thought, this was one of the men Craig had told her about and if she ended up having sex with him later, the company had agreed to cover Valerie's additional fee. She wouldn't even have to figure out how to ask for money.

I'm getting way ahead of myself, she thought. "I'm Erika Holland and it's nice to meet you."

"Holland. Whose wife or girlfriend are you?"

He certainly was direct. "I'm no one's wife or girlfriend. I'm just enjoying a delightful evening." Erika wondered how she was to act. Should she be forward or let him make any moves?

"Wonderful." Jonas took her free hand and tucked it into the crook of his elbow. "Then I can monopolize your time without anyone getting angry with me."

It didn't seem that she would have to make any moves. "You certainly can, Jonas." During the cocktail hour, Jonas kept her amused and exclusive. They spoke on many topics, and he liberally sprinkled his conversation with clever double entendres. He kept the table of eight at which they had dinner entertained with long amusing stories and a few witty off-color jokes. He was thoroughly delightful.

While Jonas was enjoying his second cup of coffee, Erika took a moment to find the ladies' room. As she sat at the mirror reapplying her lipstick, a tiny Oriental woman came into the room. She was lovely, with deep almost-black eyes, and black silky hair swept on top of her head with soft wispy curls at her temples. Crouching, she peeked under the door to each stall to make sure they were alone, then said, "Hi. I saw you at the party, so I assume you must be Erika. Valerie described you to a tee, classy, handsome and smartly dressed. I'm Mei Lee. Valerie suggested that I introduce myself and answer any questions you might have about anything." She settled on the stool beside Erika and took a lipsitck out of her silver evening purse.

Erika looked Mei over in the mirror. She looked like a tiny Oriental doll with smooth pale skin and wide-set black eyes. She used her makeup extremely well to deepen her eyes and emphasize her brows and surprizingly generous mouth. Although not a stunningly beautiful woman, Mei had done a fantastic job of accenting all her assets.

"It's nice to meet you. I've been admiring you." Mei's haltertop dress was black crepe de chine, full-skirted, and demure, yet it dipped just low enough in front to make a man think he might get a glimpse of something naughty, although he never actually did. To add to the effect, she wore slender silver and onyx earrings and a matching silver and onyx pendant, which hung in the cleavage between her small breasts, occasionally getting caught beneath the fabric. "I've been making mental notes on how to look classy and sexy at the same time. You have really done it."

"Thanks. That's a nice thing to say and I make a real effort to do just that." Erika watched the other woman give her the once-over. "You're terrific to look at too. Valerie always knows how to pick them."

"Thanks." *There's a strange camaraderie here,* Erika thought.

Mei fumbled in her tiny purse and finally found her lip liner. She used it to outline her full lips, then filled in with her lipstick. "Valerie says this is your first excursion. Is there anything I can do to help?" she asked, gently blotting her lips.

Erika marveled at the lack of any feeling of competition between the women. "I'm not sure yet. This is all very new to me. How long have you been doing this sort of thing?"

"About two and a half years, with time off to have my baby. Frank, he's my husband, doesn't really like what I do, but I'm only out one night a week. He likes the money I earn so he allows me to continue. He says that we've got our son's college partly paid for."

To say Erika was surprised was an understatement. "You've got a family?"

Mei pulled a professionally taken photograph from her purse and handed it to Erika. A nice-looking Oriental man held a toddler on his lap. "That's Frank," she said, pointing to the man, "and he's holding Cory who's fourteen months." She handed Erika a second photo, one of the three of them. Mei, in her everyday clothes, with her hair caught in a pony tail looked like an ordinary housewife. Frank was smiling into the camera while Cory looked as if he had been cleaned up for the photographer and wasn't happy about it at all.

"What a wonderful family," Erika said.

"I can tell you're surprised and I guess that, in our line of work, it is a bit of a shock, but Frank loves me and takes care of Cory while I'm out." Erika suspected from her tone that all wasn't as smooth as Mei indicated, but she didn't pry.

Another woman entered the ladies' room, so Erika and Mei fussed with their makeup until she was gone. "I see you've made quite an impression on Jonas Stewart. He seems really nice. Not all of them are, you know."

"Is that a warning? Have you had bad experiences?"

"Oh, not what you're thinking at all. I've never been in trouble, just bored and frustrated occasionally. Some of these guys don't have a clue about good lovemaking and I'm not hired to teach them, although I've done that a few times too. Some are just lousy in the sack, if you know what I mean, but you put up with it and deposit the cash later."

"What about the guy you're with? Have you hooked up with a nice guy?" Erika asked.

"Claude Fortier. Is that a name, or what? Sounds like a detective out of a French mystery novel. He's one of the money guys Craig McDonald singled out so I'm in biz."

"Have you made plans to go out afterward?"

"Not yet. That usually takes place with the coffee and cordials. It gets pretty predictable after a while. It's like a symphony with the notes rearranged." She deepened her voice. " 'How about having a nightcap in my hotel room? I really don't want this evening to end yet.' Or something like that."

Erika remembered that Paul had said something very similar after the Cadmire dinner. "I guess there aren't many ways to say, 'I want to fuck your brains out' without actually saying it."

"You're too much." Mei said, nodding. "I'm really going to like working with you."

As another woman entered the room Erika glanced at her watch. "I guess we should be getting back."

Mei leaned over and kissed Erika on the cheek. Then she whispered, "Welcome to the sorority, and I'm sure we'll meet again. I live on Long Island and I only come into the city when I have a party, but maybe you can come out to my place and meet my guys. I know Frank and Cory would love you. And I could tell you stories . . . Why don't you give me a call sometime. I don't have a pencil and paper, but you can get my number from Valerie."

"I'd love to. Thanks for the invitation and let's see whether we can work it out." Arm in arm, the two women left the ladies' room and returned to the party.

As he sipped his brandy Jonas asked, "What are you doing later? I'd love to continue our conversation. You're a wonderful listener."

She thought about Mei's comments on how to invite a woman to a man's hotel room and tried not to laugh. "I'd love to hear more about your adventures, Jonas," she said, looking into his eyes. "Here or anywhere else." Did that corny come-on line come from her mouth?

"Great. Why don't we go back to my hotel room?"

Jonas's hotel room was, in reality, a large suite, with two bedrooms and a well-furnished living room done in shades of beige and wedgewood blue, with a thick beige-and-blue tweed carpet. He opened the refrigerator behind the bar in the corner and pulled out a bottle of Chardonnay. "Is this all right for you?" he asked.

"That's just fine," Erika said, settling in a deep-beige velvet side chair trimmed in pale wood.

"How much are you being paid for this evening?" Jonas asked.

Erika gasped. Well, that answered one question. "What makes you think I'm being paid?"

Jonas crossed the room and handed her her wine, then sat in the matching chair at right angles to hers. "I've been through this many times before. It's a pretty recognizable pattern. Large dinner party thrown by men who want me to invest in their company, several very attractive, unattached women and bingo. They think that with a little sex, I'll be putty in their hands."

Erika sipped. It did sound very tacky when put that way. "So why did you bring me back here?"

Jonas had poured himself a cognac and he swirled the amber liquid in his glass. "Why not take advantage of what's offered?"

"Actually that sounds just as tacky." Erika slammed her mouth shut. He was the customer and the customer was always right. It wasn't up to her to criticize.

After a moment's hesitation, Jonas's laugh was rich and full. "You're absolutely right, Erika, I'm being just as tacky as they are." He leaned forward and pulled his wallet from his pants pocket. He fished out a handful of bills and handed them to her. "I like you, Erika. Very much. You're a straight shooter and I admire that."

From a quick glance Erika saw that there was more than five hundred dollars in her hand. She put the money on the table beside her. "I'm glad of that, at least. I'm afraid I flunked Enticing 101."

He laughed again. "Not in the least. I find you very enticing, witty, and clever with a quick mind, and deliciously honest to boot. I thoroughly enjoyed you as a dinner partner and I anticipate a delicious time taking advantage of all you have to offer."

Shit, she thought. He was treating her like a hooker, which was exactly what she was. The phrase *bought and paid for* echoed in her mind, and it didn't make her feel good at all. However, she had made a deal, both with Jonas and with Valerie, and she wasn't about to renege. Whether she'd ever do it again was another matter.

She sipped her wine, totally unsure of what to do next. "I'd like to see what I've bought," he said. "Please remove your clothes. Slowly."

Oh God, Erika thought, *I don't know whether I can do this*. She swallowed a lump the size of the Rock of Gibraltar and stood up. She knew her trembling fingers couldn't possibly handle the long zipper at the back of her dress, so she turned her back to Jonas. Clearing her throat, she said, "Would you help me?"

"I'd love to, my dear." She crouched before his chair so Jonas could slowly lower the zipper until her dress was open down the back. She stood, keeping her back to him. She thought about all the movies she'd seen over the years in which someone stripped.

Tease. That's what a strip was, a tease. At that moment the whole thing became a game. How well could she tease her customer, her john? She remembered Natalie Wood as Gypsy Rose Lee and Demi Moore in *Striptease*. *Damn it*, she thought, *if I'm going to be a hooker, if only for one night, I'm going to be the best one I can be.*

She slowly allowed the top of the dress to slip down her arms until it hung from her breasts. The melody to the song "The Stripper" played in her head and she slowly moved her ass and felt her skirt swish against her legs. "Umm," Jonas said. "Nice, but I want to see more."

She turned so her side was to him, allowing him to see one bra-covered breast, as her dress slipped to the floor. Glad she had taken Brook's advice and invested in some outrageous lingerie, she slid her palms over her hips, enjoying the feel of her silky half-slip. When Jonas reached out to touch her she moved away, just out of arm's reach. "You tease like a pro," he said.

Bravo to me! "I am a pro," she said, somehow not ashamed of it.

"Turn around, pro," Jonas growled.

She turned, her hands in front of her concealing her lace-covered breasts. The cornflower blue bra and panties she wore were more lace than fabric, and she knew her nipples showed, peek-a-boo fashion, through carefully placed openings. The cups were also arranged to push her breasts together, creating a deep cleavage. His eyes seldom left her breasts, while he said, "Take that slip off." Erika hooked her thumbs over the slip's waist-elastic and drew it down, bending over so Jonas could get a good view of her cleavage. When she stood up, she watched Jonas's eyes, fastened on her bra cups.

"Very nice. You've got great tits. Leave the bra on, but get out of those panties."

She should have been shocked both at his orders and her willingness to obey, but she wasn't. She realized that she was actually having fun. She lowered the pitch of her voice. "You're certainly in a hurry, Jonas. You really need to slow down." She was being outrageous, and she loved it. "You're wearing decidedly too many clothes," she purred. "Let me help you."

She moved between his spread knees, but when he made a grab for her breasts, she playfully slapped his hands. "Not yet. Slow down." She put his hands on the arms of the chair. "Keep them there and let me make you more comfortable."

"You're making me very *un*comfortable," he said, rubbing his crotch, "but I'll let you run the show for a while." He replaced his hands on the chair and Erika could see his knuckles whiten as he gripped the wood.

"Very good." She bent over, moving so her lace-covered breasts were only inches from his face. She untied his bow tie and pulled his studs through the openings in his shirtfront. He was naked beneath and she combed her fingers through his thick black chest hair, listening to him moan. He leaned forward and nuzzled the deep valley between her breasts. *He's definitely a breast man,* Erika thought. She moved so her right breast pressed against the side of his face and rubbed against his cheek. He closed his eyes and sighed. She'd found his sexual weakness, and she intended to use it to give him more pleasure than any other hooker ever had.

She pressed the heels of her hands against the sides of her bra cups, deepening her cleavage, and encouraged Jonas to bury his face in the valley for long moments. "Yes, baby," she purred. "Would you like to hold them?"

His voice was hoarse and broke as he said, "Yes."

She took his hands and replaced hers with them, then reached down and grasped his hard cock through his tuxedo pants. On a hunch, she asked, "Would you like to fuck my tits?"

He leaned back and stared at her, his eyes glazed. Without a word, he pulled off his jacket and shirt, then his trousers and shorts followed. As he sat back in the chair, Erika watched his fully erect cock dance in his lap. Jonas grabbed the front of her bra and pulled her toward him. He yanked the straps over her shoulders and dragged the cups down. "Make your nipples hard," he growled. "Pinch them."

She did as he asked, twisting her nipples through the lace until they tightened. Although she wasn't particularly aroused, she was enjoying watching Jonas's excitement. She heard his jerky breathing as his fingers grabbed for her breasts. "Panties off. Now!" he managed to say.

She quickly removed her panties and knelt on the thick carpet at Jonas's feet. She arched her back and lifted her breasts so Jonas's mouth could fasten on one nipple, sucking and biting. She guided his hands to the front fastening of her bra and felt him unhook it, then he grabbed for her crotch, burying his fingers in her pussy. Breasts free, she rubbed her hard nipples over his chest and he pulled his fingers from her body, leaned back and groaned. Eventually, after weaving a deliberately torturous path down his chest and belly, Erika cradled his erection tightly between her breasts, pressing them together. Fluid leaked from the tip, lubricating the warm valley. She rubbed up and down the length of his cock, her gaze on his closed eyes and panting mouth, gauging his reactions to what she was doing. Yes, he was in esctasy.

She bent over and flicked her tongue over the slippery tip of his penis each time it drove upward between her breasts. She felt him throb, his hips thrusting. With a deep moan, thick white semen erupted from his cock, spilling on his belly and flowing over her flesh.

Erika was triumphant. She had excited Jonas so much that he came. She had sensed his desires and catered to them, without concern for her own excitement. Her arousal hadn't mattered, still didn't matter. This wasn't lovemaking, it was a job. She looked at his well-satisfied expression. It was obvious that she had done the job well, given him the pleasure he had paid for. Why shouldn't she be well rewarded for it?

In the bathroom she washed herself, then took a warm face cloth and returned to Jonas, bathing his belly, cock, and balls. "My God, woman, you're certainly a pro. No one's ever picked up on my desires so quickly. And you're obviously an expert at tit-fucking."

"I'm good at giving pleasure, whatever the needs." *I am good at it!* She couldn't help grinning. "And I enjoy it."

"That certainly shows. Listen, consider what I gave you a tip and charge Regency Software, too. You deserve it."

"Thanks, but no. They paid for my dinner and will pay for the rest. That's more than enough."

"An ethical prostitute. Fabulous."

She found a slip of paper on the table and scribbled Valerie's number on it. *We should have business cards*, she thought as she began to dress. "Call any time you want more company. I'll be happy to oblige."

"Oh, by the way. I just thought you'd like to know that I had already decided to invest in Regency before the dinner. I don't intend to tell them that, however," he said with a satisfied sigh. "I'll let them think it was your doing. My little joke."

"Why not? It will be great for my reputation."

"Your reputation needs no hype. You're fabulous."

Now fully dressed, Erika said, "Would you like me to tuck you in?"

"No, I think I'll just relax here for a while and think about your beautiful, talented boobs."

Erika lifted one breast from her bra and rubbed it across Jonas' face. "For luck."

He sighed, kneaded her flesh, and bit her nipple. "For luck."

Valerie called the following evening. "I spoke to Craig McDonald a few minutes ago. You made quite a hit with Jonas Stewart. He's raving about how wonderful you were."

"Let's just say we hit it off. I discovered his weakness and we both loved it."

"He told Regency that you deserve to be well rewarded by the firm and, since he's going to be an investor, they listened. They're paying you another thousand. Before taxes, of course."

"You take out taxes?"

"From the escort part of the fee, yes. Any money you get in cash is like a tip. You give me my twenty percent, then decide what you want to report to the government. I run a legitimate business as far as the government is concerned. Escort services and such. So yes, I take out taxes."

"No health benefits?"

Valerie laughed. "Only for our clients. What are you going to do with all your new cash?"

"I'm going to go to France and see my daughter. We've got a lot of fences to mend."

"Great. Are you interested in more jobs?"

She thought about Jonas and her reaction to him and to the situation. "I certainly am."

"Okay. It might not be for several weeks, but I'll call you when something comes up, as it were." The two women were laughing as they hung up.

Chapter
5

"Hi, honey. How was your week?" Erika said into the phone the following Sunday when her daughter arrived on the line. It was early December and the school was getting ready for winter vacation.

"Hello, Mother," Rena said, a nasty edge to her voice. "How was *your* week?"

Sometimes Erika wondered why she made the effort to call her daughter each Sunday. On the good days, Rena was short and uncommunicative. On the bad days, like today, she was sullen and frequently downright nasty. How had they come to this? she wondered. It was partly that her daughter was now fourteen and suffering from the natural problems that came with the age. Erika had bought several books on living with teenagers, but, of course, she didn't live with her daughter, merely tried to maintain some kind of a civil, if long-range, relationship. Of course, a great deal of the difficulty lay with the past and nothing could change that.

The summer Rena had turned six, Rick had decided that it would be good for all of them if Rena started first grade at an exclusive boarding school in France. "Many of the daughters of the partners go to school overseas. It rounds them, educates them in the world that they will be expected to join. I've already enrolled her in the school that Greg's and Mark's children attend."

He was kidding, right? "You mean those on the top of the corporate ladder?" Erika asked with a sneer.

"Of course. Rena is my daughter and I'm making more than enough to support her there even before I become a partner. She needs to mingle with all the right people."

"Rick," Erika said, trying to sound reasonable, "she needs to be with her mother. She was perfectly happy in kindergarten here. The schools in West Hampton are rated among the best in New York and she's made some good friends." He wouldn't send Rena away, not if Erika had anything to say about it.

"No one makes real friends at six years old," he said, sounding callous, "and those kids won't be of use to her when she's older."

She panicked as she realized sadly that his decision was firm and that he was digging his heels in. "She needs friends, not children who will be of use to her!"

"Wrong. And besides, think of the time you'll be able to devote to becoming part of the corporate wives' group. It's important to my career, and my career is important to you. After all, that's why we moved to the Hamptons."

"I don't like those women. All they do all day is shop and attend charity affairs. I hate bridge, tennis, and golf. It's all so useless." All she had ever wanted to be was a mother, a job she loved and was good at. "I was looking forward to helping out in Rena's classroom as I did for her kindergarten."

"That's a very selfish attitude," Rick continued, his voice calm and measured. "I put up with this ghastly commute to the city just so we can be near the partners and become part of their social clique. You need to help out too. There's more to my becoming a partner than just my work."

The argument had gone on all that summer until finally, totally worn down by Rick's continual wheedling, Erika gave in. "On one condition. We'll try it until Christmas break, then we'll talk to her. If she likes it then she can stay there. If not, you promise to let her come home and go to school here."

"Of course, but I know she'll love it there."

Rena arrived home from France at Christmas a different child. Where before she had been sassy and bright, now she was serious and contemplative. She called her parents Mother and Father and spent considerable time with the first-grade reading materials she had brought with her. She spoke English but worked on her French from a workbook. Occasionally she answered a question with *Oui* or *Non*. Erika found that she had little in common with this six-year-old.

Without much discussion Rena returned to France after the break. In April, she phoned home, asking for permission to go home to Switzerland with a school friend for the summer. When Erika said, "No," Rick grabbed the phone and told Rena that they'd talk about it and phone her back.

"She'll have nothing to do here," Rick maintained, a slight whining tone in his voice.

Erika felt Rena slipping away. "She'll have the beach and the country club. And she'll have us!"

"Yes, but she won't have any children her age to play with. This trip to Switzerland will be so much healthier for her. She'll be exposed to more European culture. She'll love it." Soon, Erika's arguments became less and less forceful until eventually it was easier just to agree. By the time Rena was in fourth grade, Erika spoke with her twice a month on the phone and saw her only a few weeks a year. During those visits, although Erika made a great effort, she and Rena had little to say to each other so the visits to museums, zoos, and parks were awkward, the conversation stilted. By the time Erika and Rick split, there had been few ties between mother and daughter.

* * *

Erika sighed and pressed the telephone against her ear. Everything had gone so terribly wrong between them. Could it ever be mended even with the trip to France she had saved so long for? Rena's voice buzzed at her across the miles. "I hear you're becoming quite a party girl." There was a nasty edge to her voice.

Momentarily Erika panicked. What did she know about her evenings? "Party girl?"

"Daddy says you went to a dinner with some of the partners. All dressed up as though you hadn't a care in the world." She hesitated. "Don't you care about him any more?"

"Care about your father?" Erika combed her fingers through her hair. She had never told Rena about her difficulties with money or Rick's insistence that his daughter remain in France. "He and I are no longer in contact. After all, he's got Sandy and he's making a new life without me."

"Well, you're not supposed to go out," Rena whined.

Funny, Erika thought, occasionally there's a little girl beneath all that sophistication. "Sometimes I need to be with people."

"You have your job. That should be enough. Daddy doesn't party."

"He doesn't? I'll bet he's out several evenings a week with friends or business associates, with and without Sandy. I don't have that kind of business life."

"You should only have women friends."

She heard Rick's thoughts coming from her daughter's mouth. Should Rick only have men friends? If only she could share everything she knew about what a stud Rick had been during the last years of their marriage, but it would serve no purpose and drive a wedge between Rena and her father. "I have women friends and that's fine, but sometimes I need to go out with men too."

"No, you don't! It's slutty."

"Where did you learn a word like that?" From Rick no doubt.

"Okay, time to change the subject. I've been saving my money and I think I've found a discount fare to Paris. I thought I'd come over during winter vacation and spend a week with you."

"You don't have to." Rena's voice was flat.

"I know I don't have to. I want to see you. It's been a very long time and I miss you."

She could hear Rena's long sigh. "I guess it would be okay. I had, of course, intended to spend my vacation with Janice."

"Janice?"

"Oh, Mother, keep up, will you? Janice Kirby." Rena went on to explain that Janice was the daughter of two well-known movie stars.

"I didn't know they were married," Erika said.

"They weren't. At least not to each other. She's a love child. Anyway, her mother's got a villa in Italy near a fabulous ski resort and I'm invited to spend the vacation with her."

"I'd rather you spent part of it with me."

"I guess I could postpone Italy for a few days." They discussed timing, arranging for Erika to arrive in the small French village during the first week in January, four weeks hence.

"I'm looking forward to seeing you. It's been such a long time." When Rena said nothing, Erika continued, "I'll call you next Sunday."

"You don't have to. If I'm going to see you, I'll talk to you then."

"I'd like to call anyway." Tears slipped down her cheeks. She was begging her daughter for time.

"Suit yourself."

Valerie called the week before Erika's trip to France. "Are you interested in a job next week?"

Erika explained about her trip. "I'm really sorry I have to say no the first time you call me directly, but I just can't."

"Of course. I understand. I hope you have a wonderful time with your daughter."

So do I, Erika thought. "I'd love to get together," she said. "Maybe we could arrange dinner together after I get back."

"I'd like that a lot," Valerie said. They picked an evening in the middle of January, after Erika's return from France. "Mondays are usually slow so unless you hear from me to the contrary, let's plan on it. How about that place we met the last time? It's a bit out of your way, but it has the best garlic bread."

"I remember. You can't eat garlic when you're working."

Valerie laughed. "Right. How about meeting at seven that Monday?"

"See you then."

Just after the beginning of the new year, Erika arrived at the school and met a young woman she didn't really know. Rena was now fourteen, tall and good-looking with wonderful thick brown curly hair and her father's wide-set hazel eyes. She was almost Erika's height and had an already lush body, evident even though she was covered with a loose sweatshirt and jeans. There were clumsy moments when Erika tried to hug her daughter and Rena quickly backed away. Trying to brush it off, Erika took a few pictures, then the two had lunch together at a small bistro within walking distance of Rena's school. They spent an awkward hour discussing their lives in the most cursory terms. Finally Rena said, "Aren't you going to ask about Daddy?"

Erika felt the pit opening beneath her feet. "How is he?" she said, her voice tight.

"He's fine, and so is Sandy. They're getting married, you know." There was a hard edge to her voice that Erika couldn't seem to soften.

"I had heard."

"She's not pregnant, if that's what you're thinking."

"Why would I think that?"

"That's why you married Daddy, isn't it?" Rena's tone was nasty and spiteful.

If it hadn't been so tragic, it would have been funny. Her trapping Rick. She remembered that late summer afternoon at his folks' house. He had been twenty-three then, and Erika just twenty, a junior in college. They lay on Rick's bed, petting and kissing, making the most of their last day together before he headed back for his last year at Harvard Business School, after which they wouldn't see each other for months.

"Come on, baby, just this once," Rick whined as he stroked Erika's bare belly. "I know it's dumb of me not to have a rubber, but I have to go back to school tomorrow. Anyway, you just had your period, so you can't get pregnant."

"You know I want to," Erika said, unable to catch her breath with Rick's hand rubbing all the places he knew made her crazy, "but it's so dangerous."

Rick leaned over and licked the joining of her lips. "Baby, you know I'd never hurt you. It's just that we'll be apart until Christmas."

Erika's sigh echoed throughout her body. "I know. But . . ."

She'd miss Rick tremendously while he was at school, but she'd focus on the fact that by this time next year they'd be married. God, she couldn't wait. Okay, she admitted to herself, they weren't engaged exactly and she didn't have a ring. They hadn't actually talked about setting a date, but she knew that once he was finished with classes and had been hired by a top firm, he'd be ready to commit himself to their life together. After she and Rick were married next summer, she could finish her senior year at night while Rick made a name for himself in international business.

How was she going to live for another entire year without him? She wouldn't date anyone and knew that Rick was faithful too. Sure, there were a few women in the graduate program and he must be tempted by gorgeous undergraduates too, but he swore to her that she was his only girl. He certainly hadn't deserted her this past year. They had talked once a week and written almost daily. Well, she had written daily, anyway. He'd only managed a letter every week or so, but she knew he loved her. When he had arrived back in San Diego, he'd called her up almost immediately and they had been together at least once a week since. She knew that he wasn't seeing other girls like some of her friends had told her. She just knew it. He was seeing only her.

"Come on, baby," Rick whined. "I just want to show you how much I love you. Don't you want to be with me?"

"Of course I do," Erika said, awash in erotic feelings as Rick's hand stroked lower. Earlier Rick had removed his shirt, then unbuttoned her blouse and parted the sides, stroking her naked breasts with his knowledgeable fingers. Now he was caressing all the spots that made it so difficult for her to think. "It's just that I don't want to take any chances."

"You're so beautiful that it's impossible for me not to want you. I know it's just a little risky, but I want you so much."

"I'm glad you think I'm beautiful, but I just can't."

Rick pulled his hand back and, with a loud sigh sat up and turned his rigid back to her. "It's okay," he said, his entire body shuddering. "I understand. You know I'd never do anything that you didn't want."

Erika reached out and stroked the length of his naked, steel-hard spine. "Oh, sweetheart, don't be like that."

"It's nothing. You girls don't understand anyway. It's just rough on me to love you so much and want you so much and not be able to do anything about it."

Erika knelt on the bed beside him, grasped his shoulders and turned him toward her. His hazel eyes gazed deeply into her pale brown ones, areas of light and shadow making his face look mysterious and sexy. With a tentative hand she stroked his cheek, sliding her fingertips over his lips.

He grabbed her wrist and yanked her hand away. "Don't tease me! If you're not going to let me love you, don't go around touching me and making me more crazy than I already am." He turned away again and started to get to his feet.

"Okay, Rick." She sighed. "If you really want to, and if you're sure it's not dangerous . . ."

Eagerly he stretched out against Erika's body, his hands dancing over her belly. "Oh baby, that's why I love you so much." He quickly unzipped the front of her shorts and his fingers easily found her mound, pulling her pubic hair slightly.

Her breath caught in her throat and her heartbeat sped. Of course it was all right. After all, they were going to be married anyway and Rick wouldn't do anything that wasn't okay. It wasn't as if they hadn't made love lots of times and it always felt so good. She watched him remove her pants, and then deftly pull off his own. She stared in fascination at his engorged cock, sticking out so rigidly from its nest of curly brown hair. The sight of him, fully erect, always made molten heat flow through her, gathering like a storm ready to break between her thighs. She felt his erection slide over her mound, finding the channel it was meant for. She had never felt him naked inside of her but to her it didn't feel terribly different.

"Oh Lord," he moaned, "it feels so good to be inside of you, just skin against skin. It's so much better than with those horrible things on." As Rick supported his body over hers, she grasped his muscular shoulders and watched the play of emotions over his face. Eyes closed, an expression of near pain on his face, he threw his head back and rammed into her. Over and over he pounded, banging his pubic bone into her soft, swollen flesh. She wanted him to slow down and wait for her, yet she couldn't deny him his obvious pleasure. Knowing what would drive him over the edge, she wrapped her legs around his waist and bucked upward, meeting thrust with thrust. It didn't matter whether she climaxed anyway, she thought. Rick's pleasure was what was important.

"Yes, baby. Right now!" One final thrust and she could feel his cock pumping into her. He collapsed, then quickly rolled onto his side, bringing her with him, her legs still around his middle. "You are so wonderful," he said, his voice ragged, "and I love you so much. You make me so happy."

"And I love you, Rick. So much I ache with it."

"I'll miss you," he said, his voice already sleepy.

Oh shit, Erika thought, looking at her now fourteen-year-old daughter, *this is going to get really ugly*. She wouldn't argue with Rena about how she had been conceived, or why. What was the point? Her daughter would believe what she believed and denials would get her nowhere. Why couldn't things be better between them? "Yes, I was pregnant, but we were planning on getting married anyway. You just speeded things up."

"Really? That's not the way Daddy tells it. According to him, you got pregnant so you could hitch your wagon to his rising star."

His rising star? Erika couldn't speak. Oh, Rick, why are you doing this to our daughter? Had it always been like this between them? No! There had been good times. Early in their marriage it had been wonderful, just the three of them. Where had they gone wrong? "That's not the way it happened, baby."

"Don't call me that. I'm not your baby. You gave up that right years ago when you sent me away. You couldn't have cared less about me; all you cared about was the fat paycheck that Daddy earned. Jewelry, a house, and an apartment, the country club, a Mercedes, the good life." Erika heard the quiver in her daughter's voice. "You didn't care a thing about me and you still don't. I was a trap you set and nothing more, and once it worked, you didn't need me anymore."

"Baby . . ." She saw her daughter's glare. "Rena, that's not the way it was at all. I made some mistakes, I'll admit that. I shouldn't have sent you away to school. I never wanted to but—well it happened. I want to make it right now. I want to be with you, share with you, love you."

"Too late, Mother." Rena made *Mother* sound like a dirty word. "I told you that you could come to visit, but I've changed my mind. I'm taking the train to Rome this afternoon to stay with Janice. I'm going to enjoy the rest of my vacation before I have to go back to the school that Daddy's paying for. At least he cares enough to do that much." Rena stood up, grabbed her coat and stalked away, her back as rigid as her father's had been all those years before.

Erika sat at the tiny table for a long time, tears streaming down her face. She had expected . . . What had she expected from a girl, an almost-woman, whom she hadn't really spent any time with for more years than she wanted to admit? The chasm between them was just too wide.

She rearranged her return flight and arrived back in New York in the early morning, only three days after her departure. She cried for most of the day, then, as soon as she thought Brook would be home from work she knocked on her friend's door. Through intermittent bouts of tears, Erika told Brook all about her abortive visit. "It was horrible. I don't have any clue who she is. She's my flesh, my baby, and yet she's a complete stranger." She started to cry again. "I don't want to let her go."

Brook handed her the cup of tea she had made in her tiny kitchen. "You don't have to. Keep calling her and try to keep some communication between you."

"But she hates me." Erika shredded the drenched tissue in her hands.

"I don't think you can know that nor can she. She doesn't know you any better than you know her. Right now she doesn't even know herself. She certainly resents you for sending her away but hate—Give her a chance."

Erika took a slow swallow of her tea, using the cup to warm her freezing fingers. "I didn't want to send her away," she said, her voice small. "It was the biggest mistake I ever made."

"I know, but it happened."

"I didn't put up enough of a fight. I should have insisted that she never go to that damned school."

"Should have, would have, could have. You didn't do any of those things. Now the situation is the way it is and you'll have to move on from here."

Erika paused, then said softly, "I really fucked everything up, didn't I?"

Brook shook her head. "It's not the best situation I've ever heard of, but we'll use our pooled wisdom to try to make it work."

"What the hell to you know about children?" Erika snapped.

"Ouch. Don't beat up on the messenger."

Erika reached out and embraced her friend. "Oh, Brook, I'm sorry. I don't know what I'd do without you."

"Well, you won't have to find out because I'm here for you."

Her voice quivering, Erika said, "Thanks. I guess you're right about Rena. All I can do is keep trying."

"Good girl. Now why don't you get cleaned up and let's go have something outrageous for dinner?"

The following Monday, Erika arrived at Villa Maria and was guided to a table in the back. Dressed casually in a gray-and-rose jogging suit, socks, and sneakers, Valerie had already been served from a bottle of Chianti Classico and a loaf of garlic bread was just being delivered to the table. "I see you've already started," Erika said as she sat down.

"No reason to delay the bread and if you're not up for wine, I can always take the rest of the bottle home."

"No need. The wine's fine with me."

"You look fabulous," Valerie said, then bit off a large chunk of bread.

"Thanks." Erika had taken special pains with her appearance, wearing a pair of tailored brown gabardine slacks, a toast-colored blouse and a beige-and-brown wool vest. A tight black leather belt emphasized her slender waist. She had showered and then carefully applied her makeup covering the signs of her lack of sleep. After all, Valerie was in charge of getting her jobs and she wanted to impress the woman.

"It's obvious that you've been careful with your appearance and that's great, but you don't need to primp for me anymore. From now on, if we have dinner, it's jeans and sweatshirts. Yes?"

Erika nodded. "Deal."

"How did your trip go?"

Erika had been ready for the question, prepared to respond that it had been fine, but somehow she found herself telling Valerie all about Rena and her reactions to her mother's visit. Somehow in telling the story again, the sting of rejection lessened a bit. "I don't know why I'm telling you all this," Erika said, her eyes filled with tears. "I was all prepared to say that France was nice and move on."

"People say it's a gift I seem to have, one that I recognize in you. Neither of us asks a question without expecting a complete and honest answer. It's a talent and, frankly, it makes me good at what I do. You'll find it stands you in good stead in this business. Men want to think that a woman is interested in them."

Erika fumbled in her purse and found a tissue. She'd been using a lot of them recently. "Thanks. That's quite a compliment."

"It was meant as such. What are you going to do now about your daughter?"

"I guess the only thing I can do is to keep trying to talk with her. My friend Brook keeps my spirits up. She's amazingly supportive and helpful." Erika talked about Brook for several minutes sipping her wine and calming.

"She sounds like quite a woman. Is this a sales pitch?"

"For Brook? I don't have the faintest idea whether she'd be interested in what we do, but she'd be an asset."

"If she's a friend of yours . . . But let's talk about you. Are you still interested in our little business?"

"Yes," Erika said. "If you've got work for me, I'm interested."

"I need to ask you a few very personal questions. What sexual activities wouldn't you indulge in? I mean the really kinky stuff."

"I don't know. I haven't given that aspect much thought."

"You need to. I have customers with specific tastes and I match my ladies to those. Some of my ladies enjoy anal sex; some wouldn't do it at any price. I have women who enjoy acting out fantasies, some who can bring a toy bag to an evening and use every one to heighten the excitement, and a few who particularly enjoy threesomes and group experiences. I have women who enjoy dominance, some who enjoy being submissive, and a few who will take either side. Faking anything usually doesn't work for long. You have to be into it, whatever *it* is. If not, the customer won't get the most out of his evening and that's what I'm after."

Erika leaned forward, propping her elbows on the table. "Rick and I got into a little kinky stuff, as you put it, and there wasn't anything I didn't enjoy. I never really considered the hard-core stuff. I don't know whether I'm comfortable with pain, you know whips and stuff, either giving or receiving."

"Okay. That's fine. Actually everything's fine but being limited just reduces the number of possible appointments I can send you on."

"I need to think about the rest." She settled back in her chair. "Let's be frank. We're talking about prostitution now, not just doing escort work."

Valerie took a large bite of bread and chewed slowly. "I get a lot of calls for parties, gatherings, and dinner parties, but I also get lots of calls from horny men who want a willing woman to play with."

"Then I'd be a call girl."

Valerie wiped her fingers on her napkin and laid her hand on Erika's arm. "Don't get all tied up with labels. Remember sticks and stones? Well, names can hurt you if you let them control your behavior. If the idea of what I do offends you, that's fine. We can be friends and I can call you only for parties and such. Frankly, there's a lot more money and, from my perspective, fun to be had if you expand your horizons a bit, but it's up to you. It's a big step."

"Yes, it is." She remembered Jonas and the triumphant way she had felt when she figured out how to best give him pleasure. "I don't think I have much of a problem with it. I guess I'm hearing Rena's voice calling me a party girl."

"She's fourteen and it seems to me that she wants you and Rick to get back together so she can eventually have a normal family. I don't think children ever give up on their parents. They can't see how wrong some relationships are."

"You think so?" Erika hadn't considered that. "It's been so long since she's been part of a mommy-daddy-daughter household, and from the little she tells me, few, if any, of the other girls at the school have that either."

"She sees it on TV, in the movies, and she reads about nice sitcom families like that in books. It's natural that she would want it for herself, even if she won't admit it out loud. Does she like Rick's new lady?"

Erika considered. "Sandy? I haven't the slightest idea. She told me they were getting married."

"She's got to be pretty bitter about that. It's one strike against a normal family for her. If you're out dating, that's about it, as far as she's concerned. Family, as she sees it, will never happen for her."

"You really think that's what she wants?"

"I don't know your daughter, but it would seem logical."

Erika hadn't told Valerie about Rena's remark about why she and Rick had gotten married. "I was pregnant when Rick and I married and Rena threw it in my face. Rick and I already had plans to get married so my pregnancy just advanced the date a few months. At least that's what I tell myself." Erika tried to be honest. "Maybe she's right about one thing. I know I didn't get pregnant to trap him, but maybe he felt trapped. Maybe he's resented it all these years."

"Who knows? Does it really matter now?"

"Rena thinks it does."

"It sounds to me as though she's doing everything she can to hurt you. Creating this wall of hate is almost as valuable to her as loving you, and much less risky. It gives her a consistent emotion, something that's always there, comfortable almost. It's difficult to know whether it's real or not, but that's not really important. She might also be testing you to see how bad she can be without you leaving her."

"She's certainly making our relationship as difficult as possible."

"I'm sorry. It must be hard on you," Valerie said wistfully, "but in some ways I wish I had your problems. Derek and I never had children."

"I didn't realize you were married."

"I was married. He died several years ago. Cancer."

"I'm so sorry."

"It was awhile ago and the pain eventually recedes. He's why I got into this business in the first place."

Erika leaned back. "Tell me, if you don't mind."

"About eight years ago he was diagnosed with colon cancer. We were devastated, and broke. He was a freelance artist and I held only temporary office jobs. We had no health insurance." Valerie sighed. "A guy in one of the offices I worked in had been hitting on me. I kept refusing but he was persistant, finally offering me money. The idea horrified me, but when Derek and I talked about it, the money was hard to resist. The guy wanted something quite special, so I asked for as much as I thought he'd be willing to pay. He went for it and my husband didn't object too loudly. The evening went okay and the guy told a few friends and the rest, as they say, is history."

"Something special?"

"He wanted a dominatrix." Valerie smiled. "Actually it was all a misunderstanding. It was midwinter and the weather had been awful, freezing rain and sleet for almost a week. Each day I had shown up at work in black jeans and a dark turtleneck sweater, with high-heeled black boots and a wide, heavy silver belt Derek had gotten me for my birthday. The guy thought he was reading an invitation."

Erika tried not to look shocked. "You're kidding. He thought you were a woman who enjoyed making men crawl?"

"He did. And you know what? I found out that I enjoyed it. We spent the evening with his face in my pussy, giving me some of the best orgasms I'd ever had."

"Had you ever done anything like that before?"

"No, but the week before our 'date' I read lots of stories in kinky magazines to prepare me. That's not a bad idea, by the way. There are lots of slick paper magazines that specialize in various"—she searched for a word—"art forms. He had told me clearly what he wanted so I read up on it. Derek and I discussed it and he was actually quite helpful. When I came home after that night, Derek and I talked about it and he admitted that he'd wanted to try something like that for a long time. We played a few times after that." Erika could see Valerie swallow hard. "Until he got too sick." Valerie straightened her spine. "Anyway, that was the beginning. The rest was just establishing contacts and trusting my instincts. I managed to earn more than enough to support us both and help out with medical expenses."

"That's quite a story."

Valerie looked at Erika. "It doesn't shock you?"

"Maybe a little," Erika said. "A year ago it would have blown me away, but I'm a much more grown-up person now and knowing you and the things I've done—well, I've mellowed a lot. I think your idea of reading stories about sexual options is a good one. Let me do a bit of browsing at my local newsstand and I'll let you know what activities are off limits."

"Great."

On her way home from work the following afternoon, Erika stopped at a huge newsstand and browsed through the X-rated magazines. She had the current copy of *Cosmo* in her hand and any time anyone came into the back of the shop, she dropped what she had been looking at and flipped through *Cosmo*'s pages. As she looked over the shelves of periodicals her eyes widened. There were magazines devoted to everything from diapering to incest. Trying not to look too interested, she selected a few and was glad when, looking bored, the salesman put them all in a flat brown bag.

She was sitting in her living room reading a story about the proper way to flog a submissive when Brook knocked on her door. "Hi, babe," Brook said as Erika let her in. "I was wondering whether you'd like to go out for dinner."

"I'm doing my homework."

Brook's jaw dropped as she saw the display of magazines arrayed on the coffee table. *Diapered and Dominated, Tickling Stories, The Spanking Journal.* "What the hell is all this?"

Erika told her about her dinner with Valerie. "I need to understand what's beyond the pale for me. Once I do that, Valerie will have jobs for me. Actually I mentioned you, too. You're interested, right?"

"I think I might be." She plopped on the sofa beside a copy of *The Red Connection.* "What's this one about?"

"It's one of the few that turned me off. It's about activities that actually draw blood and it's more than I want to deal with."

Brook made a face. "I don't think I could do that either. Have you found anything else that's off limits?"

"I know I shouldn't judge, but urination and such are definitely out. Most of the rest, however, although it's really bizarre, if it turns some guy on, I could enjoy sharing his pleasure. If you're really interested in working for Valerie if the occasion arises, you should do some thinking along those lines too."

Brook leaned back and propped her feet on the coffee table and picked up a copy of *Lesbian Diaries*. "Ever done it?"

"No, but I'm in the 'not sure' camp. If something happened, maybe a man requested a threesome, I think I could do it, if I were a bit mellow and really hot."

Brook uncrossed and recrossed her ankles. "This conversation is making me very uncomfortable. I had a lesbian experience once and, although women don't turn me on, I won't say I wouldn't try it again. However, I don't ever want you to think that I fantasize about you." Brook shuddered. "Shit, now I'm worried that from here on, this conversation will create some kind of strain between us."

"Oh Brook, of course it won't. I don't think of you that way at all. Let's just put that entire thing off limits. I wouldn't jeopardize our friendship for anything."

Brook grinned. "Me neither. I'm just curious. Have you ever thought about being with a woman?"

"I have thought about it, but the situation hasn't come up and I don't know what I'd do if it did. Maybe I'd run screaming."

"I doubt that."

Erika paused. "Okay. I'll admit it. Although I have no interest in you sexually, you've piqued my curiosity. Tell me."

"My senior year in high school I was a cheerleader and we all changed in the same locker room. Anyway one of the girls came on to me so we met at her house and made out. Mostly I was curious. I'd been with dozens of guys and I just wondered what it would be like to be with another woman."

"What was it like?"

"It was okay. Just okay. She wasn't very experienced and we fumbled. It wasn't much different from fumbling with some guy, except she was softer."

"Did you ever do it again?"

"No. I'm not going to put it down out of hand; it's just not my first choice. Or my tenth, for that matter. Have you?"

"Never. I've been curious from time to time, but I've never even considered acting on it." She took a deep breath. "Phew. This conversation is scaring me a bit too. I don't want anything to louse up our friendship. If I hug you hello, I don't want either of us having funny thoughts."

Brook extended her hand. "Deal."

Erika shook it. "Deal."

Brook put the lesbian magazine back on the coffee table and picked up one with a photo of a man tied to a chair. "How about this? Any interest in tying some guy up?"

Erika shrugged. "That's Valerie's thing, and I think I could enjoy it too. Being in control. Watching him get hard and not be able to do anything about it without my permission. It was sort of like that with Jonas. I loved watching him want me."

As they continued discussing the pros and cons of various sex games, both women agreed that, if a customer was interested in something really unusual, most things would probably be okay. Finally, Brook's stomach rumbled. "Time for dinner. Want to come with me?"

"Sure. Chinese?"

"Done."

Valerie called about a week later. Erika told her what she had discovered about herself. "Sounds like you've given this quite a bit of thought," Valerie said.

"I have. This is serious stuff. I wouldn't want to get into a situation where I had to disappoint someone."

"I don't always know in advance, but I try to anticipate a man's desires. I can usually tell from the questions a new guy asks on the phone. It's funny, some come right out and ask for what they want. 'I'd like a tall black woman who'll spank my bottom and call me a naughty boy,' one man said. I happened to be able to oblige. Another wanted someone who would pee on him. I had to turn that guy down.

"Others hem and haw, but I can usually get enough information to match him with the right person. Speaking of which, are you free Friday evening?"

Erika's heart began to pound. "Yes. Got someone?"

"I do. He's an old friend."

"A friend of yours?"

"I call all my customers friends. It makes the language easier and there's less chance of being overheard and misunderstood."

"Or understood."

"Right. Anyway, Randy Castner is just what his name implies. Randy. All the time. He likes new faces and I thought you two would hit it off well. He's quite rich, great in bed, and deliciously kinky. Nothing you can't handle, I promise. He enjoys long dinners with lots of sexy conversation. Anticipation is his fetish."

"You've been with him?"

"Several times, but I'm not an adventure for him anymore. He's got a great sense of humor, he's not bad to look at, and he's got a platinum credit card. Interested?"

"Sure. If he's as nice as you say, though, why does he have to pay for dates and sex?"

"I asked him that once. He goes out on regular dates, but he considers them work. Be charming. Go slowly. Be on your guard for gold diggers. This way he knows what the deal is up front."

Erika thought about it. "I'm not sure I understand, but I don't have to. If he's willing, why look a gift platinum card in the mouth."

"Right on. I'll check it out with him and call you with his phone number."

"How come you're not going out with him?"

"I'm busy Friday evening and, as I said, he likes new faces. And new bodies. The entire evening will be billed as escort services at fifteen hundred dollars. That okay with you?"

Fifteen hundred dollars. "More than okay."

"Yeah," Valerie said, "the money's sensational. Don't give up your day job yet, but eventually you could be making quite a bit more in the evenings than you do in the daytime."

"From your mouth to God's ears."

Valerie called back with Randy's phone number. Scared and excited, Erika dialed. "Hello, Randy? My name is Erika Holland and Valerie DeShields suggested that I call."

She could hear the deep breath. "Hello. I was expecting your call, Erika. Tell me a little about yourself."

Erika had decided what to tell men and what to keep to herself. "I'm thirty-four and divorced. I work as a 'girl everything' at an insurance agency."

"What do you look like?"

She wanted to ask why that mattered, but instead she said, "I'm about five foot five with a nice figure, brown hair, and light brown eyes."

"You sound like just my type."

"What exactly is your type?"

She could hear Randy's laughter. "Breathing with a pulse, actually. And willing." He named an upscale restaurant in midtown. "How about meeting me at seven on Friday? Then we can see how compatible we really are."

How could she put this delicately? I'm on the clock? "You know I work for Valerie," she finally said.

"I do and you'll get paid even if we don't hit it off. I want someone for company, not just for sex, although that's important too."

Erika silently shook her head. This was getting really strange. He paid for company. "Right. I understand." She didn't.

"Great. I'll see you at seven. Just ask for my table."

At seven o'clock on Friday, Erika asked for Randy Castner's table. She was guided through the elegant restaurant to a damask-covered table along one wall. The man seated on the banquette was about forty, with prematurely gray, carefully styled hair, a small moustache, and a wide, slightly mischievous smile. Although he wasn't particularly good-looking, he had a comfortable aura as though he was happy with himself. He stood and helped the waiter slide the table forward. "You must be Erika." He patted the banquette beside him. "Sit here and let's get to know each other."

Erika moved around the table, swept the skirt of her gray wool dress beneath her, and settled onto the soft cushioned seat. For a second she remembered sitting next to Jarred on her first night out after Rick. She'd come quite a way since then. "It's nice to meet you," she said.

"Would you care for a cocktail before dinner?" the waiter asked.

"I usually drink Scotch, but if you want a bottle of wine . . ."

Erika had been to this restaurant several times with Rick and she knew it had a great wine cellar. "Have your Scotch." She looked at the waiter. "You used to have a Fume Blanc I particularly liked by the glass."

"Of course, madam, I know just the one. Sir?"

"Johnny Walker Black on the rocks."

"Immediately."

"You've been here before," Randy said.

"Several times awhile back, with my ex-husband. He particularly liked the wine list."

"I'll have to give it a try next time."

Over drinks, the two talked. Erika found out that Randy had never been married, had a huge collection of nieces, nephews, aunts, and uncles scattered around the country and loved his work. "I design and program computer games," he said. "At first I sold a few, but when I realized how little they paid me and how much the company made I started my own business. The computer chips have been getting so much faster and capable of so much more that my little enterprise has done nothing but grow over the past few years."

Erika listened attentively as he told her the outline of his latest adventure quest game. "It sounds really exciting." She studied the glow in his eyes. "You love your work, don't you?"

She watched his face light even more. "Yes, I do. I can't imagine making this much money for playing with toys. It's all I've ever dreamed of and more."

"It sounds fabulous."

They studied the menu as the waiter arrived. "What would you like?" Randy asked.

"I think I'll have the sole. You?"

"I'm having a steak." He looked at the waiter. "Blood rare." His gaze returned to Erika. "You raved about the wine list. What shall I order?"

"You want me to pick?"

"Sure. You seem to know this restaurant."

"Okay. I'm going to have another glass of the Fume Blanc. For a man as definitive as you seem to be, I'd recommend the BV Cabernet. It's strong and should hold up well against the meat."

"Done." He nodded to the waiter who completed their order, then disappeared. The conversation didn't lag during the meal. Each had been to Europe several times and they compared notes on their favorite places. "Florence," Randy said. "When I arrived at the train station on my first trip it was as though I had come home. In my opinion, it's the most beautiful city in the world."

"I loved Florence too," Erika said, "but my then-husband thought it was too provincial." They had finished their main course and sat side by side sipping cordials. After two glasses of wine, the liquor was making her head buzz.

Randy extended his arm across the back of the banquette and stroked her neck. "He's wrong. Florence is almost as beautiful as you are." When Erika looked at him questioningly, he continued, "You're beautiful and sexy and you turn me on, lady."

Erika felt him teasing her ear. "Boy, you change gears in a hurry."

"Too fast for you?"

"No, it's just surprising."

As Randy continued to tickle her ear, his other hand found her knee below her skirt. As he rubbed her stockings, he said, "You're not wearing those awful panty hose, are you?"

Her breath caught in her throat as his hand slid up her inner thigh. "No."

His fingers reached the skin above the top of her stocking. "Good. Now go and take your panties off for me."

Erika couldn't have been more surprised if he had asked her to do a swan dive onto the dessert tray. "What?"

Randy's grin made her tingle. "Go into the ladies' room and take your panties off, and when you get back, hand them to me. Leave everything else just as it is."

Without a word, a trembling Erika made her way to the ladies' room. *This is crazy,* she thought, *deliciously so. So naughty, but no one will know except the two of us.* She closed the stall door, pulled off her panties, and slipped them into her purse. It was a wonderfully decadent feeling walking back to the table across the restaurant, her pussy naked, her damp lips rubbing against each other. She slipped in beside him, tucking her skirt and slip beneath her.

Randy held out his hand, palm up. Without a word she opened her purse, withdrew the panties, and put them into his hand.

"Good girl," he said, stuffing the tiny bit of nylon into his jacket pocket. His hand found her thigh and slipped upward beneath her dress. When his fingers brushed her pubic hair, she jumped. "Relax. Just sip your drink and pretend nothing is happening."

She lifted her brandy and sipped the warm brown liquid while his fingers played with her clit. Unable to swallow, she said, "I can't pretend anything when you do that."

"I know. That's the idea. I just wonder how excited I can get you when you can't let anyone know what's happening. Do you scream when you come?"

"Don't be ridiculous."

"Ridiculous? You mean you don't think I can make you come or you don't scream?"

"Neither. Let's just get out of here."

"Not a chance," Randy said, a salacious grin lighting his face. "I'm enjoying myself and I'm paying, after all."

His fingers were alternately squeezing and releasing her clit finding her exact rhythm. Her entire body trembled as his other hand returned to the back of her neck. "You're very quiet all of a sudden. Isn't it your job to make scintillating conversation?" he asked.

Erika floundered, unable to frame a coherent thought. "I can't say much of anything with you doing that."

"Good. That's what I had in mind."

He kept playing with her clit until she was sopping wet and on the verge of climax. "You're going to come, aren't you?"

"If you keep doing that, yes."

"I knew you'd be easy," he said, laughter bubbling just beneath the surface.

She gazed into his eyes, then, on impulse, reached over and unzipped his slacks beneath the long tablecloth. Concentrating as his fingers continued their playing, she said, "Two can play this game." She spread his fly and worked her hand under his shorts. He was hard, fully erect, and the tip of his cock was wet.

"Now we have a problem," she said, her breathing rapid. "If you make me come, I'll do the same to you." She wrapped her fingers around his cock and rhythmically squeezed, exactly as he was doing to her clit. "If I come, it's not difficult to hide. If you do, it will make a mess in your carefully pressed pants."

Randy's sudden laugh was rich and full. "You're quite something." He withdrew his hand. "Let's get out of here."

They could barely wait until they were inside Randy's apartment. Clothes littered the bedroom floor and they fell on each other on the bed. Naked, he used a condom from the drawer of the bedside table and, without hesitation, drove his erection into her waiting body. He came quickly; then, still lodged inside her hot body, he rubbed her clit until she came as well. Silently they lay side by side until their bodies calmed and their breathing returned to normal. "That was fantastic," he said.

"It certainly was. I have to say that game you played in the restaurant was the sexiest thing I've ever experienced."

"I've played it a few times and no one's ever turned the tables as neatly as you did. Bravo!"

They made love again an hour later and finally, at one, Erika dressed. "You can keep the panties if you like," she said.

"I intend to. I didn't even check to see what kind they were. I only know they're black."

"Bikinis, of course." She winked. "With lots of lace and a very wet crotch."

"Of course. Can I see you again?"

"I'd like that. You play the most delicious games."

He stretched out on the bed like a cat. "So do you, Erika, so do you."

Chapter

6

A week later Erika was relaxing over hot and sour soup and fried dumplings with Stuart. They had discussed the problems of the current administration, the difficult situation in the Middle East, and the newest exhibit at the Museum of Modern Art. Erika loved her evenings with Stuart. The conversation never lagged. Rather they both vied for space to bring up some new and fascinating discovery about the world. Finally, Stuart said, "Now that we've solved all the world's problems, tell me about you. How are you really?"

"Some of me is great and some not so good," Erika said, pouring dumpling sauce on her plate.

"Okay, let's get the not-so-good part out of the way." Stuart sat back and concentrated on Erika's face.

"I told you on the phone that my trip to France didn't go well."

"That's an understatement. No progress with Rena since?"

"None. I got her phone number from the school, and I called when I got back and again this past weekend. She was monosyllabic at best. It's like talking to a wall." Erika's shoulders rose and fell as she heaved a great sigh. "She hates me and she's not going to forgive me."

Stuart looked genuinely puzzled. "For what?"

"Don't defend what Rick and I did. It's not like you to be dishonest." She put her chopsticks on the table and folded her hands in her lap. "We shipped her off to boarding school. That's such a cliché, but it's exactly what we did. We got her out of our way so we could be a good little corporate couple. I look back on it now and regret it tremendously, but it was just as much my decision as Rick's. Rick, however, seems to have become the good guy to Rena while I'm the heavy. She slammed me in the gut with her crack about my getting pregnant to trap him. She couldn't have just sucked that idea out of the air. She must be getting it from him."

"I wouldn't put it past him to try to win this tug of war any way he can and filling Rena's head with lies."

"They aren't lies. He's just putting his spin on them." When Stuart started to protest, she held her hand up. "Don't. I've come to terms with what happened and now I just have to keep trying to establish some kind of relationship with her in spite of it. And, teenagers are difficult to deal with under the best of circumstances."

"Believe me, you're right about that," Stuart said with a rueful smile. "Mine are right around Rena's age, and according to them, neither Lorraine nor I have a functioning brain cell between us." Stuart finished the last of his soup and signaled to the waiter to remove his bowl. "You said that some of you is great. Tell me that part."

"I've really hit it off with Valerie. She's a wonderful woman and we've been doing some business together." Erika had already had two dates since her evening with Randy. One, a party for a rock musician, went well with some fast sex in a back bedroom and the other, a date with an out-of-town salesman for a plastics manufacturer with "entertainment" in his hotel room. In both cases the sex had been uncomplicated and not stressful.

"That's fantastic. Good money?"

"Great money. I'm already seeing something going into my savings account for a change. For so long, I thought it was a one-way street, all outbound."

Stuart reached across the table and grasped Erika's hands. "That's wonderful. I'm so happy to see you succeeding. Do you enjoy Valerie's line of work? I hope you're not doing it just for the money."

"I would do it for the money alone, but it's really enjoyable too. All my clients have been nice people interested in fun sex. Valerie's very careful and we've set a few guidelines between us. She's so sane, somehow."

"Funny," Stuart said as the waiter put steaming plates of kung pao chicken and fried rice on the table between them and removed Erika's empty soup bowl. "That's the exact word I would use to describe her too. It's such an insane business, but she just keeps her cool and makes it all happen."

The waiter put a red-and-white-patterned dinner plate in front of each of them and they helped themselves. They made small talk over dinner and too soon the check was paid. "We've let too much time go by between visits," Stuart said as he helped Erika on with her coat. "Let's not let it go this long again."

"Definitely not," Erika said. "Give my love to Lorraine and the kids."

They kissed each other's cheek. "I will."

As she walked back toward her apartment, she realized that she was very lucky. She had Brook, Valerie, and Stuart. How many other people could boast such good friends?

Erika's life became predictable. Aside from the first frantic week after her return from France, she limited herself to one or two evenings out per week, mostly on the weekends. She had a day job that gave her a steady paycheck, and she couldn't do her best work when she had been out until all hours the evening before.

Eventually, however, the lure of the fun evenings with great money became irresistible. By May, she was dating three or four evenings a week. Several men, including Jonas, had become regulars, calling whenever they were in town. Between her two jobs, she had managed to build up a considerable bank account. She called Rena every Sunday, but when she suggested that they spend some time together over the summer Rena flatly refused. "Mother, I've made my plans and I just don't have time." When she had pushed, Rena had become so obdurate that Erika had let the issue drop.

She had dinner with Stuart almost every week and spent quite a bit of time with Brook, whose love life was as fleeting as Erika's relationships. Although Erika and Valerie had dinner once a month and talked about Brook, Valerie's business had just the right number of escorts so Brook was never needed.

One Wednesday evening Erika was sitting in a white leather lounge chair in her newly decorated living room, flipping pages in *Time* magazine. She subscribed to both *Time* and *People* and made it a point to read both each week to keep her conversations lively. The small room was dominated by a long navy sofa with a small white pattern and matching side chair. The coffee table and two end tables were covered with bits and pieces that Erika had acquired over the past year: a pair of ginger jar lamps with soft vellum shades, a small carved jade elephant with its trunk raised in triumph, an empty glass vase in a deep shade of rose and several Southwestern planters filled with greenery. There were also two pictures of Rena as a child in small silver frames and a larger one of the two of them in France framed in a carved wood frame, a gift from Stuart.

When the phone rang, she distractedly reached for it. "Hello?"

"I'm in a jam, babe," Valerie said. "Both Mei and Sherry are down with the flu and I've got a big summer party tomorrow night. Every available one of my girls is booked. I've called around, but as you know weeknights are tough. I've gotten a few answering machines but so far no luck. I know you were out both nights over the weekend and last evening, but I'm stuck. Can you help me out?"

"Of course. You know I'll help whenever I can."

Erika could hear Valerie's sigh through the receiver. "Terrific. That's one down. This gig is a trade show party hosted by a large drug manufacturer and both Mei and Sherry were supposed to be there. You've often mentioned your friend Brook, but the time's never been right before. Do you think she'd be interested now? I'm waiting for callbacks, but there are only two other girls who aren't either already booked or definitely out of the question."

Brook had said a few times that she'd be available for escort work, but . . . "I won't even presume to speak for her. Let me ask and I'll call you right back."

Erika slipped on her shoes and ran up the two flights to Brook's apartment. She knocked and Brook answered the door, reading glasses propped on her nose, a copy of *Smithsonian* magazine in her hand. "Hi. Come on in." She closed the door behind her friend. "What's up?"

Brook's apartment looked as it always had, totally chaotic. Erika moved several sweaters from an overstuffed chair and sat down. "I just got a call from Valerie. She's got a problem for tomorrow evening; she needs two more women for a party. I'm up for it, but that still leaves her one short. Interested?"

"Me?"

"Sure. You've always said that's you'd love to be paid for what you now give away for free. I've spoken of you to her many times, but the time was never right before. Tonight she mentioned you and I said I'd ask."

"Wow, I'd love to." Brook slumped in the corner of her brown leather sofa. "I guess."

"Cold feet?"

"You seem to have such a great time, and the money's hard to turn down. It's just . . ."

"I know. You never thought of yourself as a prostitute."

"That's harsh." She hesitated. "But accurate. *Phew.*"

"Take your time. You have five minutes to consider it." Erika walked into Brook's tiny kitchen and filled the teapot with hot water. As she put it on the stove, Brook arrived at the kitchen door, her eyes large and round. "I'd really like to do it."

"I know."

"But I'm scared stiff."

Erika turned on the burner beneath the teapot. "I know that too. Is it the sex?"

"Actually no. For me that would be the easy part. To be brutally frank, it's the people who frighten me."

Erika leaned back against the counter. "I'm not sure I understand."

"You wouldn't. It all comes to you so naturally. It's the manners, talking to folks who earn more in a day than I do in a month. Making small talk about the bond market and the price of commodities."

"Is that what you think we talk about?" Erika said. "Most of the time we talk about things I know nothing about, like sports. I've had to bone up on the Rangers and the Yankees just to be able to nod at the right time."

"I thought you enjoyed sports. We talk about it from time to time."

"To be honest, I pick your brain. I memorize something you say about the Knicks needing a power forward or the Met's chances to make the playoffs." She shrugged her shoulders. "I wouldn't know a hockey stick from a golf tee."

"You're kidding. More than a year together and I never knew."

"I talk a good game, and that's all it takes. So what do you say about tomorrow evening? You're a bright woman with so many interests that you could make clever conversation with a mummy."

Brook rubbed the back of her neck as Erika put tea bags in two mugs. "If you think so."

"If it's not the sex, then I do think so. Shall I call Valerie?"

Brook took a deep breath and nodded. "Yes. Do it. Will you help me with the wardrobe and stuff? I never use makeup and my hair could use a bit of help for something that important. It's tomorrow evening? Oh shit."

"I've got a great idea," Erika said. "Let's each call in sick tomorrow and make a day of it."

"Call in sick just because? I almost never call in sick."

"I know, neither do I, and that's why we can do it tomorrow. Call it a mental health and beauty day. I'll call Valerie back, then we'll raid my closet and find something to make you look ravishing. Or maybe that's ravishable. How about an afternoon at Marcel's? You can take it out of your earnings. I'm afraid we don't have time for the works, you know, body wrap, massage, but we can get your hair styled and your nails done. They can even give you makeup lessons."

"I don't usually wear makeup."

"I know, but in this business, the way you look, and the way you show that you care about the way you look, is very important."

"Right." After only a moment's hesitation, Brook said, "Okay. Let's do it."

After a quick call to Valerie, Erika and Brook went through Erika's closet. When Brook found a pair of white linen dress trousers, Erika said, "I never wear slacks when I'm working for Valerie." When Brook looked puzzled, she continued, "I want men to feel I'm available. Accessible. You know what I mean. It's like panty hose."

That remark made Brook smile. "What else?" she said, putting the slacks back into the closet. "Give me Erika's tips on playing a party."

"During evenings like this one, I never stand talking to another woman for more than a few moments. It's more difficult for a man to break in on a duet than it is for him to try to assist a woman alone and looking a bit out of place. I do out-of-place very well."

"You're certainly right about that. I do the same thing when I'm out looking for male company. Men just love the 'lone woman in distress' idea. Sadly, the world seems to travel in pairs so most men are only too happy to help us single women out."

"Another thing," Erika said, remembering her first dinner with Valerie, "I always watch for onions or garlic in whatever I nibble. Actually I usually eat enough beforehand so I'm not hungry. Nothing ruins a lovely beginning more quickly than bad breath."

"You really have thought all this through."

"Valerie has been a great teacher. I guess I treat my dates like a business. This is money, mine to earn and theirs to spend. The more careful I am, the more often men will want to see me again and will be willing to spend for that. The more they spend, the more I make. It's simple."

"Okay. One more question. How do we explain our presence at something like this? I can't very well say, 'I'm a hooker hired to be here for your pleasure.' "

With a grin, Erika dropped onto the bed. "Not very likely. If they ask, which they seldom do, I usually just say that I came in with someone, but he seems to have left without me. Seldom, if ever, does a man want to know about the competition.

Conversation isn't usually a problem from then on. Just assume it's a guy you've picked up; ask about him and let him do most of the talking."

Brook stared at her. "Aren't you getting a bit cynical?"

"I try not to and I really do enjoy most of the men I'm with. Sometimes, however, it's just a job to be done as competently and as efficiently as possible."

They pored through the closet and selected several dresses that would suit Brook's fair coloring. "I never liked this dress on me," Erika said as Brook tried on a slender, cocktail length, muted green dress of soft cotton gauze. It was modest, with a scoop neck top, a gathered cummerbund-style waist, and slightly flared skirt.

Brook stroked her hand over the fabric. "This is the softest thing I've ever had on, but what's wrong with it for you?"

"It's not my taste and not really my color. I've worn it a few times, but I just don't feel that I look good in it."

"Hey, if you've got no interest in it, I sure have." She held the dress against her and turned this way and that in front of Erika's full-length mirror.

"I'm not giving it away, babe," she said, "just letting you wear it."

Brook stuck her lower lip out. "Rats."

Erika relented. "Well," she said, "if it looks as good on you as I think it will, I just might let you have it. The great thing about this job is that, although you need knockout clothes, like that dress, you don't need too many different outfits. You seldom see the same folks twice. And anyway, no one remembers."

"Oh, they'll remember this dress," Brook said with a grin. "Especially with me in it. Do you expect that there will be other opportunities for me to wear it?"

"If you're asking whether Valerie might have more jobs for you, I think she will. The guys will love you and she'll love you too. You're very attractive, intelligent, well read, and certainly not a prude."

The following afternoon Brook and Erika were "squeezed in" at Marcel's, a famous salon in midtown Manhattan. Since Erika now frequented it, Marcel himself took charge as Brook took her place at an operator's station. "Erika, my love," Marcel said, his lisp and carriage making him a caricature of the lifestyles of the rich and gay. "Who's this delicious creature?"

"This is my friend Brook."

Marcel ran his fingers through Brook's long blond hair. "Wonderful. You can't get this color or texture from a bottle. But, my dear, who has been cutting this, or have you been doing it yourself with hedge clippers?"

When Brook looked horrified, Erika jumped in. "Ignore him, Brook," she said. "If he doesn't say anything totally outrageous and insulting every hour, he gets hives."

Brook relaxed and Marcel giggled. "Now darling, I do not." He crushed a handful of Brook's hair in his fist then looked closely at the ends. "Wonderful hair. Fine, yet with some body and no split ends." He turned to the stylist. "Denise, do nothing to these beautiful strands. Leave the color alone." He looked at Brook in the mirror, then threaded his fingers through her hair and fluffed it forward. "You'll want something you can style and restyle, you know, long one day, up and sexy another. I'd suggest we cut it to here," he said, indicating a spot on Brook's arm several inches below her shoulder, "and let it curve in toward your jawline." He pulled it forward over her neck. "Yes, Denise. Like that."

When Brook nodded, Marcel peered into the mirror, then forced her head up with a finger beneath her chin and stared at her cheek. "Good skin and great pores, but what a waste. Why don't you wear makeup?"

"I've just never gotten into the habit," Brook said, looking chagrined. "Oh, maybe some lipstick. That's about all."

"Criminal. Denise, she needs cool tones for those delectable blue eyes. And what blonde goes out on the street without doing something about her lashes and brows. They almost disappear." He waved a hand. "You know what to do, Denise, but keep it light. Let's not destroy that Kansas farm girl image. She'll love it." He picked up Brook's hand. "And do the nails, of course."

"Of course," Brook said, a bit overwhelmed. "I use a computer all day so don't do anything with my nails that will get in the way."

Throughout all the discussion Erika stood off to one side, watching. "How do you feel about it all, Brook?" she asked.

"Nothing he's suggesting is permanent so if I hate it, off it comes."

"Hate it?" Marcel shrieked. "Nothing we do here could ever be less than perfect. You'll love it. I guarantee it."

Erika had dealt with Marcel several times over the past few months. "Money-back guarantee, Marcel?"

"Of course not. I may be perfect, but I'm not a fool."

Marcel walked out to the sound of everyone's laughter. After several hours of pampering and primping, Erika returned to Brook's cubicle and gazed at her friend. As Erika could have predicted, there was no danger of anyone wanting her money back. Brook's hair was carefully cut, curving in at the sides, falling like a golden curtain down her back. Denise had used hot rollers to add just a bit of fullness in the front and had feathered a few strands to form wispy bangs. She had skillfully applied cosmetics and, as Erika stared, Brook beamed.

"I'm staggered," Brook said. "Look at me, Erika. I'm gorgeous. To my fingertips." She held out her hands and waggled her fingers as Erika examined her carefully polished, daytime-length nails.

"You're a knockout," Erika said, "and I'm not bad myself."

While Brook had been pampered in one area of the salon, Erika had had her hair trimmed and highlighted with a slight auburn rinse. She had also had a facial, a manicure, a pedicure, and a leg wax. Now the two women stood at the cash register. When they saw their bills, Erika watched Brook blanch. "When I have my hair cut, it costs twenty bucks with tip. This is outrageous." She gazed at herself in the mirror behind the cash register and grinned. "Worth it, but outrageous."

"True," Erika said, handing the receptionist her credit card, "but Marcel is the best."

"But of course," Marcel said, suddenly appearing behind them. "I am always the best." He bussed each woman on the cheek. "And you two ladies look fabulous. Brook, you are pleased?"

"I certainly am."

"Of course you are," Marcel said.

"Of course," Erika said. "We are all always the best."

The two women climbed into a taxi at seven that evening and Erika gave the address of a large midtown hotel where a medical convention was being held. Valerie had told Erika that the gathering the two women were to attend was an after-show party arranged by a drug manufacturer. They were to hang out at the hospitality suite and "entertain" any of the out-of-town doctors and hospital staff who might be likely to place large orders. "Do we have to decide who's worth our time?" Brook asked as the cab made its way downtown.

"Nope. They pay us and take their chances. No one actually knows whether this increases sales or anything, but it keeps the visiting royalty happy and that's the object of the game."

"Are we engaged for the entire evening?" Brook asked, her meaning clear despite her slightly cryptic wording.

"Until midnight, or as long after as we're needed. The fee is more than generous."

The two women found the double-size hotel suite filled with suit- and tie-clad men juggling canapés and glasses. Brook was wearing the green dress she had selected and had added the "lucky" gold jewelry that Erika had worn to the original Cadmire dinner and on her first evening for Valerie. Erika wore a deep plum cocktail dress with a V-neck, cap sleeves, and full skirt that closed with a long row of tiny matching buttons down the front. She had added silver sandals, a multistrand silver necklace, three bangle bracelets, and long silver earrings. They quickly got glasses of wine from the bar.

"Take good care of yourself," Erika said under her breath.

"Take good care of yourself, too," Brook said, then they separated.

As a uniformed waiter passed with a tray, Erika took a napkin with a tiny puff of pastry filled with shrimp dusted with fresh dill. As she bit into it, a voice behind her said, "Try the paté. It's really much better than the shrimp."

She swallowed her tiny mouthful and said, "This really isn't bad." She sipped her wine to clean her mouth. "I'm Erika."

"Hello. I'm Casey Kemp and you're smashing."

She turned. Casey was in his mid-forties, with long brown hair tied at the back of his neck with a leather cord and steel-rimmed glasses covering magnificent deep-blue eyes. His face was long, with a heavy jaw and prominent chin. His hands were wide with blunt fingers and his broad smile revealed white teeth that contrasted with his deeply tanned skin. She inclined her head. "Thank you, sir." She let her gaze wander from his face down the length of his well-structured body to his hand-tooled loafers. "You're not bad to look at yourself."

His laugh was loud and immediate. "I must admit that I've never been given the once-over before."

"You've just never noticed. A man who looks like you has gotten the once- and twice-over many times, I'm sure."

He inclined his head. "I thank you, dear lady. I wasn't looking forward to being here, but now I think this is going to be a delightful evening. Are you alone?"

"I'm afraid so. I came with an acquaintance, but he seems to have slipped off without me."

"His loss is my gain."

Erika smiled at him, wondering how many times she had said that same line, and how many men had responded with the same retort. "And mine, I think. Tell me a little about you."

"I'm married."

"And I'm not. Now that we've got that out of the way, tell me something else about yourself."

They stood and talked for over an hour. Casey was the CFO of a large hospital in Indiana and they spent a significant amount of time discussing the future of medicine and managed care. "You really seem to understand," Casey said at one point. "Are you in the health care field?"

"Not at all. I'm the lord high everything else at a small insurance agency."

"Lord high everything else. That's *Mikado,* isn't it?"

"You know Gilbert and Sullivan?" Erika asked.

Casey beamed. "I used to sing with a musical theater group that did two of their operas each year. Is *Mikado* your favorite?"

"Actually, I love one that's really not very popular. Did you ever perform in *Iolanthe?*"

Casey's smile widened. "That's my favorite too. 'While you're lying awake with a dismal headache . . .' One of my best patter songs."

At about eleven the crowd began to thin. Erika glanced around, looking for Brook, but she was nowhere to be seen. *Well,* she thought, *we'll compare notes tomorrow.* "I don't suppose you'd let me take you home," Casey said.

Erika had long ago decided that she wasn't going to let her business dealings spill over into her personal space. Early on in her adventures she had considered bringing men to her apartment, but she always found a way to avoid it. "I'm going quite a ways, but I could drop you first." That had worked so far.

"Thanks. I'm here at the hotel." He paused. "Would you like to come upstairs and have a drink with me?"

"I'd love to. The party's winding down, but I'm not really ready to go home quite yet. You're such great company."

Chapter

7

Erika went to work the following morning almost asleep on her feet. All through the day, she wondered whether it was finally time to "give up her day job." Between phone calls and policy investigations, she calculated what she was making from Valerie and was pleasantly surprised to realize that she now made more from escorting than she did from the insurance company. And much of that was off the books.

That evening, she changed into leggings and a red-plaid shirt, then called Brook and invited her to share the steak and potato she had picked up at the local market. "I assume you've got salad makings? Bring them down and we can compare notes over dinner." A health food guru, Brook always had vegetables and whole-grain bread in her refrigerator.

"I can't wait to hear about your evening," Brook said as she dropped a container of arugula on the counter. She wore gray sweatpants and a Minnie Mouse T-shirt. "I brought a great new fat-free dressing too."

While they prepared dinner together in Erika's tiny kitchen as they often did, Erika told her about her evening. She and Casey had made uncomplicated love twice in his hotel room.

"He was really a hunk," Brook said. "I saw the two of you, heads together, deep in conversation. Are you going to see him again?"

"This is a tough business in that respect, you know. One of three things usually stops that cold." She made a fist in the air, then extended one finger. "Many of the guys are geographically undesirable. Casey's from Indiana and, of course, as is often the case, he's married." She extended a second finger. "Some are from around here and those who know I'm a pro are surprised that I'm not interested in continuing a relationship for free." A third finger joined the other two. "Occasionally I meet a nice guy who doesn't know I'm a pro. If I'm interested in seeing him again for free, I usually don't. Eventually he's bound to learn about my job and I don't think it would go over very well. I'm not going to leave myself open for the disillusionment and eventual crash."

"You sound bitter."

"I'm not really. I've had a marriage and I'm not anxious to begin that merry-go-round again." The microwave oven dinged, and Erika reached inside and squeezed the potato to see whether it was done.

"What about the guys you see over and over?"

"Oh sure. I see guys who know I'm a pro and are interested in continuing a relationship for money, and that's great. As you know, I have several guys who call me when they get the itch or when they're in town. We have great times together and that's that. Casual dates with hot sex afterward. That's about as permanent as anything I find through Valerie can be." She turned the knob on the microwave to give the potato another minute, then dropped the steak into the hot, salted frying pan.

"That's depressing."

"Not for me. I'm not really interested in anything more permanent. I've given it a lot of thought and this kind of relationship is really all right for me. At first I wondered whether I was justifying things and I really wanted something more, something permanent with a man, but you know, I'm really happy this way. You're still looking for Mr. Right, aren't you?"

"Yeah," Brook said, breaking the lettuce into two bowls. "I want the home and family. You've had that, but I haven't." She stopped and sighed. "I'm thirty. I always thought I'd be married and settled by now. Maybe there's just no guy out there for me."

"Hogwash. There are lots of guys out there, any one of whom would make a great family with you." She turned the steak over in the pan. "You have to kiss a lot of frogs to find one handsome prince."

"I know," Brook said, "and I've certainly kissed my share."

"Speaking of princes, how did things work out last evening."

"Actually it was fun. Great sex and no stress wondering whether he might be *the one*. Simple somehow. I knew what I was there for and so did he."

"Did he know you were a pro?"

"He asked me right off. He was a buying agent for a large medical group and clinic in Seattle and had been to lots of these before. He knew they sprinkled the party with paid women, so he just asked me. I said yes, and it was so much easier. No beating around the bush."

Erika lifted the steak from the pan, put half on each of the plates, added half the potato and carried the plates into the living room. Brook followed with the salads and two oat bran rolls she had brought. "This is quite a mixed message for my stomach," Brook said. "Salad, oat bran, baked potato, and cow. I'm not sure my system will survive our dinners."

"I know, but they sure taste good." The two women settled on the sofa and put the plates on the coffee table, where they had already put napkins, steak knives, and forks. "How about a red wine," Erika asked, "to celebrate our evening?"

"Why the hell not? My body's hardly a temple tonight."

Erika made quick work of opening the wine and pouring two glasses. She handed one to Brook, then began her dinner. "Okay, babe," she said, a mouthful of steak on her fork, "tell me all about last evening."

"It was quite a ride." Brook chewed, and drifted back to the previous evening.

Once she and Erika had separated, Brook accepted a glass of champagne from a passing waiter and wandered around the room. There were small groups of men wearing everything from serious business suits to jeans and Western shirts. She sipped her drink and tried to look a bit lost. *Tried?* she said to herself. She was a little lost.

After several minutes a man in gray slacks and a well-tailored pale-green shirt reached out from a nearby group, grabbed her around the waist, and pulled her against his side. "Gentlemen," he said to the others, "this is . . ."

"Brook," she said. The guy was rather homely, with lots of shaggy sandy hair, bushy eyebrows, and a thick sandy moustache.

"Well, Brook," he said, "these are my friends Ken Connor, from Tyler, Texas, Mark Chang from Chicago, and Walt Perrelli who's here from Atlanta. I'm Jim Barclay and I'm in town from far-away New Jersey. We're all in the medical field, always anxious to help a lady in distress."

Brook straightened her back and, remembering why she was being paid for the evening, said, "It's very nice to meet all of you." She looked at each man, carefully implanting names in her mind.

"You were looking a bit out of place. Are you here with someone?"

Brook remembered all of Erika's advice. "I was, but he seems to have disappeared."

"That's great news. Walt and Ken are doctors. Mark runs a small clinic in a very bad neighborhood, and I'm in medical purchasing. Are you in the drug business?"

"Not at all. I work for an advertising agency, but I gather that most of the people here are in the health care field. You're from places that are so far apart. Do you get together often?"

"Just this convention every year, but we've known each other for a very long time," Jim said.

"Speak for yourself," Walt chimed in. "I'm not that old."

"It must be difficult coping with all the changes in the industry." Brook was suddenly glad she had done a bit of surfing on the Internet and read a few articles on the changing health care system. "What do you think managed care is going to do to your businesses?"

"A lady with a very good question," Mark said. "Frankly, Brook, I think, in the long run, we're fucked."

Jim turned to Brook. "Don't mind him. We just sat through several sessions on the future of health care in the U.S. and we've been drowning our sorrows ever since."

"I don't mind the language if that's what you're apologizing for. I frequently have the urge to let out with a few expletives when the situation warrants, and it would seem that this situation calls for it."

"Bravo," Ken said. "A lady who understands the value of an expletive. I don't know about you, but I'm going to hit the food table."

"Are you hungry?" Jim asked.

"Not really. I'm enjoying the conversation."

For a good part of the evening, Jim and Brook shared their views on health care and many other topics with anyone else who would listen, often engaging in heated arguments. Jim kept a proprietary arm around her waist as several other people, both men and women, joined the discussion then wandered away. At about nine-thirty, the room slowly began to empty out. "Your friend hasn't returned."

"My friend?" Brook said, puzzled.

"The one who brought you, then deserted you."

"Oh, him," Brook said, trying to remember her cover story. "He's not a very reliable guy."

Jim leaned close to her ear. "There is no guy, is there?"

"I don't know what you mean."

"Of course you do. You're being paid to be here this evening, aren't you?"

Brook was a very poor liar and Erika hadn't said that her occupation was a secret. "Busted," she said. "I'm here to be decorative and entertaining."

"Well, you certainly are decorative, and as for entertaining, you've done really well so far. I assume you're paid for the entire evening." Brook had no idea how to answer that so she remained quiet. "Can we go up to my room and continue the entertaining there?"

Brook looked into his eyes. He was a very charming and direct man with strong views on all subjects, which he wasn't reluctant to share. He was well read, very intelligent, and he had a great sense of humor. "Funny," she said, gazing at him. "If we had met under other circumstances I would be quick to take you up on your suggestion and, as a paid escort, I guess some men expect it."

"I don't expect it. That was a yes or no question."

"Good. Right now I'd rather I wasn't being paid, so you'd know that I'm interested in you as a person, not a client."

"If that's a line, it's a very good one, Brook," Jim said. "I'm flattered. Let's get out of here."

In the elevator, Jim said, "I can't decide whether you're very good at this or very new."

"I don't understand," Brook said.

"You seem so genuine, not jaded as I would expect. Is it an act?"

Brook sighed. "If you want me to be honest, this is my first time doing this."

"You're kidding."

"I've always been interested in men and I date a lot. I have a friend who's in the business, so to speak, and she invited me along this evening."

"Why did you agree? Don't tell me you've got a sick mother who needs an operation," he said, making her laugh.

"Not at all," Brook said. "I love meeting men. I love the dance that follows. You know the one, done to the tune of "Getting to Know You." I love the expectation that makes your palms sweaty and your skin tingle, the wondering whether the evening will end with that fabulous first adventure in bed. I just thought I might as well get paid for it."

"An honest woman. Is the money good?"

"Better than nothing," she said, sliding her arm around his waist, "and you meet the nicest people, at least so far."

Jim hugged her against his side. "I think I love you."

Brook rested her head against his shoulder and relaxed completely. Amazingly enough, she was able to be herself and earn a paycheck too. In his room, Jim hung their coats in the small closet, then settled in a soft chair. "Come here," he said, and pulled her down on his lap, unzipping the back of her dress in one easy motion. Then he slipped his hand beneath the fabric and stroked her side, finding the edge of her breast. His lips found hers and they kissed as her arms twined around his neck. He held the back of her neck as he placed feathery kisses on her eyes, her cheeks, her ears. *God*, she thought, *he's a really good kisser.* He pulled the pins from her hair and let it spill over his hand.

Jim pulled back and gazed at her. "You know what I'd like to do? This hotel has the most outrageous bathrooms you've ever seen. Mine has a huge double shower. I'd like to climb in it with you, get all wet and slippery and fuck your brains out."

"Umm," Brook purred, "sounds wonderful."

Together they entered a lavish bathroom large enough to land a small plane. It was all done in black and white, with two sinks, two toilets, each enclosed in a small room, and a stall shower the size of Brook's entire bathroom. The towels, four of each in three sizes, were thick and dazzling white, with black edging and the initials of the hotel prominently embroidered on each. "Wow," Brook said. "Quite a room." With only momentary embarrassment, she quickly took off her clothes. As she stood, surrounded by mirrors, Jim just looked. "You're gorgeous, you know that?"

She glowed beneath his gaze. "Thanks. I'm glad you think so."

Jim turned on the water in the black-and-white-tiled shower stall. There were two shower heads and a fine mist came from perforated pipes set in the wall as well. "Is this a gas or what?" Jim said, sounding like a small boy with a new toy. "The company pays for the room, although it's only an hour from here to my house. They know, however, I wouldn't come to this fiasco without a few perks and when I do attend I always manage to find ways to save them money. Therefore, this is worth it for them."

"And not a bad little vacation for you," Brook said. "Are women like me part of the perks you're talking about?"

"Of course." *Okay*, she thought, *he's used to picking up the women who attend these things. He's more experienced than I am. Amazing.*

Jim stripped off his clothes and Brook admired his trim body, his penis only partially erect. *Good*, she thought, *they'd be able to play before he became too needy.* "You keep in good shape. Do you work out?"

"Racquetball and tennis." He unwrapped two small bars of hotel soap, grabbed a face cloth from the rack, then stepped into the shower. "You're not going to be upset if your hair gets wet, are you?"

"Not at all," Brook said as she stepped beneath the spray. *He's got this all down to a routine. He's obviously done it all before. Hell*, she thought, *I don't care. He's leading and that's great.*

Jim soaped the cloth, then said, "Turn around." She turned

her back to him, and he slowly stroked her back with the soapy cloth. As she braced her hands on the tile, he rubbed down from shoulder to buttocks, then up again. He knelt, then soaped the backs of her thighs slowly sliding toward the insides, rubbing the slick cloth just to the edges of her pussy lips, then back to her knees. He soaped to her cheeks again, then stroked between them, rubbing her anus, making her knees buckle.

"Turn around," he said, his voice a bit shaky. She turned and he soaped her belly and chest, paying particular attention to her breasts. Dropping the cloth on the floor of the shower, he soaped his hands and swirled the lather around her stomach and ribs, then lifted her breasts and cupped them in his hands. Water streaming down his face, he licked the tips of her nipples, then took the entire areola in his mouth. She held the sides of his face as he suckled.

When he paused, she said, "My turn." She picked up the cloth and rubbed it over the bar of soap. She began with his hands, slowly washing each finger then sucking it into her mouth as if it were his penis. His cock got harder with each finger. Grinning, she washed his arms, shoulders, and chest. "Turn around," she said and slowly stroked the cloth over his back and buttocks. She knelt at his feet and washed his legs and thighs, working her way up to his cheeks again. Then, as he had done to her, she slipped the soapy cloth between his cheeks and fingered his anus, listening to his raspy breathing.

She grabbed his hips and turned him so his cock was level with her mouth. Her mouth danced over him, licking the underside of his wet shaft, then tickling his balls with the tip of her tongue. "God, you're good," he moaned.

"I hope so," she said, taking him deeply into her mouth.

"Enough, woman," he growled. "I'm not ready to come just yet."

Again he turned her around and soaped her buttocks and anus. "I never assume," he said. "Is this way all right with you?"

Brook had indulged in anal sex before and had neither enjoyed nor hated it. "Not without a condom," she said.

"Way ahead of you," he said, reaching out for the foil packet he had put on the floor just outside the stall. He quickly covered his rampant erection, then placed her hands on the wall of the shower. Water pouring over them, he added more slippery soap, then placed his latex-covered cock at the entrance of her rear opening. Slowly he pushed.

At first there was some pain, but as Brook focused on relaxing, his cock slipped inside. She expected him to plunge deeply into her, but instead he pulled out. Again and again he pressed his cock into her, then pulled back until her body accepted him easily. Finally he pressed deeply inside and held still.

Brook's nipples tightened, her pussy swelled and she trembled. God, she felt so full, so hot. "Touch yourself," he said over the sound of the water. "I know you need to come and I want to feel it. Touch yourself. Come for me."

She reached down and slipped her fingers between her swollen outer lips, finding her erect clit. She swirled her middle finger over the tip, then stroked the length to her hungry opening. "Yes, baby," he said, "I can feel tiny muscles move, getting ready to come. Rub it, baby. Stroke it. Put your fingers inside and fuck your sweet cunt."

His words heated her still further and she did as he asked, inserting two fingers in her channel, then pulling them out and rubbing her slippery clit. She marveled at the difference in feel between the water and her copious juices and the incredibly filled, stretched feeling his cock created. "Yes," Jim's voice drove her on, "finger your clit, fuck your beautiful cunt. Do it. Do it."

Over and over she touched, pressed, felt herself outside and in. Soon, she could hold back no more. Jim's fingers found her nipples as her orgasm overwhelmed her. Trying to keep her knees from buckling, she came, her fingers pressed into her pussy. "Good girl," Jim said. "Now don't stop. Don't stop!"

As spasms continued to crash over her body she felt Jim's cock twitch, then throb as he came. All too soon his deflated penis slipped from her body. Slowly he slid to the floor of the shower and sat propped against the cool tiles, panting. "Oh God, oh God," he said. "That was glorious."

Brook rinsed herself off, finger-combed her hair under the spray, then stepped out of the shower, turning off the water. She put on one of the thick snowy white terry cloth robes she found on the back of the bathroom door, then handed the other to Jim. He picked himself up off the floor, wrapped the robe around his torso and almost staggered into the bedroom, dropping onto the bed like a stone. "Shit, Brook, you've done me in completely."

Brook settled on the edge of the bed. "I'm glad. You're gorgeously sexy."

"Can I see you again? I know you're a professional and I'd expect to pay."

"I really like you so there would be no fee."

"Listen," Jim said, raising himself onto his elbows, his breathing still rapid. "I really enjoyed this evening for a slightly unusual reason. I've been to these things before and been with pros before, but you're a wonderful combination of great sex and honesty. When I say I'll pay, don't be a dope. Take the money. I can afford it, and it makes me feel free somehow. I don't have to worry about courting or saying or doing something wrong. I can fuck your beautiful ass and I don't have to apologize or worry that you'll be offended."

Brook smiled. "You're quite a guy, Jim. Thanks for all the kind words and for the advice." She took the pad from beside the bed and wrote down her name and phone number. "I'll look forward to hearing from you." She took several minutes to put on her clothes and, by the time she was completely dressed, Jim was asleep. She placed a soft kiss on his forehead, then left.

* * *

"You're quite right," Erika said, finishing her wine and pushing her empty plate to the far side of the coffee table. "That was quite a ride. It seems you've gotten a steady customer."

"I hope so. How often do you find a man who's great at sex and anxious to pay for it?"

"Not often, in my experience. I wonder why he doesn't find some woman, get married and get all the sex he wants for free."

"Free?"

"That's what Rick did. He got the use of my body and my services in all areas, then took the money and ran."

"Your bitterness is showing. Jim's not interested in anything more than an occasional night of playing. He told me that he was married once and it left a bad taste in his mouth. Nothing steady for him."

"You know that men like these aren't marriage material. I guess that's the one difference between this and your evenings of bar hopping and one-night stands. These guys will be anxious to see you from time to time, but make no serious demands. No marriage proposals, no full-time relationships. Is that okay for now?"

Brook grinned. "Yeah."

"There's something I've been meaning to talk to you about," Erika said. "I've been doing a lot of thinking and I've decided to quit my job at Proxmeyer. Last night I got only about three hours sleep so I was totally trashed today. Over lunch I did a lot of figuring. I calculated that I'm averaging almost two thousand dollars a week from Valerie."

Erika said it with awe, but Brook didn't look surprised. "I told you that you were silly not to quit."

"I know, but I'm never sure this will continue. What if I never get another client?"

Brook merely raised a quizzical eyebrow. "Right, and maybe the sun will rise in the west tomorrow."

"That's the way," Erika said with a grin. "Make fun of a poor scared girl."

"Poor? Be honest with yourself for just one minute. How much money do you have in the bank?"

"Enough." She paused and, when Brook didn't say anything, she amended, "More than enough, and if my clients continue the way they are going, I can make enough from Valerie to pay my bills and continue to save. I'll never again be dependent on any man the way I was when Rick left. Period."

"Might there be more work if you don't have to get up the next morning?"

"I think there might be. I know some of the girls go off on trips and such, things I can't do now."

"Trips?"

"Sure. There are men who need, or just want, decorations to travel with, women who can make him part of a couple at business weekends or important sales trips. Or just rich, bored, lonely guys who want to play for days at a time."

"That sounds too good to be true," Brook said. "Just remember me when that happens. I've got a lot of vacation saved up at Juskowitz."

"So you don't think I'm nuts to give up a steady paycheck?"

"Not at all. You enjoy the entertaining and we both know that you hate it at Proxmeyer."

"I don't hate it exactly, but . . ."

Contrary to her worries, over the next year Erika's bank account flourished. In the following calendar year, her income from her activities with Valerie grew to over two hundred thousand dollars. Brook was also seeing clients once a week or so, although she had not yet made the break from her day job.

Valerie had also become dependent on Erika's skills in the business world. Erika was great at smoothing over difficult or embarrassing experiences with Valerie's clients. She usually held on to accounts in spite of the occasional woman who didn't show up or the man who was dissatisfied with his evening. Her charm and skills as a natural negotiator pushed Valerie's business into more and more lucrative areas, including populating parties for musicians and entertaining after film openings and awards ceremonies. The two women had become closer as she saw more of the business side of Valerie.

For several months Erika idly looked in the Sunday *Times* Real Estate section and the following summer, she found a perfect six-room apartment on Riverside Drive. It had floor-to-ceiling windows overlooking the Hudson. Although it was empty, as she looked around she could see the potential—large, airy rooms, high ceilings, and a highly polished wood floor in the dining room. Because she had frequently wanted to bring a man to her apartment but didn't want anyone knowing where she lived, she decided to keep her old apartment strictly for entertaining.

Brook was terribly upset when Erika told her the news about her new apartment, but within a year, Brook had also moved, into a building only two blocks from Erika's apartment. They both used Erika's old apartment from time to time so, with only a bit of preplanning to avoid bumping into each other, they both had a place to entertain men when they needed it.

In late spring of that year, Valerie and Erika met for lunch at an English pub–style restaurant in midtown. They ordered fish and chips and chatted. When the lunch dishes were finally cleared away, Valerie leaned forward, propped her elbows on the table and said, without preamble, "I wanted you to be the first to know my secret. I met a very special man about six months ago. He learned what I do for a living and he didn't care. We've been seeing each other ever since, and now he's asked me to marry him. I've said yes."

Flabbergasted, Erika said, "You didn't tell me."

"I know and don't be hurt. It was mean of me to keep this to myself for all these months, but it was sort of private, if you understand."

"Of course I do," Erika said, smiling warmly. Valerie glowed and looked ecstatic and Erika couldn't be happier for her.

"Good. I don't want you to think I've been keeping secrets."

"Valerie, that's great news. I'm so happy for you. Tell me all about him."

Valerie extolled the virtues of Madison Hackett for fifteen minutes. "We're going to pick out a ring this afternoon," she said, "but these"—she indicated the large diamond studs in her ears—"are an engagement present." She leaned forward. "One and a half carats each, blue-white and all that. The man's not only wonderful, he's loaded."

"The earrings are magnificent," Erika said. "I have only one question. Does he have a brother for me?"

Valerie laughed, and continued, "There's one minor problem. He wants me out of the business and away from anyone I might have met over the years."

Erika raised an eyebrow. "Our clients come from all over the country. How will you manage that without living in a cave?"

"Madison knows there might be times when things get awkward, but he wants me as far away from here as possible. We're moving to his ranch somewhere in the boonies of west Texas."

Erika was shocked and speechless. It had never occurred to her that the business wouldn't go on forever. There were always lonely, horny men who needed TLC of the kind the business could provide. Valerie took her hands. "I want to turn the business over to you to run."

Erika gasped. "What?"

"You know everyone and how to deal with the customers and my ladies. The only part of it that you're not intimately familiar with is the bookkeeping and such, and that my accountant and I can teach you in a few days. Actually you might even have more efficient ways of doing it. My system dates back more years than

I care to count. I'll give you all my records and contact lists." She sat up straighter. "It's a bitch of a job. As you know there are always problems, changes of plans, hurt feelings, embarrassments. I think you can handle it and I've got twenty-six other women who will need your management skills. I can't bear to think of them out of jobs."

"Valerie, I don't know what to say."

"Say you'll do it. You can get Brook to help, of course, but you and I have a special flare for this." She gazed intently at Erika. "All I ask is that you put twenty percent of the profits for the first three years in a bank account in my name." She closed her eyes, then opened them again. "In case this all doesn't work out, which it will of course. Will you do it?"

Could she do it? Erika wondered. Run Valerie's business? She'd never even considered it, but as she turned the idea over in her mind she realized that she could probably handle it all as well as anyone. She now had the computer skills to work with the spreadsheets and lists she knew Valerie kept on her computer. She also knew about the second set kept on disk in the safe in her apartment. She should think about it, consider all the ramifications, but she found she didn't have to. "I'd like to do it."

"God, that's a load off my mind. If you hadn't been willing to do this, I don't know what I would have done. There's no one else who could run it successfully. I couldn't very well sell it, but I couldn't put all those women out of work either."

"How soon?"

"Madison and I want to move in about three months. I think that would give us ample time for the switch-over."

It was actually closer to five months later when Erika and Brook stood at Kennedy Airport with Mrs. Valerie Hackett and her husband of six weeks. "I'll miss you so much," Valerie said. "Call me a lot, will you?"

"Of course," Brook said. "We'll call you so often you'll start to let the answering machine pick up just to avoid us."

When Erika saw that Valerie was about to dissolve into tears, she kissed Madison on the cheek and pushed the two toward the security gate. "Hustle, or you'll be late."

As they walked down the carpeted hallway toward the gate, Valerie and Madison turned and waved several times, until they were finally out of sight.

Near Thanksgiving, almost six years after the dinner with Stuart that began her career, Erika was again having dinner with him at their favorite Chinese restaurant. "I have something I have to tell you," he said as the waiter brought the hot and sour soup. "Lorraine's got cancer."

Erika couldn't speak for a moment. Then she reached out and placed her hand over his. "Oh Stuart, I'm so sorry. What can I do to help?"

"Nothing. Just being here with you and hearing your support is enough."

"Have you known long?"

"We found out last week."

"You should have called me. Has she been ill?"

"She's been getting weaker and has had some gynecological problems, but we thought it was just change of life happening a bit prematurely. She's only forty-three, after all." His eyes filled and he blinked several times. "Anyway, she went to the doctor and he did tests. There's nothing that can be done."

"Do the kids know?"

"We told them. They're really adults now. Mostly I think they're upset that they couldn't present her with grandchildren. I told you that Kevin is getting married in three months," he said, referring to his middle son, "but Lorraine doesn't have that long. She won't even make the wedding."

That fast? "Oh God. How are you holding up?"

"Actually I'm falling apart. That's why I wanted to have dinner with you. You're always good for my mood and I need lots of support right now."

Erika was glad she could give him something. She knew Lorraine mostly through Stuart, but she had always seemed to be a sensible, together lady. *Shit,* Erika thought, *shit, shit, shit.* "I don't know what to say? My mind is whirling, trying to find just the right words that will make everything better."

"There are no words and I need a break from all of it. Tell me about one of your recent dates, preferably an outrageous one." He picked up his spoon and scooped up some of the soup.

"Do you really want to hear this?"

"It will be great medicine. Tell me a story."

Over the years, Erika had, without violating any confidences or revealing any identities, told Stuart about many of her more unusual dates. "I had a guy a few weeks ago who could only get it up if I rubbed olive oil all over his body. Extra virgin, no less."

Stuart's laugh warmed Erika's heart. She continued, "He didn't want intercourse, just a hand job. It smelled so good that it was difficult to think of him as anything but a well-dressed salad. I kept wondering how he'd look with a crouton in his navel and slices of raw onion around his cock." She couldn't tell whether Stuart was laughing or crying.

"Do you know how much I love you?" Stuart said. "I can't imagine anyone else telling me something like that. Got another?"

"Always. Actually I have one of Brook's. She had a guy who ordered cherry tomatoes from room service in his hotel, stuffed them one by one into Brook's pussy, then ate them right from there. The following week he wanted to play kinky games with jalapeño peppers, but she drew the line at that one. No hot peppers on her delicate parts. He got really pissed but eventually she found another way to satisfy him."

Stuart was literally holding his sides laughing, tears coursing down his cheeks. "The ultimate food fight. What did she do?"

"It turned out he was willing to settle for olives. But only green ones."

Stuart wiped at his streaming eyes. "You're making this up."

Erika held her hand up, palm out. "I swear. One man's appetizer is another man's fetish. I'm not sure I'll ever look at a tray of hors d'oeuvres the same way again."

As Stuart calmed, he said, "As the corny line goes, 'Thanks, I needed that.' "

Throughout dinner Erika regaled Stuart with more stories. She noticed that he ate little, and she didn't do much better, but finally the waiter brought slices of orange and fortune cookies. While Stuart pulled his open, he said, "Remember that evening years ago when your fortune said that there were new and wonderful things waiting for you? It was right. You've changed so much from the frightened woman whose husband had just left her."

"I have, haven't I? And most of it thanks to your help and your introduction to Valerie."

Stuart read his fortune aloud. " 'You will endure.' It's almost as though that fortune was picked for me. What's yours."

She chuckled. "Some things never change. Mine says, 'There are new and wonderful things waiting for you.' I guess they still use the same cookie company."

"I'm sure it's true," Stuart said. "You determine your own fate. Always remember that."

Erika held his hand across the table. "So can you. You'll endure. You have your kids. Family is the most important thing in this life." She thought about Rena, but pushed the thought from her mind.

"And I have you," Stuart said. "You're as much family as anyone else."

"Thanks, Stuart." They paid the check and, as they walked to the door of the restaurant, Erika wrapped her arms around Stuart's shoulders. "If there's anything I can do to help . . ."

"I won't hesitate to call you. This dinner has been really good for me. Thanks for being what I needed. You."

"Give Lorraine my love and tell her to call me if she wants to talk or anything."

"I will."

Just nine weeks later, Stuart called to tell Erika that Lorraine had passed away in her sleep having been kept comfortable and relatively pain free. Erika attended the funeral on Long Island, along with many of her ex-husband's business partners. She held Stuart's hand for a few moments, then sat alone at the back of the church. She watched Stuart and his children huddle together, their mutual grief obvious.

As she listened to the eulogy, she looked around at the big shots from Cadmire. They had dutifully said hello to her as they passed in the moving mass of mourners, but her identity hadn't really registered. They hadn't changed much, Erika thought, not nearly as much as she had. When Rick left she had been a small dependent wife, leading a useless existence. Now she ran her own business, the escort service she had christened Courtesans, Inc. She had the responsibility of managing almost thirty women and, added recently, three men. Now that Valerie was in Texas, married to her soul mate, as she had put it, Erika ran everything and did it well. Brook helped, of course, but most of the responsibility was Erika's. Brook was great with clients and with the other escorts, and she handled the computer bookings, but in the final analysis, it was Erika's baby.

Erika's baby. It had become her only baby since the final blowup with Rena two years earlier. Erika had purchased a ticket on Air France to attend her daughter's graduation from high school and had called Rena, then almost eighteen, with the news. "I'll be arriving the Thursday before the ceremony."

"I'd rather you didn't come," Rena told her, her voice sounding tight despite the thousands of miles of phone wires between them. "Daddy's going to be there and he's getting the two tickets

I'm allowed. There won't even be a way for you to get into the auditorium."

Erika swallowed hard. For weeks she had had fantasies of her reunion with her daughter. Although she hadn't been welcome for several years, she saw herself being greeted at the airport by a grown woman, now clearly understanding what Erika had gone through and willing, if not to forgive, then at least to give them another chance. "You gave the tickets to your father and Sandy?"

"Not Sandy. Where have you been? Sandy and the baby live in the States now. She turned out to be just like you, interested only in Daddy's money. He's coming with Angela. I like her and she likes me."

"But . . ."

"Listen, M— Just listen. I don't want to have anything to do with you. I've been accepted at college in Chicago and I'm going. Two of my friends from here are going there too, and Daddy's in full agreement. He's going to help with tuition and I'm going to study whatever I want."

"What college? What are you going to major in? We talk every week, but you obviously haven't told me anything."

"We don't talk each week, you talk and I listen, or don't. You seem to have a life for yourself and that's just great. So I think it's time for you to leave me alone."

"But honey."

"Don't, Mother. Just forget that you have me and let's let it all drop. It will be much less painful that way."

Her words sounded so much like Rick. "Is that the way you feel, or are you just parroting your father?"

"This is all my decision. I'm eighteen now and capable of being my own person." She was almost shrieking now. "I don't need you and I don't want you."

I don't need you and I don't want you. Those words sounded so final. She had discovered her daughter's address in Chicago and, for a year and a half, had sent cards and letters each week. And she'd continue. She didn't know whether Rena was reading them, but although she got no response, she had to keep trying.

As the final words of the service echoed through the room, she stood with the assembly, squared her shoulders and walked outside toward her waiting car and driver. In the fall, she and Stuart resumed their dinners together and, on an icy night, just over four years later, Erika climbed into a taxi in front of the Waldorf Hotel.

Chapter
8

The Present

Stuart twisted in the uncomfortable chair in the ICU visitors area and watched through a seldom-washed window as the sky lightened. There had been no word, so he had to hold on to the fact that Erika was still alive. The doctor said that if she made it through the first forty-eight hours, she had a good chance. He reflexively looked at his watch although he'd looked at it only a minute before. Well, he sighed, she'd already made it through three hours. Only forty-five to go. He combed his fingers through his salt-and-pepper hair and pushed his glasses up toward the bridge of his nose. What if she didn't make it?

No, he berated himself for the hundredth time during this interminable night, he wouldn't allow himself to think about the what-ifs. Erika was going to be fine and that was that. He stood, straightened his slacks and made the now-familiar journey to the coffee machine down the hall. Depositing a dollar in the "Please contribute" container, he pushed the red lever on the front of the machine and moments later pulled the cup of hot water from beneath the spout. He took a tea bag from the basket beside the brewer, unwrapped it, and dunked it in the steaming water. He usually took his tea without sugar, but tonight he needed the energy so he opened a white packet, poured sugar into the tea and walked back toward the waiting room. He used to drink coffee, he remembered. It had been Erika who had converted him to tea.

The almost empty waiting room was nondescript, with green tweed–covered furniture, Formica tables, green industrial-strength carpeting, and mustard-yellow walls. The room smelled of antiseptic and deodorizers—the smell that most people immediately recognized as "hospital." The tables were littered with well-thumbed magazines, the newest of which was six months old. Although the conditions for the families of patients were Spartan, the hospital had one of the highest ratings in the city and Stuart was content that Erika was getting the best care available anywhere.

As silently as he could, he walked across the room and gazed at two bodies, one stretched out on each of two sofas. An hour earlier he had found a nurse and gotten two cotton blankets, tucked one around Brook's shoulders and draped the other over Shara's sleeping form.

As he settled back into the uncomfortable chair, Brook sat up. "I'm not asleep, Stuart, just trying to blank my mind," she said softly, moving to the end of the sofa so she could sit beside him. She finger-combed her long hair and, with graceful movements flipped it over her shoulders, then rubbed her reddened eyes.

"I wish I could stop thinking," he whispered, attempting not to wake Shara.

"So do I," Brook said, rubbing the back of her neck, "but I just keep going over and over everything, trying to find something someone could have done to prevent this."

"There's nothing anyone could have done," Stuart said. "It was an accident. Even the police said so. The freezing rain is the only real culprit. The taxi was going slowly, as was the SUV. The one good thing about it all is that no one else was hurt."

"Damn SUVs," Brook snapped. "The driver is at home with her family, the cabbie's off duty, and Erika's in critical condition. It doesn't seem fair." She sighed and shook her head. "I'm sorry, Stuart. I'm certainly glad everyone else is okay. I guess I just want to blame someone." She dropped the crumpled blanket on a side table and watched as Stuart stood and automatically folded it. "You're so like her," she murmured as she stood and walked toward the hallway. "Keep me company?"

"Sure," Stuart said, following Brook back to the coffee machine. "They've only got Lipton."

"That's why I always keep tea bags with me," she said, a small smile on her face as she pulled a plastic bag filled with assorted herbal teas from her purse.

"Always prepared," he said.

"I try. Thanks for being here," Brook said as she pressed the spigot and filled a cup with hot water. "I think this has been the longest night of my life."

He leaned against the counter in the tiny kitchen area as Brook dropped a bag of herb tea into her Styrofoam cup. "You know," he added, "I never liked tea, but Erika convinced me to try it." He blinked several times to control the tears clogging his throat.

"Yeah, me too." A wistful smile crossed her face. "She taught me to like lots of things."

Stuart's expression softened. "I can imagine."

Taking Stuart by surprise, Brook reached out and enfolded him in her arms. "Oh, Stuart, it's really too bad we've never spent much time together."

Deeper friends than they had ever been, they separated. "I know," Stuart said, moved by Brook's friendship. "I guess we just became two different compartments in Erika's life." He paused, then said, "I love her very much, you know."

"I think I know that better than Erika does."

"I'm afraid that might be so. She thinks of me as a good friend and part-time sex partner, but I'd like it to be more."

"Is there much more than that? Love and sex is more than many have to build a relationship on."

"That's true as far as it goes, but I want her to marry me."

Brook looked surprised. "She never told me that you had asked her."

With a rueful smile, Stuart said, "I never actually asked her right out."

"Stuart, although we've never really gotten to know each other in person, I feel as if I know you very well from listening to Erika talk. Let me be blunt about this. Does this desire to get married have anything to do with the fact that Erika's in critical condition? It's really easy to confuse the terror we all feel, and the love we all share with her, with something else."

Brook was right as far as it went, but his feelings for Erika went so much deeper. Since Lorraine's death, Erika had filled a giant void in his life, but she was more than just a replacement for his late wife. She was there for him when he needed a friend, and when he wanted a sex partner. They knew just about everything there was to know about each other and each accepted the other, flaws, weaknesses and all. They enjoyed each other's company, spending evenings together at Broadway shows and movies on nights she wasn't otherwise engaged. Sometimes they merely had long quiet dinners together, discussing everything from her business to global warming and the political problems in Northern Ireland. Occasionally they went to Erika's apartment and sat in the living room, each with a book, reading in companionable silence.

Although he hated the term, he felt they were soul mates, parts of some whole that was only complete when they were together. "You're a good friend, Brook, to her and now to me, but no, I've been thinking about it for a while now."

"So why haven't you asked her? Is it the business, the fact that she has sex with lots of men for money?"

"Blunt, aren't you? No," he tried to assure her, "it's not the business. Actually I feel partly responsible for Courtesans, Inc., and I'm glad for that. I've watched it grow over the past ten years and as it did I've watched Erika change from a dependent woman to the person she is now. It's been a wonderful experience just seeing it. The business has been a big part of that and I wouldn't begrudge her that for anything."

Brook sipped her tea. "So? Why marriage and why haven't you told her how you feel?"

"Lot's of reasons. The first time we made love I was terrified that it would change our relationship, maybe for the worse. If it hadn't worked out, then I would have lost not only a woman I could make love with, but my best friend. I guess proposing gives me the same worries."

"The changes that going to bed together made were good ones, right?"

His face softened and he could feel himself flushing. "Oh, yes."

"I remember that it was many months before Erika confided in me that you two were sleeping together. She never told me any of the details. Care to share?" Despite the smell of antiseptic in the air and hospital personnel bustling around them, Brook waggled her eyebrows. "Huh? Huh?"

Stuart remembered so well. "Not a chance."

"Rats," Brook said, standing straight and slowly making her way back to the waiting room.

Tea in his hand, Stuart leaned his hip against the counter, rested his elbow on the small microwave oven and allowed his mind to wander to that Chinese restaurant two years earlier.

"You're looking well," Erika had said as they met outside the red-laquer doors of the Pagoda Palace one late fall evening. It had suddenly gotten cold and Stuart watched the puffs of vapor as she spoke.

"I'm feeling well. The job's good and the kids are great. Kevin's wife is pregnant," he said, referring to his middle son. "I'm going to be a grandfather." He opened the door and guided Erika into the warm interior. "That should make me feel old, but somehow it doesn't. I guess it's the 'life goes on' thing." He helped her off with her calf-length black wool coat and handed it and his leather jacket to the coat checker. He looked at Erika, dressed in a green-plaid wool shirt with a green turtleneck beneath and a pair of well-worn jeans. He never tired of looking at her, he realized.

"Good evening Ms. Holland, Mr. Dunlop. It's nice to see you again. Your usual booth in the back is available. I'll get your wine and an order of fried dumplings as soon as you're seated."

Although Erika now lived on Riverside Drive, they continued to meet several times a month at the restaurant around the corner from her old apartment. Erika leaned toward Stuart. "It's nice to be treated as one of the family when we come in, but I'm afraid we're becoming too predictable, like an old married couple. What if we didn't want dumplings?"

Old married couple, he thought, and felt his body stir. If they were an old married couple, they'd finish dinner and go home together to share a bed. Mentally Stuart shook himself, then whispered, "We'd have to eat them anyway, I'm afraid. George would be so disappointed if we didn't."

Erika smiled ruefully. "I suppose so."

"We could meet somewhere else, you know. Maybe we should have lasagna or curry once in a while."

"And break this wonderful habit? Not a chance. It's so comfortable."

Comfortable. Recently that word had been bothering Stuart a lot as he thought about his relationship with Erika. It was comfortable, but he was starting to dream about more than comfortable. He was beginning to fantasize about them in bed, teasing and playing some of the games she told him about. He'd like to tell her of his feelings, but he always chickened out. Erika had always viewed him as a good friend and maybe he should be content to keep things that way. Anyway, who knew what can of worms he'd be opening if he suggested they make love. He loved touching her so, with a hand in the small of her back, he guided Erika to their booth, then sat across from her. Comfortable.

The wine and dumplings arrived quickly and, as they talked, he finished his Cabernet and, contrary to his usual one-glass limit, ordered a second. As Erika talked about the latest political scandal involving a prominent senator, he watched her mouth. She had the most sensual lips, he thought as he watched her form words. Her mouth had been playing an increasingly prominent role in his erotic dreams recently. At first it had seemed disloyal to Lorraine to think sexual thoughts about Erika, but he began to understand that his wife had been gone for almost eighteen months and she would have wanted him to have a life of his own. After all, although he was going to be a grandfather, he was only forty-seven.

He gazed at her long fingers as Erika picked up her chopsticks. Having erotic thoughts about Erika felt like incest. After all, they had been friends for almost eight years and she had become like a sister to him. He watched as she took a bite of her kung pao chicken. She handled her chopsticks like a native as she lifted a pea pod to her mouth. He watched her tongue as she licked a bit of sauce from her lower lip. God, everything she did was erotic. He felt his body react and he squirmed in his seat.

"Earth to Stuart," Erika said, wiping her mouth with her napkin. "Do I have a sesame seed caught on my teeth?"

Stuart fought to keep his voice level. "Not at all." He wanted to eat his dinner, but he knew he wouldn't be able to operate chopsticks with his hands shaking as they were, so he took another swallow of his wine.

Erika put down her chopsticks and leaned forward, propping her elbows on the white tablecloth. "Stuart, what's wrong? You've said almost nothing all evening and you've barely touched your dinner. Is it this grandfather thing?"

Stuart wondered how to answer. He had dated a few women since Lorraine's death, but he had found himself comparing every woman he spent any time with to Erika. Was she as classy, as good a conversationalist, as charming, as sexy? No one had passed the "Erika test," but what was he to do? If he said anything, made a pass at her, it would change everything. He might lose a friend and their friendship meant everything to him. "It's nothing," he said, not saying the words he wanted to say. "Have you read the latest John Grisham?"

"You just changed the subject awfully abruptly. Are you sure you don't want to talk about it?"

"I don't know yet. For a little while, allow me to change the subject."

"Done. I won't pry. The latest Grisham? Actually I just finished it." They proceeded to exchange views, but again, Stuart's mind wandered. What to do? How big a risk was he willing to take? As Erika so often said, in for a penny . . .

Sometime later the waiter removed their dishes and, as they sipped their tea, Stuart's attention was again attracted by Erika's mouth. He watched her lips, now devoid of lipstick, brush the edge of her cup and imagined that mouth on his cock. She would lick him, play with him, do things he'd never done before. Was that the allure? The new, forbidden? No, he realized. The attraction was doing them with Erika. He swallowed. "Do you know you have a very sexy mouth?"

He watched Erika freeze, her eyes gazing into his. After a long pause, she said, "Thanks." She made a sound not unlike a small cough and set her teacup on the tablecloth. "I didn't know you cared," she said lightly.

Stuart felt his mouth go dry and his palms get sweaty. He couldn't tell how she had meant that remark. Gently, he said, "I do."

Their gaze held. "I feel like my entire world just tilted," Erika said. He could hear that she was making an effort to keep her words light. "Did you feel that too?"

"I've been feeling that for a long time now." He hoped they were talking about the same thing. He loved her like a sister, but right now he wanted her as a lover. "Erika, this is really difficult." He stretched out his hand across the table, palm up. With a small smile, Erika placed her hand in his. "You know that I'm your friend."

"My best friend, Stuart," she said, twining her fingers with his. When he couldn't say more, she continued, "Are you wondering whether there's more?"

God, she'd said it. If he were going to turn back, it had better be fast. He didn't want to turn back. He wanted . . . "How is it that you can read my mind?"

Erika's chuckle was open and inviting. "Because I've been wondering the same thing."

Stuart's mouth dropped open and he felt his world spin. "You have?"

Erika placed her other hand over their joined ones. "Stuart, you're my best friend, but you're also an attractive, sexy man. I've hesitated to say anything for fear of ruining what we have and, after all, I have sex with men for money so I'm really nervous about this."

He had expected any reaction but this. "You? Nervous? Why in heavens would you be nervous?"

He watched Erika's shoulders rise, then slump as she heaved a big sigh. "You, of all people, know that I have a reputation. Every time I spend an evening with a man I'm on trial. He's got expectations and I have to live up to them or I don't get paid and my reputation is shot. Can you understand what that's like?"

Stuart shook his head. "I don't know. I've never thought of it like that."

"I'm sure you haven't, but let's be honest. Have you ever imagined doing some of the things I tell you about with me? Do you ever think, 'Lorraine and I never did that. What have I been missing?' "

Stuart found himself unable to dissemble. "I suppose I have."

She squeezed his hand, her smile wide. "Thanks for being honest. All right, let's go one step further. Have you dreamed about what it would be like? I'd do all the right things, know all the right moves? Make the earth move?"

Stuart's body reacted to the images rushing through his mind, so he shifted his position on the seat. "I don't know."

"I just watched you move to adjust your body to make your slacks more comfortable. Remember it's difficult to fool me on sexual issues. I read body language all too well, and maybe, in our case, that's not such a good thing."

Stuart pulled his hand away and leaned back against the plastic. "Okay. Let me be brutally honest, at the risk of, well, of everything. I've been having increasingly erotic dreams about you recently." The words came rushing from his mouth. "Is that bad? I listen to your stories and I get excited. You're experienced in ways I've only dreamed about. Is it so unreasonable that I wonder how we would be together?"

Her smile was wistful. "No. Not at all. I just don't want to make a gigantic mistake. It scares me to death that I might louse it up in bed and thus lose you both as a lover and as a friend."

"It scares the shit out of me too," Stuart said, "but what scares me more is the thought of missing out on something that could be so wonderful." He paused, trying to gather his scattered thoughts. "There was no one before Lorraine or during our marriage. I've dated since but . . . Yes, it scares me that you're a pro at this."

Erika's eyes fastened on his. "I can imagine. You must feel as if you're being judged against every other man I've ever been with."

Stuart nodded slowly as he felt his skin heat. "That's really awful, but true."

Erika's gaze was unwavering. "I never compare. I make love to every man I'm with as if he were the only man in the world. That's what makes me good at what I do. With you, I'd be making love to my best friend, and I have to tell you that I've dreamed about it."

"You've dreamed about me? What was it like?" Stuart asked, not sure he wanted to hear the answer.

"Hazy? I just know that after the dream I wake up wet and hungry."

He had taken the risk and he'd won. His spirits soared. She was wonderful and he should have known she'd never hurt him. "Me too."

"This is really strange. Friendship and lust make strange bedfellows." She moved around and sat beside him in the booth. As she placed her palm against his cheek, he felt the heat of her long fingers. She smiled. "I don't want to lose you."

He covered her hand with his. "I don't want to lose you either, but . . ."

She moved closer, until their lips were almost touching. "But it would be a shame not to try."

He cupped the back of her head and touched his lips to hers. Her mouth tasted as sexy as it looked. He wanted to lose himself in the kiss, but he pulled back. "This isn't the place."

"I know."

"Your old apartment is just around the corner."

Erika moved back to her side of the booth as Stuart signaled for the check. "I keep that apartment for business and you aren't a customer. A quick taxi ride and we can be at the place where I live. I've never invited a man up there, but it's the only place I want to make love to you."

His hands trembled as he pulled out his credit card. As the waiter left, he said, "I'm as nervous as a schoolboy."

"Me too," she said, and her smile made everything all right.

They kissed and held hands in the taxi and in the elevator to her floor. In her apartment, they threw their coats onto the sofa and stood in the middle of the living room. She slipped her hands around his neck. "Tell me what you've been dreaming about."

Shit. How could he tell her about the nights he awoke, covered with sweat, his erection almost painfully hard, images of her naked body filling his mind? How could he tell her about his hand surrounding his cock as he imagined her straddling him, wearing a tight corset, her breasts bare, long garters holding up black stockings. He'd see her head thrown back, her screams filling his ears, the smell of her arousal in his nostrils, the feel of her silky stockings against his thighs.

He swallowed, unable to speak. She slid her hands into his hair. "I want to make this good for you. For us." She kissed him, again the aggressor. The thought that she had probably done this hundreds of times flashed through his mind for an instant, but he found he didn't care. He wanted her and he loved it that she was taking the initiative since his mind refused to focus on anything. "I want you," she whispered.

"Lord, Erika, I want you so much," he said, cupping her face and pressing his lips against hers. "I can't think straight."

She took his hands in hers and guided them to her breasts. "Don't think, just touch me."

She pulled off her shirt and her breasts were full, her nipples hard beneath the thin cotton of her turtleneck. He kneaded her flesh while his lips played with her mouth. Beneath his palms he could feel the pounding of her heart and the shaky rise and fall of her chest. Needing skin against skin, he pulled his shirt off as she yanked her sweater over her head. As she reached behind her to unfasten her tiny lacy bra, he stopped her. "This way," he said, slipping the straps down her upper arms and pulling the lace from her breasts. Now her beautiful breasts were supported by only the wire of her bra. "I've imagined you this way."

Like a cat in heat, she rubbed her hard nipples against his lightly furred chest. Everywhere the nubs touched, ribbons of heat penetrated his skin to the very heart of him. He released his belt and unfastened his pants and she unzipped her jeans. "I never wear slacks of any kind when I'm working, but taking pants off this way is very erotic too." She stopped suddenly. "I'm sorry. I shouldn't talk about working."

"No, actually it's good that you do." She was Erika, a delicious mixture of lover and prostitute. He winked. "I have a friend who's a professional at this, you know. I would be delighted if she taught me some of the tricks I never learned. Then I could make all of *your* fantasies come true."

Erika giggled. "Stuart, you're wonderful."

As she pulled down her jeans, Stuart saw that she wore tiny lace panties. He knew she wouldn't be wearing stockings and garters but maybe next time. If there was a next time. As he removed his slacks he wondered what she saw when she looked at him. He wasn't in bad shape for a man in his late forties, but she'd been with . . .

"Don't do that," Erika said, cupping his face in her palms and staring into his eyes. "I can read your mind. I'm not thinking about the bodies of the other men I've been with. I'm right here with you, one hundred percent." She pointed to his shorts and growled, "Now take those off too."

Quickly he was naked and they were in her bedroom. She threw the bedspread on the floor and sat on the edge of the bed, still wearing her panties and bra. Taking a condom from her purse and placing it on her bedside table, she said. "I want you to know that I've never been in this bed with any man but you."

He sighed. "I'm glad." He pushed her onto her back and stretched out beside her. "God, I want you." His cock was fully engorged and he rubbed it against her side, feeling the heat of her body against it for the first time. He was afraid he might come just from the pleasure of that. He turned onto his back, his cock sticking straight up from his groin. Sensing his mood she crouched beside him. "This way?" she whispered.

He grabbed her by the waist and lifted her over him, then slid his hand between her spread legs. Her panties were soaked. Through the fabric, he found her clit and stroked over its swollen surface, watching her face as her hips moved sinuously against his fingertips. "Yes, Stuart," she said, "like that."

Through the sexual haze, he realized she had called him by name. She was making love to him, not to some nameless, faceless customer. He rubbed, finding her rhythm, discovering exactly where and how she enjoyed his fingers. Soon he could wait no longer and sensed she was close to orgasm as well. He found the condom and handed it to her. He wanted her hands on him.

Slowly, ever so slowly, she unrolled the cold, wet latex over him, then guided his cock toward her steaming opening. She pushed the crotch of her panties aside and lowered her body over him. Her breasts spilling out over the wires of her bra, her panties still in place yet with his cock deeply imbedded within her—it was like his fantasy but so much better. He watched her face and held her hips as her body rose and fell on his. When she threw her head back, dug her nails into his skin and screamed, he felt the spasms of her body on his erection. He felt his climax rocketing through him and he let it take total possession.

With his penis still deep within her, Erika fell forward, her naked breasts against his chest, her breathing as fast as his, their hearts pounding in the same rhythm. He held her in his arms, totally content.

They lay just that way for several minutes, somewhere between awake and asleep. Finally she propped herself on her hands and looked down at him. "God, that was sensational, Stuart."

"You're sensational, Erika. It's amazing but that was exactly what I've been fantasizing about for months. You're so beautiful, so erotic."

He allowed his penis to slip from her body and she handed him some tissues. They cleaned up, snuggled together, and Erika pulled the covers over them. "Can you stay with me tonight?"

"Yes," he whispered. "I'd like that."

With a deep sigh, Stuart returned to the present, the coffee maker, and the visitors area. And the awful waiting. He had never told her how in love with her he was, although he thought that she knew. Did she also know that he wanted to marry her, make their arrangement official and permanent? He'd tell her when she woke up. If she . . . No! No ifs! When she woke up.

He tried to focus on the news that Erika had survived the night and that was what the doctor had called a "good sign." He remembered his first terrible visit to her bedside at just after 6:00 A.M. Although he had been warned, he was shocked at the sight of the fabulous, vibrant woman he knew lying pale and unmoving, her head swathed in bandages, a machine breathing for her, her suddenly vulnerable body surrounded by tubes and equipment that beeped and whined and whooshed, keeping her functioning while her body tried to heal itself.

He'd sat at her bedside, holding her limp hand, stroking her pale fingers, and talking to her in hushed tones. "I love you, Erika," he had said. Now he could say it. Where had the words been for the past year, since he'd known how deeply he felt? Now they spilled out. He told her of all the things they would do when she was better. He made promises to God that he knew he couldn't keep, yet if Erika pulled through, who knew what he could do?

All too quickly a nurse clad in a bright purple scrub top and plaid scrub pants had tapped him on the shoulder and told him it was time to leave. He had kissed Erika's palm then placed her hand on the stark white sheet. As he walked from the room, he thought that the nurse's bright colors were so incongruous, yet appropriate. Erika would have hated white.

Slowly he'd walked back into the waiting room and sat beside Brook. It would be all right. It had to be.

At seven-thirty, when Shara awoke, Brook convinced her to go home and get some rest in a real bed. "I'll call you if there's any news. I promise."

By ten o'clock, Mei Lee and Carolynn Bruno had joined Stuart and Brook and now the four sat talking in hushed tones. As they made small talk, each trying to cheer up the others, a tall, slender woman dressed in well-fitting black denim pants, a crisp white shirt with a thin red stripe, and well-worn blue-and-white running shoes walked into the waiting room, a small suitcase in her hand, a computer carrying case over her shoulder, and a heavy ski jacket tucked under her arm. Her hair was slightly lighter than Erika's, almost pale enough to be called ash blond, the short strands lighter at the ends. Her eyes were the same odd shade of brown as Erika's, the color of well-aged brandy.

This had to be Rena, the resemblance was too marked. Brook must have called her. Erika would want her daughter here, but Stuart was a bit surprised that Rena had come all the way from Chicago. He looked the young version of Erika over. She wore no makeup and no jewelry, so unlike her mother, yet her resemblance to Erika was obvious for those who knew her mother well. It wasn't just in her appearance, but in the way she moved. She held her head cocked to one side, Stuart saw, the way Erika did when she was slightly unsure of her surroundings, one hip slightly thrust forward. He smiled despite himself. He was seeing what Erika probably had looked like when Rick had fallen in love with her. He quickly calculated that when Erika was Rena's age, Rena was already two years old. He and Brook stood simultaneously and crossed the room.

"You must be Rena," Brook said extending her hand. "You look so much like your mother. I'm Brook Torrance and we spoke on the phone last evening." Reflexively Rena touched Brook's hand briefly.

Stuart reached forward and took the suitcase from Rena's hand as the younger woman dropped her coat and computer on a chair. "My name is Stuart Dunlop. I'm an old and dear friend of your mother's. Brook and I are so glad you came. I know your mother would be, too."

Rena's shoulders drooped and she looked bleary eyed. Stuart guessed that she hadn't slept the previous night. "I guess she's still alive if you're all still here," she said, her voice tightly controlled.

Stuart watched Brook's shoulders tighten. "She's in critical condition, but she's resting quietly."

"Is she going to make it?" Rena asked, her tone curious rather than worried.

"They don't know yet. One relative or friend is allowed to see her for five minutes each hour. I'll arrange for you to have the next visit."

"Don't go to any trouble," Rena said. "She won't care whether I'm here or not."

"She'll care," Stuart said softly. "More than you can possibly understand."

Stuart heard Brook's hesitation, before she said, "Come over here and sit down. You must have made a flight at the crack of dawn."

"Although I didn't know she had one, you must be Erika's daughter," Mei said, trying not to stare. "I'm Mei Lee, and you look so much like her."

"Carolynn Bruno," the other woman said. Carolynn, a redhead in her early thirties, with eyes that were almost violet and a peaches and cream complexion that could have put her in a commercial, extended her hand. "I didn't know Erika had a daughter either. You're so lucky to have a wonderful woman like Erika in your life. I've only known her for a year or so, but I know she'll be so glad you're here."

"I doubt it," Rena said, so softly that only Stuart and Brook could hear. She settled on the sofa beside Mei.

"Can I get you come coffee?" Stuart asked. "It comes from a machine, but it's not too bad I understand. I think there are a few doughnuts left as well."

"I had breakfast on the plane," Rena said, with a deep sigh, "but if they have tea I'd appreciate it."

"They do," Stuart said, smiling inwardly. Tea. "Let me guess. Sweetener. Half a pink packet."

Looking a bit puzzled, she said, "That's right. Thanks."

When Stuart returned from the coffee area, Brook stood talking to a nurse, informing her that Ms. Holland's daughter had arrived and should be allowed at her mother's bedside as soon as it was feasible. "Ashley, just let everyone know and make a note on Ms. Holland's chart if you would."

"Of course, Brook," the pink-clad nurse said. It was amazing how quickly Brook got on a first-name basis with people.

As Stuart handed Rena her Styrofoam cup, the nurse beckoned and she stood up. "You can see her for a few minutes right now, if you like," Ashley said and, as Stuart watched, Rena placed the cup carefully on a small table, straightened her shoulders, and took a deep breath. He caught Brook's eye and shrugged as Rena disappeared down the corridor toward her mother's room.

Rena followed the short older woman in the pink scrub suit through the heavy doorway and alongside a busy nurses' station toward a room at the end of the open area. Olkowski, her badge said. Ashley Olkowski. As Rena looked from side to side, she could see men and woman through the glass walls of each cubicle she passed. All were surrounded by the trappings of the very ill, machines that breathed, that regulated heartbeats, that dispensed life-continuing medications. Little had she ever suspected that she'd be in one of these places, visiting her mother, of all people.

"It's right here," Ms. Olkowski said, motioning her into a large room filled with machinery. On the bed lay the woman Rena had hated for so long, looking frail and vulnerable. *Why am I here?* she wondered. *What compelled me to come and see for myself that the bitch was dying? Why couldn't I have left well enough alone and stayed in Chicago? Oh, Mother.*

Rena looked at her mother, so white, so devoid of life. Through her mind flashed images of the woman she had loved as a child, the woman who had run behind her as she learned to ride a bike, played cards and board games with her, cut the crusts off of her peanut butter sandwiches, tucked her in and kissed her good night, the woman who had all but given her away at the age of six.

The nurse pulled a straight chair beside the bed, and Rena dropped onto it, suddenly weak and exhausted. "I'm sorry but I can really only let you stay for a few minutes," the nurse said. "Talk to her. We don't know that she can hear you, but it couldn't do any harm. Keep it all upbeat. The mind plays a very large part in recovery." With soundless footsteps, Ms. Olkowski left the room.

Rena sat in silence for several moments listening to the machines, watching her mother's chest rise and fall to the rhythm of the ventilator. Her mother didn't feel anything now, but why should that be any different. Erika hadn't felt anything for her daughter in years. "What can I say to you, Mother?" Rena finally said in a whisper. "Shall I tell you what I see when I look at you? I see a woman who couldn't make the effort to keep her daughter with her. Why, Mother? Why?" She blinked several times. *No. I won't cry. Why should I?*

"Okay. Let me be honest. I'm not totally stupid," she said, her voice tight. "I can see Daddy as he really is. Controlling, driven. If I were to be honest, he's probably the one who wanted me gone so he could push and shove his way up the corporate ladder with you at his side." Slowly her eyes filled. "Why didn't you fight for me? Was I so hateful that you gave up easily? Did you ever want me or did you get pregnant to trap him the way Daddy says?"

Tears flowed freely down her cheeks. "You started your mysterious business and became just as driven as he is, with no time for me in your life." She straightened and swiped her hand over her cheeks. "Well, now look at you. Weak, vulnerable the way I was back then. Now I have the ability to push *you* away. Paybacks are a bitch, aren't they, Mother," she snarled.

She sat silently for a few minutes until Ms. Olkowski tapped her on the shoulder and said, "I'm afraid I'm going to have to ask you to leave now. Your mother needs her rest."

As she stood, Rena mouthed, "Paybacks are a bitch." Silently she made her way back down the long hallway.

Now that she had seen her mother and gotten that particular monkey off her back, she walked back into the waiting room and looked at the people sitting and talking quietly. Brook was a handsome woman, not beautiful exactly but with a strength and character in everything from her hairstyle to her carriage. Her blond hair was beautifully styled, its careful shaping enabling it to avoid looking as if she had slept in it, as she undoubtedly had. Her blue eyes were like small pieces of sky.

The man named Stuart looked far worse. He sat in a chair that was a bit too small for him in a pair of rumpled slacks and a crushed light-green dress shirt. He wore no belt and looked as if he had dressed in about three seconds. Yet with all his dishevelment, he looked to be a comfortable, fatherly looking man who appeared to care a great deal for her mother. Were they sleeping together? Of course they were and why not?

The others in the room, the two women who had been there when she came in and a really dark, gorgeous man who had obviously just arrived, looked at her expectantly. They all seemed to care deeply about her mother. "Any change?" the woman named Carolynn asked.

"I don't know how she was earlier, but she's not responding to anything at the moment."

The group appeared to slump. Interesting people. Her mother certainly had a loyal group of friends. "I'm so sorry," Mei said. The petite Oriental woman with long straight hair that fell like a satin waterfall down her back dabbed at her eyes. "I can imagine how difficult this must be for you."

I don't need your pity, lady. Dryly, Rena said, "You have no idea."

"Can you stay for a few days?" Brook asked. Brook. Her mother had spoken of her often in the old days when she had called each Sunday. God, how she had dreaded those calls, hearing that voice and being reminded of what might have been, but never was.

"I'm not sure. I left my return ticket open and I might just fly back to Chicago this afternoon."

"Without knowing how she's doing?" Carolynn said, standing and prowling the room with long strides. "Oh you can't do that. We could call you often but still, it's not the same as being here and, well, knowing." She must be a professional model, Rena thought, with her statuesque height and perfect figure.

"I think I could deal with it," she said, trying not upset the group with her feelings. Willing to take the easier path for the moment, she would let them continue to think she was her mother's loving daughter.

"Do you have to go back to your job?" Brook asked, obviously unwilling to admit that she had no idea what Rena did.

"Actually I brought work with me." Rena moved her jacket aside and settled into her chair. She patted her computer case. "Right here."

"Oh, that's good," the newest addition to the group said. *Boy,* Rena thought, *tall dark and handsome doesn't go nearly far enough for you.* "We haven't met. I'm Alex Kosta." His voice like liquid silk, flowing over her and all but seducing her where she sat. He appeared ageless and almost impossibly good-looking, like the dashing heroes of the romance novels Rena enjoyed. Like those larger-than-life men, he looked dangerous somehow, with his brooding Mediterranean eyes and long, soft black hair that he wore almost touching the collar of his tan cotton shirt. His tight khaki pants fitted his lean body as if he had been poured into them. *Phew,* Rena thought. She could have sexual fantasies about this man for months. *Damn,* she thought. *How can my brain be in so many fragments? I'm thinking sexy thoughts about a total stranger and hateful thoughts about my mother. I have to admit though that I'm also concerned and curious about the woman who engenders such loyalty from her friends.* She tore her gaze from the man called Alex. *Don't spoil the image of the dutiful daughter, at least not yet.*

"Listen, Rena," Brook said, "I know your mother would want you to stay at her apartment." She reached into her purse, pulled a key off her ring and handed it over. "Here. Take this and you can settle in any time you want. I'll call the doorman and square it for you." As she fumbled with her purse, she surreptitiously wrote the apartment's address on a piece of paper, palmed it and passed it to Rena. Interesting. Brook obviously didn't want to let the others know that Rena had no idea where her mother lived either. Very interesting and very protective. Of whom? Her? Erika? "If you'd like, why don't you head over there now and drop your things? Then you can come back later and get another chance to see your mom."

Stay in her mother's apartment? See where her mother lived? Rena felt the walls closing in. Her throat tightened and her skin prickled. She wiped her sweating palms on the thighs of her jeans. None of these people could possibly understand. Her mother might appear to be a wonderful person, but it seemed that only Rena knew the truth. *She was a monster. She is a monster! Would seeing her mother's apartment change that?* She didn't want to challenge the image, but these people were making everything difficult. Suddenly needing to escape, she stood, shouldered her PC case, grabbed her suitcase and coat and, without another word, fled toward the elevator.

In the busy lobby of the hospital she found a small seating area and dropped into an ersatz leather chair. She schooled her breathing. In, out, in, out. Slow. Slow. She had to think this all through, and this wasn't the place to do it. She took the scrap of paper Brook had handed her from the pocket of her jeans. She realized that, for some reason, she needed to remain in New York for a day or two at least.

Having made that basic decision, she asked herself whether she could stay in her mother's apartment. What harm could it do? Humanize the monster? Okay, her mother slept in a bed, wore clothes, brushed her teeth. She was still the woman who sent her daughter away, forever.

She looked down at the scrap of paper. Why the hell not? Beard the lion in her lair, as it were. Certainly Rena could spare a few days and then, when her mother regained consciousness, they would have it out once and for all. That was why she needed to stay. She'd get all this off her chest and be a healthier person for it. Rena never considered that her mother might die. Erika couldn't die; she was too tough.

Rena felt her body slowly relax. She looked at the people around her, some rushing around, some merely waiting, all deeply involved in the lives of others. Patients, nurses, doctors, family, friends, and she was none of those. Where exactly did she fit? What was she doing here?

She lifted her chin, stood up and pulled on her jacket. Since she had never been in New York City before, she knew she should figure out how to get around using public transportation, but for now she grabbed her bags and walked out the main entrance. Clutching the address, she flagged down a taxi. She climbed in and read the words aloud to the driver. Ironic, she thought. Her mother had probably done the same thing the previous evening and now she was lying in that ugly room with all those friends hovering. *Fuck you, Mother. Fuck you.*

Chapter

9

During the taxi ride, Rena tried to free her mind of the issues whirling inside. She used a few relaxation techniques she had learned from a friend and finally managed to appreciate the ride through Manhattan. The weather had cleared completely and the sky was now deep blue, what she could see of it between the skyscrapers lining both sides of the streets and avenues. As the taxi made its way through Central Park, she gazed at the naked trees and brown grass. Pigeons flew and perched and waddled everywhere. Since it was lunch time, traffic was heavy. It took more than half an hour to weave across town to Riverside Drive.

As the driver pulled up before a dark-green awning, Rena gazed to her left, at the view of a strip of park and, beyond, the Hudson River and the Palisades. The water was still rough and filled with small whitecaps left over from the previous evening's storm. For a moment she watched a tugboat pushing a long barge chug its way upstream. Finally, the driver cleared his throat. She gathered her belongings and paid him. As she reached for the door handle, the building's doorman quickly opened the door for her and extended his hand to assist her out of the cab.

"Yes, ma'am. May I help you?" he asked, reaching to take her suitcase and PC.

"I'm Erika Hughes's, I mean Erika Holland's daughter."

"Of course. You're Ms. Rena. Ms. Brook called and told us to expect you." He patted her hand. "I was so sorry to hear about her accident. Please, tell your mother that Walter sends his best and wishes her a speedy recovery."

Taken aback by his obvious sincerity, she stammered, "T—thank you. I will."

"Will you be staying long?"

"I don't know yet."

Walter pointed toward a uniformed man who stood beside the mail boxes. "Well let me or Martin, he's the concierge, know if there's anything we can do for you. We're all very fond of your mother and are anxious to do anything at all for you." Efficiently, he carried her things into the lobby, guided her to the elevator and pushed the button for the sixteenth floor. He motioned to the man he had called Martin. "This is Ms. Rena Holland. She'll be staying in her mother's apartment for a few days."

"Of course, Ms. Holland. I'll be sure to tell all the others that you're to be given complete access. Is there anything else that Walter or I can do to help you settle in?"

As she entered the elevator, she said, "No thank you, and it's Hughes. Rena Hughes."

"Of course, Ms. Hughes. I beg your pardon."

The doors silently slid closed, and Rena stood in the luxuriously appointed elevator gazing at the scrupulously clean walls of mirrors and deep-pile navy blue carpeting as it rose. "Phew," she muttered. "Some place my mother has here. I wonder what it costs a month." She left the elevator at the sixteenth floor and, as the note from Brook said, selected the door to apartment two, one of only three doors on the floor. She unlocked the door and stepped into the black-and-white-tiled entry, flipped on the light, and closed the door behind her. She couldn't control the long low whistle that escaped her mouth. "This is amazing."

From the entryway she could see into a large living room all done in shades of burgundy and moss green. The floor was covered with an Oriental rug over thick carpeting, inviting a visitor to remove her shoes and enjoy the softness underfoot. The chairs and sofa looked so soft that you wanted to curl up and put your head back. The walls were decorated with prints in oversized silver frames, flowers, waterfalls, cityscapes, and the end tables each had an array of green plants, their leaves spilling onto the wooden surfaces.

Rena set her suitcases down and prowled. On the other side of the foyer was the dining room with an antique table that seated six. In the center was a large flower arrangement that looked like the florist had slaved over it for hours. Chrysanthemums, baby's breath, and a few spectacular blossoms Rena had never seen all nestled in a sea of greenery. Prints similar to the ones that covered the living room walls covered one of these walls, hung at irregular heights and distances from each other. Two elaborate silver candlesticks sat on the highly polished surface of the chest that stood beside the door through which she had entered. Above the chest hung an oil landscape lit with a small, carefully placed spotlight. She opened the top center drawer of the chest and found a complete silver service for eight and assorted linens in the drawer below.

The third wall contained doors that lead to the kitchen and a linen closet and the fourth wasn't a wall at all, just three floor-to-ceiling windows with a view of the Hudson River and the high rock cliffs beyond. With the noonday sun overhead, the view was even better than from ground level and made Rena catch her breath. For several long moments, she just gazed from the window watching toy boats lumber up and down the river. *I'm lucky I don't live here*, she thought. *I'd stare out this window and never get any work done.* With a sigh, she turned and looked around.

Despite the opulence of the furnishings, there was a deserted feeling, as if no one used these rooms.

She wandered back to the entry and down the hall that led to the three bedrooms. Two were quite obviously guest bedrooms with the comfortable yet sterile look of rooms seldom if ever used. The third bedroom was obviously her mother's. Funny, she thought as she entered, here she was surrounded by her mother's things yet she couldn't feel her, couldn't feel anything. This room seemed somehow much more comfortable than the rest of the apartment as if someone actually lived here: a wide brass bed covered with a crazy quilt made from swatches of fabrics of all colors, prints, and textures, a lounge chair upholstered in soft gray velvet, a small refrigerator in the corner.

There were knicknacks on the vanity and a collection of bottles of perfume and body lotion. To her amazement, on the wall were more than half a dozen silver-framed photos of her, taken at various ages, some of her alone, and some with one or both of her parents. Most had been taken before she moved to France, but a few were more recent. There was her high school graduation photo and one taken at her senior prom in college. She idly wondered how her mother had gotten hold of them. She certainly hadn't sent them to her.

Rena walked over to the vanity and picked up a simple silver frame. Inside was a photo she remembered well. It showed the two of them in front of a small bistro on the main street of the town near her school.

She closed her eyes, remembering that visit. Why had her mother waited so long to come to France? She had claimed that she was broke, but her father had left her with plenty of money. He had told Rena that in so many words, so why hadn't Erika visited? Her eyes clouded. Why did she leave me all alone?

She closed her eyes and, when she opened them again she was drawn back to the picture. Her mother's arm was draped lightly around her shoulders, her smile bright, maybe too bright. There was something around her mother's eyes, the look of an abused woman waiting for the next blow, Rena thought. Not understanding what she saw, Rena's gaze switched to her image in the photo and she shook her head. Her expression was sullen and she stood with her coat pulled tightly around her, held with both her hands. Her body was straining to keep from touching her mother's. None too gently, Rena set the photo down on the vanity's mirrored surface.

The light was flashing on her mother's answering machine. She had three messages. Without much thought she pressed the *play* button. "Hi Erika, it's Clay. I just wanted to tell you what a blast I had last evening, as always. I know you know, but just to make it official, charge my credit card. I think I'll be in town around the twentieth of next month, but I'll let you know the exact date. Thanks."

There was a beep. I wonder who Clay is and what that was about the credit card, Rena thought. Another message began. "Hey, Erika, Greg Haslett. I left a message last evening about the group thing next month being canceled. Well, it's on again, for sure this time. I need three women. One requirement. One man has peculiar tastes. He's into Asians, specifically ones with long hair. I know you've got one particularly gorgeous girl, I think her name's Mei. Is she available? Call me later."

Rena dropped onto the edge of the lounge chair. *This can't be what I think it is. It's some kind of mixup. I mustn't jump to conclusions.*

One more beep. "Erika, baby, it's Marty. Thanks ever so for the black gal with those great tits. Those boobs of hers are worth every penny. Make a note that next time I call, send her. Love you." The message ended with loud kissing noises.

There wasn't a mistake, was there? These messages were from men about prostitutes, weren't they? No, there had to be another explanation. She played the messages again, trying to catch her breath while the damning words filled the room. There was no room for error. She couldn't be misunderstanding. Her mother was a madam, a whore. Rena looked around. A well-paid whore, but a whore nonetheless. "A fucking whore." Her sardonic laugh echoed from the walls. "Right. Fucking. Slut. My mother the hooker." *Little Goody Two-shoes*, she thought. *So good, so motherly. No wonder she didn't want me around.*

She thought back to the people she had met at the hospital, Mei and Carolynn. Whores. They must be hookers. And what about the men? Them too? The one called Stuart didn't look like a male prostitute. Neither did Alex, but of course he was so good-looking—God, she realized, he must be. I was attracted to a male prostitute. That's disgusting. She mentally shook herself. Maybe they all weren't in the business. Maybe he is just a friend. What about Brook, her mother's best friend and, most probably, her business partner? Maybe there was some rational explanation for all of this. Brook would know everything, but could she ask? What could she say? Excuse me, Brook, but do you and my mother run a brothel?

Her thoughts unable to resolve themselves, she walked into the vestibule, collected her things and walked back down the hallway. She couldn't live in that room, so she settled into one of the guest rooms. Her hands shaking with questions and feared answers, she wandered into the kitchen, curious to learn everything she could about the woman who had given birth to her yet she didn't know at all. She opened the refrigerator to find it was almost empty. A package of English muffins, half a loaf of bread, a jar of peanut butter, two bottles of fat-free salad dressing, several restaurant containers of leftovers, four bottles of Perrier, and a door shelf full of condiments. Rena took a bottle of sparkling water and twisted off the cap. *Shit. What the hell do I do now?*

Bottle in hand she made her way to her mother's bathroom. The room was neat, toothpaste in a holder on the wall beside a toothbrush, small towels folded on the back of the toilet surrounding a box of tissues with a silver cover. Even the shower was neat, with only a bottle of shampoo and one of body wash.

The scrubber hung on a small hook on the wall of the stall. *No men's gear,* Rena noticed. *Well, obviously she lives alone.* Of course she didn't often sleep alone, but men probably came and went with such speed that no one had time to leave any personal items.

Curious, she opened the door to the medicine chest. Inside she found the usual assortment of digestive aids, headache remedies, first-aid supplies, and cold care products. On the bottom shelf were three boxes of condoms, one plain, one ribbed, and one mint-flavored. There was also a tube of spermicide and a diaphragm. "She doesn't take any chances, does she?" Rena muttered. *No more children for her. No more? Who am I kidding? No children at all.*

Her mother's closet was next. Rena spread the doors wide and gazed in awe at the collection of high-priced clothes for all occasions. Cocktail and evening dresses, sequined tops and long skirts, business suits and soft silk blouses, all in an assortment of shades, from bright primaries to pastels. Many of the outfits were black, with classic lines that screamed of their high price. Rena checked the labels and found everything from dresses by Herve Leger of Paris and Gigli of Bologna to jeans from The Gap and shirts with tiny images of Mickey Mouse on the pocket. There were classic-looking shoes from Manolo Blahnik and Gucci on the floor and several Fendi purses on shelves at one side.

She walked to the dresser and opened the top drawer. It contained ordinary, yet obviously costly bras, panties, and slips in all colors and nylons in a rainbow of shades. The drawer below was filled with kinkier objects; bustiers, bras with cutout fronts, and crotchless panties. Rena wondered at the lack of panty hose and nightwear. There were no negligees or erotic transparent robes anywhere. She opened the bottom drawer and quickly realized that it was filled with sex toys. She closed it with a hard push.

Rena dropped to the floor, sinking into the pearl gray carpeting, her gaze falling on the shoes on the far side of her mother's closet. Mixed with the designer shoes were strappy sandals and slides in all colors, several pair with extremely high stiletto heels in gold, silver, and black. Unable to resist, she scrambled to the closet and peered at the floor toward the back. Patent leather boots in red and black with laces up the front stood in neat rows. "Whorehouse shoes," she said aloud, moving to the bed and collapsing on the quilt.

She glanced at the window and saw the sun, streaming through the glass, then looked at the clock radio bedside her mother's bed. It was already after three o'clock. The phone rang, but she didn't consider answering it. She let it ring, then, after several moments, the answering machine picked up. Her mother's voice said, "Hi, you've reached Erika Holland and Courtesans, Inc. Please leave a message at the sound of the beep and I'll return your call as soon as I can." There were several tones, then the messages she had already heard played. Finally, the machine said, "I will erase your messages." After a few more beeps, a woman's voice said, "Hi, this is Brook Torrance. Erika won't be able to answer her messages for a while so please leave messages on my answering machine at two-one-two five-five-five two-four-seven-seven." Courtesans, Inc. Good name for a whorehouse, Rena thought.

A moment later a second phone rang. "Hi, it's Erika. Leave me a message." A voice followed. "Rena, it's Brook. If you're there, pick up the beige cordless phone on the bed table." There must be two answering machines, Rena thought, one for the business and one for her personal calls. Obviously Brook would be taking all the business calls for now. "Good," Rena said aloud, a nasty edge to her voice, "the business won't suffer. All those horny guys will get their fucking without my mother."

"Rena, pick up the beige phone if you're there."

Not wanting Brook to know she had been snooping, she waited a moment, then picked up the phone and, trying to sound breathless, said, "Hello?"

"Rena, it's Brook."

Hoping Brook would buy the act, she said, "Sorry it took so long for me to answer. I was in the guest room lying down."

"I thought you'd like to know that things are pretty much unchanged with your mother. I also fixed it so you won't be bothered with phone calls for her."

"Thanks." What more could she say?

"I thought you might be napping. I hope the phone didn't annoy you."

"Except for you," Rena said honestly, "there haven't been any calls."

She could hear a deep sigh. "Great. Are you coming back to the hospital today? I thought if you were going to be here about dinnertime we could take a walk, get a bite to eat, and talk."

Talk. Yes, there was quite a bit to talk about. "I wouldn't miss that for anything," her voice hard-edged.

There was a slight hesitation, then Brook said, "That's fine. I'll wait for you."

Rena glanced again at the clock. "I should be there around five-thirty. I guess I have to take a taxi."

"Not really." Brook gave Rena instructions on how to use the city buses to get to the hospital. "Until later," she said.

"Right," Rena said, then replaced the receiver.

Exhausted, yet determined to find out all she could about her mother's business she took a quick shower, dressed and headed to the hospital.

Several hours later Rena and Brook sat in a small luncheonette only a block from the hospital. Rena had arrived back in the ICU waiting room to find half a dozen women and two men, in addition to Stuart and Brook, all talking quietly. As she was introduced, she tried to imagine each as a prostitute but couldn't. She had to be wrong. She must have drawn the wrong conclusions from the information she had, but what other conclusion was there?

Before leaving the hospital with Brook, she had spent five minutes at her mother's bedside just staring and trying to integrate all the pieces of information she knew. As she left the ICU, she received a brief update from her mother's doctor. "Nothing's really new, but the fact that she's still with us is encouraging." The doctor also said, "If and when she regains consciousness, however, it's impossible to know the amount of brain damage she's suffered. The bleeding into the brain could have had little effect or it could leave her with considerable deficit." Rena tried, but couldn't imagine her mother as anything but fully alive and well.

After her visit to her mother's room and her conversation with the neurologist, everyone in the waiting room crowded around to hear her relay the doctor's words, each patting her shoulder or holding her hand, telling her that they would help in any way they could. At the words *considerable deficit*, there was an audible gasp from the group.

Now, half an hour later, she sat across from the woman who could give her some of the answers she needed about her mother's life before the accident. Neither woman had much appetite, so they had each ordered only a salad. Small talk waned and finally Rena said, "Tell me about your business."

"Business?"

During the taxi ride to the hospital, Rena had decided to be honest with Brook. "I heard you clearing the answering machine."

Brook's body slumped in her seat. "I'm sorry I didn't think of it earlier. I'm sorry you had to find out that way, but now you know."

"I'm not sure what I know, so you'd better tell me."

"What do you think?"

"We're dancing." When Brook didn't respond, Rena said, "I think you're a whore."

Rena watched Brook's eyes close and her body sag still more.

After a long silence, she opened her eyes and leaned forward. "Your mother and I run an escort service that provides company for lonely men and women."

"In other words, you run a brothel," Rena snapped.

"We provide escorts for parties, quiet dinners, any time someone wants intelligent company and interesting conversation."

Through gritted teeth, Rena said, "Conversation. Is that what they're calling it these days?"

"If the escorts make arrangements with patrons afterward, that's their business."

"Right, and pigs can fly on alternate Saturdays. Come on. I'm not that naive. Be honest for just a few minutes. Your business is high-class prostitution."

She watched Brook swallow hard. "I really think you should be having this conversation with your mother."

With a rueful glare, Rena said, "That's not really possible right now, is it?"

Brook was spared the need to answer when the waiter arrived and put two chef's salads on the table. She lifted her fork, played with a bite of lettuce, then replaced the fork on the plate. "I'm not going to justify what we do. I don't feel I need to. Let me just say that if a person is lonely and wants companionship, and the counterpart is willing, what's the harm?"

"Harm?" Rena hissed, slamming her fork onto the Formica table. "It's immoral and disgusting."

"Why?"

Rena hesitated. She wasn't going to get into a debate about the pros and cons of running a brothel. "It just is." She took her napkin from her lap, put it on the table, and stood. "Did you get her into this?"

Brook looked totally deflated. "Actually she invited me to join her."

Rena pulled her wallet out of her jacket pocket, withdrew a

bill, and dropped it onto the table. "Well, bravo for her. I hope you two are happy."

"Actually," Brook said, looking Rena in the eye, "we both are happy. The only serious problem was Erika's inability to break through the walls you've built up." Brook reached out and caught Rena's hand as the young woman turned to leave. "She really loves you, you know."

"No, I don't know and I don't care." Trembling, Rena pulled away, jammed her arms into her ski jacket and stormed out of the restaurant. For almost an hour she walked the streets of Manhattan trying to calm her anger. *How dare that woman try to justify what they did? It was illegal and immoral. It was an insult to every loving family.*

Her breath making small puffs of vapor in the cold air, Rena finally found herself back at the hospital. She entered the warm lobby and again sat on one of the utilitarian sofas. During her walk she had decided to stay over that night at her mother's apartment, then fly back to Chicago the following morning. "You're Maureen Hughes, aren't you?"

She jumped. No one had called her Maureen since she was a child. And who would know her here? She looked up as a man in his mid-thirties sat down on a chair across from her. He had an ingenuous smile with a shock of bright red hair and, of all things, a face full of freckles. He wore a gray-and-black-plaid flannel shirt over a gray turtleneck sweater and gray slacks. A black trench coat was draped over his arm. "It's Rena. Do I know you? Are you one of Mother's friends?" She couldn't keep the sneer from her voice when she said the word *friend.* Was he one of her male prostitutes?

"My name is Sean Fredericks and I'm an acquaintance of your mother's in a way." He extended a wide-palmed hand. "It's nice to meet you." She took his hand. His grip was firm, his hand soft. "How is she doing?"

"About the same." She started to stand. "How did you know who I was?"

"I overheard one of the nurses call you by name. I think we need to talk."

"I'm afraid not. If you'll excuse me, I'm going to head back to her apartment."

"I really wanted to chat with you." They both stood and Sean picked up Rena's coat and held it for her. "Maybe tomorrow."

"I'm flying back to Chicago tomorrow, so I don't think we'll get that chance."

Rather than looking shocked at her defection, Rena thought Sean looked almost triumphant. "If you're leaving tomorrow, I think we need to talk tonight. Let me buy you a drink. Then we can share a cab across town."

She had to admit that she was curious, but she didn't want to talk to anyone about her mother. She just wanted to go back to Chicago and forget this whole ugly day. "I don't think so, but thanks for the offer."

"I know a few things about you from the research I've done on your mother. I know you haven't seen her in several years and I'm sure that you're none too happy with what you found about her business. I think we have a few things in common."

Rena sighed and zipped her jacket. This was big bad New York and she was the daughter of a hooker. Maybe he thought she was in the business too. "I'm sorry. I don't think we have anything in common and I have to go now."

He was several inches taller than she was and he stood close enough to be able to lower his voice to almost a whisper. "I can read people very well and I would be willing to bet that you've just found out about your mother's activities and you're pissed. I don't blame you. She runs a brothel for the disgustingly rich and famous, and I've been trying to get her to shut it down for several years."

It was all right for her to think of her mother as a madam, but it made her flinch to hear someone else say it. "Good night Mr. Fredericks." She turned and headed for the door.

"I don't want to arrest her or anything," he said, keeping pace with her. "I just want her to leave this line of work."

Rena stopped and looked at Sean. "Are you a cop?"

His laugh was rich. "Not a chance. Let me be perfectly honest with you, Rena, if I may call you Rena. I write for the *National Informer.*"

"That scandal sheet?"

Sean had the good grace to look embarrassed. "Yes, that scandal sheet." He looked around, and as Rena followed his gaze, she saw that several people were listening to their interchange. "Can we talk?" he asked. "Please?"

Resigned to hearing what Sean had to say, Rena nodded. "Just for a few moments. It's been a very long day."

"I can imagine." Sean slipped his coat on and led the way out the front doors of the hospital. They walked for less than a city block and then he motioned her toward a small bar. "It's noisy, and a good place to talk without anyone listening. All right with you?"

When she nodded, he opened the door. They stepped inside a warm, rather cosy bar with a noise level, Rena thought, that would eventually deafen any regular customer. Sean took her coat and then guided her to an empty booth in the rear. "Can I get you a drink?" he asked, standing beside the table.

Rena leaned back against the maroon leather seat realizing how tired she was. "I'll have a beer."

"Do you want to pick a kind? Remember this is the big city."

"Chicago's hardly the sticks," she said, annoyed at his characterization of her city. "Just whatever light beer they've got on tap."

He made his way to the bar, said something to the bartender, then returned looking abashed. "Sorry, for putting down Chicago."

"I'm not a fan, just a resident."

"I'm still sorry. It was thoughtless. The waitress will bring our drinks, and I ordered a snack. I haven't eaten yet this evening."

Not up to small talk, Rena said, "Fine. Now what's your interest in me?"

"Let me be perfectly frank. I know about your mother's business and I've been interested in it for quite a while. She has a client list that's made up of lots of people in the public eye. I want that list and some inside information that you can get for me."

"I'm afraid I know less about her business than you do."

"I know, but you're in a position to find out all kinds of things, that I'm not."

"Things?"

"Sure. The whos and whats and hows. You know. The juicy details that the people who read the *Informer* want to know."

"Why should I want to get this information for you?"

"Because if I had her list and some interesting details about sexual preferences and such I could get your mother out of the madam business. Judging from what she charges, I'm sure she's got enough money to last her forever so she can retire gracefully."

"Retire? If you expose her and her clients, she'll go to jail. Sorry, no dice."

Before she could get up, he continued, "There's not a chance she'd get arrested. She's got police, politicians, lawyers, and judges in her pocket. She supplies a bit of tail for free and they look the other way."

Rena was surprised how this slimy man offended her, but if she were honest with herself, whether she had contact with her mother or not, she did want Erika out of the business. She didn't want to be the daughter of a hooker. "What makes you think I care enough about her to give a damn whether she's doing what she does or not?"

Sean waited until the waitress put the two beer glasses and the snack plate containing mozzarella sticks and mini pizza rolls, with a cup of red dipping sauce, on the table and left. "I think you do. I don't know about all your past history with your mother, and I'm sure you have your reasons for feeling less than the dutiful daughter. I also know that having a mother who runs the most notorious escort service in New York would make my skin crawl."

Horrid little man, Rena thought, *but he's right about me not wanting her to run a brothel.* "What do you want from me?"

His eyes narrowed. "I want names and specific kinky stuff. You know my newspaper so you know the kind of things I need."

"You'd keep my mother out of it entirely?"

"Of course."

Rena raised an eyebrow. "I'm not a child anymore. How can you guarantee me that she won't be harmed by all this?"

Sean looked wounded. "You mean you don't trust me?"

She felt the first smile in many hours soften her face. "No farther than I can throw a grand piano, Mr. Fredericks."

He laughed. "If I can give you some sort of assurance that your mother wouldn't be harmed by all of this, are you interested?"

"I don't know yet. Let me give it some thought. You have to think about what you can do to guarantee me that my mother won't be involved. And maybe Brook Torrance, too. Of course there would be no reference to my involvement either."

Rena could tell that Sean was making an effort not to look too triumphant. "Okay, let's see what you come up with and then we can deal."

What did she care if he got something he wanted. She would be getting something she wanted, too. "It's not quite that easy. I want an ironclad guarantee, like maybe a five hundred thousand dollar bond to insure complete anonymity."

Sean hesitated, then said, "That can be arranged."

When Sean agreed so quickly, Rena knew she hadn't asked for enough. She leaned back and sipped her beer. She had heard about the million-dollar deals and hundred-million-dollar lawsuits that rags like the *Informer* paid. "Let's say half a million each, for my mother, Brook, and myself if there's any harm done to any of us because of anything you print."

"Phew," Sean said. "You're talking big bucks, even for just getting the bond. I'll have to talk to a few people."

"You do that."

"While I do, you spend some time getting chummy with the folks who work with your mother. Get cozy. I know they'll feel close to you since Erika's in such bad shape. They might be willing to talk about their experiences. I want everything you can get hold of." He paused. "In addition, for each article I write, there will be a twenty-five-thousand-dollar bonus for you."

"That's quite a lot of money," she said, thinking about her bank account, almost empty now that she'd bought her last-minute airline ticket here from Chicago. "How many articles would you be writing?"

"One for each celeb you can get information about. Just talk with people and learn as much as you can. I need specific names, dates, and places, details I can verify, or at least attempt to verify."

Twenty-five thousand, and her mother out of the business. That was quite an incentive. Could she gather enough information? Could she tell this smarmy little man the lurid details? She didn't have to decide yet, just investigate. "Let me see what I can do, and you talk to your lawyers about that bond."

Sean finished his beer, grabbed a mozzarella stick, and stood up. As he put on his coat he said, "I'll call you on Erika's private phone, but if you don't answer I won't leave a message. I don't want anyone else possibly knowing about our little arrangement." He fished a business card from his wallet. "If you get anything or need me, you can reach me here." He scribbled on the back. "My cell phone, pager, e-mail address—it's all on there. For you I'm available twenty-four hours a day."

She slipped his card into her purse. "Remember that this is just to get my mother off the hook."

"Right. Of course." Sean dropped a twenty dollar bill on the table and extended his hand. Rena shook it and for several minutes after he left she remained sitting, sipping her beer, and staring into space. She hated her mother, so why did she care whether she was a hooker or not? Why did she care about Brook? She thought about it and couldn't fathom her reaction. She didn't want to have anything to do with her mother, but she didn't want her to be a madam.

When Rena found herself unable to unknot her feelings, she stood, put on her coat, and walked out into the frosty evening air. Exhausted, confused, she was deeply conflicted both about her feelings toward her mother and her opinion of Sean Fredericks and what he had asked her to do. All she could be sure of was that she didn't want to be the daughter of a whore. After several minutes staring into space, she hailed a cab and headed across town.

Chapter

10

Rena awoke the following morning neither refreshed nor rested. She had tossed and turned for much of the night. When she had slept, she had had dreams of being pulled in two directions or parented by faceless aliens. Standing beneath the shower spray, she decided not to think about any decisions and just talk to people and try to gather information. Whether she gave Sean anything or not didn't matter yet.

Rena arrived at the hospital just after nine and before coping with Brook, she slipped past the waiting room and sat beside her mother's bed for several minutes. Then she stopped at the nurses' station and found the resident in charge of her mother's case. Dr. Petrie was about thirty, with a dark-blond crewcut and a boyish face with hazel eyes and prominent ears. "I'm really happy to be able to tell you that your mother spent another quiet night. She's still in a coma, giving her body a chance to heal, but her vitals are all quite good. Every injured body reacts differently so we don't know when, or even if she'll come out of it, but we're all feeling upbeat. She could come out of it today, or tomorrow, or not for several weeks or even months. Until she awakens, we won't know anything about her mental condition." He patted Erika's shoulder. "I think you can be encouraged, however."

"That's wonderful news. Thank you, Doctor." She had known all along that her mother was too tough to let a little thing like a head injury stop her from doing whatever she wanted.

When she arrived in the waiting room, Brook was sitting in the corner talking to a man and woman Rena hadn't previously met. Funny how she now looked at every friend of Brook's and her mother's as if they were hookers, although these two definitely didn't look the part. As she crossed the room, Brook stood up and the couple turned toward her. The woman looked to be in her forties, reed slender and medium height with curly black hair and lightly tanned skin, wearing jeans and a sweatshirt with a Texas flag on the front. She wore no makeup to enhance her deep brown eyes or to cover the deep purple circles beneath. *She's got perfect eyebrows,* Rena thought. *Just the right arch, just the right thickness. Now why am I noticing eyebrows?*

The tall man sitting beside her had strongly chiseled features, with intense green eyes, a sandy brown, neatly trimmed beard, and slightly graying hair with deep waves curving across the top. He was also wearing jeans, with a light blue tailored shirt and one of those Western string ties with a silver slide. His belt was held closed with a silver and turquoise buckle that matched the band on his watch.

Anxiously, Brook said, "I saw you talking to the doctor. How is your mother this morning?"

"The doctor's encouraged, but they won't know anything until she wakes up, if she does."

She watched Brook heave a great sigh and scrub her hands over her face. "She will. I'm sure of that now. Does the doctor have any idea when that might be?"

"Unfortunately no. I checked a few Web sites on comas and they say that it's impossible to tell when a person might wake up."

"I know it will be a slow process when she does begin to come out of it, but I just know she's going to be fine. Soon she'll be awake and joking with us all." This morning Brook was also without makeup and looked as if she hadn't slept any better than Rena had. Like the new couple, she too wore jeans, and her bright red sweatshirt had a picture of Tweetie Bird on the front. "I thought you were heading home this morning."

She would have to tread gently to get everyone to accept her after the negative impression she had made the previous day. Without their acceptance, she would never be able to find out the things she wanted to know. "I decided to take your advice and stick around for a few days. I make no guarantees, but maybe I need some time to try to understand everything." She looked at the other couple, unwilling to talk about Erika's business in front of them.

Brook reached out and took her hands. "I'm so glad. I know how much she cares about you. I hope that, if you give it all a chance, you and she can reach some kind of understanding."

"I can't make any promises," Rena said. "About anything."

"I understand."

The couple had remained silent but now the woman smiled and said, "You have to be Rena."

How many people had her mother talked to about her? "That's right. How did you know?"

"I'm an old friend of your mother's and she's showed me your picture many, many times." She extended her hand. "My name is Valerie Hackett and this is my husband, Madison."

"It's nice to meet you," Rena said, returning the woman's firm handshake. She nodded at the man, wondering where they fit in her mother's life. "You say you've known my mother a long time," she said, taking a seat on the small sofa. "Where did you two meet?"

Brook smiled at Valerie. "You can be frank," she said. "She knows all about Courtesans, Inc."

"I ran the business until I found Madison." Valerie took her husband's hand. "He was one of my customers and he decided that he wanted to make it a permanent arrangement." She smiled at Madison with such obvious love that, for that moment, it excluded everyone else in the room.

"You owned the business before my mother?" Rena said, totally nonplused.

"You know, that's the kind of reaction I would have expected from Erika's daughter. You're so like her. I remember the night we first met. She found it difficult to believe that I was a prostitute and a madam."

Rena swallowed hard. "I guess I do too." Although she was an attractive woman, she certainly wouldn't turn heads.

"I understand. It's a common reaction." She grinned. "Not that I tell everyone about my previous life, but the ones who know are always surprised."

Madison spoke for the first time, his voice warm and friendly, his fingers laced with his wife's. "The first time we met, she was mingling with lots of men in tuxedos at an international oil traders convention. I'm in commodities, you know, and I took one look at her and decided she was going to be my personal commodity."

"When he found out that I was a paid escort," Valerie continued, "he handed me a thousand dollars, grabbed me by the arm, and all but dragged me to his room. We didn't come out for three days, and I didn't even charge him extra." The two sounded like they had told this story many times and had the dialogue down pat.

Rena was amazed. "So you two eventually married and he took you away from all that."

As Madison answered he patted her hand. "She was ready for a different kind of life and I think she's been happy." He gazed at his wife. "Have you ever regretted giving it all up?"

"Not in the least. I loved it while I did it, but now I just love you." Valerie leaned over, bussed Madison's cheek, and then refocused her attention on Rena. "I was so sorry to hear about your mother's accident. We flew in last evening, but by the time we got here you had already left."

"How long are you two staying?" Brook asked.

"Madison has to get back tonight, but I've got a room at the Plaza for a few days. I'm hoping to be here when she wakes up, but I have to be back on Thursday. As strong as you two are," she said, looking first at Rena, then at Brook, "Erika will need all the support she can get. It's going to be a difficult time for her. She's not a woman who can lie around in bed." Realizing her unintended double entendre, she looked chagrined.

"Thanks," Brook said. "It will be good to have you here."

"Is there anything I can do while I'm here, Brook?" Valerie asked. "Can I field phone calls or fight fires for you?"

"I'm keeping all the balls in the air, so to speak." She turned to Rena. "Courtesans, Inc. takes a tremendous amount of managing, something your mother was"—Brook paused, took a deep breath—"I mean is, extremely good at."

Management, Rena thought. *That's one word for it. I guess this kind of business isn't covered at the Harvard B School.* She chuckled inwardly. *I can just see it in the course catalog. Brothel 101, or How to Run a Bordello and Make it Pay. Among the things covered will be bribing police and tax evasion. Subtopics will include working the room and working the phones.* To avoid saying what she was thinking, she merely nodded, then leaned forward and propped her elbows on her thighs. "When did my mother take over your business?"

"More than five years ago when Madison and I got married."

"That must have been quite a financial sacrifice for you," Rena said, trying to get an idea of how much her mother made. Could she survive without the business as Sean had said?

"Not really. I was well compensated with a percentage of the profits for three years thereafter. It worked out really well all around."

If my mother lived on the proceeds while she paid off Valerie, the business must be doing quite well. But how much was from her personal clients? Obviously the man named Clay on the answering machine had been a customer of hers the evening of her accident. "I guess it did," Rena said. "I'm still a bit confused. Does my mother still do a lot of entertaining herself?"

"She goes out one or two evenings a week," Brook answered. "She's got so many regulars that she seldom gets an opportunity to meet anyone new anymore."

"Regulars?"

"Men who ask for her specifically. Courtesans, Inc. isn't just parties, although we want the government to think so."

A look passed from Valerie to Brook, but Brook said. "Don't worry, Val, Rena deserves to know the entire story, especially if she's going to get to know Erika."

Valerie nodded. "True." She turned to Rena. "It must be difficult to accept all this, but your mother needs you and your understanding now."

"I know," Rena said, not really knowing anything. Pulling the conversation back to the business, she continued, "Don't you all have to worry about the cops and all?"

Brook answered. "Not really. We make it very clear to official people that we're an escort service not a house of prostitution. We only deal with long-standing customers or people recommended by long-standing customers. There's usually a party or dinner involved so we can maintain that we're just supplying a charming, intelligent woman for conversation. Nothing more."

"What about taxes and stuff?"

Valerie uncrossed and recrossed her long legs. "We always give the government exactly what they are entitled to." She winked. "All the escorts are independent contractors and we give them Ten-Ninety-Nines at the end of the year. If there are tips for extracurricular activities, that's between the ladies and their accountants."

Valerie looked at her husband. "I don't know about you, but I'm really hungry." She turned to the other two women. "Most people lose their appetites when they're stressed, I eat. Since we're here in New York, I'm dying for a bagel and lox, and I know just the place." She stood up and shrugged on her sheep-skin-lined leather jacket. "Would either of you care to join us?"

"I had something at home," Rena said, remembering the slice of toast and cup of tea she had had earlier.

"I'm not very hungry," Brook added. "You two run along and enjoy your bagels. We'll see you both later." She stood and embraced Valerie. "I hate it that you disrupted your life," she said, a catch in her voice, "but I'm so glad you're here."

"Me too, babe," Valerie said. "Later." Hand in hand, Valerie and Madison headed toward the elevators.

"Tea?" Brook asked.

"Sure." In the coffee alcove, Brook said, "You look like hell. Did you get any sleep?"

"Some. I'm really shocked by the whole idea of Courtesans, Inc. and it will take quite a bit of getting used to."

"I can imagine," Brook said, carrying her Styrofoam cup back toward the waiting room.

Rena followed, cup in hand. This morning another corner of the room was occupied by a young couple, tearfully waiting for news about a loved one. She needed information so, as she dropped into a side chair, she asked, "How did you get involved?"

Brook settled on the sofa she'd been occupying and sipped her tea. "Your mother and I met the first day she moved into that tiny apartment off Broadway. Neither of us have any family to speak of, except you, of course, so we kind of clung together. I helped her get her job with the insurance agency and we spent a lot of time just walking around the city."

"How did my mother start doing what she does?"

"That was Stuart's doing, actually."

"That man who I met yesterday?"

"Yes. He works with your father, you know."

Realization dawned. "Of course. Stuart Dunlop. He's a partner now."

"Right. Well, the firm needed a woman to fill in a dinner party so Stuart suggested it to your mother." Brook recounted the story of Erika's first dinner party and her meeting with Valerie. "And, as they say, the rest is history."

"And you?"

Brook told Rena about the first evening she had been invited to a party as a paid escort. "It was a gas. I was suddenly being paid for doing something I had always done for free."

"That's sick." As the words came out of her mouth, Rena regretted them.

"No, it's not," Brook said calmly, "but I can understand that you must think that. Let me tell you what I've told a few people since. It's really simple, but if you think about it without all the knee-jerk overtones, maybe you'll begin to understand. Men often pay for sex. They pay with dinners, movies, whatever, expecting the woman to put out at the end of the evening. Maybe not on the first date, but the second or third. There's no love, no long-term commitments, just a guy, a girl, and sex. Of course, if things go well, then it continues for additional dates. It's not good or bad, it's just the way of it."

She's trying to justify being a whore, Rena thought. *It's amazing the way a woman who seems as reasonable as Brook can make prostitution seem like a normal and natural thing to do. Like dating, indeed.*

"This way," Brook continued, "it's all up-front. Cash changes hands and everything's predetermined."

Needing Brook's goodwill, Rena gritted her teeth and said, "Interesting point of view."

"Just let it rattle around in your brain for a while and see what comes out." She looked at the couple in the far corner of the room and lowered her voice. "This isn't street hooking. We don't pick up unknown guys and give blowjobs in the front seats of cars. And it isn't just sex. All of the people who work for Courtesans, Inc. are college graduates or at least behave as such. We all can make conversation about almost anything, or look interested if the topic is new. Most of us read at least one newspaper a day, plus several magazines each week. We can talk about books, movies, TV shows, politics, international problems, the sciences, whatever a partner wants to talk about. We get paid for being much more than something a man can climb into bed with."

Rena wondered whether Brook actually believed the propaganda she was spouting. As she heard Sean's voice asking about the unusual sex practices of the clients, she deliberately relaxed her shoulder muscles and said, "You must have to cater to kinky stuff from time to time."

"We do things with clients that they wouldn't do at home, if that's what you mean. Many of the men I've been with complain that their wives aren't interested in creative sex so they pay me to play."

"They're cheating, going outside of their marriage."

"True and I try to convince them to talk with their wives, but they aren't interested in taking the risk. With me there's no risk that I'll think they're deviant. They don't care what I think; they just get to do what they want. Most of the time."

"Most of the time?"

"There are things I won't do and I make that really clear upfront. One of the things Erika does is keep that straight. She tries to match the desires of her clients with the tastes of the escorts. Some women like heavy stuff; some don't. Some enjoy domination, some are basically submissive. Some want to teach; some enjoy being taught. Of course, the male escorts, too, need to be paired with the right women."

"I never thought about male prostitutes." She pictured Alex with some homosexual man, grunting in a hotel room somewhere. He was so attractive and sexy. What a waste.

"Not at all. Actually, Alex is a devout heterosexual. One of the other male escorts is gay and entertains men who want that kind of sex, but Alex and Paul are straight as they come."

Straight. Alex was straight. She was surprisingly relieved although she shut her mind to the fact that she was attracted to a professional. Not her, no way! "Oh."

"Alex is special, isn't he? If he were a few years older, he could slip his shoes under my bed for free." She paused. "You should talk to him. He's got some stories you won't believe. Actually you should talk to a few of our employees, get them to share some of their experiences. You might understand your mother better that way."

"That sounds like a good idea." A great idea actually. She'd be able to gather information and possibly feed it to Sean if she decided that was the right thing to do. She suppressed a grin. "How about you? Have you had some unusual moments?"

Brook snorted. "Who hasn't? I've fulfilled a few odd fantasies in my time, and probably will continue to."

Not if I have anything to do with it, Rena thought. "For example?"

Brook gazed at Rena. She was such an enigma. On the one hand, she seemed concerned about her mother and on the other she appeared to hate her, both for their shared past and because of Courtesans, Inc. Brook had the feeling that the concern was less real than the animosity, but she seemed naturally curious about the business and the seamier side of sex. *Do I have stories?* Of course, but for now Brook didn't think Rena was up to the really kinky. "I remember a man who was crazy for gadgets and for me in funky clothes. Let's call him Sloan so I don't have to be discreet. I hope you don't mind."

"Not at all," Rena said. "I'll admit that I've become really curious about what goes on."

"Well Sloan loved it when I surprised him with an outrageous new outfit or a toy or gizmo. I remember I arrived at his apartment one night dressed in a tight red latex body suit that zipped all the way up the front. I brought one for him too, and we played in the shower, plastic to plastic. Another evening, I gave him a masturbation tool, a sort of vibrator shaped like a hand that fitted over his erection and—well, you can picture the rest." Brook grinned at the memory. "He came twice that evening, once playing with the toy and once, later, with me."

"I hope it's not too crass," Rena said, "but I have to ask. How much did you get paid for an evening like that?"

Brook was surprised that the question hadn't come up sooner. "Usually between a thousand and fifteen hundred dollars for dinner and whatever. Since there was only the whatever," Brook said with a twinkle, "Sloan paid only a thousand."

"A thousand dollars? For an hour?"

"Or two. That's all Sloan wanted, but with other men the entertainment could last for an entire evening and into the wee small hours. It's whatever they want." She leaned forward and dropped her voice still more. "For parties the base cost is about a thousand for each girl and after-activities are extra."

"A thousand dollars or more?" Rena said again and Brook could see her mind reeling. "Does Courtesans, Inc. get part of that?"

"We take twenty percent for making the contacts, managing all the craziness and lots of other overhead. The folks who work with us are free to do whatever they want in their spare time, of course, and occasionally someone decides to try to cut us out. Erika and I decided early on that we would take a nonaggressive position, but if someone begins to freelance with one of our customers they're on their own. We never get them work again." Brook smiled. "It's usually just not worth it for them to try to go it alone and twenty percent isn't really much."

"Phew. Those are big numbers."

"The men and women who employ us can afford it and they know what they're getting."

"What are they getting?"

Brook considered her answer, wanting Rena to understand. "Men like Sloan pay for a particular woman with particular tastes that mesh with theirs, and we make it worth every cent each time. Other men are looking for decorations to hang on their arms at parties or women strictly to impress others. With some it's simply privacy. Many of the folks who pay us have famous faces and need to be anonymous. With us they can be sure we won't go running to the newspapers with the kinky details." The image of Sean Fredericks's face flashed through Brook's mind. "Lots of people are really voyeurs at heart. They enjoy finding out the details, publicly condemning us and privately wishing they could do what the rich folks do."

"Sloan must be able to afford you. What does he do?"

"He's the CEO of one of the more successful dot-coms and he's certainly not lacking in the money department."

"How many times have you seen him?"

"He lives in Connecticut, but he has an apartment on Fifth Avenue that he uses during the week. We've been seeing each other maybe once a month for almost two years so you can do the calculations."

"Is he married?"

"Yes, but his wife just isn't interested. According to him, she's strictly into missionary position, but he loves her and doesn't want to press her to do anything that might make her uncomfortable. So he scratches his itches with me—and others I guess.

Aside from those evenings, however, I suspect that he's a good husband."

"Good husband? He's cheating."

"Yes, he is, but I'm not the morality police. If he weren't with me, he'd be with someone else. So I don't make judgments . . ." She grinned. "Just money."

"So it's all about the money?" Rena said, a nasty edge to her voice.

"Not at all. Yes, I like the money, but I enjoy pleasing men too, and I'm good at it."

"I guess you're right," Rena said, obviously not convinced. "What about Sloan?"

"Do you really want the details? It gets a bit over the top."

She watched Rena consider, then say, "Yes, I want to hear. I might as well know everything."

"Okay. I actually do a lot of extra work for him. I pore over catalogs and roam Web sites looking for new things I can surprise him with. I remember one evening in particular last summer. I showed up at his apartment at around nine o'clock. I had dressed specifically for him, with a light silk raincoat over my clothes. I had used a lot of mousse on my hair, then kinked and fluffed it. I wore deep-red lipstick, dark eyeliner, and mascara. I added heavy gold hoop earrings and a thick gold necklace. I was quite a sight.

"When Sloan answered the door he was wearing a pair of jeans that had been washed almost white and a tight navy blue T-shirt." She smiled wistfully. "He's in his forties with his hair carefully combed to camouflage his receding hairline." She leaned forward so she wouldn't have to raise her voice, laced her fingers, and remembered the evening as if it were yesterday. "He opened the door for me . . ."

"You look sensational, Brook. Come on in." Sloan closed the door behind her, then said, "What, no brown paper bag?"

"Nothing that simple," Brook said. She reached out and grabbed his hard erection through the zipper of his pants. "Disappointed?"

"Frankly, yes. I always enjoy your little surprises." He enfolded her in his arms. "However, you're delicious enough without any special treats." He kissed her full on the mouth. "You surprise me. I thought ladies like you didn't kiss on the mouth."

"Don't believe everything Julia Roberts says," she said. "I love your mouth." She wrapped her arms around his neck and licked the opening of his lips with her tongue. "Kissing is too wonderful to pass up." While they kissed, Brook pressed her pubic bone against his cock, rubbing and wiggling. "Come here," she said, sinuously rubbing her body against his.

"You're driving me to distraction, Brook," he groaned.

"Is that bad?" she purred.

He arched his back and, with a hand splayed in the small of her back, pressed her more firmly against his groin. "Not at all." He grabbed at her coat. "Take this off."

Coyly, she stepped back out of his reach. "You're in quite a hurry, aren't you?"

He grabbed for her as she danced away. "You bet. I've been thinking about you all evening."

They played chase around the bedroom for several minutes, both giggling like children. Finally Sloan grabbed her raincoat sleeve and pulled. As the coat fell away he just stared. Brook was wearing a skintight white leather skirt that ended about eight inches above her knees. Her cropped, short-sleeved top, which came only to the middle of her ribs, was made from a tight stretchy fabric the color of ripe watermelon. She had put a pushup bra beneath, creating deep shadowed cleavage above the low scooped neck. Her shoes were clear plastic with four-inch heels. "My God," he whispered. "You look like the poster child for hookers anonymous."

"Do you like me?"

"Shit, Brook, you're a gourmet feast for a starving man. Get over here."

"Not yet." She pushed against his chest and he fell back onto the bed. "Let me show you what you're getting tonight." She stood beside the bed and put her foot on the spread, allowing Sloan a good view of her crotch. "Like these shoes?" When he nodded she said, "I picked them up just for you." She waggled her foot. "I know you're kinky for ankle straps. Want to unbuckle me?"

As she watched, he used his trembling hands to unfasten the straps on the shoes. She grinned as she saw the effort it took for him to drag air into his lungs. "You really know how to make me crazy," he said, his voice hoarse.

"Lots of things make you crazy and I try to enjoy every one." She dropped the shoes on the floor but left her foot on the edge of the bed. "How about helping me take off these hose." She sighed. "They're so hot."

"Shit, baby, so am I," Sloan said. He slid his hands up her thigh until he reached the gartered top of her stocking. When his hands started to slide higher, she slapped his playfully. "Not so fast. Just the stocking."

"You're so hard on me."

Brook grinned, then leaned over and grabbed his erection through his slacks. "That's not the only thing around here that's hard." She stood back up. "The hose."

Slowly he pulled one garter and stocking down her leg, working it gently over her foot. She changed feet and he removed the stocking from the other foot. Then, still standing beside the bed, she pulled the top off over her head, revealing a dark pink lace bra that lifted her breasts and pushed them tightly together. Still wearing her skirt, she straddled his hips and pressed her tits against his face, burying his nose and mouth in the cleavage.

She felt his hands slip inside the bra and scoop out her flesh, pressing his face deeper into the valley between. "God, you could feel slashes of heat rocket through her body. *Amazing,* she thought, *that I come here to tease and please and I end up getting so much pleasure myself.*

After long minutes of sucking noises and heat, she stood up, helped him pull off his clothes, then removed her skirt. Naked, he lay back on the bed, his erection sticking straight up from his groin. Brook got her purse and found the two items she was looking for and placed them on the table beside the bed. Ripping open a foil package, she unrolled a ribbed condom, turned it inside out and stretched it over his erection. "I hear that those ribs feel great on the cock. You'll have to give me a solicited testimonial."

"Your panties?"

"Not to worry," she said, as she straddled his hips and slowly lowered her now-soaked pussy onto his shaft. The spilt crotch of the panties divided, allowing him to penetrate deep inside of her.

"Watching you with those panties on, and my cock buried in your sweet pussy is a gas." As she lowered herself fully onto him, he asked, "What the hell is that?"

"Ah, you feel my little friend." She knew he was now aware of the egg-shaped vibrator buried deep in her channel, resting against the tip of his cock. She grabbed a small electronic device from beside the bed and slowly pushed a slider.

"Oh my God," he said as the egg vibrated against him.

"Shit, that's fabulous," she said. "I've never turned it on before." She raised and lowered her hips and each time he reached her depths, she felt the vibrator pressing against him. It took less than a minute for him to bellow as he came.

She rolled over and he snuggled her against his side. "That little friend of yours is dynamite."

"I thought you'd like it. I bought it just for you."

"It's always an experience with you, Brook. A terrific experience."

"Wow," Rena said, whispering as Brook had so no one else in the visitors area would hear. "That was quite an evening."

Brook looked at Rena, a grin splitting her face. "That was one hell of a night."

Rena shook her head, obviously baffled. "You obviously enjoy what you do."

Brook sat forward and looked carefully at the younger woman. Somehow it was important for her to help Erika's daughter understand. "Listen, Rena, you'll have to make up your own mind as you meet some of the people who work for Courtesans, Inc. but just throw your preconceived notions out and listen. Like all the men and women who work with your mother and me, I enjoy the hell out of what I do. I go to expensive restaurants and lavish parties. I wear designer clothes and have my hair and nails done every week. I meet fascinating men with varied interests who, on the whole, treat me like the lady I like to think I am. I make great money so when I'm not out with a man I can do what I want, when I want."

"But where's your self-respect?"

"I have no problems with self-respect. I'm a terrific person who's worth every cent I'm paid. For the most part, the men I'm with respect me too."

"Some don't?"

"Occasionally I get treated like a piece of meat. However, if a man just wanted a place to put his erection, he could do it for a lot less than what I charge."

Rena shook her head. "I hear what you're saying but I just can't deal with it."

"You don't have to. All I want is for you to keep an open mind and judge for yourself. I hope you can do that."

"I can try."

Chapter

11

As Rena listened to Brook's story, she found it impossible not to be titillated by the overt sexuality. Rena had to admit that Brook certainly seemed to enjoy it. Who wouldn't? Hot sex and all that money. But it was short-term pleasure with no long-term goals, no ultimate payoff. No marriage and happily ever after. Okay, she didn't really believe in happily ever after, not in the real world. But what about stability, shared interests?

She thought about her father. He and Sandy had married and had a little girl, but it was only a year until they were embroiled in a long, acrimonious divorce. Rena was sad that, after all the animosity, she had a half sister whom she hadn't seen in several years. Vowing he'd never marry again, her father was now dating women almost as young as Rena, living on every dime of his enormous salary. He never came to the U.S., but invited Rena to spend weeks with him in a rented villa in Italy or a leased flat in London.

Maybe Brook was right. Live high and fast and suck as much juice out of things as you can. Maybe there was no brass ring. She pictured her mother living as Brook had described. No! It was just plain wrong. Her mother was fucking guys of all ages and tastes. Fucking, not making love. There was no love anywhere. This wasn't life; it was a sham. She suddenly knew she had to get her mother out of it. Sean could make it happen. Between the two of them they would shut Courtesans, Inc. down. She only had to gather information.

She refocused her eyes. "I'm sorry, Brook, I guess I just drifted away for a moment. If you think it's a good idea, I'll spend some time with a few of the"—she searched for a comfortable word— "employees and try to keep an open mind."

"Thanks. I know your mother would like that and it's the most either of us can ask." Brook stood. "Good morning, Stuart. You look like hell."

Rena stood also and turned to greet the man who had walked in behind her. "How is she?" he asked. Dressed casually as he had been the day before, today in slacks and a multicolored knit sweater, he looked strained and pale.

"The doctors are encouraged," Rena said, then repeated her earlier conversation with the neurologist.

"I'm glad," he said, letting a slow stream of air out of his lungs. "I'm delighted to see that you're still here, Rena."

"I decided to stick around for a few days," she said. "I've got everything I need with me on my laptop. I can work here as well as anywhere else." The three sat back down.

"Stuart," Brook said, "you'll never guess who showed up this morning. Valerie and Madison."

Stuart's smile made him look almost handsome. "I had a feeling that nothing could keep them away." He turned to Rena. "Did you get to meet them?" When she nodded, he continued, "What did you think?"

"They certainly aren't what I would have expected." For a retired prostitute and her husband. Although she didn't say them aloud, the words hung in the air as if they had been spoken.

"They're good people," Stuart said softly, "and that's a lot in this day and age."

Brook glanced at her watch. "It will be visiting time in a minute. Do you want to see her, Rena?"

"I've been there already so you go ahead." When Stuart nodded his agreement, Brook walked slowly toward the doors marked ICU.

Stuart's in love with my mother, Rena realized. *He knows what she is yet he loves her.* She shook her head. How could he? There were several minutes of awkward silence, then Rena said, "Brook tells me that you got my mother into her business." Despite her efforts, there was a nasty edge to her voice.

"Yes. She attended a dinner party with members of your father's firm and was compensated for the evening."

"Oh." Struggling for some conversation, she looked around, then said, "It's pretty quiet this morning. There are usually several people here by this hour."

"It's Sunday morning, Rena. Most of your mother's friends were out late last evening."

"Oh right," she snapped. "Big date night."

"Yes, that's right," he said softly, unwilling to be provoked.

"How can you put up with it? You seem to care about my mother so how can you let her do this?"

"Let her? This is her life and I've got no right to tell her how to lead it. I love her very much." His shoulders lifted as he sighed. "I feel really badly that I never really told her how much." He took off his glasses and rubbed the bridge of his nose. "When she's better, I'm going to ask her to marry me."

Rena's heart leaped. This was the solution. He'd get her out of the business and she wouldn't have to deal with the slimy Mr. Fredericks. "You won't let her continue doing what she's doing after you get married, will you?"

He slowly put his glasses back on. "First, I don't know whether she'll say yes. Second, it's her life and she can do what she wants. I wouldn't even consider asking her to quit."

"You wouldn't mind being married to a prostitute?"

"Rena, Erika's the woman I love, the way she is." He shook his head. "I know this thing shocks you and you'd prefer that she wasn't what she is, but it's not my business and not yours."

Why couldn't he understand? "From my perspective, it's the job of people who care about my mother to try to get her to see that what she's doing is wrong."

Stuart smiled. "Are you saying that you care about her?"

Shit. "I don't know what I'm saying, but I know that this is immoral."

"Morality is in the eye of the beholder."

"Ridiculous. There are certain things that are just wrong. Killing is wrong for example. End of sentence."

"Killing is wrong. What about in self-defense? What about killing to protect the lives of your children?"

"Of course. That goes without saying . . ."

"So killing isn't always wrong. I will admit, however, that there are things that are categorically wrong." Stuart's voice was low yet adamant. "Abusing someone who's weaker than you or who, for whatever reason, has no choices. Child abuse, spousal abuse. But here we have consenting adults. I find your point of view a bit narrow."

"You would," Rena said, now furious. "You and Brook justify what my mother does and it won't work." Her voice dropped to a loud hiss. "She's a whore and no one's going to convince me that it's okay." She grabbed her jacket and stormed toward the coffee alcove.

Standing in front of the coffee machine, she fisted and unfisted her hands, unable to understand their attitude. It wasn't okay. Not her mother. She knew that her feelings were bouncing back and forth, and she couldn't stop it. Did she hate her mother for being a prostitute or for being a bad mother? All she could be sure of was that she didn't want to be the daughter of a hooker. Trembling, she tried to relax her shoulders and slow her breathing.

Slowly she put on her jacket and spent several hours walking the streets of New York, trying not to think about anything. When she returned to the hospital, she sat at her mother's bedside for her allotted five minutes listening to the rhythmic whine and throb of the machines, smelling the disinfectant, watching the angular pattern of the readouts. "Oh, Mother, how could you? I understand that you were young and scared, but you didn't have to turn to prostitution." Tears rolling down her cheeks, she continued, "You had me. Why did you do this to me?"

When the nurse finally insisted that she leave, she found the ladies' room, splashed cold water on her face, then wandered back into the waiting room. Only Mei Lee sat in the sterile room, reading a magazine. She looked up as Rena entered. "How is she?"

"About the same. The doctor told me this morning that he was encouraged, but it is still a long road back to who knows where."

"I'm so sorry. How are you holding up?" She seemed genuinely concerned.

"I'm okay." Maybe now is the time to start doing some investigation. "Listen, I am a bit hungry. Do you know any place around here where I could get a bite of lunch?"

"Sure. There are lots of luncheonettes and stuff."

"Would you like to join me? I've been doing lots of talking to Brook and she thought it would help me understand everything here if I talked to some of my mom's . . ." she fumbled, ". . . friends."

"Friends. Yes, we're all friends, and we work together. Is that what you want to talk about? Courtesans, Inc.?"

Rena took a deep breath. "I'm sorry. This isn't easy for me."

Mei took Rena's long-fingered hand in her tiny one. "Don't be upset. If I were in your shoes, I would be having a real hard time with this too. Most of my family has no idea what I do. My husband knows, of course, but my folks would absolutely freak."

"You're married?"

"Yup. Chuck's home with the kids so I can be here with Erika. I know she isn't aware of who's around, but somehow I need to be here. I've already eaten, but I'd be happy to sit with you. Maybe I can give you some insights into your mother that you couldn't get from anyone else. I remember when she first started with Valerie."

Rena pulled on her jacket and together the two women found a place for lunch. Since it was already after two, the place they found was quiet and they sat at a table in the back where they could have relative privacy. Rena ordered a tuna sandwich and tea while Mei had a Diet Coke and a salad.

When the waitress left for the kitchen, Rena asked, "If you were around when my mother began, you've been doing this for a long time. You look like such a baby."

"It's said that Oriental women don't show their age. Actually I'm thirty-six."

Rena was flabbergasted. "I would have guessed about twenty or so."

Mei beamed. "I know. I don't know what it is, but I still get proofed when I order wine in a restaurant. It's been quite an embarrassment from time to time, on dates and stuff. When I go out with Chuck and the kids, and they call me Mommy, I get the strangest looks, like Chuck robbed the cradle or something. My boys are twelve and ten."

"Amazing." She wanted to tread lightly. "Tell me about your husband."

"He's an accountant and he's recently started his own tax business so he works at home. It's great for the boys to have him at ball games."

"Sounds like he's quite successful." She fumbled. "Why?"

"Why do I continue working? Frankly, because I like it and the money pays for college for the kids, long summer vacations for all of us, a really nice house on the island, and lots of things we wouldn't be able to afford otherwise."

"Doesn't your husband object?"

"Not usually. Sometimes he gets a little jealous, particularly with some of my regulars, but I usually tell him about my evenings and that leads to a night of great sex. It really turns him on to hear about my escapades."

"You're kidding."

Mei's giggle was charming. "Nope. There are many men who are turned on by sexy stories."

"About you and other men?" Rena didn't get it.

"Amazingly enough, yes. You have to realize how it began with us. I had two kids and was already working when we met. I told him right off what I did for a living and that I had children to support and wasn't going to give it up. He had real trouble at first, but eventually he adjusted and asked me to marry him. Once we were married, we discussed my retiring, but he found he could deal with it, and the money's a seductive lure. Maybe I'll quit eventually, but for now I'm having too much fun."

Rena shook her head in wonder. Here was another woman who loved being a prostitute. "Brook told me how much she enjoyed it, but it's really hard for me to wrap my mind around it."

"I can imagine. When some of us get together and talk, it seems so bizarre, but it works."

"If it's not prying, I'd be interested in hearing about some of your experiences."

"Sure, if you think it would help you to understand. Erika's such a wonderful person, but I can see that it would be a bit of a shock for you."

"Shock is a small word for it."

Mei stared at Rena. It wasn't difficult to sense that all wasn't good between the younger woman and her mother, and that surprised Mei tremendously. She could think of nothing more wonderful than having Erika for a mother. She wasn't about to tell this almost stranger about all the times Erika had helped her through tough moments when she and her first husband were still married. He had been all for her job, but had also reasoned that if she was a prostitute, she should be able to satisfy all his needs, whether she wanted to or not. Seven years earlier, when he had become physically abusive, Mei had left with only her pocketbook, a diaper bag, and two small children. She had lived with Erika for almost three months until she was on her feet, then Erika had helped her find a lawyer who settled things with her husband and got him out of her life for good.

She had met Chuck a year later when she enrolled in a college literature seminar. She had taken the course both for enjoyment and to become better able to discuss books with her steady customers, and Chuck had been enrolled for pure pleasure. He had asked her out for coffee after class one evening. On Erika's advice, Mei had told him on their next date what she did for a living. To her surprise, he hadn't been shocked or disgusted. He had met her boys and quickly fell in love with her and with them. They had married six months later. The past five years had been pure pleasure for both of them. He still loved the idea of a ready-made family, with Little League and the PTA.

The waitress arrived, put their food on the table, and disappeared into the front of the restaurant. "Have you been with any famous people?" Rena asked.

"Sure. That's a lot of what we do. I've got a number of regulars whose names you'd know."

"Tell me what it's like, maybe a typical evening."

Mei grinned as she forked some lettuce into her mouth, chewed, and swallowed. "There aren't really typical evenings, but I can tell you about a recent one if you'd like to hear. Let's just refer to the guy as Joe. I know he wouldn't want his name revealed."

"Don't worry. I have no intention of telling anyone."

Mei took another bite of salad and wondered how much Rena was ready for. "Do you want all the lurid details?"

Rena leaned forward. "Maybe I'm a bit perverted, but I think I'd like to hear the details."

"You're not perverted at all. I last saw this guy a few weeks ago. As I always do, I called him about three in the morning, fifteen minutes before I was due to arrive." She remembered it all vividly.

"Hi, sugar," she said into the phone, her voice pitched low and breathy.

"Mei, baby," he said. "I can't wait to see you. You're not going to be late, are you?"

"Not at all. I was just wondering whether you were ready for me."

"Ready? I've got a hard-on the size of a tree trunk."

"I have a surprise for you, but I want you to do something for me first."

"Okay, baby, anything."

"While we talk, I want you to take off your shirt so your beautiful hairy chest is exposed."

She heard him put the phone down and clothing rustle. "I did it, baby."

"Now your pants and shorts. Do it for me, sugar." Mei waited, twisting a strand of her long black hair around her finger.

"Done. I'm buck naked."

"Good. Stand up and look down. Can you see your cock?"

"Sure, baby. It's sticking straight out, looking for you."

"I'll be there soon enough. I want you to take the phone in your right hand and hold your cock with your left."

"Hold my cock?"

"Slowly wrap your fingers around it. Come on, sugar. Do it for me."

She heard Joe hesitate, then he said, "Okay. I've got my hand around my cock."

Mei grinned. She loved phone games. "You wouldn't kid me, would you?"

She heard a great sigh. "No, baby, but I don't want to shoot my load before you get here."

"Are you really that hot?" Mei asked.

"I'm hot as a pistol."

"Well, I wouldn't want you to ruin everything by coming too quickly. Maybe you'd better slow down a bit. After you hang up, I want you to go into the bathroom and take a nice relaxing shower. I want you squeaky clean and ready to last a long time. You know how we like to play."

"I can't wait."

"Oh, in case you're not out of the shower when I get there, unlock the door for me, will you, sugar?"

"Oh baby, I can't wait." When she heard him hang up she put her cell phone back into her purse and picked up her travel case from the floor just outside Joe's hotel room. She heard the door latch click. She knew he would do what she had asked, so she waited half a minute for him to turn on the shower, then entered the hotel suite. The room was done in elegant simplicity, with classically designed furniture, Turkish carpeting with several modern paintings on the wall. In the Presidential Suite, at $750 a night, she reasoned that the art work was genuine.

She hung the *Do Not Disturb* sign on the door and locked it, then crossed the room, kicking off her shoes so she could move silently. At the bathroom door, she set her case down, quickly removed all her clothes, then quietly went inside and put her case on the gray and red granite counter. The room was white tile with red and gold floral tile insets, gold fixtures, and thick yellow towels. There were two yellow full-length terry cloth robes hanging on the back of the door, with the hotel logo on the pocket. Ignoring all the luxury, she opened the case and withdrew a flesh-colored dildo with a wide flange around its base. Over the sound of the shower she could hear Joe humming.

Putting the dildo on the floor where she could easily reach it, she moved the curtain aside and stepped into the shower, pressing her back against the wall to postpone the moment when he became aware of her. Still oblivious, Joe soaped his arms. Silently she reached around him, took the soap from him and pressed her breasts against his slippery back. "Hi, sugar. I thought you might like some company." She lathered her hands, then grabbed his only partially erect cock and rubbed.

"I love it when you surprise me, Mei," he said, looking down, "but I want to make this last, so you'd better stop that."

"Don't worry, sugar, I won't disappoint you." Water streaming over them, Mei released his now fully erect cock and soaped his back and buttocks. "I just want to play in the water." With lathered hands, she picked up the dildo and rubbed soap over the surface until it was slippery. "Put your hands on the wall, spread your legs and lean forward," she said. "I wouldn't want you to fall."

When he had done as she had asked, she rubbed a soapy finger over his anus, then turned the water off. "Ready, sugar?"

"Shit, Mei. I'm always ready for you."

Mei reached around and held his erection as she set the scene. "Okay, here's the situation. You're a man who's never been penetrated before. You've been taking a shower and your roommate, a handsome guy with a gigantic cock that you've admired, slips into the shower behind you. Can you picture that?"

"Shit, yes. Describe him for me."

Mei knew Joe's preferences well. He wasn't gay, but the idea of being with a man excited and repelled him simultaneously, a particularly arousing combination. "He's very dark, with black hair and eyes almost as dark. He's got a full beard and moustache and his chest, arms, and legs are covered with dark hair too. He's at least six feet five and built like a football tackle, huge shoulders, arms and legs. All you can think about is his muscular body, but it also embarrasses you to think of how he turns you on." Mei could feel Joe's rising excitement as his cock twitched and throbbed. He groaned softly.

"He's behind you and you can hear his heavy breathing, feel his hot breath on your back." She licked his skin. "He reaches around, grabs your cock, laughs, and says, 'I knew you'd be easy.' You're not easy, are you, Joe?"

"No. I don't want to be excited by him, but I am."

"I know, and he knows too. His cock is enormous. You can't see it, yet you know. Your mind is filled with the image of his gigantic dick. You know what you want and what he's going to do, yet it terrifies you." She felt him tremble, glad his hands were braced to prevent falling. "He knows you want it." She placed the tip of the dildo against Joe's anus. "You try to stop it, hold every muscle tight, but it's no use. He's too powerful for you." She pushed the dildo against his tight sphincter until it released, allowing the plastic to enter his body. "It's impossible for you to keep it out," she purred, the stall adding its steamy heat to the arousal of the moment.

"Oh, God," he groaned, his body shaking.

Slowly she pushed the dildo deeper, squeezing his cock tightly as she did so. She slid her fingers to the base of his shaft and circled it with her thumb and forefinger. As she tightened her grip, she knew she would prevent his ejaculation. "He's pushing his hard cock deeper and deeper into your body. You want him to stop, yet you don't because it feels so good. Admit it. Tell him how good it feels." When he remained silent, she held the dildo still. "Tell him. Do it."

"Oh God," he groaned. "It feels so good."

"Should he stop?"

"God, no."

She pressed harder until the dildo was lodged firmly in his ass.

Then she began withdrawing it, and forcing it back in, using her body weight to drive it deeper. "You want to come, don't you?"

"Yes."

Mei smiled. She knew exactly what Joe wanted and often created scenarios to increase his excitement. "He's laughing at you, sugar. You're so easy. He knew he'd be able to fuck your ass and he knew you'd like it. You want more. Tell me what you want."

"I want . . ."

"You want what?"

"I can't say it."

"You want him to fuck your ass. You want *me* to fuck your ass. Say it." When he hesitated, she said again, "Say it."

"I want you to fuck my ass," he said, the words exploding from him.

Mei released her grip on the base of his cock and he screamed as he came, semen erupting in great spurts. Slowly, as he calmed, she withdrew the dildo. In silence, they soaped, rinsed, and dried each other, then swathed each other in thick towels. Barely able to walk, Joe collapsed on the bed. "I'm sure you're the devil," he said.

Mei's laugh was soft. "I certainly am, and you love every minute of it."

"Every minute. There's an extra three hundred on the dresser for you," he said. "For services above and beyond."

She dressed, then pocketed the money. "Call me whenever," she said, then slipped from the room.

"You knew exactly what he wanted, didn't you?" Rena said when she finished her story. This was exactly what she'd wanted, but she needed to know who this personality was and when and where it had happened. Tread slowly, she told herself.

"Of course. That's my job, and my pleasure."

Rena leaned forward. "I know I shouldn't ask, but is his name really Joe?"

Mei whispered. "I know I shouldn't tell, but after all, you're Erika's daughter. His name's Mickey Hernandez."

"The guy from that soap?" Rena couldn't help being impressed. Mickey Hernandez starred in *The Passions of Darnley Place*, a new and phenomenally popular daytime series, and was on the cover of every magazine in the supermarket.

"The very same."

"I thought he was very straight."

"That's what everyone's supposed to think and actually he is. He just enjoys the fantasy, being forced to do something he views as really evil. "

"People are excited by something that repels them?"

"On occasion. It's what I refer to as delicious fear. The situation is exciting and so is the fear."

Rena considered what Mei said, then realized she needed details. "I'll bet he's changed recently. I mean that evening was quite awhile ago."

"Several months ago, as I remember it, but we've been together so many times that I can't keep exact track."

Although Rena didn't have exactly what she wanted, she sensed that she couldn't push any further, and she did have her first piece of hard information for Sean. To cover her grin, she took a bite of her sandwich, which had been untouched until then. Fabulous. Just fabulous.

She called Sean that evening, and they arranged to meet at the same little bar they had gone to earlier in the week. He told her that it was easiest for him since he lived just three blocks away.

He arrived at the table a few minutes after Rena, soaking wet from the cold rain falling on the city. He ordered two beers from a waitress he obviously knew named Betts, then snapped, "Okay, what have you got for me." When she raised her eyebrows, he apologized. "Sorry for being so abrupt. I'm really stressed. My wife and kids were being a pain in my ass all day and I've been overrun with in-laws. God, even in this rain it's a relief to be out of that apartment."

His wife? She didn't think of him as being married. "Your wife doesn't mind that you go out at night?"

"We lead pretty independent lives. As long as I help her take care of the kids, and bring home a paycheck, she's okay with whatever I do." His face softened at the mention of his children. *Okay, he's a family man*, Rena thought. It made him more human somehow. Sean asked, "So, how's your mother?"

"She's still in a coma, but they say she's improving. Personally I don't see it, but the doctors seem enthused. I'm really sorry to have gotten you out on a Sunday evening, but I was just so excited."

"No problem." He took a long swallow on his beer. "Thank God the in-laws are gone, and my kids were in bed and fast asleep when I left. My wife was watching a movie I've already seen so I told her I had a business contact to meet. I don't even think she noticed."

Sean handed her a folder thick with papers. She scanned the pages and, although she was no lawyer, she found the paragraphs she thought relevant and read them through twice. It seemed to say that if any harm came to Erika Holland or Brook Torrance, through the actions of Sean Fredericks or *The National Informer*, the bond would be paid.

"That's your copy," Sean said, impatiently. "You can read it over twenty times later."

Since it all seemed in order, Rena handed Sean an envelope. Since she couldn't imagine telling Sean about Mickey Hernandez and Mei in the shower, she had typed it all out. "It's about Mickey Hernandez, kinky sex, some time several months ago."

His eyes widened. "Mickey Hernandez? That's fantastic. He's got a reputation for being Mr. Clean." He skimmed the page of printed data. "Sometime several months ago?" he snapped.

"Couldn't you have gotten more hard facts? I mean dates, places. Things he can't easily deny."

Mildly deflated, she said, "I got what I could. I certainly couldn't appear to be pumping Mei for information. Give me a few days and I'll find out the rest."

The annoyed look on his face vanished to be replaced by a rueful smile. "My turn to apologize again. I know you're doing the best you can. It's just that I can't write stories without some facts to hang it on. Without specifics, this isn't publishable."

Disappointed, Rena said, "Okay. I'll see what I can do."

"Listen, thanks for all that you've done so far." She watched his deliberately ingenuous smile show his smooth white teeth. He wasn't Mr. Congeniality, but he didn't have to be. He was a means to an end for her, as she was for him. He leaned back and stuffed the envelope in his jacket pocket. "I can't wait to read your notes more carefully and I know you'll get additional verifiable stuff to make it all stick. I want to be able to connect it all to Courtesans, Inc. so we can put it out of business once and for all. Do you think you can get more for me?"

We make really strange bedfellows, Rena thought, then smiled inwardly at her double entendre. "I can try. Everyone's being really cooperative, trying to help me understand what my mother does."

"Do you understand it?"

Did she? She had to admit to herself that she was a bit more open-minded than she had been twenty-four hours earlier. But she still didn't want her mother having any part of it. "No. Not really and certainly not for my mother." She took a few sips of her beer, then got up to leave. "I'm really beat so I'll let you get back home."

He remained seated. "I hang out here pretty regularly so I think I'll stick around for a while. You know, unwind before I go home and cope."

"Sure." She slipped her coat on and said good night. As she

approached the door, she saw him reopen the envelope, read the contents and smile. As she left, he waved at her and gave her the okay sign.

Several minutes later she returned to the bar to retrieve the umbrella she'd left on the floor beneath the table. As she left for the second time, she saw Sean wander toward a pair of women, a slightly overweight redhead and a slender woman with ebony skin, seated at the bar. They looked barely old enough to drink. He deftly slipped between them, draped an arm over each woman's shoulder, and ordered another beer.

Chapter
12

During the day on Monday, the doctors ran another battery of tests and later met with Rena and Brook. "Things look better than we had expected," Dr. Freed said. "The body's an amazing machine and often we doctors only have to support it while it takes care of itself." He looked at Rena. "Your mother's coma is lessening and we hope that during the week she should be starting to return to us."

"You mean she'll wake up?" Brook said.

"Not all at once. Emerging from a coma isn't like what you see in movies. The patient doesn't just open her eyes and ask for lunch. If things go as we expect, she'll start to be able to respond to simple commands, open her eyes, squeeze a hand, and slowly, probably over a period of days, she'll be able to communicate. Only then will we know how much residual damage there is."

"That's wonderful news," Rena said, surprised at the elation she felt.

"Things still could surprise us and turn sour, but we're all very hopeful."

"What kind of residual damage might there be?" Rena asked, unsure whether she really wanted to hear the answer.

"I won't kid you," Dr. Freed said. "There could be any one of a number of problems. Partial paralysis, speech difficulties, problems with concentration, memory loss. I wouldn't borrow trouble right now, though. Try to stay upbeat until we know more."

"Thanks, Doctor," Brook said.

Without taking his eyes off Brook, the doctor said, "I'm heading down to the cafeteria. Do either of you ladies need to eat? You have to keep up your strength."

"Actually," Brook said, "I was just going down there myself. May I join you?"

Rena looked from Brook to Dr. Freed and felt distinctly like a third wheel. There was some kind of chemistry at work and she wasn't part of it. "Thanks, I ate a little while ago. You two go ahead." She couldn't help but wonder whether Brook would tell Dr. Freed about her "occupation."

Over the next few days, Rena managed to work on a few of her ongoing projects, e-mailing back and forth with her Web site customers, all of whom were very solicitous and cooperative. She also called Sean several times, saddened that she hadn't been able to get any new information for him. Although he had sounded impatient, he encouraged her to keep trying. On Wednesday she had dinner with Valerie and Brook before the older woman left to return to Dallas.

Brook appeared and disappeared, carving out time from the business to be at the hospital several hours each day. Stuart spent almost all day and evening in the waiting room or at Erika's bedside and he and Rena talked a great deal. Rena couldn't help but like the older man and learned the depth of his feelings for her mother.

When Rena visited Erika's bedside, the nurses suggested that she try to get her mother to respond by squeezing her hand or making some sound. So far, nothing had penetrated Erika's coma.

On Thursday afternoon Rena returned to the waiting room

after spending time with her mother. She thought she had felt her mother's hand tightening on hers on command, but she couldn't be sure.

Shara sat off to one side, working on a piece of needlework. "How is she?" she asked. Although Rena knew Shara was also twenty-three, today she looked very much like a beautiful sixteen-year-old, wearing scuffed sneakers, jeans, and a green and black sweater with a black shirt beneath. Her chocolate skin needed no makeup and her almost black eyes were wide with concern.

"My mother's being moved to something called a step-down unit tomorrow," Rena said. "With the ventilator gone, there's really no need for the intense monitoring. It's almost a week and I'm hoping she'll come around soon."

Shara took Rena's hands in her long slender fingers. "It must be frustrating for you."

It is difficult, Rena thought. *All I want right now is to finish with Sean, see my mother regain consciousness, and go back to Chicago.* Yet somehow, going back to Chicago didn't sound as good as it had a few days earlier. She'd begun to like Brook and Stuart and, she had to admit, some of Erika's employees too. *No*, she thought, *not employees, Erika's friends.* "Thanks. As I get to know you folks, I realize that it's just as difficult for you."

"We all care very much. Erika's been like a best friend to many of us."

Rena took a deep breath. This might be a good time to try for more of Sean's information. "We haven't gotten to spend much time together and I've been trying to get to know about my mother's business. If you don't mind my being nosy, tell me a little about you."

"It's not nosy," Shara said. "I can understand how confusing this must be for you. Brook confided in me that you didn't know about what your mother did until you got here."

Might as well admit it. "We haven't been on the best of terms for several years, and I didn't know about Courtesans, Inc., until this week. It is taking a bit of getting used to."

Shara laughed, then said, "Getting used to? That's probably the understatement of the year."

Rena shook her head ruefully. "Yeah. It's been hard."

"So, about me. I'm not married or anything. I have a boyfriend and we see each other once or twice a week between business evenings but I'm still free and available."

"Does he know what you do?"

"No. He's not important enough to me to tell him and endure the hassle that the information causes."

"What kind of hassle?"

Shara raised an eyebrow. "You're not that naive, are you?"

Rena smiled. "No. Sorry. How long have you known my mother?"

"About two years. I was a secretary in her accountant's office. I knew what she did for a living of course, but when I first saw her I couldn't help but be impressed by her friendly attitude. She's such a nice person and she didn't even complain when she had to wait for almost an hour one afternoon. While she waited, we talked and hit it off immediately. The next time I saw her I asked about her business and whether she ever needed ladies of color."

"What did she say?"

"She told me that color didn't enter into much of what she did. Sometimes she had a call from a man with a particular ethnic preference but usually it wasn't important. She asked whether I was interested, and I was. That was about it. I've been working for her ever since."

Rena wanted to steer the conversation around to Shara's clients. "Do you entertain many famous people?"

"Sure. That's what many of my dates are, celebrities who want it simple and anonymous." She winked. "And who can afford it."

"I know. A few other women have told me about the need for anonymity. Why do they need to pay for sex? Don't these guys have all the women they can handle, so to speak? I mean with groupies and such, I would think that famous people like that could get anything they wanted."

"The key is anonymous. They don't want to be splashed on the front page of every tabloid in the world because some sweet thing kisses, then tells all. Their privacy is one of the most important things to them."

Rena tried not to feel guilty about the spying she was doing. "I never thought about it that way."

"I've been with politicians, even a state governor. That was quite something. I was whisked into the state house in a limo with all the windows so darkly tinted I could barely see out. I was hoping to do it on the governor's desk. I thought that would be a gas, but instead I did the Monica Lowinsky thing in a broom closet, then was whisked away again."

"The governor of New York State?"

"No," Shara said, obviously unwilling to divulge any more details. "I've done it with a visiting sheik or something in the presidential suite at the Waldorf and the head male dancer, whatever you call it, from a ballet company. I always thought of ballet dancers as gay. Boy, let me tell you, he sure wasn't." With an exaggerated movement, she fanned herself with her hand.

Shara leaned forward and lowered her voice. "I guess I can brag just a bit. Last week I was invited to a party given by Kisses. You know, the rock group."

"You're kidding," she said.

Shara giggled. "Think about it. Six cute, sexy guys in their early twenties and they can't even go to McDonald's without being mobbed. What do they do for entertainment?" When Rena remained silent, Shara continued with a wide grin, "They call me, of course."

"Can you tell me about it?" Rena asked. She needed dates and places. "Last week, you said?"

"Actually it was last Thursday, the night before your mother's accident. Their business manager had called Erika and told her that the guys had a night off between concerts at the Meadowlands and wanted to throw a party. They were using the manager's big house in Westchester and he wanted three girls. I thought I'd died and gone to rock star heaven when Erika called. I had another date, but Erika had worked everything out for me. We were paid two thousand each, but I think I would have done it for free."

"She knows you're a fan, I guess."

"A fan? Me? Kisses? Who wouldn't be?" She lowered her voice a notch more. "I know they are supposed to appeal mostly to teenyboppers, but I have all their albums."

Rena thought that, although Shara was little more than a teenybopper herself, having been successful in the business for a while, she was also probably more grown-up than many adults. "Did you get the guys to sign them?"

"You know, I actually thought about it, but no, I'm too much of a professional to do that. They sent a limo for the three of us. In the car going up the parkway, Carolynn, Alissa, and I all admitted that we were more than a little excited. The house was enormous with iron gates that had to be opened by a uniformed guard. There was a driveway so long that it was almost five minutes before we got to the house.

"We were shown inside and there they were. It was all I could do not to collapse. All six guys were stripped to the waist, already partying, if you know what I mean. I tried to look cool and calm but my heart was pounding."

"Partying?"

"You know, women draped all over the room, lots of booze and stuff."

"Stuff? Do you mean they're into drugs?"

"I didn't see anyone take anything, but I think all those rock people are into something. I talked to Sammy Seven a month or so ago."

Sammy Seven had more than a dozen gold records and several Grammy awards. "Sammy Seven," Rena sighed, trying not to sound like the groupie she felt like. She'd had a crush on the handsome singer for years.

"Sammy and I talked for a while afterward. He had done a lot of cocaine and I asked him why he needed that. He said, 'Can you imagine what it's like to have to go out on stage, night after night, whether you've got a stomachache or a head cold. You gotta be on. You have to sing your heart out and sound just like you sound on the records. No improv, no nothing.' I asked him why and he explained, 'Everyone in the audience has my records and has memorized every track. They want me to sound exactly like the song they're playing in their head. Sometimes I'm just not up for it, so I take something to improve my mood.' You know," Shara said to Rena, "somehow I sympathize."

"For all that money," Rena said, with a note of sarcasm, "there have to be some sacrifices."

The remark seemed to go over Shara's head. "They do go through a lot. Anyway, it's not up to me to judge their lifestyle, just to be there when they want company."

"So tell me about Kisses." She had two of their albums, and could picture the six hunky guys half naked.

"At your mother's suggestion, I was wearing a light pink beaded tank top and a long flowered broomstick skirt. She didn't want me to appear too sophisticated, yet not too young either so I wore only light makeup. Have you met Alissa?"

"Not yet," Rena said.

"She's about my age and Carolynn, you met her didn't you? Well she's a bit older."

Rena remembered that Carolynn was probably almost thirty.

"Anyway, the house was tremendous and we were shown into

a huge room with a wall filled with sound equipment and a giant-screen TV. It was tuned to MTV, but the sound was turned way down. One of Kisses' albums was playing real loud." Shara allowed herself to be transported back to that night.

"Hi, ladies," Chad said, his body draped around a slender blonde as she bent over the pool table in the corner. "Join us." Shara watched him reach around and tweak the blonde's nipple as she drew the cue back.

"Stop that," the blonde giggled. "How do you expect me to make my shot with you doing that?"

"I don't. That way I win, both the game and you."

As she listened to the blonde giggle again, she looked at her clients for the evening. All six rock singers were dressed in jeans, and nothing else. They all had their trademark golden kiss logo around their neck, a two-carat diamond between pursed gold lips. She looked for the tattoo, the Kiss'n Lips, on each man's biceps.

Shara was handed a glass of champagne and settled on a long white leather sofa between Hector and Patrick. "Hello, gorgeous," Patrick said. In person he had a trace of a British accent and Hector's "You're quite something," had a bit of a Spanish flavor. Ricky, the tall, bald drummer seemed to be trying to teach a half-naked redhead how to correctly hold a pair of drumsticks while BJ and Ken quickly monopolized Carolynn and Alissa.

"I think this one's mine," Patrick said, blue eyes gazing at her beneath almost feminine blond lashes.

"Who says?" Hector snapped back, deep brown eyes flashing. He grabbed Shara's head and kissed her, tongue insinuating itself deep in her mouth.

Shara shivered. *I'm being fought over by two members of Kisses.* "Listen, guys," she said, pulling back slightly, "there's plenty of me to go around. I'm Shara."

"Yeah. We can all party. I wouldn't leave out my best friend. I'm Patrick, and he's Hector."

She saw that Patrick had no tattoo. "Where's your Kiss'n Lips?" she asked without thinking. It wasn't up to her to ask anything about anything, but the words were already out.

Hector roared. Through his laughter, he said, "Patrick here's afraid of needles so his 'tattoo' is inked on before every show."

"Shut up, asshole," Patrick said. "These lips are the only ones that matter." He pressed his mouth against Shara's.

Patrick's kiss was just as deep as Hector's and she tunneled her fingers through his surfer-blond curly hair. "Yes," Shara said when Patrick came up for air, "they certainly are."

Running long thick fingers through his shoulder-length almost-black hair, Hector looked at Patrick. "Wanna play? I mean really play?"

"Always," Patrick said. "What delicious thing are you cooking up?" He turned to Shara. "He's the creative one of the group."

"I'll just bet," Shara said. She was in heaven.

"I've got a great idea. I've always wanted to play in that exercise room of Burt's." He stood up, grabbed Shara's hand and pulled her up beside him.

"That's not the kind of exercise I had in mind," Patrick said.

"Me neither. Trust me."

"You've got the creative mind," Patrick said with a deep mock-bow. "Lead on."

With Shara's hand firmly clutched in his, Hector led the way through the house and down a flight of rear stairs. An exercise room had been set up in a room larger than many health clubs. There was a treadmill, a weight bench with a huge set of assorted weights, and exercise machines to tone every part of the body. "You guys must use this stuff a lot," Shara said, gazing hungrily at the sleek upper torsos of the two men.

"Actually," Hector said, "I'm the workout nut. Patrick here is a confirmed couch potato." He grabbed the hem of Shara's top. "Take this stuff off."

With no hesitation, Shara removed her tank top and skirt.

"Leave the rest," Patrick said. "You make me hungry just that way."

The walls were all fully mirrored and Shara glanced at herself. She wore white stockings and sandals, with a lacy white bra and matching panty, all of which stood out against her cocoa skin.

"I'm in heaven," Hector said. "I've always fantasized about using this room for a different kind of exercise." He walked over to a leg-press machine and patted the seat. "Sit here."

Shara settled on the seat. "Let's see how good you are," Hector said.

"At what?" Shara said with a glint in her eyes.

"Everything." He explained how the machine worked and Shara put her feet behind the bar. "I'll give you just a little weight." Hector said. "Now lift with your lower legs."

Shara extended her legs until they were parallel to the ground. "Okay," Hector said, "now the idea is that you can't let the weights down."

Since there was only slight downward pressure from the light weights, Shara held the legs straight with little difficulty. "No matter what," Hector said, moving behind her.

Quickly Hector's hands were cupping her breasts while Patrick, quickly getting the idea, straddled her upper thighs and pressed his mouth against hers.

Unable to move, Shara kissed Patrick, moaning slightly deep in her throat. Hector's fingers slipped inside her bra to fondle her naked tits. With her legs still outstretched, she cupped the back of Patrick's head and deepened the kiss, her tongue dueling with his.

After long minutes, Patrick leaned back. "God, lady, you've got a great mouth."

"Great boobs too," Hector said, and Shara realized that her bra was gone. Hector's fingers pinched her nipples hard, making her jump and causing her legs to fall. The machine dropped with a clang.

"I'm not used to getting this kind of a workout," Shara said as she massaged her thighs.

"Let me do that," Patrick said, getting off her lap and using his long fingers to knead her quaking muscles. Hector crouched beside her until he could take one turgid nipple in his mouth, rolling it over his tongue and pressing it against the back of his teeth. Shara just relaxed and let the men play, feeling her pussy swell and fluids seep out between her inner lips.

All too soon, Hector stood up. "This one," he said, patting the seat of an inner thigh machine. Shara sat on the seat and Hector lifted one leg onto each extension of the machine. The object of the machine was to work out the inner thighs by pressing your legs together against the resistance of whatever weight the trainer felt appropriate. It was an awkward position, legs spread, held apart at the inside of the knee and ankle. Hector adjusted the seat back until it was slightly reclined, then used an elastic strap to bind her to it just below her breasts. "That will keep you from moving," he purred.

"God," Patrick said, looking at Shara's vulnerable body, "she looks like a feast set out for a starving man."

"Two starving men," Hector added. He turned some control and the machine stretched her legs wider apart. "That should do it," he said. "Now the object is to try to pull your legs together."

Shara strained, but couldn't move her legs. "I think there's a bit too much weight."

"Not for what I have in mind."

Shara tried again to press her legs together but to no avail. Experimentally she tried to lift her legs off of the supports, but she was spread at such an awkward angle that she couldn't get her legs off the machine. Although she was restrained at chest and legs, her arms were free and she wasn't nervous. Just very turned on.

"I hope you didn't want these panties," Hector said, approaching her with a pair of shears. Quickly he cut across the crotch of her panties. When the cold metal touched her steaming pussy, she groaned.

"Have you ever seen a more beautiful display?" Patrick asked. "Look."

He pointed to a mirrored wall and Shara saw herself, wide open, available, arranged for a man's pleasure. Both men had brought their drinks with them, and Hector took a mouthful of ice and cold liquid. Then he knelt between Shara's legs and, his mouth still full of chilled alcohol, licked the length of her slit. The shocking cold almost numbed her tissues and she nearly screamed. As the heat dissipated, the warmth of his mouth heated her entire body.

While Hector alternately froze and heated her pussy, Patrick removed her shoes and stockings and began to suck on her toes. She had always had extremely sensitive feet so both men were driving her crazy. Quickly both men removed their jeans and Shara definitely appreciated the fact that neither man wore underwear. Two giant, erect phalluses bobbed and bounced, ready for their own exercise.

Patrick took his place between Shara's legs and his tongue danced over her soaked pussy, while Hector stood beside the machine rubbing his cock over her nipple. Shara watched in the mirrored wall, becoming more aroused at the sight of her body being ravished by the two handsome men.

"Mouth," Hector announced.

"Good. I want cunt," Patrick said. "Whoever holds out longest wins."

Shara suspected that this was a game that the two men had often played. Well, she'd be the winner. Hector rubbed his thick phallus over her face, then pushed it between her lips, while Patrick donned a condom and thrust his cock into Shara's pussy. "One, two, three," Hector said.

The two men drove into her body in similar rhythms. Having no particular favorite, Shara decided to play with both of them, wondering whether she could control them enough for them to ejaculate simultaneously. She twisted slightly and grabbed Hector's balls in one hand and Patrick's in the other, squeezing and scratching until both men were near coming. Then she tightened her vaginal muscles and flicked her tongue.

"Shit, baby, I can't stop!" Hector yelled, while Patrick just groaned. They had come at almost the same moment. The two men collapsed on the carpeted floor, and laughed, deep, joyful laughs. "You're too much, girl," Patrick said. "You did that on purpose."

Shara allowed some of Hector's semen to dribble from between her lips, swallowing the rest. "Of course," she said with a grin.

"So no one won."

"I did," Shara said.

"We all did," Hector said, releasing Shara's body from the machine.

"Holy cow," Rena said as Shara finished her story. "A sex contest."

"It was a gas," Shara said. "They told me I'd be invited to their next party too."

Rena was already composing a note for Sean, which she would give to him as soon as she had it written up.

Sean sat in a booth in the back of the bar and waited for Rena Hughes to show up. She had promised him on the phone that she had exactly what he was looking for and he was anxious to see what she had come up with. If her information was as lame as the stuff she had already given him, that would be the topper to a terrible day, he thought. He and Leslie had had another argument, but this time she had asked him to go for marriage counseling. "We have to try to work this out, if only for the sake of the children," she had said. Marriage counseling was the last thing he wanted, but he loved his boys and thus would put up with some busybody poking into his "interpersonal skills" and his ability to "get in touch with his emotional side." He almost snarled. Well, he loved his boys and so he'd do whatever Leslie wanted for now. The last thing he wanted was to be a weekend father.

To make the day even worse, Haverstraw had called him on the carpet for getting a bit creative with the Cancer Cure story. *What a crock*, he thought. *The Informer tells the truth only when it prints the date and the names of the owners on the masthead. So he had adjusted a few quotes. What the hell? Well, if this stuff with Courtesans, Inc. worked out, Haverstraw'd have to eat his words and lots more.*

He spotted Rena as she walked into the noisy room. He schooled his features to appear pleasant and benign and half-stood in the booth. She spotted him, pulled off her jacket, and hustled over. Boy, she was a looker, Sean thought. She was the image of her hooker mother. Great body with acceptable boobs. He liked them a bit bigger, but she'd do. She slipped into the far side of the booth and he signaled the waitress. "What can I get you?" he asked.

"I'll have a beer," she said.

"How's your mother?" he said after ordering.

"She's coming around, slowly. She can open her eyes, but she doesn't really see anyone yet."

"That's wonderful," Sean said. Actually he wanted all the information he could get before Erika regained consciousness and made peace with her daughter. "Let's get to it. You said on the phone that you had something for me."

Rena pulled a thick white envelope from her purse. "I wrote it all out." She put the envelope on the table between them. "I'm still not sure about all of this," she said. "I want my mother out of this business, but I'm getting a bit worried about revealing all this. These are not bad people, just men who want some fun in true privacy."

She had mentioned that this had something to do with Kisses

and what the fuck did he care about some twenty-something, clean-cut good guys, if they were good guys. Yet he had to mollify his source, something he was truly good at. "When guys like that decide to become famous personalities, they accept the problems that go with it. If they stray from the straight and narrow, someone's going to find out. If it helps you to get what you want, then it might as well come from you."

Rena kept her hand on the envelope. "I know, it's just so sneaky and it's not like me. I just want to protect my mother, but am I going too far?"

Sean reached into his pocket, found his wallet and rummaged through it for the Christmas picture of his boys. Somehow, people with information that they were reluctant to part with reacted better if they thought he was a humble writer with a family to support. He handed Rena the photo, his fingers itching to get his hands on the envelope. "I understand family," he said. "These are my boys." He pointed to the one on the left. "That's Jason, he's three, and Bobby beside him, he's almost six. If anything threatened their welfare the way your mother's business threatens her, I'd do just about anything to protect them."

Rena took the picture and looked from it to his face. "They look like you," she said.

He found the all American family shot and passed it across the booth. "That's all of us last summer. My wife's a great mother." The sickly sweetness of that phrase almost made him choke.

She handed the photos back, then passed him the envelope. "I guess you're right. I do want her safe."

Resisting the temptation to rip the envelope open with this teeth, he slowly tore it open and withdrew several sheets of paper. "May I read it now, in case I have questions?"

"Of course," Rena said.

As he scanned the pages, the waitress arrived with their beers and he reflexively took a sip. First, he read the names, date, and location of the party. *Shit*, he thought. *This is great stuff. Kinky sex in the basement of the manager's estate, maybe drugs? Could he say that on just an assumption? He'd decide later.* His eyes roamed the pages. *Patrick's tattoo was a phony? Fabulous. The screamers at the concerts will just love to hear that their idol is that much of a sissy. Afraid of needles.* He turned to the final page. "What's this about Sammy Seven doing coke?"

"Just something I heard."

"This is really good stuff, Rena. Really good." He slipped the envelope into his inside pocket. This was going to make his career. No more having to get financial help from his wife's family. He had it made! "If you don't mind, I'd like to take this home and go over it more slowly. Call me in a day or so but it looks like this is exactly what I—I mean, we—wanted. I can't thank you enough."

"Getting this business over with is all the thanks I want. Do you still need more?"

More. Shit as long as she was willing to gather great stuff. "As long as you're comfortable doing a bit of investigating." *Investigating sounds so much better than digging up dirt,* he thought.

"Okay," Rena said, slipping from the booth, her beer untouched. "Let's see what I can come up with. I'll call you."

Sean watched her back as she headed for the door, then he downed his beer in a few swallows. He really needed to read the contents of the envelope carefully, but why waste a beer and why go back to his apartment so quickly. His boys were long asleep so there was nothing there but Leslie.

He stood, grabbed Rena's untouched glass and wandered over to the bar. He scoped out the territory and settled on a stool beside a nice-looking young woman he'd seen around the neighborhood. "Hi, I'm Sean. Haven't I seen you around here before?" He arranged his face into his most ingenuous expression. "Sorry, that sounds like a pickup line, but I mean it. Don't you live around here?"

Chapter

13

Although it was only five o'clock on Friday, it was already dark when Rena entered the waiting room. She had sat beside her mother's bed for almost half an hour, glad that she had been transferred to a less restrictive room. Erika was now easily able to squeeze her hand and open her eyes when asked, yet she was not truly conscious. She was unable to connect with anyone or respond to a question. She soon would, the doctors and nurses assured her, and then they would know more about her ultimate prognosis. Rena hadn't forgiven Erika, but she decided to be as cheerful as she could, both for her peace of mind and in case anyone walked in. Therefore, while she sat, she talked, telling her mother all about her years in school, her vacations, her friends, all the things she had wanted to tell her throughout the years they had been estranged.

As she got up to leave her mother's bedside, Stuart walked in. He looked haggard, but in good spirits, and so obviously in love with her mother that she had to smile. "She's doing better, isn't she?" he said. "It's really great." He took the chair that Rena had vacated. "I'm glad you've been spending so much time with her," he said, taking Erika's hand. "She'll be so glad you've forgiven her."

"I haven't forgiven her," Rena said, softly, "but everyone tells me she'd care that I was here, so I sit here."

Stuart sighed. "Okay. Maybe you've just opened your mind a bit and that's a first step. And everyone's right, she would care. Thanks for being here, whatever the reason."

Drained, Rena walked to the open area at the end of the hall where she saw Brook, Shara, and Alex sitting together, talking quietly. Brook had a sheaf of papers and made a few pencil notations as they talked. They looked up as Rena entered. "Did she look at you?" Brook asked, barely able to contain the grin on her face.

"She opened her eyes and looked at me, but she didn't really see me."

"Me neither, but she's better each day. She's going to be okay. I can just feel it."

Rena sighed. She wished she could be as up as Brook was. Maybe her mother would be okay physically, but she was still a madam, unless Sean could change that.

The only available seat in the small crowded room was beside Alex so Rena settled into it. She had seen him two days earlier seated in the waiting room when she arrived, but she had slipped out of the hospital before anyone spotted her. Was she avoiding him? He was the only male prostitute she had met, although she knew there were two more. Why hadn't she tried to get his story?

She knew the reason too well. She was unprepared for her body's immediate reaction to his incredibly masculine aura. Did he create it or was it as much a part of him as his almost-black hair or the small rakish scar on his chin? This chemistry he exuded was obviously why he was so good at pleasing needy women. The fact that she was attracted to him annoyed her. She kept having to shake herself to make herself remember that he was a male prostitute, not some attractive guy with whom she could hope to have a relationship.

She almost jumped when Alex spoke to her, his voice deep and caring. "I'm really glad things seem to be going well," he said, taking her hand and squeezing it. "How are you holding up?"

"I'm doing okay," she said, barely able to take in enough air to answer. She'd had quite a few relationships with men but never had one affected her as he did. It must make him a fortune in stud fees.

Brook broke the spell. "I know you've been talking to some of Erika's friends and I thought you might want a male point of view. Maybe you and Alex could get together sometime."

Totally flustered, Rena said, "I'm sure that Alex has better things to do with his time than to chatter with me."

His deep brown eyes fastened on her. "Actually, I'm not busy this evening. I know you're having a really difficult time dealing with your mother's business and maybe I can help."

"Really, it's not necessary."

Still holding her hand, he said, "I know it's not necessary, but I'd like to share some of my thoughts with you. I care a lot about Erika and I know how she'll need everyone when she comes out of this. You're important to her. How about we get a bite to eat someplace where we can talk?"

Why did that sound like a dare? She pulled her hand from his but was unable to form a coherent excuse. When she didn't answer, he continued, "Good." He turned to Brook. "You and Shara can finish up without me. I've as much on my plate for the next month as I want so I can't be of much help anyway."

"Too true." Brook looked at Rena. "Listen. I'm really sorry I haven't been able to spend more time with you this week, but getting this schedule straight is a nightmare. I don't know how your mother does it and I'm hoping to give it back to her as quickly as possible."

"If you have your way," Shara said, "you'll stuff those pages in her hand as soon as she can hold a pencil."

"Too true," Brook said. "Alex, thanks for entertaining Rena. That way I don't feel so guilty."

"It's no trouble at all." He picked up Rena's jacket and held it while she slipped into it. "Has she seen the apartment?"

"What apartment?" Rena said. "I'm living at my mother's place."

Brook straightened. "When she moved to Riverside Drive, your mom kept the apartment she had when she first arrived here from Long Island. The business pays for it and some of us use it from time to time."

You mean bring johns there, Rena thought. She gritted her teeth to keep her thoughts to herself. Alex said, "No one's there tonight, right, Brook?" When she shook her head, Alex turned to Rena. "Let's have a bite to eat and I'll show it to you. It's been redone since she lived there ten years ago, but it still might give you a picture of your mother back then. If you like Chinese food, there's a nice place just around the corner from the apartment."

Unable to think of a reason to demur, she slipped her arms into her jacket. Alex put on his bright blue and red ski jacket, then placed his hand in the small of her back to guide her toward the elevator. Why didn't she have a longer coat so her back would be protected from the heat of his hand. She moved a bit more quickly so his hand fell away.

Half an hour later, after a taxi ride filled with inane small talk, they sat opposite each other in the Pagoda Palace. After they ordered a pu pu platter and glasses of Cabernet, Alex looked at her. "Is it just what I do for a living or is there some other reason you don't like me?"

Stalling for time, Rena said, "Blunt, aren't you?"

"Look. I know that you've been through a lot in the past week and I sympathize, but I really think you should cut your mother and me some slack. We're professionals, doing a job that wants to get done and doing it to the best of our abilities."

God, he was so gorgeous, but his blunt words brought her back to earth. Her voice came out as harsh whisper. "I have been cutting my mother lots of slack since I was six. I'm out of slack."

"I'm sorry to hear you say that."

She was saved from the necessity of answering by the arrival of their wine and appetizers. As she took a sip of her wine, her eyes were drawn to Alex's mouth. She watched as his lips curved around the crispy wrapper of a spring roll. She set her glass down and swallowed, hard. "How did a guy like you get into all this?"

"A guy like me?"

She sat, a spare rib partway to her mouth. "I mean, well, it would seem that you can have any woman you want. You're attractive, bright. Why this?"

"I could say, Why not? but I'll try to give you a straight answer." He popped the rest of the spring roll into his mouth, chewed slowly, and swallowed. "I love women. I love the way they feel, the way they smell, the way they taste." He licked the thin coating of grease from his fingers. "I grew up in Manhattan and I've had lovers since I was thirteen. Since I've been old enough to drive, women have wanted me to be there for them full time, and have given me gifts to guarantee that. At first, I returned the presents, thinking that I didn't want to be indebted, to be paid for being a friend and sex partner, but it didn't help. They kept giving and eventually I took. I cared for them all, every one. Every time I had to tell a woman it was over, it really saddened me, gifts or no gifts."

Rena nibbled at a spare rib so she would have something to do with her hands. She could picture women begging him to stay, wanting what he could provide.

"When I was twenty-four, I met a woman named Jennifer and we hit it off. She invited me to move in with her, and I did. She lived in a penthouse in midtown and, although I worked as a waiter for minimum wage, she introduced me to the good life. She taught me to appreciate fine wine, gourmet food, the feel of silk shirts and cashmere sweaters. Jen introduced me to classical music and fine art. Then she introduced me to some of her friends and encouraged me to relax and enjoy their company, too. In all ways. She set up threesomes with both men and women, and showed me the joys of kinky sex of all kinds. Jen threw parties that quickly turned into orgies, with free-flowing champagne and designer drugs." He sighed and sipped his wine. "Then I found out that Jen was charging her friends for my services. I was furious."

"I can imagine," Rena said.

"I was twenty-seven and I was a whore. I moved out that evening. I had saved a bit of money so I took a small apartment on the Upper East Side, and tried to figure out what to do with my life. That's when Erika and I got together professionally."

"How did you two meet?"

"She had been an acquaintance of Jen's. Erika and I had met a few times at dinner parties and such. When Erika discovered I had moved out she wheedled my phone number from Jen and called me. We met for dinner. Here, as a matter of fact. We talked and she told me about Courtesans, Inc. From time to time she had been asked to provide a male escort for a woman wanting company so she asked me whether I'd be interested. I thought about it for several days. I could do what I enjoyed, entertain women, and get paid for it. What could be better? That was the beginning."

"Do you just entertain women?"

"I'm a confirmed heterosexual and, as I found out when I was with Jen, men don't curl my toes. I meet a woman and usually there's a chemistry, something that just ignites inside of me. It doesn't happen with men."

Again swallowing hard, Rena asked, "Does it happen with all women?"

"Of course not, but it does with a surprising number. I see a woman, shake her hand, look into her eyes, and I begin to wonder how it would be to make love with her, to give her pleasure, hear her moan, watch her thrash around in the throes of an orgasm I helped create." His eyes locked with Rena's. "I can't help it; it just happens."

Rena's breath caught in her throat and she had to change the subject. "So you've been with my mother for quite a while."

"About four years." He sat back against the red plastic booth, his gaze still locked with Rena's. "Doesn't that ever happen to you?"

"What?" The question came out more like a croak.

"Some man looks at you and your nipples get hard and your panties get wet?"

Unable to speak, she shook her head.

"Liar," he said, and laughed, "but we can let that pass."

Throughout the rest of the meal, Rena was barely able to concentrate on the small talk Alex made and was almost totally unable to eat. Did he know what he was doing to her? He had to. As the waiter removed their plates, with considerable food still remaining, Alex handed him a credit card. "I would like to split that check with you," Rena said.

"No need. Next time will be on you." Next time? Within a week she'd be back in Chicago and Alex would be nothing but a delicious memory. "Ready to see your mother's old apartment?"

They walked around the corner to a large apartment building. The lobby was a bit shabby, but clean and well kept and the elevator smelled lightly of a pine-scented cleaner. As the elevator rose to the third floor, Alex said, "Brook lived on the fifth floor. That's how they met, you know."

"Brook told me," she said. Being in a small confined space with Alex was making her pulse race and her breathing quicken. She knew he couldn't miss it, and she found she was embarrassed. She was becoming one of Alex's admirers. She pictured herself begging him not to leave her as those women long ago had, but she wouldn't pay for it as they had. Ever.

The apartment looks like any other apartment, Rena thought as Alex followed her inside. Wood-framed overstuffed furniture in shades of mossy green and soft rose complemented by a thick sage green carpet, beige silk wall covering, wooden tables covered with terra cotta bowls filled with ivy and ferns and coffee table books, a television, and a VCR. "Doesn't look like a bordello, does it?" Alex said. "No beaded curtains, velvet sofas, or flocked wallpaper."

"That's not what I was thinking," she said quickly.

"Liar."

"Okay," she said with a sigh and a hesitant smile. "That's exactly what I was thinking."

"We're not like that. This is just a comfortable place to bring a date on occasion. None of us want our friends to know where we live so we come here. People get strange and there are quite a few cuckoos out there so we've all learned to play it safe."

Rena pulled off her coat and dropped onto the sofa. "Let's be honest," she said as Alex sat down beside her. "Here's what I just can't understand. You are paid to have sex with women. How can a woman get any pleasure out of sex if she knows she's paying for it? It's not real, there's no relationship."

"Do you mean that there has to be a relationship for you to enjoy sex? Wouldn't you like, just for one evening, to be with a man whose only job is to please you? Nothing is required of you other than just lying back and enjoying."

"I'm not as virginal at this as you seem to think. I've been with my share of men, some of whom were very good lovers, but there has to be something there besides sex for me to enjoy it."

Alex was silent for a few moments, then he hooked his finger under her chin and forced her to look into his eyes. "Does there really?"

She controlled her erratic breathing enough to say, "Yes. There does."

"I know I'm going to regret this," he said, "but it's hard to resist." He leaned forward and brushed his lips against hers. "There has to be a relationship, you say?"

She couldn't think. What had he said? She allowed her eyes to slide shut. Relationship. Right. He teased her lips, his tongue licking their joining. "Wouldn't it be wonderful for a man to touch all the places you want to be touched." His breath was warm against her wet mouth. "All those hot, hungry places."

No! She pulled back. "This is wrong. You're—well you're a professional."

"I'm someone who wants to give you pleasure. Can't you feel the chemistry, the hunger? It's such a wonderful feeling." He slid his palms along her cheeks, tangled his fingers in her hair and drew her close. "I can give you so much because I know what you want."

"No," she breathed, yet her words lacked conviction.

"Yes," he said as his mouth covered hers. She felt heat coil low in her belly. This was wrong, her mind called.

His tongue slowly penetrated the dark moist cavern of her mouth, played with her, thrust in and out in a primal rhythm. She heard a groan and realized that the sound came from her.

His thumbs caressed her jawline as his fingers massaged her scalp and he adjusted the angle of his face to deepen the kiss. Without conscious thought, her hands slid up the front of his shirt and snaked around his neck. His mouth was driving her crazy. Mindless pleasure. What was wrong with just enjoying?

His lips left hers so he could nibble along the tendon at the side of her neck. Her shudder echoed through her entire body and her head fell back. His mouth moved to the hollow at the base of her throat. "Do you want me to stop?" he murmured, his tongue swirling across her skin.

"Yes." Her body slumped. "No," she said and threaded her

fingers through his long black hair, using her arms to press his body against hers.

His mouth never left hers as he gently pressed her back against the sofa cushions, moving so he was kneeling on the floor beside her. His crafty fingers unbuttoned her shirt and quickly unsnapped the front clasp of her bra. In seconds he had bared her upper body and, as his teeth continued their magic journey across her collar bone, his fingers plucked at her erect nipple.

Heat slashed through her, devouring her, making her hips writhe and her breast press against his hand. "God, you are so hot," he whispered. "So responsive."

A tiny voice wondered whether he said those words to every woman he made love to. She moved to try to push him away, but then his mouth and teeth found her nipple. The pleasure was so intense that she ceased caring where it came from.

"Oh, baby, so good," he murmured. "You taste so good." The words caused tiny puffs of air to blow across her wet flesh, tightening the bud of her nipple. Still tangled in his hair, her fingers pulled him closer as she arched her back to take more. And yet more.

He quickly dragged her shirt and bra off and out from under her, then unsnapped her jeans and, along with her tennis shoes and socks, pulled it all off. Clad only in bikini panties, she lay across the sofa. She grabbed the front of his shirt and started to unbutton it, but he drew her hands away. "You're being serviced by someone who only wants your pleasure. Let me show you."

"Serviced," she moaned. *He's a prostitute and he's servicing me.* While she tried to think, his fingers found the soaked crotch of her panties and stroked. "I can't think when you do that."

"Don't think," he said, "take. Feel what it's like to be loved by someone who will quickly know your body as well as you do. Better." He explored, moving his talented fingers over her folds. She opened her eyes and looked at him as he intently watched her face. Every time she moved in response to his ministrations, he smiled.

She watched as he mapped her body, learning where she needed to be touched. His teeth nipped at her nipples, then he blew cool air across her damp flesh. He kissed his way down her belly, licking, biting, rubbing his lips over her. She lifted her hips to allow him to remove her panties.

Then his mouth was there, his tongue delving into the deep creases, insinuating into her deepest secret places, causing shards of pure pleasure to knife through her. His fingers teased her opening as his tongue danced over her clit. She grasped the edge of the sofa cushions and dug her fingers deep. Her heart pounded and she felt unable to catch her breath. She couldn't keep her body still, but as she moved his mouth remained fastened against her clitoris.

She almost died of pleasure when one of his fingers pressed inside of her, to be followed by another and another. She held on tightly and rode the waves of pure ecstasy. He drove her higher and higher and she was completely out of control.

"Let go," he whispered. "Take the pleasure and use it, let it lift you toward ecstasy, propel you up and up and up until you think you'll fall. But you won't. You'll soar. Go with it."

So high and driving higher. Colors. So many colors. Swirls of brilliant crimson, glowing orange, sulfurous yellow, all whirling, combining and separating and she was part of it. She was color. She was joy. She was ecstasy. And she came, screaming, crying, unable to control herself. For long minutes she soared toward the sun. Then, as she began to descend, he drove her up again. And yet again.

Eventually she pushed his hands and mouth away, unable to take anymore. She lay, eyes closed, listening to the rasp of her breathing. She heard him leave and water run. Then she felt a warm cloth stroking her most delicate places, and his rough cheek against the soft skin of her belly. "God," she said. "I don't know what to say."

"Don't say anything. Just float." He left her again, and returned with another warm cloth. He gently cleaned the sweat and juices from her body, then placed a glass of cold water in her hand and drew a soft afghan over her cooling body.

Finally her mind was able to think. "You did that on purpose," she said. "To teach me a lesson."

Alex sat on the floor beside the sofa, still fully dressed. "I guess I did. It didn't start out that way, but as I thought about you, I reasoned that you needed to understand why. Do you?"

"Why prostitutes? Yes, I do. That was amazing. Just amazing. You're a talented man," she said.

"I've been studying most of my life," he said, winking. "I told you, I love women. Few things give me greater pleasure than what we did tonight."

"You didn't get anything for yourself."

"Of course I did. But if you mean that I didn't climax, you're right."

"Didn't I arouse you?" she said, suddenly, inexplicably hurt.

"Of course you did, but I wanted to show you that it can be wonderful in so many different ways. I didn't reach orgasm, but I got an incredible amount of pleasure from your orgasm. The power of it for me is immense."

"Power?"

His knowing smile lit up his face. "I can do that for you even though you didn't want it at first. It's wonderful."

Suddenly Rena wanted to do it for Alex, but she didn't know how. She had never learned all the tricks a pro would know.

"Do you know that everything you're thinking is written on your face?" When she looked surprised, he asked, "Do you want me to teach you?"

She felt the heat rise in her face.

"Don't be embarrassed. It's pointless with me. No one was

born knowing. Nothing would give me more pleasure than to feel your hands on me, to show you what I like, to give you the power I feel when I give joy."

Rena closed her eyes, then looked at him. Slowly she reached out and opened the first button on his shirt, watching the smile light his face. He took her hand in his and kissed her fingertips. "Touch me," he groaned.

She unbuttoned the rest of the front of his shirt and parted the sides. His chest was covered with soft black hair and she threaded her fingers through it. She found his flat nipple and scratched it with her fingernail. It beaded tightly and his breath caught.

She flipped off the afghan and, heedless of her naked body, leaned forward and licked his lips with the tip of her tongue, her hand sliding over his chest. She pushed his shirt from his shoulders and unbuckled his belt. She had never taken the time to really look at a man and she found she wanted to now. He hooked his fingers in the waistband of his slacks. "Would you like me to take this off?" he asked.

"Yes," she said and watched him stand and remove his clothing. He extended his hand and drew her up. Together they walked into the bedroom. He flipped off the quilted spread and stretched out on the sheet. Rena stood beside the bed and gazed at his naked body. His chest was well muscled with a slender line of hair that arrowed down to the nest in his groin. His cock was semi-erect, lying against his belly. "Do you like what you see?"

Embarrassed she dropped onto the edge of the mattress and stared at the carpet. He cupped her face so she was forced to look at him. "Don't deny yourself any pleasure you want," he said. "If you want to look, do it. I like it when you look at me."

She allowed her gaze to roam his gorgeous body and watched his cock harden from only her gaze. "See what you do to me?" he said. "That's the power I was talking about before. The power to arouse, the power to please. You can excite me just by looking at me. Imagine what you can do with a touch."

Rena was amazed. She had never thought about the power of giving, but now she not only understood but reveled in it. She slid her palm down his abdomen and watched his cock twitch and move of its own accord. She reached out with one finger and stroked his erection from base to tip. She grinned as he moaned. And his cock grew.

What now? How did one touch a man? She felt his eyes on her and looked into them. "Take your palm and stroke me. Just your palm. Gently, like you would caress a baby."

She did as he asked and watched his breathing quicken. "Yes," he purred. "Like that. It would excite me if you touched my balls too."

"How?" she whispered.

He took her hand and placed it between his spread thighs, sliding her fingertips over his testicles. "Like that," he said, his voice no more than a harsh whisper. "Oh God, just like that." He took his hand away and left her fondling him.

She placed her other hand on his cock and hesitantly grasped him. "Show me," she said.

Again, he placed his hand over hers and showed her how he liked to be caressed, from base to tip. Then he reached over, opened a drawer in the bedside table and pulled out a bottle of lubricant. "Make your hand slippery," he said in a hoarse voice.

Rena squeezed a large dollop of goo into her palm, then again wrapped her fingers around him and stroked from base to tip, then back down to the base. When he said, "Tighter," she squeezed and rubbed him with one hand, still fondling his balls with the other.

His cock was so hard, rigid, his hips thrusting it through her fingers. "Don't stop," he said, then jerked and Rena watched as milky semen spurted from the tip. She'd never watched a man come before and she lamented what she had missed. It was magic, and she had done it. He thrust for several more moments, then his body stilled. "Stay there," she said, releasing him. In the bathroom she washed her hands, then soaked a facecloth in warm water. Back in the bedroom she washed him, slowly stroking his belly and cock.

As she finished, she became aware of his laughter. "God, Rena, you're a quick study." He grabbed her wrist. "Meaning no disrespect but have you ever thought about becoming a professional?"

She gasped, then couldn't resist his deep laughter. She tried to control a chuckle, but found herself unable to. They laughed together. Laughed. She realized that she had had a wonderful evening having casual, loving sex just to give and take pleasure. "You're terrific," she said. "I took a writing course in college and they always said, 'Show, don't tell.' Well, you certainly showed me."

"Can I confess something to you?" he asked.

"Uh oh. What?" She felt her entire body tighten, as if waiting for a blow.

"Well, neither of us had much dinner and I'm hungry. What say to a late supper?"

She couldn't control another burst of laughter. She was hungry now, too. "Sounds great, but I need a shower first." She grinned at him flirtatiously. "Care to join me?"

"Absolutely," he said.

Chapter

14

After Alex took her back to her mother's apartment, Rena stayed awake for a long time. Part of the time she relived the delicious evening, including their second lovemaking session after their second dinner. Not only was Alex a talented lover, but he brought things out in her that she hadn't imagined. They played with sex, giggled like schoolchildren and experimented. Rena took his cock into her mouth, something she had never done with any man before. Her mind was boggled. That wasn't the way she had thought sex was supposed to be, but she had been wrong. She fell asleep around three and slept soundly for the first time since her mother's accident.

"Oh, Rena, we've been trying to get you," Shara said the following morning when she arrived at the hospital.

Rena felt the bottom fall out of her stomach. "Has something happened to my mother?"

"She's awake," Shara said, her eyes glistening. "Brook and Stuart are in with her now. The doctors say it's amazing how quickly she's become so lucid. She remembers nothing of Friday at all, and, they say, probably never will, but there's no paralysis, no other lasting effects. She's a bit fuzzy, having trouble gathering her thoughts, but she recognizes all of us. It's like a miracle."

Rena felt herself getting teary. She couldn't forgive the past, but maybe she had begun to understand the present. "Can I go in?"

"Of course."

As she walked the length of the hospital corridor, she considered all she had learned over the past week, culminating in her evening with Alex. It certainly hadn't been love, but it was caring and it must be what many of the courtesans felt about their customers. Even if they didn't give a damn, what difference did it make. They gave pleasure. Who was the victim? All of these people, both employees and customers, depended on Courtesans, Inc. for so much. Was she wrong to try to put them out of business?

She pushed open the door to her mother's room and stood in the doorway. Brook and Stuart sat beside the bed talking softly to her mother, who lay propped up on several pillows. "I've taken care of everything," Brook was saying. "All the business matters are under control. Clay has called almost every day, somehow feeling that he was responsible for your accident. He's really very upset."

"He shouldn't be," Erika said, her voice soft and a bit halting.

"I know that, and you know that, but you'll have to call him when you're up to it and reassure him. He thinks that he should have gotten you a different taxi or something."

Erika looked a bit confused. "I lost that whole day. I don't remember."

"That's to be expected. Now you rest." She stood and took her coat from the back of the chair. "We really should be going. You just concentrate on getting better."

"And," Stuart said, "I have to talk to you seriously when you're a bit stronger."

At that moment, Erika focused on the door and caught sight of her daughter. "Rena?" she whispered.

"Hello, Mother," Rena said, taking a step into the room. "I'm glad to see you're awake." She started to tremble, unable to keep her hands still. Tears trickled down her cheek and she kept swallowing. Stuart stood and guided her to the chair Brook had just vacated beside the bed.

"You're here," Erika said, her speech a bit halting.

"I'm here," Rena said as she lowered herself into the chair.

Erika looked questioningly at Brook.

"She knows everything," Brook said.

Erika's gaze returned to Rena's and she paused as if gathering her thoughts. "I'm sorry."

"It's all right now," Rena said. "I'm beginning to understand. You found something fun to do after you and Daddy . . ." She couldn't continue. The wounds were too deep. Why had she mentioned him at all? Why couldn't she just be supportive? After all, her mother was just beginning the long road back. She might need physical therapy. She might have memory lapses, reading problems. There was so much.

"Listen, Rena," Brook said. "It's not my place to try to mediate this thing between you two, but whatever you feel, this isn't the time or place."

"Yes," Erika said. "It is." When Rena shook her head, tears almost choking her, Erika continued, "Say it."

From the depths of her soul, Rena sobbed, "Why didn't you ever love me?"

"I always loved you." After each phrase she stopped, her eyes closing, then opening. "I was wrong to send you away. But I always loved you."

Brook interrupted. "Erika, this can wait."

"No. Now!" Erika said.

"Why didn't you ever visit me?" Rena sobbed.

"I came," Erika said, tears forming in her eyes.

"You only came to France that one time. I know I was horrid, but why didn't you try again?"

It was obvious that talking was exhausting Erika, so Brook patted her friend's hand. "She flew over that one time and you made it clear that you didn't want her. She called and wrote every week, but you wouldn't respond to her letters and were pretty much nonresponsive over the phone, when you took the calls at all." Brook swiped at the tears flowing down her cheeks. "Eventually, after your graduation, she pretty much gave up. She had been beating her head against a wall, and the wall won."

"Why did she wait so long to come over to see me after she and Daddy split?"

"Trips to Europe are expensive and she had no money. The job she had at the insurance agency was just barely paying the bills."

"Why? Daddy left her lots of money."

"Did your father tell you that?" Stuart said. When she nodded, he said, "I was the one who helped your mother pick up the pieces after your father decamped with that bimbo."

"Stuart," Erika said, a stern warning in her voice.

"I'm sorry," he said, "but it's the truth. Sandy saw something she wanted, your father, and went after it. Eventually she convinced him to leave the U.S. and take her with him." He stared at Rena. "Let's get a bit of fresh air in here. Your father disappeared one afternoon without telling your mother that he was leaving. No word, no nothing. She was panicked that something had happened to him until she got a call from his lawyer. He had transferred all the assets he could manage into his name and had all the statements sent to Switzerland. He left Erika with a mortgaged house, furniture, a car with a large remaining loan, and not much else."

Brook continued, "He even took most of her jewelry."

"That's not true. And anyway, he supported her. There was alimony and all that."

"He was outside the U.S. so the courts had no power. He paid her nothing."

Rena sat silent for a few moments trying to digest. "He told me that he left her well-provided-for."

"He lied," Stuart snapped.

Rena was totally confused. All the things she had believed over the years were built on lies. Her father's lies. "She didn't tell me."

"What would have been gained?" Stuart said. "You would have had no one to hold you together. This way you had your father."

Rena tried to absorb what she was being told. "She could have gotten a real job, earned a salary."

"Doing what?" Brook said, her voice hard. "I remember her in those days. She had no skills, couldn't even use a computer. But she learned, practiced, and eventually got a job that paid enough to cover her rent."

Erika dragged a tissue from the box on her bedside table and dabbed at her eyes. "Baby, I loved you." When Brook tried to break in, Erika grabbed her hand. "Let me." She took a moment and collected herself. "I was young. Naive." She paused to concentrate. "I couldn't have managed without Stuart and Brook." She took Stuart's hand. "I got stronger."

Erika reached for the water glass and Brook handed it to her. As she sipped, Rena tried to make sense of everything she'd heard. Her father had always told her that he had left Erika well-provided-for. Although he never said it in so many words, he intimated that she didn't come to visit because she had better things to do. Rena began to put the pieces together from what she knew of her mother's life. She had lived with her parents until she had married Rick; then he had taken charge of her life. She pictured herself in the same position. It must have been difficult trying to live alone for the first time.

"Did you get pregnant to get Daddy to marry you?"

Stuart gasped and Brook held Erika's hand and answered, "I

know that's what your father told you, but your mother told me about that time." Erika closed her eyes as Brook continued. "It was the only time they hadn't used protection, and that was because your father wanted to 'feel her' not because she wanted it."

Erika opened her eyes. "Not all his fault. I loved him so much. I had you. I was never sorry." She took a deep breath.

"I'm afraid all this is too much for your mother. Let's let the rest wait."

"No," Erika said. Brook and Stuart argued, but Erika was adamant. "What else?"

Rena squared her shoulders and asked the most painful question. "Why didn't you want me to live with you after Daddy left?"

Signaling Erika to rest, Stuart said, "She did, very much, but your father said he would only pay for your schooling if you stayed in Europe. If your mother brought you back to the U.S. he wouldn't pay a dime. She wanted the best for you so she sacrificed her needs and left you there."

"Maybe I was wrong," Erika said. "Maybe we could have made it. I was so scared. I hurt you, but I didn't know what else to do."

"So you became a . . ."

"Prostitute." Quiet sobs shook her body.

"Erika," Brook said, "try to calm down. This isn't the time for this. You're just starting to get better."

Erika swallowed her sobs. "Now. We need to get it all out." She looked at Rena. "I made mistakes. Forgive me?"

Rena pressed her forehead against the cool sheets. "Oh, Mama, it's been such a long time. For your sake I wish I could say that all is forgiven like it is in the movies, but it's going to take a while for me to digest all of this." She lifted her head. "I think I understand a lot of things I didn't before, and I know that I care about you now. Maybe the past isn't really important. We all make mistakes." She thought about the envelope she'd given Sean. *I've made a monstrous one.*

The two women held hands, then the doctor arrived to clear the room. "You can all come back this evening, after she's had time to rest. Resting is most important now, to give her body a chance to continue healing." With kisses all around, they left.

While Stuart and Brook went to the end of the hall to celebrate with Shara, Rena paced the hallways. She had been so wrong. She had believed everything her father told her. Maybe her mother had made some mistakes, but as she thought about it, she wondered how she would have reacted under the same circumstances. Hardly past thirty, a teenage daughter, no money, no job, and in her mind, no way of getting one. She might have done the same things.

What about Sean? She knew now she couldn't let him publish all that information she had given him. She found a pay phone and dialed Sean's cell phone number. "Sean Fredericks," he answered

"Sean, it's Rena."

"Great. Have you got more for me?"

"No, and I don't think I will. My mother's regained consciousness and we talked. I've been wrong about a lot of things. I don't think you should write about any of that stuff I told you."

"I'm disappointed that you have changed your mind, Rena. So you're going to let your mother continue to be a whore? Isn't there something I can say? "

The word *whore* echoed through her head. She wasn't a whore. Not with all the levels of meaning that word had. She gave pleasure and what was so wrong with that? "I need the material that I gave you back."

"I still have some work to do with it, but in a month or so that information will be the basis of several great articles."

Desperation invaded her voice. "I don't want you to use it. I'll deny everything and so will Shara and Mei."

"Who cares? I've checked on some of the dates and it all fits. Denying it won't help. It's a done deal." There was a moment's silence. "And thanks," he said and, laughing, hung up the phone.

Alex showed up at the hospital at about five and he sat with Rena, making small talk. Suddenly she had to tell someone. "Alex, I've done something terrible and I'm afraid it can't be un-done." Through more tears she told him about her meetings with Sean and the terrible phone call earlier that day.

"Why?" Alex asked.

"I though it was all so immoral that I would be doing her a favor. I wanted her out of the business. She'd retire, like Valerie did, marry Stuart, and be out of my life. I didn't think about any-one else, just her. I couldn't deal with the fact that my mother was a hooker. I couldn't deal with it."

Alex wrapped his arms around her and held her while she cried. "We've got to tell Brook about this. Stuart, too. We've got to think of some way out of this mess."

"Oh God, I'm so sorry. Everyone will hate me."

He sighed deeply. "If they're anything like me, they'll under-stand. Part of me is furious with you, but most of me understands how you felt. I can also imagine how well Sean played you. He worked on your history, your feelings when you found out about Courtesans, Inc."

"I wish you'd yell at me," Rena said, fishing a tissue from her purse. "What I did was unforgivable."

"Only you can decide whether to forgive yourself, but what you did is certainly understandable."

At that moment, Stuart and Brook walked into the waiting room. "They have to be told," Alex said and Rena nodded. "I'm afraid we've got a big problem and we need to talk," Alex said and, in a few words, he explained what Rena had done.

"I was so hurt," Rena said, "and I will understand if no one ever speaks to me again."

Brook looked at Stuart, then said, "I'm surprised and disappointed, but who knows what a shock like finding out about Courtesans, Inc. would have caused me to do."

"I don't know what I would have done in your position," Stuart said, "if Sean Fredericks had come to me and offered what he did."

Rena was again unable to control her tears. "Damn it! Stop being nice to me," she said. "I'm a monster."

"Maybe," Brook said with a twinkle, "but you're our monster and we love you."

"I, of course," Stuart said, "have never made a mistake. Like telling your father that his little affairs wouldn't hurt anything as long as he kept it all quiet."

"You told him that?" Rena said.

"When he first came to work at Cadmire. He liked the ladies even then, but everyone just winked and looked the other way. It never occurred to me that you and your mother would be so badly hurt."

Brook took a deep, calming breath. "We need to tell Erika. It concerns her most of all and she deserves to know what's happened."

"She's not strong enough," Stuart said. "We can deal with this, figure some way out."

"She's stronger than any of us give her credit for," Rena said. "She's my mother and she's put up with all I've done to her. We must be able to figure a way out of this. Let's give her another day; then Brook's right, she has to be told."

The following evening Rena, Brook, and Stuart arrived at the same time. They were delighted to see that Erika looked a lot more like her old self. She had put on makeup and wore a navy blue bed jacket Brook had brought her several days earlier. Although she had no recollection of anything after her conversation with Brook before dinner she was much better able to concentrate. She laughingly lamented that she was sorry that she had forgotten what must have been an evening of great sex.

It had been a bit of a job to ferry visitor's cards down to the lobby but eventually Alex arrived with Mei and Shara. Rena knew that Alex had already told them about Sean. Finally, with the six friends gathered in Erika's room, Rena slowly explained everything that had happened to Erika. "Oh God, Mom, trying to do something that I thought made sense, I really screwed everything up."

"It's strange," Erika said, still speaking softly, but in much more complex thoughts. "For years I knew I had made a terrible mistake where you were concerned and yesterday I thought we'd made a first step past that. We can get past this too, baby. And we've got a lot of help right here in this room."

Rena sat on the bed beside her mother, her face still stained with tears. *Every time we are together,* she thought, *I cry again. For the waste of so many years, for the harm I've done, for so much.* She felt her mother's arm snake around her shoulders and squeeze. "I know," Rena said. "I thought I knew what was best for you, just as you thought you knew what was best for me, all those years ago."

Erika hugged her daughter close. "At different points in our lives, we each seem to have decided unilaterally what was best for someone else," she said, slowly. "That's really presumptuous. In my case though, I did what I did for me too. I didn't think I could handle you and myself."

"And I wanted to get you out of the business and out of my life. I didn't want to get to know you and take a chance of learning that I might have been wrong about you. My anger had grown too comfortable."

"Oh Erika," Mei moaned. "I didn't think there was any harm in telling Rena what I said."

"Of course you didn't," Erika said. "What's done is done. Now, how do we fix it?"

Rena looked around the hospital room. Shara and Mei stood side by side, holding hands. Rena realized that her maliciousness would probably destroy their way of earning a living and threaten their safety. Alex stood off to one side, one shoulder propped against the wall. His eyes were shuttered, allowing Rena no way of knowing how he felt. She sighed. Why question it? He undoubtedly hated her and she deserved it. She had used them all.

"I'd like to say something first," Rena said. "I know that what I did was wrong. I don't expect you to forgive me. I'm leaving for Chicago as soon as we have this settled and you won't have to see me again. Any of you."

"Stop the breast beating," Brook said. "There's not one of us here who hasn't, at some point, done something we're ashamed of. Life goes on. If we're smart, we learn from it and move on."

Mei smiled weakly at Rena. "Shara and I were just as wrong to reveal what we did. We're both to blame as well." Shara nodded her agreement.

Brook sat forward in one of the two bedside chairs. "Let's end the blame game. The important thing is to think of something we can do to make all this go away."

From the other plastic hospital chair, Stuart said, "I don't think there's anything we can do through legal channels. He lied to Rena and he's a despicable bastard, but if those were jailable offenses there'd be no one on the outside."

Rena's heart sank. "Asking him for the stuff back is a waste of time, too, I'm afraid. I tried."

"Rena's right," Brook said. "He won't willingly give that stuff back, not with that much money involved. I've been wracking my brain for something we can do, but I've come up empty."

"I understand that he's a louse," Rena said, "but he comes across as such a sincere, serious kind of guy. A nice wife, a couple of kids. Just trying to make a living."

"A saint, I'm sure," Shara said.

Rena remembered what she had seen when she returned to

the bar for her umbrella. "He's certainly got an eye for the ladies, especially younger ones," she said, then told them about his attempts to pick up women at the bar. "I don't think things are all sweetness and light at home."

"An even nicer man than I thought," Mei said. "Have any of you ever read that paper?" Looking a bit embarrassed, she continued, "I never buy it, mind you, but I read the rag while I'm on line at the supermarket. He and his colleagues slash anyone and everyone with innuendo, rumor, and in some cases, downright lies."

"Don't people sue when they are lied about?" Rena asked.

"You're a wonderful woman, Rena," Brook said, "and we all love you like a member of our family, but you're really naive. First, if you sue, everything they've written becomes newsworthy and gets broadcast on every gossip show on TV. And it's really difficult to win one of those suits. Since the people he writes about are public figures, they can't talk about invasion of privacy; they have none. You need proof that they lied and the articles are usually worded so carefully that that's next to impossible to prove. Even if you are victorious in court, they appeal and appeal and appeal; and as each court decides, you're news again. Lastly, if you ultimately win, your victory is published on page fifty-three, buried beneath the classified ads. And, of course, the ones who make out well financially are the lawyers."

Rena hung her head. She probably was naive, but she was learning fast. "So what can we do?" She explained about the half-million-dollar bonds. "I thought that might help protect you."

Erika squeezed Rena's shoulders again. "It might come in handy," she said. "I think the ultimate answer has to be blackmail, but I'm not sure exactly how."

"Right," Stuart said. "We need something that he will be willing to trade for the information Rena gave him."

"Trade isn't good enough. We need something that we can

hold over his head indefinitely," Brook said. "Something that he knows will be revealed if he publishes anything."

"Let's lure him into a kinky sex party," Shara said. "We can handcuff him to the bed and take pictures."

"Not strong enough. He won't care if we have pictures of him. Right track though," Erika said.

"We could threaten to show the photos to his wife," Shara continued.

"Better," Mei said. "But we need something more. Something he has to lose if we show the pictures."

Alex straightened away from the wall he'd been leaning against. "I think I have an idea," he said, then spoke for several minutes.

Brook's eyes locked with Erika's and the two women nodded. "I think we've got the basis of a plan here. Let's put our heads together and think of how we can best carry this out."

They grilled Rena for half an hour, extracting every ounce of information she had about Mr. Fredericks. Finally, when they felt they knew the man as well as they could, they began to concoct their cover story. Together they created a juicy story about a fictional local Oregon judge. The details were exciting enough that Sean would believe that it was real and, since he wasn't knowledgeable about West Coast politics, he wouldn't immediately suspect it was created for his benefit. They hoped he'd never get to research it.

They refined the story until finally Rena went home and wrote it out on her laptop. Then she called him and apologized for her previous frantic phone call. "I thought I could make peace with my mother, but I was wrong," she said, her voice filled with bitterness. "She's embarrassing and this whole thing makes my skin crawl. I sit in her room with all her prostitute friends and—well it's sickening."

She hoped she hadn't overplayed her hand, but Sean merely said, "So why are you calling me?"

"I want her out of this disgusting business. Once she's," she paused, "retired, then I can go back to Chicago and forget about her once and for all. I've got something really good to put the icing on the cake as far as Courtesans, Inc. goes. I can't talk about it. I need to do a bit of research and write it all down. Can we get together tomorrow evening? Same place?"

Sean quickly agreed.

When Rena arrived, she spotted Shara seated at the far end of the bar, nursing a glass of white wine. She and the group from Courtesans, Inc. had discussed her cover story and what she should wear until both were perfect. Shara had selected a soft silk blouse the color of ripe wheat and a long black skirt slit to the thigh with high-heeled black pumps that showed off her gorgeous legs. The outfit was tempting but not overtly invitational. Since, from her observations, Sean liked his partners young, Shara's carefully planned dress and makeup made her look youthful, yet dressed up for a really big date. As Rena looked around for Sean in the crowded room, she saw Shara glance at her watch and signal the bartender.

Rena spotted Sean sitting at his usual booth in the rear and hurried over. "This is the final installment," she said as she slid into the booth. If this doesn't finish Courtesans off, nothing will." She hoped that he'd buy her conversion, but he seemed so anxious to get his hands on her information that he was oblivious to all else.

"Great. What have you got?"

"I was talking to one of my mother's employees, last evening." She sneered. "Melinda St. Ives. Is that a name that sounds like a hooker?" She shook her head. "Anyway, she told me about an evening several weeks ago. She was very tight-lipped about the identity of the guy involved and I thought it wasn't going to be useful." She handed Sean a thick envelope. "She let slip that she'd called him M. Scott so I did a bit of research on the Net. Mark Scott Paulsen is not only a well-known judge in the Oregon

State Supreme Court, but rumor has it he's on the short list to be named to a federal judgeship when the next vacancy appears." She leaned closer and lowered her voice. "This one's really good. It seems there were three paid women and him in the penthouse of the Carlisle several months ago along with quite a bit of Ecstasy."

"Dates," Sean said. "I need dates I can verify."

"I know and it's all in there, together with the details of who did what to whom. And there was a lot of doing, including playing in the hotel pool. I gather from Melinda that he's quite a fan of paddles, and the picture she painted of him stretched across her thighs, with all three women . . . Well, let's just say it was really hot." Rena tried not to grin at the sight of Sean getting flushed at the thought of the games. She tapped the envelope lying on the table between them. "You've got to read this."

Sean cleared his throat. "Oh," he said, "I will. Thanks for all the great stuff you've gotten for me."

"You're welcome. I realize now that I can't be happy until I get my mother out of this horrible business."

Sean winked at her. "We will. You can bet on it."

"I won't keep you," Rena said, rising. "Let me know when to expect to see something in print."

"Just keep an eye on the *Informer*. It won't be for several weeks, but I can assure you, your stories will be there."

"Great." She watched Sean slip the papers out of the envelope and Rena knew he had ceased paying attention to her as he started to read. She made her way to the door and, as she slipped her coat on, she took a moment to look for Shara. She was still sitting at the far end of the bar and a disappointed causally dressed man was just leaving the stool next to her. She crossed her fingers. So far all was going just fine, but the next five minutes would make or break their plan. As she walked toward the door, she saw Sean avidly flip to the next page.

Chapter
15

Shara watched Rena leave and sipped her wine, alternately looking at her watch and the door. She surreptitiously watched Sean refold the pages Rena had given him, and stuff them back into the envelope, then approach the bar. She uncrossed and recrossed her legs, watching Sean settle on a seat several stools away from her. As the bartender handed him a beer, she said, "Joe, get me another white wine, will you?"

"Coming up," the bartender said.

"Are you sure you haven't seen K-Nine yet?" she asked.

The bartender's voice was calm and soothing, obviously used to dealing with distraught patrons. "I'm sure he's on his way."

"Bullshit," she said with an exaggerated sigh, again looking at her watch. "The game was over at five, and he was supposed to meet me right after he showered and changed."

"I'm really sorry," the bartender said, lingering, gazing at her youthful figure.

"I know," she said with an exaggerated sigh. "It's just that he gets to New York so seldom. Thanks, I'll take that wine now."

During her conversation with the bartender, Shara had watched the wheels turn in Sean's head. She had mentioned the nickname of one of the basketball players from the Golden State Warriors who were in town to play the New York Knicks. As expected, Sean moved to the stool next to her. "I couldn't help overhearing," he said. "Are you expecting Mark Cannady, the Golden State guard? I'm a big fan of his."

She looked at him, her deep brown eyes sliding over his body. "Expecting, yes. Will he show up? Who knows?" She turned away as her drink arrived. *Make him work for it.*

"My name is Sean, and I've followed K-Nine's career for a long time."

"Hi. I'm Shara." She extended her long fingers and clasped Sean's hand.

"How long have you known him?"

"Just a few months, since the team was here last."

"How did you meet?" Sean asked.

"Actually, we met at a bar near the Garden. God, he's so gorgeous so when he sat down next to me I was unable to talk." She winked. "Well, talking wasn't really necessary."

Shara watched his eyes light up. "Is he as talented off the court, if you know what I mean?"

"Well," she said, "I certainly don't kiss and tell. Let's just say that I haven't written a letter of complaint yet."

"He's married, isn't he?"

"I don't know and I don't care," she said. "He was wonderful. Now, however, he's on my shit list."

"I'm sorry. It must be embarrassing for you to be stood up like this."

"It's not fun." She motioned to the stool Sean was occupying. "Men keep trying to pick me up but I'm keeping that seat for *him*." As Sean made as if to get up she said, "It's okay, I guess. You can sit there. I don't think he's going to show." She allowed her eyes to mist as she faced him. "He's such a shit sometimes. He called me last week to remind me, as if I could forget."

"I certainly wouldn't stand you up if you were waiting for me."

She created a small, wistful smile, knowing she looked about fifteen. "I know you wouldn't." She patted his hand. "You're a nice guy, not a piece of basketball shit like K-Nine." She sighed as she touched his wedding ring. "But you're married."

"I'm newly divorced, but I haven't taken the ring off just yet."

Liar, she thought. "That's too bad. I guess in a way we're both at loose ends."

They talked for almost half an hour. Finally Shara said, "He's not going to show and I'm really bummed." She rubbed her lower back. "My fanny's getting tired of sitting on this seat. Any longer and I'm going to take root." She gazed at Sean. "This is going to sound really forward, but my apartment's just a quick cab ride from here and I'd love to get out of these uncomfortable shoes." She held out her leg and wiggled her ankle. "Why we women wear these is beyond me. Anyway, I don't want to be alone. Would you be interested in coming to my place? We could order a pizza and just talk."

She watched the pupils of Sean's eyes dilate slightly with passionate expectation as he heaved a theatrical sigh. "That would be great for me. All I have to look forward to is an empty apartment."

God, Shara thought, *it's a wonder he ever picks up anyone. I wouldn't stand you up if you were waiting for me. Empty apartment. Indeed.* She watched him grab his jacket from the back of the stool. "What's that?" Shara said, reaching down to pick up the envelope that had fallen from Sean's back pocket.

"Just business," he said, his eyes dipping into the cleavage Shara exposed as she handed the envelope to him. He took Shara's long wool coat from the back of her barstool and helped her on with it, his hands lingering on her shoulders, his mouth beside her ear. "But we're not talking business tonight, are we?"

"Of course not."

They had sat close together in the taxi, the length of her thigh pressed against his, making it clear that she was in the mood.

When they walked into the Courtesan's Inc. apartment, Sean didn't waste time. He pulled off his jacket, then helped her off with her coat. Throwing both on the sofa, he turned her and slipped his arms around her waist. She looked up at him and smiled. Their kiss was long and thorough and by the end he was panting, the bulge in the front of his jeans rigid. "I want to slip out of these shoes," Shara said, walking toward the bedroom. "Want to help me?"

The following afternoon Stuart, Mei, Shara, Brook, Alex, and Rena sat around Erika's bed. Erika was a bit tired from her first short walk to the nurse's station and back, but she was feeling upbeat and alive. She was still a little worried about her ability to concentrate, and she lost threads of conversation if everyone talked at once. The doctor had assured her, however, that that would clear up over the next week or so. The best news was that her recovery was so complete that the doctors didn't think she'd need physical therapy. She'd be going home soon.

"Ready," Alex said, as he set up a small combination TV/ VCR and Brook filled small paper cups with smuggled champagne. As she handed out the glasses, Alex inserted a cassette.

Erika glanced at her daughter, sitting beside her, holding her hand. Rena. This accident had turned out to be a blessing. She had her daughter back. Of course she realized that everything wasn't cured yet, but they had begun talking about everything and with communication would come, if not total forgiveness, at least acceptance.

"The only thing about all this that made me sad was that you couldn't be there, Mom," Rena said.

Mom, Erika thought. That one word sounded so wonderful. It sounded strangely right.

"So," Mei said, "we thought you'd enjoy watching exactly what happened."

"Hey," Shara said. "Don't forget who the star is here. I've

made a few porno flicks when my customers wanted to, but this one's the best."

Everyone positioned themselves for a good view of the TV, and Alex pressed the *play* button. The camera, Rena had explained, was activated by a motion sensor and had been carefully set up in the corner of the apartment's bedroom by a friend of Stuart's who was in the surveillance business. He had positioned it behind a potted plant, aimed at the bed, and made sure that the leaves obscured the camera but didn't interfere with the lens. The audio level had been set to pick up even the smallest sounds.

". . . get rid of these shoes," Shara could be heard to say as she walked into the bedroom and the camera activated. Sean trailed behind. Alex turned the sound up slightly then moved to lean against the wall, squeezing Rena's shoulder as he passed. They all sat, transfixed, staring at the action on the screen.

Shara had dropped onto the edge of the bed and bent over to unbuckle her ankle straps. "Here," Sean said, "let me help." He knelt on the floor at her feet and slowly unfastened the strap. Then, as he slid the shoe off, he kissed her instep and rubbed the ball of her foot.

"Umm," she purred as his thumbs pressed deeply into her arch. "That feels wonderful. I'll give you an hour to stop."

"And if I don't?"

She giggled. "I'll give you another hour."

"This would be better without these stockings," he said.

"I don't think it could be any better, but if you want, you can take them off."

With shaking fingers he slid his hands up her thighs until his fingertips reached the soft flesh above her stocking. "Don't get too fresh," she said, giggling.

As he unfastened her garters, he said, "Why not? Would you object if I did?"

"I guess not," she said as his fingers brushed her inner thigh.

"I'm just not in a hurry." It was obvious to the audience that Sean was.

"Then neither am I," he said, slowly pulling the stocking down her leg. He resumed his foot massage, playing with her toes and their unpainted nails. Finally he shifted to the other foot. He removed the shoe and stocking and took one foot in each hand. "You have great feet."

"Are you a lover of women's feet?" Shara asked.

"I enjoy all parts of a beautiful woman's body."

Shara stretched one leg until her arch rested against his rock-hard erection. "Umm," she purred, "I can see that you do." She bent over and unbuckled his belt and unfastened his jeans. Then she briefly squeezed his cock. "Nice."

At that moment a key could be heard, rattling in the apartment's door. "Damn," Shara said. "My roommate is supposed to be out until tomorrow. Damn, damn."

"Hi, Shara, I'm back early." They all heard Mei's voice then saw her peek into the bedroom. "Oops. Sorry if I'm interrupting."

"You are." To Sean, Shara said, "Let me just close this door."

"I'll do it." He stood and walked toward the door, clearly crestfallen to have his evening interrupted.

Shara stopped the tape and looked at Erika. "You have to realize what he saw in the living room. I'm sorry we didn't have more cameras. Mei had dropped her coat and was wearing a skin-tight bright-red halter top and a pair of very short white shorts." She pressed the *play* button again.

"Oh," they could hear Mei's voice say from off camera. "You're not Mark Cannady?"

"No, I'm not. Disappointed?"

"Well . . ."

Shara jumped off the bed and went to the bedroom door. "You planned this, you sneak. You were hoping for a threesome. Well, you'll be happy to know Mark stood me up."

"You seem to have made do," Mei said, pushing past Shara and Sean and walking into the bedroom. She focused her smile on Sean. "Hi," she said to him as he turned, "I'm Shara's room-mate. I'm Mei."

"I'm Sean. We were just—"

Mei's gaze dropped to Sean's unfastened pants. "I can see what you were just . . . Can I play?"

"Not a chance," Shara said. "And we weren't doing anything."

"Come on, Shara, be a pal. Don't I share with you?"

"You two have done this often, haven't you?" Sean asked. "Shared, I mean."

"Once or twice," Mei said, grinning.

Shara giggled. "Or more."

"Did you two plan this? A threesome with K-Nine?"

"He's such a hunk," Mei said, "and so tall. I thought there'd be enough of him to share."

"Yeah, share," Shara said and the two giggled louder

"I wouldn't object to being shared," Sean said. "I think I can handle it." He draped one arm over Shara's shoulders and one over Mei's, unable to keep the grin from splitting his face.

Shara cupped his face with her hands and pressed her lips against his as Mei pulled his pants down. As Sean and Shara kissed, Mei removed his tennis shoes, socks, and pants. Shara's nimble fingers unbuttoned his shirt and the two women dragged it down his arms. Then they pushed his naked body onto the bed.

With one woman on either side of the bed, Sean closed his eyes. Hands and mouths were everywhere as the two women kissed and licked and fondled. As the audience in the hospital room watched, Shara bit his earlobe while Mei licked the backs of his knees. Mei moved so she could suck on his middle finger, drawing it deep into her mouth while Shara pinched his tight nipples.

His voice slurred with expectation, Sean said, "Won't you girls undress?"

Quickly, Shara and Mei pulled off their clothes. When they were naked, they resumed their play, using their breasts to caress his chest and thighs. Occasionally one would lick the length of his rigid cock. "I guess, since you brought him," Mei said, "you get to do him first." She found a condom in the bed table drawer and the two women slowly unrolled it over his cock, listening to him moan with pleasure. Then Shara climbed onto the bed and straddled his hips, slowly lowering herself onto his shaft as Mei held it steady.

"Oh, God," he groaned. Shara rode his cock while Mei fondled his balls. Screaming, obviously unable to control it any longer, he came.

As Sean lay, panting, Erika could hear the apartment door, then someone cross the living room and approach the bedroom. She easily recognized Alex and watched Sean pull the bedspread over his naked body. "What the hell are you doing here?" Sean asked. "What's going on?"

"Nothing much," Alex said. "I'm just going to be sure I get the tape so I can put it away for safe-keeping."

"Tape?" Sean said, looking around the bedroom.

Erika could see Alex approach the camera and fiddle with the greenery around it. She also heard a muffled, "Shit" from Sean.

Then Rena walked in. "He's really confused now," she said. "Listen, Sean, and I'll spell it out. We've got this entire evening on tape."

"Rena?" Sean said. Erika watched his face as understanding dawned. "This is all a setup. These are Courtesans girls."

"Women, but yes, they all work for my mother," Rena said as Shara and Mei settled on the sides of the bed beside Sean, totally unconcerned about their nakedness. "Including Alex, who's just here to be sure you don't get violent."

"I'm beginning to get it. You set this all up. The stuff you gave me was bogus, right?"

"Sure. I don't want you to use any of the other material and I think that tape is our insurance policy."

"Please," Sean said. "Be real. I'm not a child and if they work for your mother these *ladies*," he spat the word out, "are of age. There's no child sex here. So what if you have it all on tape? It might prove a bit embarrassing for me, but not tragic. What guy wouldn't take advantage of two women?"

"We could publish stills in your magazine. I would guess that there are people at *The Informer* who would love to get their hands on juicy photos of their reporter digging dirt, as it were."

Sean's face was expressionless. He was obviously unconcerned so far. "Maybe they would and maybe they wouldn't, but why should I care? It's still just an awkward moment and nothing more."

"An awkward moment and nothing more?" Rena continued. "Maybe it would be something more for a married man?"

Erika watched a flicker of worry pass over Sean's face. "My wife knows I fool around occasionally. Are you planning to show this to her?"

"We might."

"She knows I'm not totally faithful. She goes along with it as long as I don't bring women home."

"I'm sure she says she does and that's your business, and hers. However, we're not going to give the tape to her or to your paper."

Sean's expression went from thoughtful to confused. "You obviously set this up, so what exactly do you have in mind?"

Rena dropped onto the chair in the corner of the room. "Well, here's the deal. I want all that material I gave you back."

"You can have all the paperwork," Sean said quickly.

"And," Rena continued, "we don't want you to publish any of it."

"Tape or no tape, I'm afraid you really can't stop me."

"I think we can," Rena said. "I'll bet that information I gave you isn't worth your children."

"What the hell do my kids have to do with this? You wouldn't hurt them."

"Hurt them? Not really. Although it would make me sad to think of them not seeing you again. Maybe it would be for the best though. You're such a bastard after all."

Sean's expression was now confident. "Not see them? Ridiculous. If you think you can send me to jail, you're sadly mistaken. That tape doesn't show anything illegal."

As the camera continued to record, Rena sighed and shook her head slowly. "Sean. Sean. Sean. You've got such a small mind with very narrow thoughts. What we intend to do is quite simple. We know that your wife is unhappy and will eventually be considering divorce. If you publish any of that material, in addition to collecting on the bond, we'll simply send that tape to your wife's divorce attorney."

Sean's eyes opened wide. "You wouldn't."

"Of course we would," Rena said. "Maybe we'll send a copy to both your wife and her lawyer. You'll be paying alimony for the rest of your life or longer, and the chance she'll let you see your kids, even a supervised visit, is small."

"But there's nothing really bad on that tape."

"You know that and I know that, but both Mei and Shara might be underage. Who will know when they can't be found to testify. If your wife has a crafty lawyer, anything could happen. Enjoy your kids while you can. And since it will certainly harm my mother and Brook, we'll collect our million dollars. I'm sure Mei and Shara can disappear for a while with that kind of money. Maybe spend a year on the beach in France."

Rena watched Sean's face crumple. The room was silent for a long time. "Okay," Sean said finally, "give me the tape and I'll agree not to publish any of the material you gave me."

"Please, Sean," Rena said, a small smile playing around her mouth. "Do you think I just fell off a turnip truck? We keep the tape in a very safe place. As long as you do nothing, we do nothing. It's just that simple."

"What if I find out any of the information you gave me on my own? That way I would have had it anyway."

"We won't know that, so you'd better be sure that nothing about any of the people I told you about or Courtesans, Inc. gets into your paper. Oh, and if you change jobs, we'll know it. So just write whatever crap you want about anyone else, but stay away from the people I told you about. Got that?"

As Mei handed Sean his clothes, he slowly nodded.

On the tape, Alex could be seen approaching the VCR and then the tape went dark. Erika grinned and looked around at the people she cared so much about. "You pulled it off. Bravo!"

She was off this particular hook. Her business had its dangers, but for now, everything was back to the way it had been, hectic and wonderful. She had her business and her friends. And, surprisingly enough, Alex had joined in for the first time. She had always been very fond of him, but he had always seemed somewhat distant. Now the strict loner had become part of the group's solution and Erika could see that he had changed a little, softened. Shara and Mei had more than made up for their lack of judgment and the bond of trust that had existed among the women was stronger than ever.

"We did. Sean couriered over all my pages as a gesture of good faith. We sent him a copy of the tape for his memory book. I think we've heard the last of Mr. Fredericks."

After short toasts had been shared, Shara and Mei had to leave, but they promised to return every day until Erika was well enough to leave the hospital. "According to the doctors," Mei said as she left, "that should be within a week." They both waved. "Remember we all love you all."

"Thanks," Erika said. Alex kissed Rena on the cheek and headed for the door. "I'll see you tonight."

"Seven at the Pagoda Palace," Rena said and Alex closed the door behind him.

"Hey, babe, are you and Alex an item?"

"Not an item, just friends."

Erika raised an eyebrow. "How good?"

"You're sounding just like a mother," Rena said, holding Erika's hand. "He's taught me a lot, mostly about me, and Courtesans, Inc. He's quite a guy."

"He's got quite a past, too," Erika said, not sure how she felt about her daughter dating someone like Alex. She smiled inwardly, understanding still more clearly how Rena must have felt when she found out about her mother's profession.

"I know about most of it," Rena said. "Don't worry. I've grown up a lot in the past few weeks."

"It seems he has, too," Erika said.

"I know," Brook added. "I was really surprised when he helped so much. I think it was good for him."

"I do, too." Erika took her daughter's hand. "You know, when you were young you always wanted to embrace everything from injured animals to friends with candy stuck in their hair. It seems you're still doing it."

"You know, it still surprises me that you remember things from when I was a kid. I still have that knee-jerk 'she never cared' reaction."

"I did care, and I do care."

"I know that now."

Erika felt herself held and hugged in a way she wouldn't have thought possible from the daughter she'd lost. "I'll miss you, you know."

"I know," Rena said, "but I'm seriously considering relocating. I might just move to New York. My business is portable, and we've missed so much. I think I could find clients here, and I'd like to get to know you better."

Erika couldn't control the catch in her throat. She swallowed several times and swiped at the tears in her eyes with the tissue Brook handed her. "I'd like that, but take some time to decide."

"Then do it," Brook said.

Rena laughed and hugged Erika again. "I'll be back later."

"I'll be here, waiting." Her smile was warm and genuine.

She looked at her best friend, hoping her expression told her how wonderful everything was. "I hear you've been seen in the cafeteria with the cute Doctor Freed. Anything happening there?"

Brook looked embarrassed. "Maybe." She fished the waist and connecting chains out of her purse. "Remember these?" she said, dropping them into Erika's hand. "You were wearing them that night. I think Ira, Dr. Freed, suspected something then. We've been talking and I told him about my job. He was shocked, of course, but we've continued meeting. I'm not holding my breath, but—"

"I can't think of anyone I'd rather see good things happen to than you."

"Thanks. I've got to go. Take good care of yourself," Brook said, using the wish they had made for each other for ten years.

"You too, babe," Erika said as the door closed behind her friend.

Finally Stuart was alone at Erika's bedside. She had a feeling that Stuart was going to get serious, so she said, "Stuart, you know I love you."

"I know. I love you too and I wanted to . . ."

"Stuart, I've been doing a lot of thinking about the future and what you alluded to before the accident. I've come to a few decisions." When he started to say something, Erika held his hand. "Stuart, I've known you for a lot of years, and I think we've been closer in some ways than old married folks. You understand me and give me the space I need. I need that room now. I don't want to have to answer you just yet. I want to be sure about my recovery." She stopped and took a deep breath, gathering her thoughts. "Will you wait for me?"

"Of course. I'll wait for as long as you want, but I will ask you to marry me each week until you say yes."

Erika laughed. "I can't give up the business, you realize. It's part of who I am."

"I know and I won't ask you to."

"Give me time, and I think I'll be able to give you the answer you want."

Stuart pulled a small velvet box from his pocket and handed it to Erika. "Keep this until you're ready."

She opened the box and gazed at the ring. It was a large sapphire, surrounded by six sizable diamonds. "No diamond solitaire, Stuart?" she said, her eyes twinkling through the tears.

"Nothing so ordinary for you." When Erika slipped the ring on her finger, Stuart said, "I thought you wanted time to think about it all."

Erika grinned. "I took all the time I needed," she said, then pulled Stuart's hand until he was stretched on the bed beside her, hip to hip, chest to chest. "I love you, Stuart." Erika closed her eyes and their lips met. Now she had everything.

Dear Reader,

I hope you've enjoyed the adventures of Erika, Brook, Rena and all the others involved with Courtesans, Inc. I'd love to know which characters or scenes you liked best, or just that you enjoyed the book. Please drop me a line, via e-mail at: Joan@JoanELloyd.com or via snail mail at: Joan Elizabeth Lloyd, P.O. Box 221, Yorktown Heights, NY 10598.

I really look forward to hearing from you.

Also, please visit my web site at www.JoanELloyd.com and find out about all my books, read some of my short stories, and discover all the valuable information about sexuality and relationships available there.

Best regards,